6501 W9-CDW-742

Paranormal / fantasy / Romance

Edison Junior High Library

DATE DUE

10/18/21			

PERMA-BOUND®

INVI

ANDREA CREMER

SIBI

DAVID LEVITHAN

LITY

Edison Junior High Library

speak

An Imprint of Penguin Group (USA)

SPEAK

Published by the Penguin Group
Penguin Group (USA) LLC
375 Hudson Street
New York, New York 10014

USA * Canada * UK * Ireland * Australia
New Zealand * India * South Africa * China

penguin.com
A Penguin Random House Company

First published in the United States of America by Philomel Books,
an imprint of Penguin Young Readers Group, 2013
Published by Speak, an imprint of Penguin Group (USA) LLC, 2014

Copyright © 2013 by Broken Foot Productions, Inc.

Penguin supports copyright. Copyright fuels creativity, encourages diverse voices,
promotes free speech, and creates a vibrant culture. Thank you for buying an authorized
edition of this book and for complying with copyright laws by not reproducing, scanning,
or distributing any part of it in any form without permission. You are supporting writers
and allowing Penguin to continue to publish books for every reader.

THE LIBRARY OF CONGRESS HAS CATALOGED THE PHILOMEL EDITION AS FOLLOWS:
Cremer, Andrea R.
Invisibility / Andrea Cremer and David Levithan.
p. cm.
Summary: "To break his curse of invisibility, a boy is helped by a girl, who is the only one who
can see him"—Provided by publisher.
[1. Magic—Fiction. 2. Charms—Fiction. 3. Friendship—Fiction. 4. Family problems—Fiction.
5. New York (N.Y.)—Fiction.] I. Levithan, David. II. Title.
PZ7.C86385Inv 2013 [Fic]—dc23 2012024514
ISBN: 978-0-399-25760-5

Speak ISBN 978-0-14-750998-7

Printed in the United States of America

3 5 7 9 10 8 6 4 2

To Casey Jarrin

(who sees me through the dark)

—AC

To Jen Bodner

(never invisible to me)

—DL

Edison Junior High Library

With special thanks from both of the authors to our families, friends, fellow authors, agents, and all of the wonderful people at Penguin, most especially our editor, Jill Santopolo

CHAPTER 1

I WAS BORN INVISIBLE.

I have no idea how this worked. Did my mother go to a hospital, expecting me to be just another normal, visible baby? Or did she believe in the curse, did she know what was going to happen and have me in secret? It's such a strange image, even to me: an invisible baby, born into the world. What was that first moment like, when I was held up to my mother and there was nothing to see, only feel? She never told me. To her, the past was invisible like I was invisible. She let it slip that there was a curse—angry early words with my father, not meant for my ears. But that was it. There was no other why. There was no other how. There was only the what, and that was my life.

Invisible. I am invisible.

I want to keep asking my parents why. I want to keep asking my parents how. But I can't anymore. They're gone now.

My father left when I was small. It was too much for him.

My mother held on for as long as she could. Fifteen years. And then her body broke. A blood vessel in her brain.

I have been alone for almost a year now.

I can never be seen, no matter how hard I try. I can be touched, but only if I concentrate. And I can always be heard, if I choose to speak. These, I suppose, are the rules of the curse. I have gotten used to them, even if I don't understand them. When I was a baby, I automatically had weight, but the more conscious I became, the more I had to concentrate on being held. I do not evaporate—part of me is still there, so I don't fall through floors or walk through walls. But to touch—that requires effort. I am not solid to the world, but the world is solid to me. The curse is its own intricately woven, often contradictory web, and I was born into it. I am an unknowing slave to its design.

New York City is a remarkably easy place to be invisible, as long as you have an absent father who contributes to your bank account from time to time. Everything—groceries, movies, books, furniture—can be ordered online. Cash never has to pass from one hand to another. Packages are left outside the door.

I stay inside a lot, but not always.

I live four blocks from Central Park, and I spend most of my afternoons there. It is where I choose to live my traceless, shadowless life. I am just another part of the expanse. I am there in the trees, in the air, by the water. Sometimes I will sit on a bench for hours at a time. Sometimes I will wander. At every moment, I observe. Tourists and regulars. Dog walkers who pass at noon each day, clockwork. Large packs of teenagers, jockeying loudly for each other's attention. Old people who also sit and stare, as if they have all the time in the world, when deep down they know the opposite is true. I take them all in. I hear their conversations, witness their intimacies. I never say a word. They are more conscious of the birds, the squirrels, the wind.

I do not exist. And yet I exist.

I miss my mother. When I was a child, she taught me how to concentrate, how to give myself weight when the instinct began to fail. That way, she could still carry me on her back, tell me to hold on. She wanted me to live in the world, not apart from it. She would not abide any mischief on my part—no thievery, no spying, no taking advantage. I was cursed, but I was not meant to curse others. I was different, yes, but I was no less human than anyone else. So I had to act human, even when I wasn't feeling human at all.

She loved me, which is perhaps the most remarkable thing of all. There was never any question. By which I mean: There were many questions, but none of them had to do with love.

She taught me to read, even though she had to turn the pages most of the time. To write, even though the simple act of typing on a keyboard can exhaust me. To talk, when only she was around. To be silent, when anyone else was around. She taught me science and math and history, and how to cut my hair and my fingernails. She taught me the stories of my neighborhood, the stories of her day. She was comfortable telling me about the sixteenth century, or about a show she'd seen on TV. The only period that was blank was the year of my birth. Or anything directly before. Or anything directly after.

She never told a soul. And because of this, she too was alone—alone with me. Like mother, like son. There were kids I grew up with, but only because I saw them around a lot, got to know them through observation. Especially the kids in my building. Alex in 7A has been around the longest—perhaps I remember him first because of his red hair, or maybe it's the consistency of his complaining. At six, he wanted the latest toys. At sixteen, he wants to stay out late, to get more money from his parents, to have his parents *leave him alone.* I am tired of him, as I am tired of Greta in 6C, who's always been mean, and Sean in 5C, who's always been quiet. I think he would envy my invisibility, if he knew it was possible. But since he doesn't, he settles for the other options, the more voluntary invisibilities. He cloaks himself in books. He never makes eye contact, so the world becomes indirect. He mumbles his way through life.

And then there was Ben, who moved away. Ben, the only friend I've almost had. When he was five and I was ten, he decided to have an imaginary friend. *Stuart,* he named him, and that was close enough to my name, Stephen, for me to play along. He'd invite me to dinner, and I'd come along. He'd move to hold my hand in the park, and I'd take it. He'd bring me to kindergarten for show-and-tell, and I would stand there as the teacher indulged his whim, nodding along to whatever Ben said about me. The one thing I couldn't do was speak to him, because I knew that hearing my voice would spoil the illusion. Once, when I knew he wasn't listening, I whispered his name. Just to hear it. But he didn't notice. And by the time he turned six, he'd outgrown me. I couldn't blame him. Still, I was sad when he moved away.

My days are very much identical to one another. I wake up whenever I want. I shower, even though it's hard for me to get dirty. Mostly I do it so I can concentrate myself into having a body, and then feel the sensation of water hitting my skin. There's something human in that experience, a communion with the ordinary that I need each morning. I don't need to dry off; I merely disappear, and whatever water that's left on my body falls straight to the floor. I go back to my room and put on some clothes, for warmth. They disappear as soon as I put them on—another of the curse's finer details. Then I turn on some music and read for a few hours. I eat mostly at lunchtime—the spell also covers whatever I put into my mouth, so mercifully I don't have to witness the effects of my digestive tract. When lunch is done, I head out to the park. I press the elevator button, then have to wait in the lobby for the doorman to open the door for someone else before I can leave. Or, if no one is around, I open it myself and assume that, if it's seen, someone will blame the door, or the wind. I pick a bench that no one will sit on—the birds have gotten to it, or it's missing a slat. Or I wind my way through the Rambles. By the ponds, I have no reflection. By the band shell, I can sway to the music without anyone noticing. By the ponds, I can release a sudden cry, causing the ducks to spring in the air. Bystanders have no idea what's happened.

I come home when it's dark, and read some more. Watch some television. Go online. Again, typing is hard for me. But every now and then, I will painstakingly set out my sentences. This is the way I can participate in the language of living. I can talk to strangers. I can leave comments. I can volunteer my words when they are needed. Nobody has to know that on the other side of the wirescape, unseen hands are pressing the keys. Nobody has to know my central truth if I can offer them much smaller truths instead.

This is how the time passes. I don't go to school. I don't have any family. The landlord knows my mother is gone—I had to call the ambulance, I had to see her taken away—but he believes my

father is still around. I will grant my father this: he has never dis-
owned me. It's just that he doesn't want to have anything further
to do with me. I don't even know where he is. He is an email address
to me. A cell phone number.

When my mother died, all the whys and hows returned. Grief
gave them fuel. Uncertainty pointed me backward. For the first
time in my life, without the buffer of her love, I felt truly cursed. I
only had two choices, to follow her or to stay. Reluctantly, I stayed.
I immersed myself in other people's words, in the park, in weaving
a nest for my future out of the loose strands that I had left in my
life. After a while, I stopped wondering about the why. I stopped
questioning the how. I stopped noticing the what. What remains is
simply my life, and I lead it simply.

I am like a ghost who's never died.

It starts with Ben's old apartment, 3B. Two doors down from my
apartment, 3D. Ben's family left when I was twelve. Since then, the
apartment has gone through three waves of tenants. The Cranes
were a horrible couple who spent all their time saying horrible
things to each other. They enjoyed their cruelty too much to get a
divorce, but it wasn't any fun to be around. The Tates had four
kids, and it was the imminent arrival of the fifth that made them
realize a two-bedroom apartment wasn't going to work. And Sukie
Maxwell was only planning on being in New York for a year,
because she only had a year to design her client's new Manhattan
apartment before moving on to redecorate the same client's house
in France. She left so little of a mark on my universe that I didn't
even notice her moving out. It's only when I see a set of movers

carrying an old, worn sofa—a sofa that Sukie Maxwell would have never approved of—that I know she's left our building and a new family is taking her place.

I walk past the movers and head out to the park without giving it much thought. Instead I focus on Ivan, my favorite dog walker, who is making his afternoon rounds with Tigger and Eeyore (a dachshund and a basset hound, respectively). From conversations he's had with other dog walkers, I know that Ivan came to Manhattan from Russia three years ago, and is sharing a room on the Lower East Side with three other Russians he met online. This is not working out well, especially because Ivan is trying to woo Karen, the live-in nanny for the younger members of Tigger and Eeyore's family. I've seen them too, in the park, and think that Karen and Ivan would make a good match, if only because he treats the dogs kindly and with a sense of humor, while she does the same with the children. But it is clearly out of the question for Ivan to stay over at the house of his employers, nor does he want to bring Karen home to meet his questionable roommates. It's a stalemate, and sometimes I feel I'm as eager to see the resolution as Ivan is.

There seems to be some progress today, because about ten minutes after Ivan comes to the park, Karen follows with the children. They seem to be aware of each other, but with the children around, they're hesitant. I follow as they head towards the statue of Alice in Wonderland, then get closer as the kids leave them to play. It's just Tigger and Eeyore now, and neither Karen nor Ivan is making the first move.

I can't help myself. I lean down, concentrate hard, and push the two dogs in different directions. Suddenly they are darting in circles, and Ivan and Karen are at the center of their leashes. They are flung together, and while at first there's shock, it's the kind of shock that ends with smiles and laughter. The dogs are barking maniacally; the kids are rushing over to see what's happened. Ivan and Karen are pressing against each other, trying to disentangle themselves.

I'm smiling too. I have no idea what it would look like, to see me smile. But the feeling is there.

There's no certainty that the little spark of the moment I've given to Ivan and Karen will become anything other than a moment. Still, I feel good as I head back to the apartment. I wait for Mrs. Wylie (4A) to come in, and I rush through the door behind her. Then we ride in the elevator together to the fourth floor, and I press three on the way back down. When I emerge from the elevator, there's a girl in front of 3B, holding three bags from IKEA. As she fumbles for her door key, all three of them drop to the ground. I gingerly walk past her, then wait by my door—there's no way for me to take my key out of its hiding place and open the door until she's gone from the hall. I stand there watching as she scoops a pair of bookends and some cheap picture frames back into one of the bags. She is either cursing at herself or cursing at the bags—I can't tell which. I am thinking about how Sukie Maxwell would have loathed IKEA objects in her perfect apartment, not really paying attention when this new girl looks straight at the space where I'm standing.

"Are you really going to just stand there?" she asks. "Is this fun for you?"

All the electricity in my body is suddenly alert, amped to a level of consciousness I've never felt before. I turn to look behind me, to see who's there.

But there's no one there.

"Yeah, you," the girl says.

I cannot believe it.

She sees me.

CHAPTER 2

I THOUGHT NEW YORK would be different. Yet here I am, sharp words zinging from my lips like poison darts. Same as every day back home. But this kid wasn't asking for it. Not really. He didn't *make* me drop the bags.

And, okay, he's not a kid. He's definitely around my age. Someone my mother would refer to as a "peer." At least once every hour during our drive east, she reminded me to search them out, as if my "peers" are an endangered species who it's my sole purpose to capture and catalog lest I perish as a result of my family's migration to this strange territory.

But I've gotten into the habit of mentally adding ten years to my own age. I'm not infatuated with the notion of my own great maturity or anything, but I haven't related to my so-called peers for a while. I assume this kid is "normal" sixteen, like all the rest of them, whereas I'm "life can, and probably will, totally screw you" sixteen.

And while I don't subscribe to the idea that anyone sporting a penis should hold doors for me or throw coats over puddles on a rainy-day stroll, he could have at least muttered "oh, that sucks" or kicked the Färm vase back in my direction. Since, after all, it rolled across the space between us and now rests by his foot.

I'm tempted to snark "Fine, keep it!" and throw the rest of the bags into my apartment, wrapping up the whole scene with a glorious door slam.

No joy for that plan, though, because I'm still kneeling in a disaster area of picture frames, throw pillows, and water glasses with names like Flukta and Varmt, which I'm convinced are dirty words that the Swedes use to mock us. I grope around the hall, trying to figure out where my keys fell.

A twinge in my chest informs me that the knee-jerk outburst has passed and now I feel bad about yelling at him, not to mention clumsy as hell.

He's just standing there, staring at me.

Guilt and embarrassment are already flooding my chest, choking my throat, making me wish I was anywhere but standing in this building that doesn't feel like home but somehow is. Instead I'm stuck; my feet have been bolted to the floor of this claustrophobic hall.

I miss air that isn't full of car exhaust. I miss the horizon. How is there a place that doesn't have a horizon? Humans evolved on a sphere that's spinning in an ever-expanding universe. Horizon simply is. It's like gravity. Yet somehow people on this weird island threw together enough steel and concrete to erase the spot where the sky touches the earth. It's like they wanted to pretend the rules that the rest of us accept don't apply. Maybe if I'd paid more attention, I'd notice they're all walking five inches above the sidewalk too.

You'd think Mom would have mentioned that in her whole *New York will be so much better than Minnesota and you want to be an artist and blah blah blah* pitch . . . but she didn't. It's not like I needed the pitch. After *it* happened, I was ready to go. We all were. There wasn't any reason to pretend New York was anything other than an escape hatch for the three of us. But that didn't make the move easy. Ever since we got here, my teeth have been grinding from the constant noise, nothing smells right, and I always feel like I'm about to get a headache.

I glance down at my shirt because the last time a boy stared at me this long I'd unwittingly popped three buttons while hauling moving boxes my mom had stacked in the living room, leaving my boobs to wink at the world shamelessly.

When my eyes shift down, I see my shirt is intact, so flashing isn't the issue. Maybe the girls he's used to don't talk like me. Girls in Blaine didn't talk like me. Being nice was more important than being honest. Except their definition of *nice* included gossip that cut like a knife in your back.

I thought maybe my rough edges would mean I'd fit better here. Obviously my *New York girls are tougher* theory isn't going to pan out. I can already hear my mom chiding me. *"There's no need to be abrasive, Elizabeth."*

That's the impression I give my mother. Her daughter: the scouring pad.

I shove my hand towards him. "I'm sorry. It's just that the subway felt like a sauna and the elevator was busy, so I took the stairs, which was a bad call. The more I sweat, the less civil I am."

He gazes at my fingers like they might be leprous and I snatch my hand back. He winces, lifting his eyes to mine. Very carefully he folds at the waist, wrapping his fingers one at a time around the vase. He takes several measured steps as he approaches me.

"Sorry . . . I . . . sorry." His words are slower than his steps.

I peer at him, wondering if maybe he isn't comfortable speaking English. But he looks American to me. Is that a thing? Can a person look American? Maybe it's just that he's what I always thought New York would look like. All sorts of different places and times mashed up into one person's body. Worldly—I think that's the word for it. In Blaine, people look like they've never left Blaine. And never will.

My throat is full of cotton and I swallow a couple of times. "No. I was being rude."

I gaze at the weird little ceramic piece he gently places in my palm rather than looking up at him again because by now I feel like a bitch, an idiot, and a possible racist because of my whole "looking American" inner monologue. The vase he's handed me resembles an egg that grew a neck. I'd thrown it into my IKEA cart on a whim, adding an item to my list of quirky tasks I would accomplish when exploring my new island home.

Find a wildflower to live in this vase. Note: wild—no garden snatching or purchase allowed. Sidewalk-crack flora acceptable.

I force myself to glance at him. "I shouldn't have tried a balancing act best left to professionals. I'm no plate spinner."

Lame. So lame. I'm blushing now, which makes it worse. Blood coloring my cheeks doesn't do anything for my complexion. On me it's not demure and sweet, just blotchy and unfortunate.

He smiles and a real person breaks through the mask of disbelief he's worn up to that moment. He's cute. The floppy kind of cute with dark hair I want to push out of his eyes and overly conscientious body movements, as if touching anything by accident would be a crisis. And his eyes . . . they're strange, but alluring. It's a color a painter might create, but only with lots of effort and an infinite palette to experiment with. They're blue, but not. It's that shade you catch right before a robin's-egg sky melts into the rust and rose of sunsets. It's the horizon I haven't seen since we entered the skyscraper forest of Manhattan.

I'm already sketching his eyes in my head and have to force myself to shift my gaze to the rest of him. Nothing else out of the ordinary, but not unpleasant either. He's wearing a plain white T-shirt and jeans and makes them look good in a way that only some boys can. I'm a little relieved to see he's sweating as much as I am.

"No. You're right. I was being stupid." He sounds sorry and he sounds kinda nervous.

I look down again. *Great.* My boobs might not be popping out, but all the sweat has turned me into a one-woman wet T-shirt contest.

Hormone-driven apology. That's typical. That's my life.

I grit my teeth because I can hear my mother's voice, like she's steering the boat that is my conscience. Telling me to play nice.

Make friends. Introduce yourself to the neighbors. Neighbors are essential in New York.

She's been doling out her brand of New York wisdom ever since she announced our move a month ago. I don't know where she's getting it from, since her own family left New York when she was five years old. I'm a little worried it's from reruns of *Friends* and *Seinfeld,* which doesn't bode well for us. But I guess it's better than the *Law & Order* marathons she's also a fan of. If that was her source of info, Laurie and I would have industrial-size GPS trackers strapped to us anytime we left the apartment.

The boy is staring at me again, biting his lip. He looks like he has a thousand questions brewing behind those watercolor eyes and I swear I'm not that interesting.

His nerves seem to be getting worse. I can hear the rasp of his quick, shallow breaths. His gaze has become desperate as if he's paralyzed by indecision. He lunges forward, suddenly on his knees beside me.

"Hey—" I start to shout, but he's moving his arm in slow sweeps, guiding the rainbow array of household décor back into the IKEA bags. His touch is so deliberate, so careful, as if he's transfixed by the process. He looks like he'd enjoy taking each object and giving it a thorough examination before putting it away.

Okay, weird. But he's probably just worried I'm still pissed off about him watching me drop all that stuff and I'd just start yelling at him again if he accidentally broke something while trying to help me.

Chagrined, I gather up the remaining items. When I have one

bag assembled, he's standing up again, holding the other two. One in each hand. He's still watching me, barely blinking. His eyes have new light behind them, like he's never had as much fun as carrying someone else's shopping.

I hesitate, awkwardly looking at him, then at the keys in my hand. Do I owe him another apology? Can I let a stranger into our apartment? But he's not a stranger if he's my neighbor, right? He must live here. Mom picked this building because of its location and its security. I guess *Law & Order* made an impression after all. I think about Mom, already at the hospital for a double shift though we only arrived yesterday. "Somebody has to pay for this swanky place," she'd said with a grin after peeking in my room at 4:30 a.m. Even in my groggy state, I'd croaked out a laugh at her joke. The apartment was nice, but I was sleeping on an air mattress with a leak in it.

"Would you like some lemonade?" I ask him. Lemonade strikes me as the ultimate heat-wave peace offering. Though I realize we have none in the fridge. I'm about to say that but don't say anything because he's gone pale in that way you do when you're about to be sick.

He closes his eyes, and when he does, something weird happens. It's like I blinked, but I know I didn't. He disappeared, in the way someone slips out of your peripheral vision. But I'm not looking at him out of the corner of my eye. He's standing right in front of me.

I'm desperate to get into my apartment because I'm sure this means I have heat stroke. I wish he'd say something so I could at least accept his refusal of my offer and leave. Then I realize I haven't introduced myself.

"I'm Elizabeth," I say, managing to get my keys into the lock. "But I've been thinking of trying out Jo."

"Elizabeth and Jo." He tilts his head and some of the color returns to his face. He speaks very softly. "You don't like Elizabeth?"

Ugh. Mom's infatuation with *Little Women* will never leave me in peace. I'm in no mood to explain my mom's penchant for literary homage via her children's birth certificates. Nor try to puzzle out with this strange boy why she decided it was a good idea to name me after the girl who dies and only made the strong survivor my middle name. Survival as an afterthought. I'm starting to think that if I don't chug some water in the next five minutes, I'm going to melt like a human Popsicle.

"Josephine's my middle name." I unlock the door, gesturing for him to go in ahead of me. "And Jo is my pen name."

He swivels around, walking backward into the apartment like he doesn't want to take his eyes off me. I probably should change my shirt before I tell him his lemonade will be water. "A pen name? You're a writer?"

"I'm not published yet," I say. "But the work I want to do is still kind of a boys' club."

"Journalism?" he asks.

I love this part. "Comics."

"You want to write comics?" He's utterly mystified . . . I think. Maybe he's sure I'm pulling one over on him. It wouldn't be the first time.

"Script, pencils, inks. All or nothing." I shove back rising defensiveness by asking him, "So you going to tell me or what?"

"Tell you?"

"Your name."

He does that thing again. His eyes are closed, but I feel like *my* eyes are going out of focus. Then he's holding my gaze and for the life of me I cannot look away.

"Stephen." I have to lean in to hear him. With the whisper of his name I feel his breath on my face. It's strangely cool compared to the sticky heat of the apartment.

"Welcome back!"

Stephen jumps and drops the bags and it's like the hallway all over again. He doesn't stoop to pick anything up. He's staring at my brother. I can hardly blame him.

Laurie is sprawled on the hardwood floor surrounded by small fans. He's shirtless, his arms are thrown over his head, and he's gazing at the ceiling.

"How was the subway? Is it as smelly as I imagine? I had this idea that cosmetic companies should abandon their department store posts and start spraying their samples on people on the train. Good, huh? I will rule this city yet."

The air conditioner is still in its box behind him and the fans. It looks like the fans are preparing to sacrifice my younger brother—a horde of whirring suppliants offering their victim to the gods of Freon.

I'm about to yell at him for not installing the window unit, but then I notice the glass of lemonade beside him. Now I want to tell my brother how much I love him.

"I'll put it in the window when the sun goes down," he says, obviously reading my first reaction and preparing for the worst.

"Yeah, yeah." I wave off his excuse. "Can you just get me and Stephen some of that lemonade? Also, write down where the store is so I can pick up anything you forgot?"

Laurie sits up. He's making the face I've never seen anyone else pull off, like he's smiling and frowning at the same time—a mixture of amusement and worry. "Who?"

"Stephen," I say. "He helped me with the bags. Sort of."

I throw a smile in Stephen's direction, wagering that a friendship might spark if we share a joke about our mutual skill at bag dropping. But he's staring at my brother and his hands are shaking.

Laurie's gaze slides to my right, where Stephen is frozen. Laurie's brow furrows and then he looks at me again. "Okay, Josie, what's the deal?"

"Every time you call me 'Josie,' it defeats the purpose of my pen name," I say.

"Whatever, Betty."

I give him the finger. "Come on, bro. As the elder child, I am entitled, nay, obliged to order you about. Two lemonades. Now."

"Why two? Aren't you a little old to have an imaginary friend?" He grins. "I know you've dreamed a dream of setting me up with my soul mate now that we've landed in this supposedly gay-little-brother-friendly metropolis, but I'm not that desperate . . . yet. Besides, my own imagination serves just fine when needed. I'll keep you posted, though."

I don't understand. My eyes flit from Laurie to Stephen and back again. It couldn't be any hotter in this stuffy apartment, but I feel like someone dumped a bucket of ice water over my shoulders.

"Don't be rude." I bite my lip because I sound like my mother.

"Uh—" Laurie starts to look genuinely concerned. "How long were you out in the heat?" He scrambles up. "I'll get you that lemonade."

My heart bangs around my rib cage like a pinball as Laurie trots towards the kitchen.

Beside me, Stephen whispers, "It's okay. I'll go."

CHAPTER 3

FOR THE FIRST FEW minutes, I try to convince myself that the curse has been broken. There was a time limit, and I've reached it. Just as easily as I disappeared from the world, I have reappeared. Nobody told me this day would come. Maybe nobody knew. But there, in the hallway, for the very first time, I am seen.

It's exhilarating and horrifying and mind-blowing. She sees me, and I assume that everyone will see me now. It just happened to be her.

My curse, my sentence, has been completed.

I try to remain calm. There is no way to express what I'm feeling. Maybe to a stranger I'd never see again, I'd feel the freedom to blurt out what's happened. But this is a girl who is now living on my hall. I must act normal. Not the normal of my own life, but the normal I've witnessed in everybody else's.

This is it, I think. *I can do this.*

The curse has been broken.

I am visible.

As it sinks in, the exhilaration and the horror and the mind-blowing ordinariness of what I am doing all combine into a fierce static of emotions. Elizabeth doesn't seem to notice this. To her, I am just a boy from down the hall.

Extraordinary.

Somehow I make conversation. Somehow I speak.

She is seeing the face I never get to see, because no mirror has ever caught me.

She invites me in for lemonade. I want to see how far I can take this. I feel like I can take it as far as I want.

Still, picking up her bags requires effort. I must concentrate, make my body present. I figure that perhaps it doesn't come back all at once. It's a shock to the system. A complete reorganization of the system. This is going to take time. I lift the bags and follow her into her apartment.

I figure we'll be alone. We can keep talking. I can continue to get used to the notion of being visible. Then I see Elizabeth's brother on the floor. Another person.

I prepare myself.

I am ready for him to see me.

I am ready.

But he doesn't.

He doesn't see me.

Now the static I've been feeling fills the room, fills the world. I see the surprise on Elizabeth's face, but it's nothing compared to the surprise that seems to be lashing at my every thought.

He doesn't see me.

But she does. She does.

"Aren't you a little old to have an imaginary friend?" he asks her.

That's what it feels like. I am trapped in someone else's imagination. Someone else's dream. And that someone is about to wake up.

Somehow, I find words. "It's okay," I say. "I'll go." Luckily, she's left the door open. Luckily, she is too confused to follow me. I run to my door, my feet not making a sound. Or maybe she hears them. I don't know. I feel I don't know anything anymore. Usually I look at least four times before putting the key in my lock. But now I don't care. Now I just need to be inside. Now I need to close the door behind me. Lock it. Breathe. Scream. Breathe.

There is a mirror in our front hallway. In all of those years, my mother never understood what it did to me. Or maybe she thought I needed a reminder, and she didn't want it to always be her.

I look inside it now.

I see the wall behind me. The bookshelves. The light from the window, set at an angle.

That's all.

It has to be her.

In the minutes that follow, I realize it isn't that the curse has been broken. It's that she's found a way around it. It's her, not me.

I need to test this theory. I wait until it's late, until I'm sure that she'll be asleep. I listen to the silence of the hallway, the silence of the building, before I creep outside.

Maybe it isn't just her. I have to know.

I head out of my building. The doorman is so busy watching late-night TV that he doesn't notice the door opening. This doorman has always been helpful to me.

It's a cool, late-summer night. There are some stray pedestrians on the Upper West Side, but not many. I head to the subway station, jumping the turnstile with ease. Nobody calls to me to stop.

The subway arrives just as I'm stepping onto the platform. The doors open and I find myself in a half-full car. I look around, waiting for someone—anyone—to meet my eye. Nothing. So I start to move. Bounce up and down. Do jumping jacks. Swing around a pole. Crazy behavior. Insane behavior. The kind of behavior that would have to make someone either look or look away.

Nothing.

I move from one car to the next. The door opens, the door closes—people notice *that*. The last car isn't as busy. Just a few people, clusters of couples and one single guy. I walk over to him. He's in a suit. Maybe thirty. His tie is off. He's got a beer in a bag at his feet, next to his laptop case. Every inch of his body reads *It's been a long night*.

I am right in front of him. I wave. I lean over so I am about an inch from his face. I exhale. He moves back a little.

"Can you see me?" I ask aloud.

Now he startles.

"Am I here?" I ask.

He's looking around in every direction. The couples are too far away. He has no idea where the voice is coming from.

"You can't see me, can you?"

"What the hell?" he grunts. Still looking around.

"But I'm right here," I tell him. Then I lay my hand on his shoulder. Concentrate.

He cries out.

I pull back. He's up on his feet now. Everyone's staring at him.

"I'm sorry," I whisper. We're at the stop I need.

I leave the train.

I am in the middle of Times Square. Lit like the inside of a video game. The crowds are bigger now—couples, yes, but also groups of twelve, twenty, thirty. Even after midnight. Teenagers crash playfully into each other. Fathers carry sleeping daughters in their arms. Cameras flash.

I want one person to see me. Out of these hundreds. Out of these thousands. I just want one of them to ask me the time. To ask me what I'm doing. Make eye contact. Dodge when it looks like I'm going to be in their way.

I stretch out my arms. I spin around. I dash up the red-lit staircase at the center of the square. I walk into photograph after photograph after photograph. I pose with tourists. I stand in the way of the camera. I'm blocking them, but I'm not. I'm in their way, but I'm not. I'm here, but I'm not.

My thoughts keep me up most of the night.

Did she really see me?

If she did, what did she see?

I must have been wearing clothes. I must have looked the right age. But still.

Was she seeing what she wanted to see?

Was she seeing what I'd want her to see?

Is she really the only one?

For days, I avoid her. I hear more furniture being moved into her apartment. I hear her and her brother in the hall. Her and her mother. I don't dare go out there.

What if she sees me again?

What if she doesn't?

All of my secrets start with the first one. All of my life is built around the secrets.

I am not ready to let that go. I am not ready to see what happens next. Because it's possible that nothing will happen, and that might break me.

I remember the days after my mother died. How I had to hide from the world. How I fell so deeply into silence that I forgot the sound of my own voice, as well as the sound of hers. How there didn't seem to be any point to one if I couldn't have the other.

Eventually, I have to leave. I am starting to feel like I'm pacing my cage. I go to the park. I look for Ivan and Karen. I look for other regulars. But the day is hotter than usual, and everyone is in a rush.

I head back home. I check the mail when no one is looking. I throw it all away, so there's nothing to carry.

I take the elevator back to my floor. When the doors open, she's right there.

There's no question: She sees me. The look on her face is half curiosity, half amusement.

"If it isn't the Disappearing Boy," she says. "I was starting to wonder if you really lived here."

I stare into her eyes. I am searching for my reflection. I am trying to discover what I look like.

But all I see are her eyes. The light of the elevator. The back wall.

The doors start to close, and I haven't left the elevator yet. She sticks her hand in their way to keep them open.

"Thanks," I say.

"Out for a walk?" she asks.

"Yeah. It's hot."

"I heard."

This is so awkward. There are a thousand things I could ask her, but not a single one of them would be normal.

I get out of the elevator, and she gets in.

"See ya," she says.

"Yeah," I reply.

The doors close.

She's gone.

I don't know if I can bear it. Everything was under control. Every-thing worked. And now this. I forget to eat. I can't read without the sentences somehow pointing back at me. TV seems flat, unreal.

The key to living with a problem is not to think about it all the time.

I am now thinking about it all the time.

On the seventh day after she first saw me, I break a promise I made to myself.

I email my father.

There's a girl in the building who can see me, I write. *How is this possible?*

That's all I can say. I don't want to know about his life. I don't want him to know about my life.

I just want an answer.

Tell me about the curse, I would plead with my mother. *It's my life. I have a right to know.*

I can't tell you anything, she would say. *If I told you, it would only be worse. It could get much, much worse.*

What's worse than this? I'd yell. *Tell me, what's worse than this?*

She couldn't hug me whenever she wanted to. She couldn't kiss me whenever she wanted to. It is impossible to know what love is like when those things are taken away. She had to wear all her care in her voice, and all her devotion in the way she looked at me.

It can be much worse than this, she'd tell me. *You have no idea. And for as long as I live, you'll have no idea.*

There was no sentence after this period. There was no story after this page. At least, not one that she would tell me.

On the eighth day, I order groceries online. It usually takes four or five hours for them to be delivered, but this time there's a knock on my door after two. This is strange—I always give explicit instructions to leave all parcels outside my door without knocking.

"Just leave them!" I yell.

"Leave what?" a voice calls back.

Her voice.

I'm stuck. She knows I'm in here. I know she's out there.

I look through the peephole and see she's alone.

"I can hear you breathing on the other side of the door," she says. "Can you open it? I don't want to have to huff and puff. My huffing and puffing can be *fierce.*"

I make a decision: I am going to let her in. I am going to pretend that everything is ordinary. She is just dropping by. Of course she can see me. Everyone can see me. This is just a neighborly visit. I can be a friendly neighbor. Especially since I don't have a choice.

I concentrate so my hand can turn the knob.

I open the door.

CHAPTER 4

I SHOULDN'T BE HERE. I've never done this before. It's the sort of thing I believe desperate, self-involved people do. I don't want to be one of those people.

But I'm angry and frustrated . . . and I'm lonely. I've been lonely for a while now. That's what happens when you start returning every "Hey, Liz," with a hostile glance, waiting for the punch line at your expense. Followed by actual punches.

Most of my friends melted away over the course of the past year. When the rumors about Laurie started, those "friends" who weren't really friends at all dropped off with the force of an avalanche. That hadn't been surprising.

The slow drift of the few people I'd really trusted was what actually hurt. A couple of my BFF girls tried to stay loyal, but in the end I had to push them off and watch them float away. I couldn't take the pitying, if well-intentioned, glances and sympathetic phone calls. I didn't want sympathy. I wanted people to be as pissed off as I was.

When my friends were gone, I'd clung to Laurie and to Mom.

And after *it* happened, just Mom, as we shuttled back and forth from the hospital to our house, all the while plotting our escape. But we hadn't gotten any further than escape in our planning. It turns out our refuge leaves me alone most of the time. Mom's at work. Laurie's at summer school since, after *it* happened, he missed the last eight weeks of classes. They both seem happy enough.

Mom has always used her workaholism to deal with stress. Laurie assures me that even after a week of classes, he's certain that two-thirds of his classmates are ten times gayer than he is. I have no idea how he's made these calculations. I speculate that his glee at being stuck in summer school is less about the relative gayness of his fellow students and more about (a) the air-conditioning in his school actually works, whereas the tiny window unit for our apartment spends more time sputtering than cooling, and (b) unlike the punitive forms of summer school back home, Laurie's attending a program for artistically inclined kids. Music, drama, literature, that kind of thing—and he's loving it. If it weren't for the fact that he'd been flat on his back in a full body cast, then recovering, he probably would be glad he missed finishing the school year since it meant he's now enrolled at his version of Hogwarts.

I kind of wished I could go with him. The school's visual arts program is kick-ass and would no doubt help me build my portfolio. But Mom can't afford to send both of us, and I *did* finish the school year—with daggers in my eyes and hands constantly balled into fists.

Like they are now. I realize I'm not in front of Stephen's door just because I'm lonely. I did what Mom wanted. I was polite. I tried to "make a friend" like a normal person would. I even offered the nectar-that-prevents-heat-stroke lemonade, so what if I didn't actually have any, to begin our new friendship negotiations. But Stephen bolted, leaving me babbling to Laurie about a boy I'd met in the hall, which then subjected me to hours of little-brother torment about my invisible boyfriend. And it's Stephen's fault. I'm here because I'm frustrated and have no one to yell at.

It takes him forever to open the door. When I finally see his face, his mouth is twitching like he's afraid or worried or annoyed. Whatever he's feeling, it isn't good. Not that I expected him to be overjoyed to see me. He's obviously been avoiding me, and that only scratches my already-frazzled nerves like a burr. I open my mouth to bawl him out, but my voice gets stuck halfway up my throat. What comes out instead is a pathetic croak. A sound that's limp and sad. It makes him grimace. His eyes drop to the floor.

I try again. This time I manage, "Hey."

He mumbles something. I can't tell, but I assume it's a greeting because he's human.

"So . . ."

He mumbles again. My anger starts to build up again.

"It's your thing, right?"

The question draws his gaze.

I force a smile. "Rudeness?"

His eyes go wide, which I find very satisfying.

"No," he says. Nothing else, just "no."

We stare at each other. It's getting really uncomfortable.

"What do you want?" he asks.

"Explain to me how that's not rude," I say.

He sighs, deep and awfully weary for this time of day. Maybe he's an insomniac.

"You're right. I'm sorry."

I don't expect that. I expect him to snark back at me or shut the door in my face.

"Would you like to come in?" He poses the question like he's just asked if I need him to donate bone marrow.

Suddenly I'm uneasy. Why did I come here anyway? I realize I was expecting a shouting match at the door, ending with my stomping back to my own apartment and spending the afternoon cursing the utter horribleness of other people. Now I have a choice: I can be the rude one and the crazy one because after all I showed up at his door, or I can accept his invitation.

"Okay." I walk past him as he steps back. His apartment is chilly, almost freezing, and I'm rubbing my arms to rid them of sudden goose bumps.

I can tell right away that his apartment is nicer than ours. The layout is identical, but our place is full of cardboard boxes and a mishmash of furniture. Mom put me in charge of organizing the apartment, which means it hasn't been done. I think she was trying to be nice by letting me decide what our new apartment would look like. But it's hard to get excited about unpacking, and we're still living like we'd arrived in Manhattan yesterday.

This apartment is neat, if sparsely furnished. What's the word? Utilitarian. Hooray—vocab. I'm guessing his room must have a little more character. The front hall and living room are stiffly adult. Whoever decorated it was deeply invested in neatness and perfunctory style. He must have a parent or two also calling the apartment home, but at the moment we're the only ones here.

"Can I get you something?"

I jump at the question. His voice is calmer now, clearer.

"Uh, sure."

"Lemonade?" He half smiles, like he's made a joke.

I want to glare at him but just nod. "If you have it."

"Make yourself comfortable." He points at the couch, watching his own hand move as if he's made a secret, symbolic gesture.

I settle against the stiff upholstery, which scratches against my bare skin. It's still hot in our apartment, so my uniform has been a tank top and shorts every day. I hope he has a better setup in his room because this couch would suck for movie watching.

I catch my own thought; my stomach clenches. I'm already imagining movie hangouts with a boy I don't even know, who obviously didn't want to invite me in but felt he had to. I squeeze my eyelids tight, hating how desperate I feel to have someone to spend time with. When did I get this pathetic?

"Are you okay?" He's standing in front of me, holding out a glass. Ice clinks against the rim, floating in the pastel translucence of the lemonade.

"Yeah." I take the glass. "Just a headache."

"Aspirin?"

"No." I allow myself a big gulp of lemonade. It's the store-bought kind, but it's still cold, tart, and good. "I'll be fine. Lemonade is the universal elixir."

He sits down beside me, close but not close enough for his leg to brush mine or our shoulders to touch. I notice that everything he does, he does carefully. He sits up straight, not lounging against the back of the couch like I do. I wonder if he thinks I'm a sweaty slob and I straighten, crossing my legs at the ankles in a way I imagine Queen Victoria would have approved of. It is really uncomfortable. Soon I give up and go back to lounging.

Neither of us speaks. The only sound is the sloshing of our lemonade as we take sips at irregular intervals. I can't decide if he is weird or if he really hates me, but God, I need someone to talk to. I have been sitting in my apartment for days, not unpacking, not decorating.

"Are you a ghost?"

He turns slowly, looking at me as if he's seriously considering the question. I assume he must be considering how crazy I am, so I keep talking.

"Or a magician?"

I breathe a little easier. He looks intrigued. I have intrigued my potential friend. All my anger at his bolting out of my apartment fizzles as I hurry on, wanting to keep this thread of interest alive.

"Not that my little brother thinks I'm anything but crazy, but your disappearing act the other day definitely reinforced his opinion."

When I say *disappearing,* he flinches.

"Why didn't you stay?" I asked. "I know shirtless Laurie can be a shocking sight, but I swear he's harmless."

He doesn't answer; he's just watching me.

I twist my fingers nervously. "If Laurie thinks I'm crazy, I figured maybe I should just accept it. This is an old building, right? You could just be a helpful spirit who welcomes new residents."

He laughs and his eyes light up.

I'm grinning. "I also thought you could be a mirage."

"A mirage?"

"It was really hot that day, and you know how they say you see mirages in the desert when you're about to die of thirst."

He nods.

"I was definitely dying of thirst and then you appeared."

"I am a mirage," he says, pausing. Then he frowns at me. "And you are?"

"I'm the girl next door," I say. "Well, the girl next door to next door."

"Elizabeth who is Jo. The girl next door to next door." He laughs again. I like it when he laughs. It seems like he gets warmer when it happens, like he's used to being stiff just like this apartment and laughing stretches him out, puts him at ease. I also like it that he remembers I want to be called Jo. This is a recent development, as I was always Liz to my "friends" in Minnesota, my mother calls me Elizabeth, and Laurie is constantly inventing permutations of my given name.

"And that boy was your brother?" he asks.

Now I go stiff. There's no reason for it, but it's a reflex I've developed. Whenever the phrase "your brother" came up back home, it ended in a screaming match or, that one time, a fistfight. I'd discovered I have a mean uppercut. Jennifer Norris was still sporting bandages at prom from her emergency nose job. Not that I'd been at prom, but word had gotten back to me.

I breathe through the tightness in my chest. "Yes. Laurie's my brother. He's fifteen."

"How old are you?"

"Sixteen."

"Me too." He breathes in and out, staring at his fingers curled around the glass of lemonade. "You didn't bring him with you, though."

"He's doing summer school," I say. "So I'm on my own most of the time."

I worry that I've been too obvious. Or careless. You're not supposed to tell strangers that you're home alone. Am I that desperate for a friend? Uh. Yes, I am.

He sits up a little straighter, looking right at me. His eyes, that intriguing blue shade capturing my gaze, are more penetrating and less evasive. "And your parents?"

"My mom is a hospital administrator," I say. "I guess her predecessor was a disaster, so she's spending all hours trying to convince her staff that she's not the devil incarnate. She's not home a lot."

He nods.

"How about yours?"

He doesn't answer at first and then just says, "Not around."

I quickly say, "Cool." I don't know what *not around* really means, but I don't want to pry. Parents are tricky. It's not like I'm looking to be friends with his mom or dad anyway.

I bite my lip, wanting to seal the deal before we head anywhere near deep, painful conversation. I'm looking for companionship; I don't want to go mucking around in the past. I want the past dead and buried in Minnesota.

"So I came over because I have a favor to ask." I'm ad-libbing now. I came over to chew him out, but now I'm back to wanting a friend. He's my best and only candidate.

"What kind of favor?"

"You know the neighborhood pretty well?"

"Yes."

Excellent. That's exactly what I'd hoped for.

"I need your help," I say.

He looks at me, suspicion dawning in his eyes.

"I swear it doesn't involve hauling boxes."

The doorbell rings. I tense up.

"Just leave them!" he yells.

"Who is it?" I whisper, as if robbers are waiting on the other side of the door.

"My groceries," he says.

"You have your groceries delivered?" I'm up and crossing the room. "I've gotta see this."

I fling open the door to find three bags of groceries lying at my feet. A delivery guy has already made his way towards the elevator, but he looks over his shoulder when he hears the door open.

He looks at me and frowns. "Huh. I thought you were a guy."

I roll my eyes and grab the bags.

"Kitchen?" I ask, heading in that direction. I assume it's in the same spot as our kitchen. Since he gets up to follow me, I assume my assumption is right.

He watches as I unpack his groceries. He takes the items that need refrigerating and puts them away.

"You know, if you want to avoid future accusations of rudeness, opening the door is a good start." I hand him a carton of eggs.

"I'll try to remember that," he says.

"So here's the deal," I say. "I'm new here, and since you abandoned me with my bags and I've now helped you with your bags, you owe me."

He looks like he wants to argue, but he doesn't say anything.

I sigh, wanting to be likable instead of demanding. "I'm sorry I'm not good at this."

"Good at what?" he asks.

"Asking for favors."

"Why not?"

My throat closes up. I don't want to talk about why not. I don't want to think about why not.

"My people skills are lacking."

"I've noticed that."

Laughing, I brush my fingers over his arm when I hand him a bag of carrots. The moment I touch him, we both stop. I'm not sure what's happened, but it's like the air has been sucked out of the room and we're just looking at each other. I don't think either of us is breathing.

I turn away, digging into the other grocery bag. What the hell was that?

"What's the favor?" His voice is soft. I can't look at him, so I look at the box of Frosted Mini-Wheats in my hands.

"I don't get it."

"I'm sorry?" He takes the box from me, but I'm still not looking at him. I'm staring at the kitchen counter.

"Manhattan," I say, embarrassed by my flushed face and my beating heart and my sucky navigation skills. "I know it's supposed to be a grid or something, but I keep getting lost and, to be honest, it's a little intimidating. I don't want to be lost in New York."

I turn to face him. When I meet his gaze, nothing has changed. The room is back to normal. I can breathe. Maybe I just imagined that moment.

"I need a tour guide," I say.

He stares at me. "You want me to help you?"

"Teach me about Manhattan. I live here now. I need to figure the city out."

I think I catch the jump of his pulse in the vein at his throat. "I . . ."

"We can start small. Just a walk around the neighborhood."

He looks away.

I try to lighten my voice. "I promise if I'm an intolerable person, I'll never bother you again. Not even to tell you how rude you are."

"Can I get that in writing?"

My smile is tingly as I realize he's going to say yes.

"What if I am?" he asks.

I fold up the empty grocery bag. "Sorry?"

"What if I am a ghost?" He leans against the counter, watching me. "Would you still want to take a walk with me?"

I puzzle over his question. Is it a joke? The words sound like they should be a joke, but his tone isn't teasing or even happy.

"If you decide you hate me, I've promised not to bother you," I say. "So how about if I decide you're a ghost, you promise not to haunt me. Okay?"

He closes his eyes and mine water, making him blur before me. I rub my eyelids; when I open them, he's watching me and I shiver under his intense gaze.

"Okay."

CHAPTER 5

I DON'T KNOW HOW I can do this. There has to be a way out of it. I could pretend to fall violently ill. I could pretend my mother is due home. I could start a small fire.

But I want to do this. I like the way we are talking. I like the way I am having a conversation.

I still want to know why the curse is playing with me.

But in the meantime, I'll play.

"How about the park?" I ask.

Nothing in real life has prepared me for this. The face-to-face. Yes, I had my mother, and even though I was invisible to her, I could talk with her all the time. But a conversation with a girl? I've never had one.

Instead I've had books. And television shows. And movies. And overheard conversations. Because of this, the rhythms and the patterns that everyone else takes for granted aren't foreign to me. This give-and-take of words, this verbal dance of share-and-withhold, confide-and-compel, is something I can try to fall into.

I have practiced for so long in my head, without even knowing I was practicing. Now I'm reaching for the words and the way to say them.

She has no idea how astonishing this conversation is to me. She has no idea what it's like to be an outsider to the outside world . . . and then to suddenly be let inside.

I want to keep saying hello. Because it all feels like a hello.

In the elevator, we chat about the elevator. She's already had a run-in with Smelly Guy from the sixth floor, but miraculously, she has yet to meet Irma from 2E, who likes to walk her cats three times a day. On leashes.

In the lobby, I try to keep us silent, so the doorman won't think anything is wrong. He opens the door for her, and I press through quickly.

Elizabeth notices the crunch. "I think you've gotten overly familiar with my heels," she says when we're outside. "Is there a feud going on between you and the doorman? Were you afraid he was going to lock you in?"

"They're all out to get me," I tell her. "Every single doorman in New York."

"Why?"

Why? It's a natural enough follow-up, the next logical step in the conversation. But I'm stuck without a next line.

"Um . . . because I once said something evil about a doorman's mother?"

The words fall awkwardly into the air. It's even more embarrassing to have my cheeks burn when I know they can be seen.

Elizabeth takes it in stride. "So how long have you lived here?" she asks.

Mercifully, an easy question to answer.

"All my life," I say. "Same apartment. Same building. Same city."

"Really?"

"For as long as I can remember, and back even further to when I can't remember. Since the day I was born, really. Where are you from?"

"Minnesota."

I love how she says it. *Minn-uh-soh-tah*.

"This must be quite a change," I say, gesturing to the speeding cabs, the endless line of buildings, the barrage of people around us.

"It is."

"Why did you leave?" I ask.

She looks away. "It's a long story."

I'm sure there's a short version of the long story, but it doesn't feel right for me to ask for it.

She asks, "Where do you go to school?"

I realize that she's starting to get stares when she talks to me. Because nobody else can see who she's talking to. And even in a city where it's commonplace to find people talking on microscopic cell phones or mumbling dialogue to themselves, it's still strange to see someone conversing with the air.

I quicken the pace. "Kellogg," I say, making up a school name. She's from Minnesota—she won't know all the private schools in Manhattan. "It's across town. Really small. You?"

"I'm going to Stuyvesant in the fall."

"Oh, Stuy. That's cool."

"Stuy?"

"Yeah. That's what everyone calls it."

"Good to know."

We're at the park now. There are more people, and she's getting more stares. I don't think she sees them, though. Or she's figured this is just the way city people are, rude and glaring. But that obliviousness isn't going to last long.

In order for this to work, I'm going to have to do most of the talking. At least now, when other people are around. I keep my voice low, so it will blend in with all of the other voices.

"So, you want to know about the city?" I ask as we start on one of the paths. "It's hard to tell you with any kind of perspective, because it's not like I've ever lived anywhere else." (In truth, I've never even *been* anywhere else. But I don't tell her that.) "I think it has a slightly different language than the rest of the world. When you live in New York, you can't help but know things only New Yorkers know. Most of it has to do with getting used to things. Like the subway. In most parts of the world, the idea that there are hundreds of miles of underground tubes with electrified rails careening cars back and forth—that would be science fiction. But here it's just life. Every day you head down there. You know exactly where to stand on the platform. If you do it long enough, you start to recognize some faces. Even with millions of people, you start to gather a neighborhood around you. New Yorkers love the bigness—the skyscrapers, the freedom, the lights. But they also love it when they can carve out some smallness for themselves. When the guy at the corner store knows which newspaper you want. When the barista has your order ready before you open your mouth. When you start to recognize the people in your orbit, and you know that, say, if you're waiting for the subway at eight fifteen on the dot, odds are the redhead with the red umbrella is going to be there too."

Elizabeth arches her eyebrow. "Tell me more about this redhead with a red umbrella."

I shrug. "It's not like I know all that much about her. She just tries to be at the subway at eight fifteen on the dot. She's probably thirty—maybe a little older. She's always reading magazines— *The New Yorker, Harper's,* that kind. Smart. One day it was pouring and she had this bright red umbrella. I probably only saw it once, but it made an impression, so now I always associate her with this bright red umbrella. You know how you do that? Create talismans for strangers, or for people you've just met? Like, he's the one with the gap in his teeth. Or she's the one who carries that purple bag. She's the redhead with the red umbrella. Everything else is just speculation."

"And do you speculate often?"

It's like she's asking me if I breathe often. "All the time!" I say, perhaps a little too emphatically. "I mean, there are so many lives around us. How can you not speculate?"

I can tell she's into this game. She points to a portly man on a bench, eating a donut. "How about him?"

"Gastroenterologist. His second wife just left him. He snores."

"Her?" She indicates a skanky teen girl listening to blaring headphones as she scowls at her phone.

"Russian spy. Deep, deep, *deep* cover. She looks up CIA

agents' favorite bands on Facebook and reports back to the Mother Country."

"That frat boy over there?"

"Poet laureate of the state of Wyoming, best known for his paeans to love between cowboys and their horses."

"The love that dare not speak its mane?"

"You know his work!"

She nods her head to gesture a little to the left. "That woman with four children?"

"Broadway actress. Researching the role of a woman with four children. Discovering a lot because her lesbian lover won't even let her have a pet."

"What about that girl?"

Tricky. She's pointing at herself.

"That girl? She looks like she's new to town. But it doesn't scare her. It excites her. She wants to see it all. And, yeah, she's also part of the Minnesota mafia. They get into gang wars over cheese."

"That's Wisconsin."

"I mean, they get into gang wars over which of the twin cities was born first."

"Wow. Hearing you is like looking in a mirror."

The woman with four children is glaring at us now, as if her mommy radar is tuned in to girls who talk too loudly to themselves in public places.

"Here, I have something to show you," I say, and run ahead.

We've hit the path that leads past the band shell, right to Bethesda Terrace. Trees that have lived for hundreds of years guard our steps, point us forward. It is one of my favorite places in the city, where nature draws a canopy over all the city thoughts, leaving you with a deep sense of leaves and light, people passing through and the world staying still. I run, and she follows. I jump down the steps to Bethesda Fountain, and she is right beside me. The angel statue greets us, magnificent in her peace, stately on her perch. The water of the fountain bows to her as musicians ring her with melodies. Behind her, lovers row their boats. Beyond them, trees run wild.

Elizabeth's never been here before. That much is clear in her expression. I have seen this look in people, this gasp of wonder. I want to tell her that this is only the first time, that there is going to be a second time and a third time and a fourth. That she will come here day after day, year after year. Because that is what I have done. And the feeling of being here, of being at the vortex of the city, doesn't diminish.

"This is amazing," she says.

"Yeah, isn't it?" a guy about two feet away from her says. He assumes she's talking to him. And from the way he's looking at her, I can tell he wants the conversation to continue.

"There's more," I tell her. I reach for her hand and then remember, no, I shouldn't try that. I shouldn't do that. Her hand will just be floating ridiculously in the air, for everyone to see.

I lead her away from the tourists and the musicians and the presiding angel. I take her over a wooden bridge, into the woods, into the silence. We reach the Rambles, where the park resists landscape and becomes a rough-and-tumble twist of secret paths. In fifty steps, you can retreat from the city, the world.

Elizabeth notices the change.

"Is this where all the serial killers hang out?" she asks.

"Only on Wednesdays," I tell her. "We're safe."

The trees close in, but because they do, I feel we can be more open. I don't have to worry as much about the way it appears to anyone but us.

"So while I easily picked out your connection to the Minnesota mob," I say, "I have to imagine my speculations missed a thing or two. Care to fill me in?"

"Oh, I'm just a simple girl," she says with a sarcastic smile, "who just happens to complicate everything she touches. I'm like Midas, only whatever I touch turns to drama. Or at least that's what my quote-friends-unquote back quote-home-unquote would say. I've never had Thai food, and only realized embarrassingly late in life that 'Thai' is pronounced 'Tie.' When I was in fifth grade, I was temporarily obsessed with tattoos, to the point that they had to hide all my Magic Markers. I was in choir for three years in order to be with my quote-friends-unquote, but I never sang a single note. I got really good at lip synching, though. This makes Laurie jealous, because if anyone should be the drag queen of the family, it's him. Only I don't think he actually likes drag. I don't think I've ever asked him."

We've arrived at a hidden bench. It has a brass plaque on it. *DEDICATED TO GRACE AND ARNOLD GOLBER IN HONOR OF THEIR GENEROSITY.*

I think Elizabeth's going to sit down, but instead she simply stops to read the plaque, then hikes a little farther before stopping to look at me.

"I think that fills you in," she says. "Now, do I get to speculate about you too?"

"Sure, go ahead."

She takes a long, hard look at me. It's unnerving. I am not used to this kind of scrutiny. I don't know what expression to make, what posture to take.

"I'm sorry," she says. "I was momentarily distracted by all your past lives. Let me focus."

She looks at me longer. Smiles.

"You're a reader, no doubt about that. You might have read *Little Women,* but didn't like it enough to go on to *Little Men.* That's okay—I forgive you. Maybe you're Twain's bitch. Or Vonnegut's. Deep in your heart, there's still a part of you that believes in Narnia and the Chocolate Factory and the Knights of the Round Table. Maybe not the Secret Garden, but I forgive you for that too. Am I warm?"

"Fiery," I tell her.

"Excellent. I have a feeling you might like math as well, especially as metaphor. You used to play an instrument—maybe a violin? You have a violinist's air about you. But you gave it up. Too much practice. Too much time indoors. You love this park—but that's not really speculation. That's already been demonstrated. Of course, this is where you take all the girls. This very spot. They fall for it every time."

"Do they?"

She nods. "It's that serial-killer atmosphere. It's an aphrodisiac."

"Like oysters."

"Wow. I think you're the first guy I've ever gone on a stroll with who knew what an aphrodisiac was. That in itself is an aphrodisiac."

I should have an answer to this, but instead I backtrack.

"Is that what we're doing?" I ask. "Going on a stroll?"

She comes a little closer. "It's undeniable, wouldn't you say?"

She's looking at me again. Studying me. I can't help but be drawn to this. Such a new experience. Such an unexpected turn. A question rises within my thoughts, and before I can stop it, I find myself asking it aloud.

"When you look at me, what do you see?"

I have never had a chance to ask this question before. And even the act of asking makes me shake, makes me feel as if I have opened up my chest and shown her what's inside. I am not ready for any of this, and I do it anyway.

"I see a boy," she says. "I see someone who's always on the verge of vanishing back into a thought. I see messy hair and full lips. I see the way you can't stand still. I see the way your T-shirt fits, the way your jeans fit. I see you unsure of what to do. And I can relate to that. Really."

"What color are my eyes?" I ask. It's almost a whisper.

She leans in to me. "They're blue. Robin's-egg blue with a few flecks of brown."

There is no way to describe what I feel. This is something I've never known. She has told me something I've never known.

We are so close right now. Neither of us knows what to do.

"What color are *my* eyes?" she asks.

Now it is my turn to lean in. Even though I already know the answer.

"Brown," I say. "Deep brown. Like coffee without any milk."

She smiles, and I don't know which words are supposed to follow these words, what moment is supposed to follow this moment.

"I like strolling with you," she says. Then she steps back, looks around at the trees. "I can't believe we're in the middle of *New York City*. This park is insane."

"I know," I tell her, and start walking again. I've lost any sense of where we are. She notices it immediately.

"Are we lost? I mean, in the middle of Central Park."

"No," I insist. "If we keep going, we'll hit the Castle."

"That's so Prince Charming of you!" She takes something out of her pocket. "Here. Maybe this'll help."

It happens too fast. She takes the compass out of her pocket and throws it my way. But I don't realize what's happening until too late. I realize enough to get my hands there, but not enough to concentrate on making them solid.

The compass falls right through my fingers.

She sees it fall right through my fingers.

"Sorry," I say. I bend over and very carefully, very deliberately pick the compass back up. I make a show of looking at it. Gauging our direction. Then I hand it back to her. When she takes it, our fingers touch. And the sensation of that reverberates all through my body, my thoughts, and too many of my hopes.

Did she see it? I wonder. *Did she see it go right through me? Or did it really look like I dropped it?*

I hear a jogger coming closer, panting on a late mile. I step away from Elizabeth. I don't say a word until he's past. She's distracted, and waits until he leaves before saying something else.

"What is it?" she asks when he's gone.

"What's what?"

"That look on your face. What does it mean?"

All secrets lead back to the big secret. To give one thing away means to give everything away.

I must be careful.

"I'm not used to this."

"What?"

I gesture to her and me. "*This*. Telling the truth and having someone hear it. Giving words and getting words back. I'm just— I'm not used to it."

She's studying me again. "You keep to yourself?"

I nod. "Yes. I keep to myself. Only now I'm not keeping to myself. I'm keeping to—you, I guess. I'm keeping to you."

Too much. Too fast. Too intense. The glass soul falls to the ground and shatters into a thousand words. The invisible boy becomes visible, and all of a sudden, his emotions blast neon.

"I'm sorry," I say. "This is just a stroll. It's not anything. I'm being ridiculous."

"No," she says. "Don't do that."

She reaches out to me, and for a moment I think she'll go right through. But I'm there. She touches me, and I'm there.

We are in the middle of a city, but for a minute there is no city. We are in the middle of the woods, but for a minute there are no woods. We are surrounded by people, but for a minute there is no fear of interruption.

"This is the beginning of something," she says. "Neither of us knows what, but that's okay. What matters is that it's the beginning of something. You feel that, don't you?"

I do. And that's just as surprising as being touched, as being seen.

She sees it in my eyes. "Good," she says. "Let's not go any further than that right now. You have the rest of the park to show me, after all."

The woods resume. The people resume. The city resumes. We return to the paths, and the paths lead us to more paths. We wander until dusk settles and the lamps are lit. Every now and then I say something, and every now and then she says something. But mostly we observe. We speculate. We steal glances of each other. Observe each other. Speculate about each other. Then wander some more.

It is only when I get home that I feel the weight again, of all the things I cannot tell her, of all the things I am.

CHAPTER 6

LAURIE'S LAUGHTER CARRIES through the closed door as I turn the key. I slide one last glance at Stephen, who's unlocking his own door. He gives me a quick wave before vanishing into his apartment. I swallow a sigh as my heart pinches now that he's gone.

My friend. More than a friend. My hope of something to be.

My hand rests on the doorknob as I fight the urge to chase after Stephen and steal another hour alone with him. I realize I never really came back to the building. I'm still out in the park with him, throwing wishes up at the angel. Wishes that this metropolis will hand me the life I'd secretly been wishing for. The angel fountain offers a perfect place for those wishes you're too afraid to admit you've locked away, even in the dusky minutes before falling into sleep, when your heart opens up like a night-blooming flower. So hiding your desires is that much harder. But standing next to Stephen in a forest that was quiet and private, qualities I'd thought impossible in this city, my wishes brimmed over and I had no choice but to lay them at the angel's feet, hoping for her mercy.

I wish I was still beside him walking through the park as if we were the only two souls exploring its hidden wilds. But it's late and Laurie will worry if I don't make an appearance. I shake off the lingering memory of the park and turn the doorknob.

I toss my keys on a still-unpacked box in the entryway. Many identical boxes occupy our apartment in various stacks according to the room their contents theoretically will occupy. Theoretically because they have to find their way out of the boxes and resume their function as lamps or art. Theoretically because Mom and Laurie are obviously waiting for me to do the unpacking—after all, I am the one who's home alone all day—but I resent their assumption. I resent being the only one whose life is on hold, who wades through the sticky weight of summer heat towards fall, where school will pull me back into life's regular rotation.

I kick the box, but my mood lightens when I snag the idea that unpacking offers me a vehicle for spending more time alone with Stephen. I almost turn around to skip, and I choke a little when I realize that I actually wanted *to skip,* over to his apartment and ask him to help me dig our spare sheets out of boxes tomorrow, but Laurie's call stops my giddy retreat.

"Hey, stranger!"

Pivoting, I abandon my impulse and trot into the living room, only to discover Laurie crouched like a cat on the back of the sofa. Sitting beside him is a boy I don't know. My brother had called me into the room, but I'm not the stranger. When I first walk in, the new boy's face is lifted up, open and smiling, but when he sees me, he folds up like an origami box.

"Uh . . . hey." I try to smile at the stranger, but he's avoiding my eyes.

Laurie slides from his perch to settle next to the cagey boy. "Sean, this is my sister . . ." He looks at me, his mouth crinkling. "What are we calling you these days?"

"Jo—oh, whatever, just call me Elizabeth." I'm tired of reminding everyone that I wanted to change my name the minute we changed places: both signifiers of a shift vital to our survival. I can be Elizabeth for the sake of ease, but I swear to myself that I will always be Jo on paper.

Laurie's crooked smile widens. "Classy. Sean, meet Elizabeth. Or at least Elizabeth for now."

"Brat," I say, and flop into a chair. The chair is next to Sean, and the moment my butt hits the cushion, he pulls back, as if he's a turtle and the sofa is a shell he's trying to withdraw into. He mumbles something. I assume it's "hello."

"Nice to meet you too." My tone is sharper than it should be, but I'm annoyed that Sean is acting like I've invaded his space when he's sitting on my couch. Laurie tosses darts at me with his glare.

"Sean lives in Five-C," Laurie says. "Two floors up, one door over. We keep running into each other getting the mail, so I thought I'd get to know one of the neighbors."

He smiles one of those only-Laurie-can-pull-off smiles and Sean uncurls a little.

"You two would be good buddies." Laurie has taken over the scene and is now directing it with the skill of a professional. "We started talking because he was carrying this around." I only notice now that Laurie has a comic in his hands, which he waves at me. The flapping pages make Sean flinch, and I like him a little more. He snatches the book out of Laurie's careless grasp.

"*Fables*." I attempt another smile for Sean. "That's a good one. Vertigo does a lot of interesting stuff."

He kind of smiles back, mumbles something at the same time he scuttles off the couch and heads for the door. Laurie follows him, and I hear my brother say goodbye as the door opens and closes.

"What was that about?" I ask as Laurie strolls back into the room and rolls himself out full length on the sofa.

"What was what about?" Laurie says.

"Why did he leave all of a sudden?" I wonder if I make that bad a first impression.

"He apologized and said he had to go to dinner," Laurie says. "Didn't you hear him?"

I absolutely did not hear anything Sean said and wonder how Laurie has already tuned in to our upstairs neighbor's secret language of undertones. But that's Laurie's gift: He wins people. Not every time, though.

"Cute, yeah?" Laurie gazes at the ceiling, but I catch the twinkle in his eyes and my stomach clenches.

I don't remember cute. It's hard to remember much of anything about Sean. I think he has black hair and is skinny but not scrawny. He was too busy trying to become one with our sofa for me to get a good sense of his looks.

"And he's a reader," Laurie says. "So bonus points there. Guess I'll be waiting for the postman a little more often . . ."

"Come on, Laurie," I say. "Do you even know if he's—"

I try to stop myself, but it's too late. The giddy flush of Laurie's cheeks washes out. He sits up, swinging his legs over the side of the sofa and looking right at me.

My throat is closing up, but I force words out. "I didn't mean . . . I'm sorry." I don't want to have this type of sucker-punch reflex. When I let fear get the best of me, I hate myself. I react like a dog who's been beaten; anytime I see a broom, I flinch and snarl.

He lets me sit in a pool of guilt for another quiet minute.

"I'm sorry," I say again.

"Forget it."

The apartment door bangs open. Laurie and I both jump up. Mom stumbles into the living room.

"I'm home! And I made dinner!" She lifts up bags of carryout Chinese. From the looks of it, she bought the entire restaurant.

Laurie hoots and bounces over to her. We spread a picnic of cartons on the living room floor. Mom apologizes for never being around, but she's glowing in a way that makes me know she loves her new job. Laurie chatters about school, and when he mentions Sean, I give him a teasing wink. He beams at me and I know I'm forgiven. When they ask about my day, I make excuses about not unpacking and mention exploring the park. I don't bring up Stephen. Something he said in the park is still racing through my veins, moving in perfect time with my heartbeat. "I'm keeping to you." I want that. I'm not ready to let anyone else near it. So I stay quiet while Laurie and Mom sketch out the shape of their lives. We don't talk about Minnesota. We don't talk about Dad. And somewhere between pot stickers and moo shu pork, we become a family for a couple of hours.

It's after midnight, but I can't fall asleep, having learned that New York mapo tofu is much spicier than the Minnesota rendition. Despite my gurgling tummy I don't mind being awake and alone in my room. Our apartment is quiet, but I can still hear the city— alive and at work—on the street below. I thought it would be one of the things that bothered me about Manhattan, the absence of silence, but I like the perpetual buzz of humanity. It reminds me of a clock that never needs to be wound; its gears are always turning, always at work keeping the pace of life moving just as it should.

I'm also not bothered by sleeplessness because I'm thinking about Stephen. I'm lying on my back, staring up at the ceiling above my bed where I've tacked up a star chart I got at the Chicago planetarium during our family vacation when I was ten. But I'm not looking at the stars like I usually do when I'm trying to find my way to sleep. I'm rewinding my day, reliving the park, Stephen's cool touch that leaves me warm all over, the timbre of his voice easing my anxiety at how unfamiliar my new home is. It is the best day I have ever had. I want to be there again and again and again.

I roll onto my side and reach under my bed, pulling out my case of art supplies. They were the first thing I unpacked. Before clothes, before pillows. I rifle through brushes, paint tubes, and cases of pastels. If I can't sleep, at least I can save the day in the best way I know. My first thought is that watercolors would be the perfect medium. The blurred colors washing into one another would fit the unsteadiness between us. But I want to feel the weight of the charcoal in my hand when I strike the page, making lines that will become a face I've already memorized. Memorized without even thinking about it.

I go to my desk and get a sketch pad. Settling on my bed, I rub my finger over the suede feel of the charcoal stick, pull it out, and begin to sketch. I draw for hours and don't remember falling asleep. I wake up when light hits my room. I'm sprawled across the bed, sheets of heavy drawing paper strewn around me. My fingers are smudged with charcoal, but I must have been dreaming before I had a chance to sketch any image of Stephen or the park. All the pages around me are blank.

I hurry through breakfast and a shower. Mom and Laurie are already gone for the day and I want to follow through with my me-and-Stephen-unpacking date idea. In less than an hour, I'm knocking on the door for 3D.

"Who is it?"

Tingles run up and down my arms at the sound of his voice. "It's me."

Unlike yesterday, he doesn't leave me waiting outside. The door opens almost immediately and he's smiling at me. I take my time looking at his hair, his eyes, his lips, his hands. My heart is doing somersaults.

"Hi," he says softly. It feels intimate, his voice low, only for me. My toes curl into the bed of my flip-flops.

"Hey." I am smiling like an idiot, but I can't help it.

"Do you want to come in?" He steps back, but I shake my head.

"I have a favor to ask," I say. "And it requires your presence at my place. I know it's a lot to ask, it being so far out of the way and all."

I'm laughing, but he looks uncomfortable. I think I know why.

"Mom and Laurie are gone all day," I say quickly. "It's just me and boxes."

He smiles at me, and I think I've levitated an inch. "Boxes?"

"I could use some help unpacking." I try to look sultry. "I promise rewards."

He laughs, and that's when I remember that sultry doesn't usually work for me; it comes off as maniacal, and now I'm blushing and kicking the frame of his door.

"I can help you unpack," he says, but he sounds a little unsure.

I'm starting to doubt my plan. Why would he want to unpack books and dishware? Yesterday he took me to beautiful places in Central Park, and this is what I suggest when it's my turn? I suck.

I hurry to salvage my idea. "We don't really need to unpack. I just need to show some evidence of progress with the boxes. I'm in charge of the boxes, and if I don't open one or two today, I might get kicked out of the apartment."

"Evicted, eh?" He grins. "That would be tragic."

"I know," I say. "It's such a nice building. Good neighbors are hard to find, I hear."

I start to back away.

"I'll be there in a minute," he says, ducking back into his apartment. I wander back to 3B and wait for him at my door. He appears a few minutes later, locks his own apartment, and follows me into mine.

We stop in the middle of the living room. His eyes sweep the space.

"You've got a box infestation," he says. "I'm afraid it's serious."

I laugh, heading for the kitchen to grab a knife. When I come back to the living room, Stephen pushes a box towards me.

"I've found it," he says. "*This* is the box for us."

"So be it." I brandish the knife and begin cutting away the packing tape. We open the box together, slowly pulling away the sticky remnants of tape. The container is filled to the brim with objects wrapped in bubble wrap. I pull out one of the mystery shapes and pop a few of the bubbles, enjoying their snapping sound, before I tear away the plastic cocoon. Stephen rocks back on his heels, watching me as if a person wrestling with over-taped bubble wrap is the most fascinating pastime on earth. His attention makes me giddy.

"Pretty," he says when I toss the protective shell away to reveal a carnival-glass candy dish that belonged to my grandmother.

"Then you can decide where it goes." I hand the dish to him. He takes it carefully, which I appreciate. Its value is sentimental only, and I think it's sweet that he's cautious about handling the glass dish.

"So when you look at me, you think 'interior decorator,'" he says, walking around the room as he searches for the candy dish's new home.

"I think you've got what it takes," I say, unwrapping a music box. I automatically wind it up, though I already know doing so will rob some of my happiness. Tinkling music flutters through the living room.

He pauses, listening. " 'Send in the Clowns'?"

I nod. "This is Laurie's."

"Yeah?"

"He's had it since he was five," I say.

"Kind of a heavy song for a five-year-old." Stephen sets the candy dish on an end table. It looks lonely without jewel-toned candies filling it.

"My grandma." I point to the empty glass bowl. "Candy-dish grandma gave it to him for Christmas because he loved music and clowns. I don't think she realized that it was a sad song. I'd be shocked if she knew who Stephen Sondheim was."

I stand up, cradling the music box in my palms.

"How is your brother adjusting?"

"Better than me." I sigh.

He flinches a little and I chew my lip.

"I don't mean . . . I feel good now," I say. "When we're together . . ."

My heart stutters. I don't want to say too much and ruin things. "But Laurie has school and stuff to keep him busy. I'm stuck with unpacking duty."

"Ah . . . the injustice." He's smiling again, and I relax.

"Right?" I say, putting the back of my hand to my forehead in mock suffering. "He did manage to snare someone else in the building already. A boy who lives upstairs . . . Five-C."

"Sean," Stephen says.

"Oh." I tilt my head, taking in his thoughtful expression. "You know him?"

He balks. "A little. I think he prefers books to people."

"I'm the last person who'd call that a character flaw," I say. "But still, he's not exactly a chatterbox, is he? I couldn't understand a word he was saying, but I'm pretty sure he's Laurie's new crush—God save us all."

I watch his reaction, which is mostly a non-reaction. His face is open, pleasant. All he says is: "Sean strikes me as very shy. Hence the mumbling."

I grip the music box a little too tightly. "Let's take a break. I'll put this in Laurie's room."

"A break already?" Stephen looks at the other piles of boxes around the room. "We only unpacked two things."

"I said I only need evidence of progress." I nod at the candy dish. "You have provided said evidence."

He shrugs. "It's your eviction."

I lead him out of the living room into the hallway, pausing to set the music box on top of Laurie's dresser. I grind my teeth, frustrated that I'm doing it again. Self-sabotage as a defense mechanism never ends well.

It doesn't help that Stephen is passing all my tests. It happened with him yesterday too. I'd kept my testing light—but it was still testing. When I mentioned Laurie and drag in the same sentence, Stephen didn't so much as flinch. And bringing up Sean and Laurie together is a non-issue for Stephen too.

I couldn't bear it if he was one of *them*. The ones who try to not make a face but inevitably do. The ones who shrug and say, "I don't care what *they* do, but I don't want to hear about it." The ones who whisper behind your back, who make excuses when you mention they don't spend time with you anymore.

My last boyfriend turned out to be one of them. Watching that relationship fizzle out wasn't any sort of epic tragedy. It would have died on its own anyway. His reaction to my brother was just a catalyst, speeding its demise.

I rarely think about Robbie these days, but when I linger outside my bedroom door, I know why I am now, though I'd rather not admit it. Association bites. But I can't deny that these skittering feelings, the creep of heat up my neck paired with fluttering in my stomach—all signs of a blossoming crush—last appeared when I crashed into Robbie while carrying an armload of supplies into the art room at our high school. I swore till I couldn't breathe and he laughed. A week later we were dating. Two months later I was screaming at him in the school parking lot while our classmates watched, whispered, and snickered.

"This is my room," I say. "Do you want to see it?" I worry I am being too pushy, that I should ask if he wants to watch a movie in the living room, but I want him to see me, and me is my room.

"If you'd like to show me," he says.

I take a breath and go inside. Despite all my pre-planning of the unpacking-with-Stephen event, I didn't work a bedroom cleanup into that scheme. The remnants of my restless night of non-creation are still scattered across my bed. My pajamas are hanging from the chair at my desk. A basket full of clean clothes waits to be folded.

"Oh," I say, and go to clear the paper and charcoals from my bed. I shove everything into my art case and slide it back under the bed. "Sorry about the mess."

"That's okay," he says. "At least it doesn't smell."

I sit on the bed, patting the rumpled blanket next to me.

He settles near me, not close enough to touch. Somehow a mallet has landed in my chest and is now pounding on my rib cage. I want to run my fingers along his forearm, from elbow to wrist, and then clasp his hand in my own. But there's something I have to do first. I have to get past my own fear.

"I hate to do this," I say. "But after yesterday—when I told you there's something here, I meant it."

"I know you did." He rests his fingers lightly on mine.

I flip my hand over, curling my fingers around his. "But I have some baggage to deal with."

"More unpacking?" He smiles slowly.

"Of a different sort." I lean back on my elbows and I'm sorry when my hand slips from his, but I have to focus if I'm going to get through this. When he's touching me, it's hard to think about anything else.

He bends forward, resting his arms on his legs. His voice gets rough. "Do you have a boyfriend back in Minnesota?"

I'm startled and it makes me laugh nervously, especially because I'd just been thinking about Robbie.

"Just a lame-ass ex-boyfriend. He claimed rebuilding motorcycles was his calling," I say. "But I never saw him get near a bike, and I'm pretty sure if I set out a crescent wrench, a socket wrench, and a hammer, he wouldn't be able to tell me which was which. Well, maybe the hammer."

I'm relieved when he laughs. "But no strings attached?"

"I cut those strings in April," I say.

"So where are the bags?" he asks.

I'm uneasy again, beginning to wish I hadn't brought this up. "You asked why we left."

"Heavy baggage?" he says.

I press my lips together, exhaling slowly through my nose. "Yes."

"Then you should tell me. It's more evidence of progress." He says it so calmly that I almost curl into a ball, wanting to rest my head in his lap. Instead I twist my fingers in the blankets.

"We moved because of Laurie."

He doesn't respond, just leans in, listening.

"My brother is gay."

Again, nothing. He doesn't blink, doesn't move, just listens. When I don't speak again, he seems to decide I need something. He nods.

"This spring, six assholes at my school jumped him." My voice starts to shake. I can't remember the last time I talked about what happened. "Baseball team hazing, they said. Hate crime is more like it."

I'm starting to feel dizzy. My stomach twists and I sit up.

"How badly was he hurt?"

"Broken jaw, broken collarbone, broken ribs, broken arm." I clutch the edge of the bed. "They had bats."

I hear him draw a sharp breath.

"He was in the hospital for weeks," I say.

"That must have been horrible," he says.

"It was. But considering Laurie was the one with all the broken bones, he took it better than the rest of us. He's always been our family cheerleader. But my mom and dad fell apart. Dad didn't take it well when Laurie first came out, but . . . what Dad did next none of us saw coming. He blamed Laurie for the assault, talked nonstop about how Laurie must have provoked them, said that they were 'good boys' and we shouldn't press charges. Mom went ballistic."

"I assumed your parents were divorced," Stephen says. "Since you moved here with just your mom."

"They will be when all the paperwork goes through," I tell him. "My dad's family is conservative, but he always claimed to be the liberal of the bunch. We didn't spend much time with that side of the family. But I guess his liberalism only stretched so far before it broke."

Stephen's shaking his head. "I'm so sorry."

"It wasn't just my dad," I say. "People didn't know how to handle it. My friends got weird—even the ones who really did care. I'm sure it was my fault too, but I was so angry. I couldn't trust anyone." I look up at him. "And sometimes I think I still don't know how."

"That makes sense."

"What I'm trying to say is that I spent the last four months learning to be alone, avoiding the world, hating pretty much anyone who so much as blinked at me," I say. "But when I'm with you, I don't want to be that person anymore."

"Thank you," he says quietly.

The anchor of pain that I've been dragging around Manhattan

with me snaps free, sinking into the past, where I hope it will rest undisturbed. He knows. He knows and he's still here. I want to laugh and cry. But I want something else even more. I edge closer to him on the bed. He doesn't move. I'm looking at his lips, tracing their shape with my eyes.

I close my eyelids and quickly lean forward. I feel the cool whisper of his breath on my face, but then I'm no longer leaning. I'm falling. I make a full face-plant against my bed, and the familiar scent of our fabric softener hits my nose. Spluttering through cotton, I roll over. Stephen is bending over me, his eyes wide. I stare at him. My stomach wants to climb out my throat. He obviously jumped out of the way when I tried to kiss him.

My cheeks are on fire, but humiliation makes my blood cold. *I'm such a moron. This is too soon.*

I'm blinking as fast as I can so I won't cry, but tears are biting at the corners of my eyes. I want to cry because it feels so good to finally have talked to someone kind about Laurie. I want to cry because the boy I like didn't want to kiss me. I want to cry because I'm in a new city and I'm lonely.

"Are you okay?" he asks.

I can't shake my head or nod. I'm afraid to move at all. Paralysis is the only thing between me and a total meltdown.

"I'm so sorry, Elizabeth, but I have to go." He's still hovering above me, his hands pressing into the bed on each side of me. "It wasn't your fault."

He fixes me with a gaze that makes my breath stop. Without closing his eyes, he leans down. Then his lips are brushing against mine, feather soft.

His kiss lingers, electric on my mouth, but he's walking out of my room.

I'm still lying there when I hear the apartment door open and close as he leaves. I'm still lying there when I realize I have no idea what he meant.

CHAPTER 7

I AM FINDING IT HARDER and harder to concentrate on myself when I am around her. If I am too caught up in her—in caring about her, in wondering about her—I forget about my body. I disappear in my thoughts of her.

This is not a problem I've had before. To escape my own story long enough to be a part of someone else's—this has never been a temptation. With my parents, there was always the knowledge of what was going on. Every interaction they had with me was tethered to the fact of what I was. All of our conversations were, in some way, about me. But with Elizabeth, I lose that tether. My thoughts are free to think only of her. But if my thoughts go too far, then my body, left to its own devices, loses its ability to touch, to hold, to stay.

I have to learn to be conscious of her and conscious of myself at the same time.

I am so new at this thing, which I deeply suspect is what other people call love.

I return to her apartment an hour later, after I've managed to rehearse my focus, practice my concentration.

Mercifully, she lets me back in. Mercifully, her brother and mother are still gone.

She has been taking out her anger and confusion on the boxes. There's a sheen of sweat on her skin, and her room is an astonishment of piles and scatter.

"What was that?" she says.

"I want us to go fast," I tell her. "But I need us to go slow."

She scrutinizes me. "Why?"

If I cannot tell her *the* truth, I can tell her *a* truth.

"Because I've never done this before."

"Never."

"No. Never."

"No evil exes?"

"No exes mark my spot. Evil or otherwise."

"Why?"

I shake my head. "It just hasn't happened."

I can't tell her she's the first person I've ever had feelings for— she's not. But at the same time, I can't tell her she's the first person I've ever had feelings for who actually knows I exist. Because she is. And that would no doubt scare her.

"You can't just leave," she tells me. "If a moment goes wrong or if something isn't right—you can't just say you're sorry and walk out the door. The next time you do that, the door's going to be locked and bolted behind you. Do you understand? I like you, okay?

But I also need to like the way you make me feel. And just now? I didn't like that at all."

I tell her I know.

"Okay, then." She looks around the room. "So who's my box bitch?"

I smile. "I'm your box bitch."

"I'm afraid I didn't hear you."

"I'M YOUR BOX BITCH!"

Now she smiles. "Much better. Let's get to work."

I focus. As I rip off the packing tape, I focus. As I fold the empty boxes into their flattest state, I focus. When she's showing me books, asking me if I like certain authors—I focus. And then when those books sentry around us in stacks, and she beckons me to hear her favorite Margaret Atwood poems, I focus. It's called "Variations on the Word *Sleep*" and at the very end the poet says she would like to be "the air that inhabits you for a moment"—hearing this, my own breathing intensifies, like breathing itself is a sense.

Time doesn't stop, but we stop. We cannot ask time to stop, but we can stop ourselves.

She turns to me, and I focus. On her breathing. Her eyes. Her lips. She leans into me, and I focus. Her heat. Her skin. Her hands.

We touch, and I focus. We kiss, and I focus.

We are the time. We are the breathing.

We are the air.

What follows is an almost perfect week.

The weather turns nasty outside, storm after storm after storm, which proves to be a perfect excuse to stay indoors. With her brother off at summer school and her mother starting work, we have the days to ourselves. Our apartments and the hallway between them become the only territory we need, the Profoundly Sovereign Nation of Us, and we alternate between the newness of her place and the long history of mine.

She discovers my parents' old board games in our hallway closet, and soon we are playing them all, sometimes two at once. Risk and Monopoly and Scrabble and Trivial Pursuit. It's been a long time since I've played them, and it makes me a little maudlin at first.

Elizabeth senses this and asks, "Do you miss your parents?"

I stop, game piece in hand. How does she know? And then I realize she believes my story, that my parents are off on some research trip for the summer. She believes I miss them in the way you miss something you know will someday return.

"A little," I say. Then, "It's your turn."

Over the board games, she tells me a lot about Minnesota, and Robbie, and Laurie, and her parents. I tell her about people in the park, residents in the building, other things I've overheard or witnessed over the past few years. It's the difference between autobiography and biography, and if she notices, she doesn't mention it. A few times, she asks me about my school, and I make things up. Or she asks me about my parents, and I give her an altered version. The mother I tell her about is still a recognizable version of my mother—the same quirks, the same laughs, the same missing family history. Only she isn't dead. And she doesn't have an invisible son.

My version of my father is a farther stretch. Or maybe it isn't. Since I don't really know him at all, there's always a possibility that the things I'm saying are true.

Meanwhile, it's not all conversation and unpacking and board games. There are sublime moments of curling together, breathing together, kissing together, feeling together. Every now and then, I manage to get lost in my own private happiness, and I realize that I've lost my focus. But then I see her eyes are closed, and she hasn't noticed. My lips, for that moment, simply seemed light to her. Or my hold on her was gentle, my caress breeze-like.

Somehow, it works.

The only source of tension is the fact that I haven't met her brother or her mother.

"They're starting to think I've made you up," she says.

I can't tell her that I saw Laurie just yesterday, mooning by the mail room, pretending to read a book while his eye was constantly drawn to the door. When I first saw him, on that first day, all I could really see was his shirtless bravado. But now, looking closer, knowing what I know about what he's been through, I manage to see the vulnerability, the eagerness, the mix of in-your-face defiance and in-my-mind loneliness. For fifteen minutes, he waited by the mail room, and for fifteen minutes, I waited with him. If he sensed my presence, he didn't let on. I saw his scars—the visible ones—and saw how breaking him had not made him any less beautiful. If anything, he stood stronger, because he'd survived. I was envious, really, of how comfortably he inhabited his body. How he wasn't going to let anyone take that away from him.

Then Sean arrived. Also reading a book. And in Laurie's face there was that flash of extraordinary nervousness, followed by the click of determination and the illusion of total calm.

"Hey, you," he said, and Sean seemed delighted to see him.

I left then. They would have thought it was just the two of them in that mail room, but I would've known I was there. And I had no right to whatever it was they'd decide to share.

Again, I can't tell Elizabeth any of this. I can't tell her that her brother has come to mean something to me, even if, as far as she knows, I only saw him for a brief conversation the day they moved in. She wants us all to hang out, for me to get to know him, and I don't really know how to address this. Then one day, it's right there in front of me. Laurie calls for his usual after-school check-in, and I tell Elizabeth to pass the phone.

"Really?" she says.

I nod, and she gives it to me.

"Laurie?" I say.

"Yeah?"

"This is Stephen."

"No way!"

"Way."

"This isn't some actor my sister's hired to impersonate her imaginary boyfriend?"

"If it is, I'm really enjoying the research."

"Gross!"

"Anyway, do you know what day today is?"

"Free cone day?"

"Close. Let's start with a day of the week."

"If I'm not mistaken, it's Wednesday."

"Correct! And what's Wednesday?"

"Um . . . the day after Tuesday?"

"No. It's the day new comics come out."

"I'm fascinated to see where you're going with this."

"It's not me that's going somewhere. It's you. You're going to Midtown Comics and picking up a copy of the special edition of *Runaways* that came out today. Your sister wants one."

"And what's in it for me, exactly?"

"Sean, Laurie. Sean is in it for you. He goes there every Wednesday afternoon at four."

There's a pause. "What has my sister told you?"

"I'm guessing that she's not the only one with an imaginary boyfriend, Laurie. Make it real. If you want to, of course."

"Thank you, my new spiritual advisor. I shall take that under consideration."

"Just do it before four o'clock, okay? And I was serious about bringing back that *Runaways* comic for your sister."

"Aye aye, Captain."

Elizabeth and Laurie talk for a little bit more. Even before she's off, though, Elizabeth is looking at me like I've done something very, very good.

"You're sure Sean's going to, um, return the affections?" she asks once the call has ended.

I shrug. "Not sure. But it's only going to hurt until he tries. And if Sean isn't into him, I'm sure he'll be kind about it."

(I do not tell her about the time I spotted Sean in his hallway trying desperately to get a wi-fi connection so he could continue chatting with a boy from Dallas.)

"Well, I think you've won my brother over," Elizabeth says.

"And you? Have I won you over?"

She laughs. "Oh, I'm not as easy as my brother."

I know it can't go on like this. I know that this bliss is built on a razor-thin foundation, and at any moment the wind could come along.

But I am enjoying myself. Enjoying her. Which makes it so easy to forget.

Elizabeth heads back to her apartment for dinner. She invites me along, but I tell her I can't. She doesn't question it too much, just gives me a kiss goodbye.

Two hours later, I am sitting on the lime-green couch, reading the copy of *Blankets* that she let me borrow, when I hear a noise at the door.

At first, I don't get it. It's not a knock. Or a delivery . . .

It's a key in the door.

I put down the book. Stand up.

The key turns in the lock.

The door opens.

And in walks my father.

He's older.

The last time I saw him was a year ago, but it was my mother's funeral, and I wasn't really paying attention.

Now, though, I see him. His hair is all gray. He's still tall, still strong—but weathered. He's wearing different glasses. Thin and silver.

"Stephen!" he calls out.

I am right here, I want to say. But instead I stand there, watching him. He looks around at the apartment. Closes the door. Puts his briefcase down—a briefcase, not a suitcase, so I know he's not planning to stay.

It's like an adult version of the game we'd always play before he left—hide and not seek. I am always the kid who's hiding. He is always the father who's not seeking.

I am right here.

He calls my name again. Shifts on his feet. He's starting to realize.

"Stephen." He says it quieter now. He knows I'm in the room.

"Hi, Dad."

It's too short—not enough to work with. He turns my direction but misses by a few feet.

"How are you?" he asks the empty space.

I can't help myself; I move farther away, so he'll feel more foolish.

"I'm fine," I say.

His head jerks to another spot.

I keep moving.

It's not a fun game for either of us.

"Why are you here?" I ask.

"I got your email," he says. "About the girl. And I realized, it's been a long time—"

"Since you've seen me?"

"Since I've been here."

"You haven't been here since she died."

He nods. "That's right."

I've stopped moving, and he's facing me now. Part of me wants to eviscerate him—to ask him how he believes it's at all acceptable to leave a teenage boy alone for a year after his mother dies. But the other part of me keeps remembering: He writes the checks. If he were to stop supporting me, I would be on the street. And it's not like I've ever wanted him here. I am happier alone.

Plus, I do feel sorry for him, in a way. All through my childhood, and into my adolescence, it would be one of the major topics in my head: Which parent are you? Meaning: If you were to have, say, an invisible son, what would you do? Would you be the one to run or the one to stay? My answer was never very consistent. Some days, I would be certain I'd be my mother. The caregiver. The one who felt the tie so acutely. The one who built the nest. And other days, especially as I got older, I'd think: *You're fooling yourself. You want to be your mom. But really, you're your dad. If you were in this situation, you'd be gone in a second.*

It would be the cruel thing to do, but I am not above cruelty. Witness me now, asking my father, "How's the new family? Are all my half brothers and half sisters half-visible?"

My mother would say, *You only hurt yourself when you talk like that.*

But she's not around anymore.

"You don't have any half brothers. Just two sisters. Margaret and Lyla. They are doing very well, thank you. They're beautiful."

"So I guess you can see them."

"*Stephen.*" Now he's getting a little angry. "I came all the way out here to help you. But if you're going to take that attitude, I can just get on the next plane back to California."

"Attitude? Why, is there something in my expression that's bothering you?"

"I have been in an airplane and a taxi for the past eight hours. I am going to go freshen up, get something to drink, then come back here to talk to you. At that time, I am hoping you will be ready to talk."

"Do you remember where the bathroom is?" I ask.

He leaves without another word.

I sit back down on the couch. I try to read *Blankets*. I try to lose myself in the words and pictures, but I am so distracted that I can barely find the concentration to turn the pages.

I know what my father is going to do. When he returns, he will pretend the previous conversation never happened.

In this, he does not disappoint.

"So," he says, his shirtsleeves now rolled up, a ginger ale in his hand, "tell me about this girl."

"Her name's Elizabeth. She moved in two doors down—Sukie Maxwell's old apartment. If you remember her from the funeral." No response. "I just bumped into her in the hallway one day, and . : . well, she saw me."

"You're sure?"

"Yes. We've spent a lot of time together these past couple of weeks. I'm positive she sees me."

He sits down next to me on the couch.

"Look, Stephen. It's natural to want to be with someone else. And maybe you've been alone here for too long. That would explain what's happening."

"What do you mean?"

"Do you go out with this girl? To the movies?"

"To the park. But mostly we stay around here."

"And she talks to you."

"All the time."

He shakes his head and looks sad.

I am nearly amazed to discover a new depth in my disappointment in him. "You don't believe me, do you?" I say.

"I want to believe you, Stephen. But you have to understand . . . nobody is able to see you."

"That's what I thought! But she does. She sees me."

"And do the other people see you? When you're out in the park?"

"No! But it still works." I see I am not winning him over. "Do you think I'm making this up?"

"I'm sure you want it to be real. And it would be perfectly understandable for you to let your imagination run wild while you're here alone all day . . ."

I can't have this conversation.

"You don't believe me?" I yell, standing up. "Well, fine. I'll show you." I head right to the phone, pick it up, and dial Elizabeth's number.

"Hi," she says. "I thought you were busy this evening."

"Look—I have a little surprise for you. My dad is in town. A totally unexpected visit. I'm not sure how long he's here, but he wants to meet you. Would you mind stopping over?"

"Meet your dad? Wow. I'm kind of in my drawing clothes right now, so if I came right over, I'm worried he'd think I was a deranged, ink-stained wretch. So give me ten minutes."

"See you in ten minutes."

From the look on my father's face, I'm guessing he wishes he were drinking something stronger than ginger ale. I don't think either of us knows what to do now—it's like both of our lives are on pause until Elizabeth arrives. We don't even attempt small talk. We just sit there. Waiting.

Finally, there's a knock at the door.

"I'll get it," I say.

My father stands up and hovers behind me as I open the door. Elizabeth's there, practically giddy. She looks right at me, says hello, and I quickly focus because she gives me a kiss on the cheek and I want it to have somewhere to land.

Then she walks past me and says hi to my father. Who is speechless.

"Elizabeth, Dad. Dad, Elizabeth."

"It's so great to meet you," Elizabeth says.

Dad's words kick in. "Lovely to meet you as well."

"Mrs. Swinton is still in London?" Elizabeth asks.

Dad looks pained, and I feel shaky. I haven't told him about that part—that Elizabeth thinks Mom is still alive.

"I wish she could be here to meet you" is how he replies.

For the first time, I look at my father and I see how haunted he is by all of this. He doesn't want to be having this conversation. He doesn't know what to do.

"Mr. Swinton?" Elizabeth asks. "Are you all right?"

He shakes his head. "I'm sorry. It was a long flight, and I fear I'm a little worse for wear."

Elizabeth gets the cue. "That's okay. I'm glad I got a chance to say hello. Hopefully I'll see you again before you leave." She comes back over to me and gives me another kiss on the cheek. "I'll leave you two to catch up."

I thank her and show her out. My father and I are silent, listening to her footsteps go down the hall, then the opening and closing of her door.

"How is this possible?" my father asks, collapsing back down on the couch.

"I don't know, Dad," I say. "You tell me."

"You don't understand. It simply can't be possible."

"The only reason I don't understand is because you've never told me why this all happened."

He shakes his head. That's not the topic he wants to be covering now.

"Is she the only one?" he asks me.

"Yes."

"You're sure."

"Yes."

"It's impossible."

"You've said that. But guess what. She sees me."

He sighs. "I wish your mother were here."

Now it comes back—the anger.

"You're not allowed to say that," I tell him.

"What?"

"That's not a wish you're allowed to have. If you really wish my mother were here, you should've been here when she was. You should've been here. Period."

"Stephen, I can't have this argument with you. Not right now. I have to figure out what's happening."

"We *both* have to figure out what's happening. Help me, Dad."

He stands up. "I will. I promise. I will try. But right now—I can't think right now. I'm going to go. I have a hotel room and—well, I'm going to go. But I'll be back tomorrow. We can have dinner. I'll come by at six. And in the meantime, I'll . . . try to figure things out."

His briefcase is in his hand. I know there's no stopping him, and he knows I'm not going to try.

He opens the door, but before he leaves, he tells me one more thing:

"Before, when I said I wished your mother were here—I meant that if anyone in the world had a right to see you, it was her. And the fact that someone else can see you . . . it would have meant the world to her. No matter what it may portend. That's all. It's unfair that this girl, and not your mother, gets to see you. But I know she'd be glad."

He's finally found the one thing I can't argue with.

CHAPTER 8

I SHOULD BE HAPPY. Most of the time I am. Most of the time *happy* isn't enough of a word to describe how I feel. I lose myself in Stephen without being lost. I find myself in Stephen when I didn't know I was there waiting to be found.

When he's talking to me, when he's touching me, I'm so oogly-eyed giddy that I worry I'll blurt out all the rose-petal, candy-heart mush that's built up in my body. I don't want to do that. It's not my style and I'm still nervous enough that I'll mess this up somehow. I haven't ever felt I needed someone other than my family. Stephen is changing that.

Oogly-eyed, goofy-grin romance aside, I'm uneasy. And this restlessness isn't the kind that's a natural partner to fear of rejection. The sense of something amiss creeps up when we're apart. I try to ignore it, pretending that I don't notice the flickering of doubt in my peripheral vision. But it's there and it's getting harder to shrug off.

I blame my family. Not in an angry kind of way, but in that searching-for-responsible-parties way. Mom, having gotten her routine at the hospital a bit more under control, is still working long hours, but she's showing up for dinner and family movie nights more often. Laurie has pronounced that his new mission is to expand our DVD collection because, even though it's a fantastic film, he cannot watch *Ghostbusters* more than twice a week. *Ghostbusters* is our fallback pick and the only movie we can all regularly agree on. My votes are for *Watchmen* or *Donnie Darko*— both of which get eye rolls from Mom and Laurie. Mom goes for foreign films, which I don't like because their idea of action seems to be hard-core brooding and Laurie says he can't follow due to his constant texting during the films. Laurie pushes Cary Grant on us, which is fine, but Mom and I get tired of black and white. So we all agreed it was a good idea when he volunteered to help our cause. I suspect it's an excuse for him to accomplish said mission with Sean as a sidekick. The mumbling couch turtle hasn't been to our apartment again . . . at least I haven't seen him . . . but I've caught Laurie murmuring into his phone a few times. When I've tried to get his attention, he gives me the *get out of here now or we're not speaking* look and I haven't pushed the issue.

But after dinner, when he reveals *The Ghost in the Shell* with a flourish, I can't keep my mouth shut. I'm snagged instantly because it's anime, and Mom is intrigued because it's Japanese. Laurie lights up with a smug grin when we both titter our approval. But there's no way he picked that movie solo.

"I guess this proves your new honey has good taste," I say.

Mom perks up. "What's this?"

"Shut up, Elizabeth," he says. "Or I'll take back the *Runaways* your boyfriend had me bring you."

My brother and I are mirror images of each other, facing off at the kitchen table. Arms folded, smiles tight, acid glares.

"I don't think we need a movie," Mom says. "Watching you two battle over secret love interests is entertainment enough."

Her gentle mocking transforms our thin-lipped anger into embarrassed blushes. She's a master of diffusing tension, which is probably why she's never had trouble snapping up the best administration jobs at renowned hospitals.

"Who's going to tell me first?" she asks.

Laurie's cheeks are like roses, and guilt from baiting him tips me into confession.

"I met this boy," I say, thinking I couldn't have put it in a more infantile way.

"He's real," Laurie says. "I talked to him on the phone."

"For the last time." I glare at Laurie again. "Why would I make up a boyfriend?"

"I dunno," Laurie says. "You're a writer . . . kind of. Maybe like method acting for character creation."

I make a sound that's somewhere between choking and a snarl.

Mom pats my hand. "What's his name?"

"Stephen." When I say it, I hear how my voice changes. I barely recognize it. Mom's smile, surprised but tender, tells me she understands exactly how I'm feeling. I don't need to say anything else.

She turns to my brother. "Well?"

"That's it?" He shoots an accusatory glance at me. "You're only giving her a name."

I ignore him.

"I'm waiting, Laurie," Mom says, cutting off any further discussion of my young romance.

Forsaking the chance to tease me for the bliss of spilling his own heart capades, Laurie smiles goofily.

"He lives in the building," he says. "Two floors up. His name is Sean. He's six feet tall. Wiry but not too skinny. He has the best hair and it falls over his eyebrows in the most adorable way. And he's sooooooo smart. Way smarter than Elizabeth even."

"Thanks," I say.

Mom grins at me. "Serious. Clearly."

I give her a solemn nod.

"You guys," Laurie whines. "Don't make fun of me. I really like him."

"We only tease from love, sweetheart." Mom laughs. "I'm happy you have a new friend."

Laurie's so full of crush-ridden ecstasy I think he might bounce out of his chair.

"Don't forget to breathe, Tigger," I say.

"Since we've heard about Sean," Mom says, "it's only fair you tell us a little more about Stephen, Elizabeth."

Unlike Laurie, for whom romance equals gushing, I get awkward. My fingers wrap around the seat of my chair.

"Ummm. He's nice."

"And?"

"He lives two doors down."

"Really?" Mom's eyebrows go up. She looks from me to Laurie. "Lots of building romance. This could become a French farce if you two aren't careful."

Mom laughs at her joke, which only gets blank stares from us. Realizing her joke failed, Mom gets serious.

"What about parents?" she asks.

"Sean doesn't get along with his parents," Laurie says. "They sound like jerks."

"You don't know them yet," Mom chides.

"I know what he's told me," Laurie says. "They're definitely jerks. We don't hang out at his place unless they're gone."

"I see," Mom says, sliding a glance at me. "Elizabeth?"

"Stephen's mom is in London right now, and I met his dad last night."

My brow furrows when I say it. I'd been so excited that Stephen wanted me to meet his dad, but it was kind of awkward, adding to my inexplicable uneasiness about where things stood with us.

"Oh dear," Mom says, lacing her fingers together. "Well, I guess I can't count on anyone else to chaperone, just like they can't count on me."

"Chaperones?!" Laurie puts his fingers up in the sign of the cross. "Gah!"

"I'm not here a lot," she says, shaking her head at him. "And I know you're responsible enough to be unsupervised. But falling for someone can lead to impulsive decisions."

Laurie and I both groan in anticipation of where this is going, but Mom stampedes right over our protest.

"I expect that if it becomes necessary, you'll discuss with me what you need to be safe. And you know I prefer it if you abstain from sexual activity until you're eighteen . . . at least. You both still have a lot of developing to do, physically and emotionally."

I think I'm going to spontaneously combust, while Laurie only looks bemused. Mom may be the queen of conflict resolution, but when it comes to anything health related, she can't get her tone past clinical.

Mom places her napkin on her empty dinner plate and smooths her skirt. "Since that's taken care of, let's clean this up and watch the movie."

Dishes scrubbed, dried, and put away, I settle onto the couch. Laurie sets up the movie, while Mom salts the popcorn, which is already glistening with melted butter, just the way we all like it—devoid of any redeeming nutritional value. Laurie is still chattering at Mom about the merits of Sean's eyebrow-veiling hair and I smile, knowing that while he jumped on me for telling her about him, Laurie has been dying to talk about his new crush. Sean's the first potential boyfriend Laurie's had, and while I'm not sure exactly what's transpiring between them, it's making Laurie happy. That knowledge makes something inside me, something that had been sharp and brittle, start to soften. A scabby old wound healing.

Laurie and I snuggle in on either side of Mom, and I am suddenly so content tears prick the corners of my eyes. The only thing I could wish for is that Stephen were here too. Having Mom know about him, listening to him talking to Laurie on the phone—and the sweetness of the gift he'd had Laurie pick up for me—I want him to meet my family.

I fish my phone out of my pocket before I remember he's at dinner with his father.

When I met Stephen's dad, it was uncomfortable. The room

felt too small, the air too stuffy. Thinking about Laurie's analysis of Sean's family, I wondered if Stephen and his dad were fighting before I arrived. But why would he invite me over then? Because he doesn't want to hide his life from me, even the bad stuff. That's the way we are together. That's why I lo . . .

The thought catches me off guard. I was thinking it. *That's why I love him.*

"Are you scared?" Laurie asks, drawing me out of my own mind. "It's just a preview."

I look down and see I'm clutching a throw pillow to my chest.

"Nope," I say quickly. "Just caught a chill."

"Seriously?" Laurie stares at me. "It's like a gazillion degrees outside."

"I hope you're not getting sick," Mom says.

"I'm fine," I say, pushing her hand away before she can feel my forehead. "Let's just watch the movie. I'm excited about it."

I'm grateful when they don't push the issue further. Still trembling slightly from the confession of feeling that shuddered its way through my limbs, I text Stephen.

The Runaways rocks. You're my hero. Probably Laurie's too 'cause he won't shut up about Sean. Hope dinner is going well. Miss you.

I want to write *I love you*, but I'm way too scared to risk it. Even thinking it is still scary.

When I go to bed, he hasn't written back. I wake up and still haven't heard anything from him. What if he read between the lines of my text, somehow seeing my wishful "I love you" sentiment in the words, and was put off by it? What if he had a bad dinner with his dad and is really upset but afraid to call? What if they were in a tragic cab accident and are even now in intensive care at my mom's hospital? My explanations for why I have no Stephen texts or phone calls in the last twelve hours get wilder and wilder. The most recent involves escaped Bronx Zoo monkeys and the Central Park horse carriages. Anxiety crawls under my skin, making me pace around the house in my pajamas while Laurie reads me the ingredients of Pop-Tarts to prove that they are 99 percent artificial.

"Then why do you eat them?" I ask, glancing at my phone for the millionth time.

He shrugs. "They taste awesome. I have an artificial fruit and preservative addiction."

"Interesting self-diagnosis," I say.

"I have uncanny skills when it comes to assessing my state of being. My current assessment being that my most serious addiction is to artificial blueberry."

"Ah."

He licks Pop-Tart crumbs off his fingers. "So when do I get to meet him?"

"What?" I'm looking at my phone again, not really listening.

"Mystery, but not imaginary, boyfriend," he says. "Stephen. You're obviously gone for him. And while the phone call was a suave first move, I'd like to make sure I approve. Said approval requires face-to-face."

I don't answer, gazing at Laurie.

"Don't you want me to meet him?" He looks crestfallen.

"Of course," I say. It's dawning on me that Laurie has given me a perfect solution to my ongoing crisis. Stephen invited me to meet his dad. That's a big move, relationship-wise. So the next step must be for me to reciprocate. Laurie's perfect. Parents are more intimidating, and I'm sure if Stephen had a brother or sister for me to meet, he or she would have been first. Plus his dad isn't always in town, so there was an expiration date on this chance to meet him.

"You have a few minutes before you need to get going?" I ask Laurie.

"I was planning to savor one more Pop-Tart," he says. "You inviting boy wonder over now?"

I bite my lip. "Is it too early?"

"Not really," Laurie says, looking me up and down. "But you're not exactly coiffed."

"Do you want to meet him or not?" I glare.

"If you're comfortable with being PJ-bedhead girlfriend, don't let me stand in the way." Laurie's Pop-Tart hops out of the toaster. He sniffs it like he's discerning the notes of a fine wine.

I am a little embarrassed to see Stephen before a shower, but I don't want to miss this chance. I'm worried about why he hasn't called and also worried that I'll lose my nerve about him meeting Laurie if I don't act on the current impulse.

I dial Stephen's number. It rings twice.

"Hey." His voice is tired.

Fail. "I woke you up. Sorry."

"No," he says. "You didn't. I'm awake. I just didn't sleep at all."

"Oh," I say. He was up all night and he still didn't text or call. My heart feels like it's caving in on itself. "Are you okay?"

"I'm trying to figure that out," he says. "How was movie night?"

His tone lightens and I smile, relieved. "Great, in fact . . ." I glance at Laurie, whose eyes are closed as he has apparently achieved Pop-Tart nirvana. "Can you stop by?"

"Right now? Are you alone?"

"Yeah," I say. "I—" Guilt dries out my throat. I'll be alone soon enough, but I want Laurie to meet Stephen. It's not too much of a lie, is it?

"Yes," he says, cutting me off. "I need to talk to you about something."

My smile vanishes and my heart is now in splinters. The talk. He wants to have the breakup talk. He somehow picked that *I love you* right out of the text, has decided I am too needy, and is coming over to break up with me. And when he sees me with unbrushed hair and tattered pajamas, he will have even more of a reason to ditch me.

I try to talk, wanting to delay him, say I've changed my mind and we shouldn't see each other. But my mouth is full of cotton and my lips have gone numb.

"I'll be right over." He hangs up.

I set my phone on the counter.

"Is he coming?" Laurie asks.

I nod. He slides out of his chair and comes to my side, frowning.

"What's wrong? You kinda look like you might throw up."

I don't want to answer because I think I probably will throw up if I open my mouth.

There's a light knock on the door and it swings open.

Laurie turns, smiling. "She must really like you if you're in the habit of just walking in like you live here."

If I wasn't shaking with the knowledge that I was about to be dumped, I would smile. I always leave the door open for Stephen. I love it when he walks in, always opening his arms to me before we even say hello.

"That's weird." Laurie is staring at the open door, looking past Stephen, who is frozen a few steps into our apartment.

Laurie looks at me. "Didn't somebody knock?"

"Stephen did." My voice comes out like a crow's croak.

Stephen still hasn't moved. He obviously doesn't want to break up with me in front of my brother any more than I want him to. But here we all are.

"Stephen, this is Laurie," I say. "He's about to head to school. I thought you could say hello before he leaves."

Why I'm trying to help the boy who is about to stomp on my heart get past this awkward first-and-last introduction to my brother is beyond me, but I don't know what else to do.

"Elizabeth . . ." Laurie frowns at me. "There's nobody here."

"Don't start with the imaginary boyfriend bit again," I say. "It's not funny."

Laurie pales. "I'm not joking."

Laurie doesn't answer but turns back to the door, staring.

"Stephen, did you put him up to this?" I ask.

Stephen hasn't moved, but his fists are clenched at his sides now.

"What the hell is going on?" Laurie rubs his eyes.

"Laurie," Stephen says, quietly but in a firm tone.

"Oh my God." Laurie jumps back. His elbow knocks his juice glass to the floor. It shatters. "Who was that?"

Stephen is looking at me now. I meet his sad gaze. His shoulders rise and fall as he sighs. Missing pieces begin to fall into place.

Something happens that's never happened to me before. Not even when I saw Laurie going into the emergency room. I start screaming and I can't stop.

CHAPTER 9

MY MIND, FOR A MOMENT, is caught in a tight loop.

This can't be happening.

Therefore it is not happening.

This can't be happening.

Therefore it is not happening.

Then Elizabeth starts to scream and I know that, yes, this can be happening, and, yes, it is most definitely happening. And all the things I thought I was going to say—apologies about my father, more lies about my mother, more lies to deflect Elizabeth's gaze from the real truth—all of these things fall away.

"It's okay," I say—perhaps the biggest lie of all. But it's one of those things you do. You say something like "It's okay" not because it is, in fact, okay, but because you're hoping these words will somehow make it okay. Even though they never, ever do.

Laurie is grabbing her shoulders, asking what's going on. He is so confused. And she is so confused. I am the only one in the room who understands what's happening.

"Elizabeth, I'm sorry," I say, getting closer.

"No," she says, pulling away. "Don't come near me."

Laurie stands between us, even though he can't see me.

"This isn't funny," he says.

"No," I tell him. "It's really not."

She's backed against the wall now. Staring at me. Laurie looks at her. Sees the intensity of her gaze.

"You really see him, don't you?" he asks.

"And you really can't," she says. It's not even a question. She knows.

"I can explain," I say. Even though I can't.

"Are you—are you a ghost?" Elizabeth asks.

"No. I'm alive. I'm just . . . invisible."

There. I've said it. I've used the word.

Laurie is over by Elizabeth now. His arm around her. Calming her. Exactly where I want to be.

"If you're invisible," Laurie asks, "how can she see you?"

"I don't know. I was as surprised as anyone by that. Nobody's ever seen me before. Nobody."

I say this to Laurie. But now I look at Elizabeth. Look right at her.

"You have no idea what that's like," I tell her. "That first day in the hallway—to have gone my whole life without a single person seeing me, and then you saying hello, inviting me in. That was astonishing. But this whole thing—you and I—it isn't just about that. It's about much more than that. And while I don't know why you see me, I am so happy that you're the one."

"Why didn't you tell me?" she asks.

"I didn't think you'd believe me. Or, even worse, that this

would happen when you finally found out, with you over there and me over here. I didn't want us to feel the way we feel right now."

"Where are you?" Laurie asks.

"Right here," I say. "Follow the sound of my voice." He starts walking towards me. "Yes. Right over here. Right. Here."

We are face-to-face. Only he can't see my face. I wonder if he'll hit me. Throw me out. But instead, he reaches up his palm. I know what he's doing. I mirror his movement. Concentrate.

When our palms touch, he jumps back, shocked. But then he recovers. I concentrate again. He touches my hand. Traces my arm. Shoulder. Neck. Face.

"Holy holy," he says. "I mean, holy holy holy."

Elizabeth is watching all of this.

"I'm real," I tell her. "It's still me."

Laurie backs away again. "How long have you been like this?" he asks.

"My whole life," I tell him. "Apparently it was a curse that made me this way. I was born invisible."

"So, really, no one's ever seen you?"

"No. No one but Elizabeth."

I'm hoping to see some tenderness emerge in her expression. Now that she has an explanation, now that she knows, I want her to show some sign that things between us are still possible. That even if I lose her as a girlfriend, that even if she never wants to touch me again, I won't lose her in my life.

But the tenderness is tamped down. Confusion and anger are still in control.

"So you don't go to school," she says. "Obviously."

I shake my head.

"And when I went over last night, your father couldn't actually see you."

"Correct."

"What other lies have you told me?"

There's a cutting, wounded tone in her voice now. And I think, *This is not how I want to tell her.* But I can't avoid it any longer.

"My mother's dead," I say. "She lived with me for most of my life. Until a year ago. My dad isn't really in the picture; he just pays for things. But my mother was everything."

It's Laurie who says, "I'm so sorry to hear that."

Elizabeth, though, is still caught up in the larger anger. "You lied about that? Why would you lie about that?"

"Elizabeth," Laurie cautions.

"No," I say, "it's a valid question. Even though there isn't really a valid answer. I mean, I don't know. That's the answer. It was just something that came out of my mouth the first time we talked about it, and then once I'd said it, I was pretty much stuck there. And, I admit, there were moments when it was nice to pretend she was still alive. Bittersweet, but nice."

"I guess I gave you a lot of chances to pretend," Elizabeth says. "Pretend to be visible. Pretend to have a mom. Pretend to like me. What a joke. What an amazing joke that must have been."

I really can't comprehend why she's saying such things.

"It wasn't pretend," I tell her. "Not with you. I'm genuine with you. More than I've ever been allowed to be. Because you can see me."

"It's not fair," she says. "It's just not fair."

Now the anger is subsiding, but it's sadness, not tenderness, that's emerging in its place.

It's Laurie who says, "I think you should probably go."

"No," I say. "Not until . . ." And then I freeze. Not until what? Not until she recognizes that the time we've had together was never a lie? Not until she says that, hey, even though I'm invisible to most people, she's happy to be with me forever? Not until someone in the room acknowledges that this isn't easy for me either? That it's never been easy for me, and this is taking all the hopes I've ever had and pulverizing them into one neat, tidy black hole?

I'm trying to think of something else to say when Elizabeth surprises me by starting to laugh.

"What?" I say.

She shakes her head. But she can't stop laughing. "It's just that—I thought to myself, 'You have to tell him you can't see him anymore.' Isn't that funny? I can't see you anymore. That's so incredibly funny."

"All right, Jo, c'mon," Laurie says. He moves over to comfort her again, but she pushes him away.

"No, Laurie—don't you think it's funny? Isn't it hysterical? My life—everything that's happened so far in New York—is a complete joke. So shouldn't I be allowed to laugh at it?"

"You can laugh all you want," Laurie says gently. "But I don't really think you find it funny. And I don't think Stephen finds it funny either."

"Thank you, Laurie," I say.

Now it's his turn to shake his head, as if he can't accept my thanks.

"Really," he says, "you have to go. Although we all know this isn't a joke, you have to admit that it is extremely, extremely messed up."

"Believe me, I know. I've lived it my whole life."

I know I have to go now. I know that by leaving the room, I am running the risk of never being allowed inside again. That's not my call to make. I know that.

"I'll go," I say. I look at Elizabeth again. "Is that what you want?"

She doesn't say a word. Just nods.

I turn to leave. But then Laurie calls out to me.

"Hey—just one more thing," he says.

"Yes?"

"Sean—he's not, like, one of you, is he?"

"One of me?"

"Like, we haven't moved into an apartment building that's secretly for mutants, have we?"

It's probably a good thing Laurie can't see my expression.

"No," I assure him. "It's just me."

"Thanks."

I concentrate on the doorknob, on letting myself out. Then, when I get to my own door, I concentrate on the doorknob, on letting myself in. I think that this might be the easiest way to live—just concentrate on the small things, and never let your mind wander to the big things. But it's a faulty premise, built on the notion that you can choose where your mind goes. Or where your heart goes.

I'm sorry. I should have said it again to her, before I left. Even though I didn't choose this, I'm sorry she's become involved. Because if she's feeling even a fraction of the loneliness I'm feeling, or even a fraction of the disappointment—well, then, she's right. It is deeply unfair.

"I'm sorry," I say aloud. And again. "I'm sorry."

But who's around to hear it?

Nobody but me.

CHAPTER 10

LAURIE GUIDES ME to the couch. I'm shivering and a little nauseated. My skin is too tight and my head throbs.

"I'll get you some water," he says.

I wrap my arms around myself, trying to rub away the chill that's settled over me.

Words that end in *ble* turn in my brain like a wicked carousel. *Impossible. Improbable. Inconceivable. Unacceptable. Undeniable.*

But it all brings me back to one word: *invisible.*

"Here." Laurie folds my hands around a glass.

I take a sip.

"You're going to be late," I say.

He laughs. "Josie, we've just learned not only is it possible for someone to be invisible, but the invisible person isn't being discussed on *Dateline*. He's your boyfriend."

I flinch.

"Sorry." His voice gets softer. "Maybe you're not ready to hear this, but I know how you get. Don't blame him for stuff that isn't his fault. Before this happened, how were you feeling about Stephen?"

I drink more water. I thought he would grind my heart up in the garbage disposal when he broke up with me.

Laurie answers for me. "You're crazy about him. Like I've never seen."

But now I am irascible because he is invisible.

I crack a slight smile at my silent joke. I don't know if it means I'm recovering or about to totally lose it.

"Don't you want to help him?" Laurie asks.

"He's invisible." I say it and my voice cracks.

"I know," he says. "It must be awful."

Laurie has done what Laurie does best. He sees the world through the other person, the hurting person. He is seeing life as the invisible boy, who watches everything without ever being noticed himself.

"When no one can see who you are, no one really knows you," he says. "The loneliness must be like an ulcer that's always gnawing at your gut."

"But . . ." I say. Guilt begins to chip away at my outrage, but pride tries to weld my indignant humiliation back in place.

"But what?" he says. "You know it's true. You heard him. No one has ever seen him. Not even his own mother."

I nod. Something in my chest is cracking and I shudder. Laurie puts his arm around me.

"No one has seen him. Except you."

He lets the words sink in. I nod again.

"That has to mean something," he says.

"What does it mean?" I whisper.

"I think it means you're the one who can cure him."

"Cure him?" Immediately I want to call Mom. She knows people at the Mayo Clinic. She can pull strings. We'll figure this out.

Laurie has seen something spark in my eyes and he grabs my hand. "No, Elizabeth. Maybe *cure* is the wrong word. Don't go there. It's not a disease. If you treat him . . . in that way you'll never see him again and his ending up on *Dateline* would be a best-case scenario."

"How do you know that?" I ask. "What if he does need a cure?"

Part of me wants a rational explanation. Something that science can drop into a textbook and let us all learn to live with because someone else claims to understand it.

"He said he's cursed," Laurie says. "Curses aren't diseases, they're . . ."

Now he starts realizing what he's about to say. He offers me a helpless sigh.

"Oh my God," I say. "Magic? Give me a break."

"He's invisible!" Laurie stands up and paces across the room.

"I know!" I draw my knees to my chest. "But magic? It's not . . . real."

"And invisibility is?" Laurie says. "Elizabeth, I could not see him. Nothing. Not anything."

"I know . . . I just can't . . . how can this even . . . ?" I dig my fists into the couch cushions.

"I thought I was having a Pop-Tart hallucination at first."

"Come on." I'm not ready for jokes yet.

"I'm serious," he says. "If you eat more than fifteen, things can get a little crazy."

"Whatever." Irritation curls around me like a blanket and I feel better. It's easier when I'm angry. Anger has been my armor for a while now and I'm comfortable slipping into it again.

"Don't." Laurie has other ideas. "Don't do that."

"I'm not doing anything," I say, withdrawing further into myself.

"Liar," he says. "Being pissed will get you nowhere."

"Don't tell me how to feel."

"Then stop acting like a baby," he says. "Stephen didn't mean to hurt you."

"He lied to me!" That's the worst part. I still can't quite believe he's invisible. I can see him. I've held him. Kissed him. But the lies are all too real.

"Can you blame him?" Laurie asks. When I glare, he says, "Obviously, you can. But I think you're taking this the wrong way."

I tear my eyes off him, staring at the blank television screen instead. I see Laurie's and my reflections on its surface like we're the hour-long drama playing out for the world to see.

"If you were in his place, what would you have done?" he asks.

I look at him, open my mouth, and realize I don't have an answer.

"No one has ever seen him," Laurie says. "Until you."

Suddenly he walks out of the room. I stare after him, thinking he's decided he's made his point and is leaving me to either retreat to anger, sulk, or come up with my own solution. But a minute later he's back with a comic in his hand. He walks up to me, thrusting the *Runaways* in my face.

"Who had me get this for you?"

"Shut up," I say.

"Stop it!" He's shouting. "Stop feeling sorry for yourself and get a clue about what's happening here!"

"Why don't you explain it to me since you have all the answers!"

"He's in love with you!" Laurie throws the comic at me. "When he figured out I was here, he could have bolted back to his place, waited for you to show, and then made an excuse about having forgotten something. He could have found a way to lie again, Elizabeth, but he didn't. He told you what he hasn't told anyone. And he told me too. He frickin' let me trace the shape of his face with my hands. How weird must that have been?"

I want to yell at him, but I can't. I can't do anything but cradle the *Runaways* against my chest.

Laurie isn't done yet. "He is in love with you and if you love him at all, you need to figure out how you're going to deal with this. He needs you to do that. And if you want me to continue to respect you, I need you to do that too."

"Okay." I say it quietly.

"Okay?" Laurie's chest is still puffed up, like he expected another round or two of shouting. "Oh."

He sits beside me.

"So what do I do?" I ask.

"I'm not sure," he says. "You're the one who knows him. What do you think you should do?"

"Apologize?"

"Probably." He smiles. "But don't overdo it. You're right about the lying. Lying is not okay. Forgiving him for it is a good idea, but I'm not happy about my sister's boyfriend being dishonest either."

I return his smile. "Thanks."

"Of course."

Questions begin to bloom in my mind. "You're serious about the whole curse, magic thing?"

"I don't know if *serious* is the right word," he says. "It's more like there aren't any other options, so let's go with this one."

"How do curses work?"

"News flash," he says. "I'm gay, not a witch. Gay *and* witch is Dumbledore, and last time I checked, he was still just a guy in a book."

I laugh and he hugs me.

"Despite my taking the high ground here, I'm as stumped as you are, Josie," he says. "I don't know what to do."

"What if he hates me now?" My mind is jumping around with the same speed as my suddenly pounding heart.

"Hang on," he says. "Let's handle one issue at a time. Remember that whole apology idea you came up with first?"

I nod.

"Try that," he says. "Then move on to step two."

"What's step two?" I ask.

"If you're lucky . . . or in his mind, if he's lucky, makeup making out—probably taking it all the way to third base. Unless you guys are already hitting it out of the park." He grins.

"Laurie!" I mash a throw pillow into his face.

"I'm just trying to give you incentives." He's still laughing. "I know how stubborn you can be at admitting you did something wrong."

My cheeks are flaming, but I'm grateful I don't feel cold and sick anymore.

"Go over there," Laurie says.

"What if he's not home?" I know I sound lame, but my anger is gone, leaving only embarrassment and renewed fear of rejection. If I wasn't about to get dumped this morning, I may have sealed that deal with my earlier outburst.

Laurie gives me a long look. "If he's not home, you come back, take a shower, and transform yourself into 'lively, attractive Elizabeth' instead of continuing to sport this 'waking dead Elizabeth' look you've got going."

Now all I want to do is take a shower.

"I'm kidding," he says, seeing anxiety roll across my face. "You look cute in PJs. It will also probably assist in that whole make-out scenario I mentioned. Get over there. Talk to him."

"Then what?"

"Did Mom not have the talk with you?" Laurie asks. "Do you not understand the principle of making out? Uh-oh . . . do you not know what third base is?"

"Aren't you supposed to be helping me?" I laugh, grateful for his teasing even if I'm blushing from head to toe.

"I am helping," he says. And he is. "After making out, you talk to him, figure out what he does know about this whole invisible issue, and then together you decide what the next step is."

"What is the next step?" I ask.

"I don't know," he says. "I'm guessing he doesn't know either. This is a first for everyone involved. Solutions will require collaboration, I'm thinking."

"Right," I say, worrying at the tangles in my hair.

"I'll wait here in case it goes badly," he says. "If necessary, I will go buy you ice cream."

"No," I say, shrugging off my anger armor and trying to find some resolve to replace it. "Go to school. I'll be okay."

"You sure?" Laurie asks. "I'll be worried about you."

"I don't want you sitting here while I try to take us past third base," I say, as much to bolster my own confidence as to tease my brother.

"TMI! TMI!" Laurie shrieks, bolting from the room.

"You started it!" I call after him.

He peeks around the corner, grinning. "All right—I'm going to school, and if I hit the subway right, I might even get there on time."

"Okay." I smile, but I'm starting to lose my nerve.

He holds up his phone. "This will be on at all times. If you need me, I'll come right back."

"Thanks," I say.

When he returns to the living room, he hugs me. "Be honest and don't pretend you're not falling truly, madly, and deeply for this guy. Denial will get you in trouble."

I wait until Laurie leaves and then I shuffle down the hall to Stephen's apartment. I feel silly wearing my pajamas, but I know stalling will only push me along the road to permanent residence in cowardville. Laurie's right. I'm stubborn and could easily nurse a grudge that keeps me from ever talking to Stephen again.

My stomach is a pretzel when I knock on the door.

There's no answer.

I shift back and forth on my feet, count to ten, and knock again.

Very softly, from the other side of the door I hear his voice.

"Elizabeth?"

"Yes," I say. My heart has climbed into my throat.

The door opens. He's standing there. Visible.

I don't know what to say. I look at him and think how unfair it is that such a beautiful face is hidden from the rest of the world.

Laurie is right. He is visible to me. Only to me. It must mean something.

All I want to do is touch him and tell him how wonderful it is to see him. That I promise to never take my ability to see him for granted.

I reach out my hand. My fingers are shaking.

He looks at me for a moment before taking my hand in both of his.

CHAPTER 11

I TELL HER EVERYTHING I know. It doesn't take long.

This, I think, is the way to thank her. This, I believe, is the way to prove that there aren't any more secrets. This, I hope, is the way to get her to stay.

I have lived with this truth for so long that I'm used to it. It's through Elizabeth's reaction that I see how strange it is. How unbelievable. How unreal.

I also see how sad it is.

"You've never been to school," she says. We're sitting on the couch, facing each other. "You've never had friends over. You've never had . . ."

"Everything was me and my mother," I tell her. "Every valentine. Every piece of homework. Every board game. Every birthday cake. Every everything."

"You must miss her so much."

I shake my head. "I haven't let myself. Not the way that you mean."

"Why not?"

"Because if I did, I would never make it back."

Already it's destroying me to say it out loud. The only saving grace is that there's someone to hear it.

"I'm sorry," I say.

She shakes her head. "Don't be."

"No, you don't understand. I'm sorry for putting you in this position. It's unfair to make anyone the only one. It was unfair to my mother. And now it's unfair to you."

I hate that she sees I have no one else. But that's part of the everything I know.

"And you have no idea why this curse happened?"

"No."

"No idea who created it. No idea why."

"No idea."

"But your father knows."

"Yes. I mean, I think so."

She looks me right in the eye. "So why don't we ask him?"

"I've tried."

"Well, this time we'll double-team him. Triple, if Laurie can come."

Just thinking about finally having the answers makes me dizzy, frightened.

I shift on the couch so I can put my head in Elizabeth's lap. Concentrate so I can try to feel some comfort there.

"You don't have to do this," I say.

She runs her fingers through my hair. "I know. I don't have to be here. But here I am."

"Why?" I ask.

"Something to do with love, I guess," she says. "Now, quiet. Let's rest for a second. We have a lot to think about."

I turn my head so I'm looking up at her. She leans down.

My kiss isn't enough. There's so much more I want to share with her.

Love.

Fear.

Gratitude.

We go to the park.

This time, she notices. The way everyone ignores me. The way they look at her if she says something to me. The way I leave no trace.

"What's it like?" she asks when we find a quiet spot under one of the stone bridges.

"It's hard to say," I tell her. But I can see that's not good enough for her, so I go on. "It isn't loneliness, really. Because loneliness comes from thinking you can be involved in the world, but aren't. Being invisible is being solitary without the potential of being anything but solitary. So after a while, you step aside from the world. It's like you're in a theater, alone in the audience, and everything else is happening on the stage."

"That's awful," Elizabeth says.

"Yes and no. Sometimes more yes, sometimes more no."

"I know what you mean about loneliness, though. I think it's more lonely when people you trust turn against you. When you're exiled. I went through that, at least a little bit. It's like being kicked off that stage, and then being forced into the audience to watch as it all goes on without you."

So there we sit. Under a stone bridge, watching people run, walk, stroll, jog by.

An audience of two, now.

When we get back to the building, she says, "I want Laurie to be there. When your father comes. I think he can help."

"Are you sure?" I ask.

"Yes. It's easy enough for me to sound all strong when I'm with you. But really? I'm not the biggest fan of confrontation. I'm not very good at it. Laurie, however, is a pro. I mean, when my dad saw us off at the airport, pretending we were going on some family trip without him, instead of leaving to build a new, dad-less life, I actually gave him a kiss goodbye. Laurie called him a jerk. Which was the right thing to do."

"The more the merrier," I say.

She goes to fill him in.

Back in my apartment, temporarily alone, I don't know what to do.

They knock on the door at five thirty. I know it has to be them because Dad would never knock.

"Whoa," Laurie says when I open the door. I have to remember that he's not used to things like doors opening on their own.

"Come in," I tell him.

"Nice place," he says, taking it all in. I don't know whether he's just being polite. It's been a long time since I've wondered what other people thought of the apartment. In many ways, over the past year it's become a museum version of itself. It's not like my mother died and I suddenly decided to order new furniture, or hang different things on the walls.

We're all a little tense, paying a little too much attention to each other. I'm studying Elizabeth's reactions, she's studying mine, and Laurie is trying to study us both, although my reactions are of course more elusive. Instead of studying my expression, he's studying the apartment, looking for clues. If there are any, I've never found them.

Elizabeth reaches into her pocket. "I know this is weird, but I brought something for you."

It's a folded piece of paper. Instead of handing it over, she unfolds it for me. Smooths it out. Puts it on the living room table.

It's a sketch. Of a boy.

"It's not perfect," she says. "I mean, it was just an exercise. To draw something from memory."

"Is that—?" I ask.

"Yes. It's you."

"He's never seen himself?" Laurie asks.

"No," Elizabeth says, looking in my eyes. "I don't think he has. Right?"

"Right," I whisper.

I don't want to see it.

I want to see it.

I see it.

There I am.

Me.

That's me. A hastily drawn version of me.

"I just thought you'd—"

"You're right. I do. Thank you."

Laurie reaches down and picks up the drawing for a closer look.

"Not bad," he says. "I mean, you look—real."

"I feel real," I say.

None of us know what to do with that.

"Can I see the rest of the apartment?" Laurie asks. In response I give them something approximating a tour. We're all waiting for the sound of my father's arrival. And at six, right on the mark, it comes.

Key in the door. My name called out.

We come back to the living room.

"Dad," I say, "you remember Elizabeth." I'm sure he remembers her, but maybe not her name. "And this is her brother, Laurie."

Dad looks bewildered. "Can he see you too?"

"No," I say. "Just Elizabeth."

We stand in awkward silence for a second. Dad offers Elizabeth and Laurie something to drink, as if he lives here. Laurie asks for some water, which gives Dad an excuse to go to the kitchen for a second.

"You've got to ask him," Laurie says as soon as Dad's out of earshot.

"What?"

"Why you are the way you are. The curse."

"He won't tell me."

"Fine," Laurie says. "I'll do it."

"Laurie—" Elizabeth cautions. But wasn't this why she brought him in the first place?

Before she can say any more, Dad's back with a glass of water. Laurie waits until the very moment it's passing from hand to hand to ask, "Why is Stephen invisible?"

Dad's hand pulls back slightly, the water overflowing the rim and running over his fingers. Then he hands the glass over to Laurie, shaking his head.

"Stephen?" Dad says. "What's going on?"

But Laurie won't relent. "I think Stephen has the same question."

"It's okay, Laurie," I say. "I can take it from here. Why don't we all sit down?"

So we gather in the living room, as if we're going to talk about a field trip I want to take, or ask him for money so the three of us can start a band.

Dad still tries to get out of it. "I'm really not sure this is the time—" he begins.

"He has black hair," Elizabeth says. "Well, really dark brown. But it looks black. And his eyes are this brilliant blue. He's got a birthmark—a small one—right before his left ear. He has really nice shoulders."

"Why are you telling me this?" Dad asks, his voice cracking.

"Because you need to know. He's a person. I can see him. He's flesh and blood, even if you can't see the flesh or the blood. I don't think you see him as a person. Not like the rest of us."

"But he's *not* like the rest of us," Dad says.

"Only in one way," Elizabeth replies. "And not to me. Here. Look."

She hands him the sketch. He doesn't know what it is when he takes it. Then he looks down and his hand shakes. He blinks back tears and puts the paper back down.

"Again, why are you telling me this?"

"Because," I say, "it's time, Dad. I know you don't want to tell me, but you have to tell me. What's happened with Elizabeth changes everything. It means—well, it means other things are possible. The curse can be broken."

Now Dad looks angry. "You're not supposed to know about the curse!"

"Well, I do. And so what?"

"You don't know *anything*."

"So tell me!" I am matching his anger now.

"Okay, both of you," Laurie interjects. "No yelling. The neighbors will hear. I mean, the other neighbors."

Dad gets up from his seat and walks over to the bookshelf. He's staring off, his back to us. Then his shoulders sag.

"Mr. Swinton?" Elizabeth asks.

He mumbles something. It takes me a moment, and then I realize what he's said.

I always thought he was blond.

Because my mom was blond.

Because maybe when he was a kid, my dad was blond too.

He's pictured me. All these years he's pictured me.

And he happened to be wrong.

"Tell me," I say. "Please. Once and for all."

He turns back to look at Laurie and Elizabeth.

"Not with them here," he says. "It's not their business."

I can see that Elizabeth's about to agree with this. But Laurie gets it.

"No," he tells my father. "Stephen needs us here. With all due respect, sir, you've left him alone for a very long time. If he needs us here, you have to let us stay."

"It's true," I say. "It can't just be me. If you kick them out now, it won't matter. I'll only tell them when you leave."

Dad's looking at Laurie, appealing to him. "I'm not a monster. I know it might seem that way to you. But there are reasons not to tell him. Knowing might not change anything. It *won't* change anything. There's nothing that can be done."

"Let him decide that," Laurie replies. "Not you. It's his life."

I see him make the choice. Even though I don't know what it is, I am sure he's about to say everything I've always wanted him to say. And as the adrenaline surges, so too does my fear. Everything is going to be different now, one way or the other. And I can no longer stop it. It's inevitable.

My father is about to tell me the truth.

"Your grandfather is a cursecaster," he begins. "I know this is going to sound unbelievable. It certainly did to me at first. But it's real. Very real. Your grandfather's a controller. And by this, I don't mean he's a controlling man—although I suppose he's that as well. When I say he's a controller, I mean that he has powers. He can do things that normal people cannot. He's not a witch or a wizard. He's not a god. It's something else, although there are qualities of all of that. I don't know that much about the background—this is your mother's father, and she didn't talk about any of it. She never talked about any of it."

He stops. I tell him to go on. He does.

"Your mother's early life was hell. Her own mother died when she was very young. It was just your mother and your grandfather. Maxwell Arbus. As a cursecaster, he was incapable of doing good. At least not in his work, and I haven't heard any evidence that he did good outside of his work. The thing about cursecasters—you have to understand this—is that they are different from spellcast-ers. Spellcasters—if there are such things—can create as well as destroy. At least that's what your mother told me. Cursecasters can only destroy. Again, I don't know how. I don't know why. All I know is that your grandfather was capable of this. And you are the proof."

He stops again, and in his pause I can recognize a lot of what I was feeling when my own truth was revealed to Elizabeth—that fear of the words being said combined with the relief at the abil-ity to finally say them.

"I'm the proof," I say.

His eyes dart to where I am. Where, to him, my voice comes from.

"Yes."

"What happened?" I ask. "Why did he curse me?"

My father shakes his head mournfully. "It wasn't you he was cursing. Or me. I hadn't even met your mother yet. It was her, Ste-phen. You have to understand. This was done long before you were born."

Elizabeth takes hold of my hand. As if she knows that will

require some of my concentration. As if she knows I need to let my father speak on.

"Tell us," she says.

My father sees the way her hand shapes itself around mine. He knows. "As I said, Stephen's mother's childhood was not a good one. Cursecasting is a powerful ability—but it doesn't actually pay the rent. So Maxwell rambled from job to job, getting angrier and angrier, which made him more inclined to lay down curses.

"When your mother was young—seven or eight—she tried to run away. As a result, your grandfather laid a curse on her, so she couldn't leave him. She had to be within a certain radius of his presence at all times, like an invisible leash. She would try to run, or would try to stand still while he was moving away, but it wouldn't work. She wouldn't feel pain—she would just be unable to get very far before her body made her follow him.

"I don't know why he wanted her around. Partly, I guess, to take care of him—make his meals, manage their squalor. And I imagine he was lonely. If I'm in a generous mood, I may even try to believe he was grieving over the loss of his wife. But at heart, he was an evil, tortured man who used his evil to torture others. His talent was cruelty. If a shopkeeper made him wait too long, he could cast a spell so that the shopkeeper would go home and start to forget his wife. Her name, her existence, everything. Or he could curse a politician into a weakness for female campaign workers, or a judge into a weakness for a certain casino. There was a limit to the power he had, but he used it when he could.

"Eventually, he loosened the leash on your mother so she could go to school, but she could never really go more than a town's distance away. The only bright side of the curse was that he couldn't do anything else to her—you can, apparently, only cast a single curse on anyone at a given time. He tried to pretend this wasn't true, and tried to threaten her with others. But she started calling his bluff. She started acting out—refusing to make his meals, refusing to do his bidding. It infuriated him. And while he couldn't curse her outright, he certainly wasn't afraid to use his fists or his voice. She couldn't go to the authorities, because even if they'd tried to put him away, she knew that she was bound to him, and that there was no way she could avoid going wherever he went.

"She didn't want you to know any of this. I feel—well, I feel I'm telling you a story that isn't mine. I know you don't think so, but I miss her every hour of every day. I couldn't stay—she understood that—but I still miss her. Some people are given relatively fair lives. But others—they carry the burden of the unfairness of the world. That was your mother. Until you were born, she could never get a break."

"But wasn't I the worst thing of all?" I can't help but ask. "I mean, that's what this is leading up to, isn't it?"

"No. You were the best thing. Even if you were . . . born the way you were. She loved you unconditionally."

"But what happened with her father?" Laurie asks. "I mean, obviously the curse was broken and she got away, right?"

"Yes. I'm getting to that. Somehow, she managed to make it to high school. She didn't have many friends—there were always places they wanted her to go that she couldn't, and she was afraid to bring any of them home, lest her father appear. She started to become obsessed with the source of the cursecasting—she tried to follow her father, to see if he met up with any other cursecasters, but he never seemed to. She ransacked their house when he wasn't there, looking for books or journals or any other record of how the cursecasting worked. But there wasn't anything, not even a stray word to go by. She had no idea how it worked, only that it kept her trapped.

"Without telling her father, she started to work after school, to save up money. When she got to senior year, she applied to colleges and got into some of them. She brought up the subject with her father, and he told her absolutely not—she was never going to leave him.

"Desperate, she resorted to what she called *playing the curse*— that is, giving in to it completely, and taking it to an extreme. If he wasn't going to let her go, she wasn't going to let him go either. She stuck by his side. She followed him everywhere. He'd yell at her, and she'd yell back. He'd push her, and she'd push back. For the first time, she started to see weakness on his part. He didn't know what to do. He couldn't cast another spell without negating the first one.

"He tried to make her promises. He told her she was born to be a cursecaster too. That he would teach her. That she didn't need college—she had another, greater calling. But she wouldn't relent. She stopped talking to him. She would still be there, wherever he looked. But she wouldn't say a word, wouldn't acknowledge him. It drove him crazy. She wouldn't let go. She played the curse harder. And eventually he broke."

My father takes a deep breath. I am still holding mine.

"I don't know exactly what happened. I don't know what led to the fight that ended everything. Your mother never told me; she said it wasn't important, that it was the accumulation of things that caused the break, not any one in particular. All the anger, all the resentment—it built and built, and your grandfather didn't have any other way to release it, except as a curse. A cruel, cruel curse.

"Your mother wanted her freedom. He said fine, she could finally have her freedom. But it came at a price. No longer would she or anyone she loved be able to see him. He would be invisible to her for as long as he lived. There would be no going back. And just as he would be invisible to her, so too would her children be invisible—not just to her, but to everyone. The old curse was over. This was the new one."

"Why didn't he just make *her* invisible?" Laurie asks.

"First, I'm not sure cursecasting works that way," my father replies. "But second—and more important—he knew what he was doing. He knew that it would be much harder to watch her own child suffer for her actions than it would be if she suffered herself. And so it was."

It hits me. I've been listening to this. It's been a story. I've been an observer—observing my father's pain as he tells me, observing Laurie's curiosity, Elizabeth's quiet. But now I feel as if my whole life has been rewritten, and it's the same pain as if all my bones have been rearranged.

I am not thinking about me.

I am thinking about my mother.

My father can't stop now. "She escaped. She left the room and never saw her father again. She could feel his presence—she knew he meant his curse—but she didn't want to stay any longer. What mattered the most was to get out of there. And to keep going. She was only sure it was over when her body let her leave. She kept going and going. She tried to erase her trail as best she could, because she didn't want him to change his mind and follow. He'd want her back. She knew it. As soon as he was truly alone, he'd want her back. But she'd be long gone.

"I think he genuinely believed that his disappearance from her life would be a punishment, that she would regret her departure. But of course she didn't. She went to college and got enough loans and scholarship money to make it through. She said her parents were dead, and nobody questioned it. She had her mother's death certificate, and said her father had never been in her life. She put the past behind her. After college, she and I met at a party. We were happy. She didn't tell me any of this—I got to know her without knowing her past. It was only after we were married, when we started talking about having children—that's when she told me.

"I didn't believe her. How could I? I was sure, from the way she talked, that something had been horribly wrong with her father. But curses? Invisibility? How could I believe that? She stopped talking about it. She decided, for a time, to love me anyway. She decided to risk it, to have a child. She got pregnant. Without telling me, she found a midwife who believed her. It was a home birth. God—I just can't go back to that night. I had doubted it, and then there you were. Only you weren't. And I discovered that your mother hadn't been lying after all."

He walks over to the couch. He can tell by the position of Elizabeth's hand where I am.

"Stephen," he says. "Look at me."

I do. I look him right in the eye.

"Your mother loved you. From before you were born, no matter what, your mother loved you. She felt she had brought this on you, but she never loved you any less. If anything, she loved you more for having to bear the weight of her curse. I tried to tell her—really, I did—that just because you were innocent, it didn't make her guilty. Some days she believed me. Some days she didn't. But she always loved you."

"I know that," I say. "You don't have to tell me that."

But maybe he does. Maybe I feel more awful now than I ever have before. Maybe they were right not to tell me. Maybe this only makes things worse.

I am thinking, of all things, about the silent treatment. The same silent treatment that my mother apparently used on her father, I would sometimes use on her. Not often. But there were times when I was really young, when I was really angry, that I would just stop talking to her. She couldn't see me, and then she couldn't hear me either. It always upset her, and now that upset takes on another dimension. Five years later, ten years later, I feel so profoundly sorry. I understand that there was no way I could've known, and that she knew that I didn't know. But still. The hurt I gave her. Not just in my very existence, but all the times I got it wrong.

I know she loved me. But I also know that her love took work. Lots and lots of work.

She'd told me all of my grandparents were dead. Instead of inventing new grandparents for me, she simply avoided talking about it.

"Are you okay?"

It's Elizabeth, not my father, who asks me this. But everyone hangs on my answer.

"I don't know what I am," I tell her. "I have no idea."

Dad paces away. Turns back to me. Wants to finish his story.

"We tried to find him," he says. "After you were born. She went back to where she'd left him, but he was long gone. He didn't leave a trail either. We hired detectives. They said it was like he'd never existed. Then she tried to track down other cursecasters, to see if there was any kind of antidote, any way of ending it. But we never found another cursecaster. Only internet crackpots, including one or two who were willing to string us along for months, even years. Nothing worked. Your grandfather was the key, and we had lost him."

"So you think that's it?" I ask. "That's what it takes to break the curse?"

"Yes," my father says. "To break the curse, you must find a man who isn't there."

CHAPTER 12

WHEN I WAS TWELVE and my family hadn't yet disintegrated, we made our annual pilgrimage to the Minnesota State Fair. Laurie bet me that I could stomach three back-to-back trips on the Tilt-A-Whirl. While my mother tried to convince me that there was no honor in regurgitated cheese curds, I couldn't bear to ignore the gauntlet my little brother had thrown at my feet.

I did it. I didn't throw up, but the world felt like it was spinning for another hour at least.

I feel that way now, off-kilter and unable to stop the ground from shifting beneath my feet.

No one is speaking. Stephen's father clears his throat, gets up, and leaves. None of us try to stop him.

"Wow," Laurie says, no longer able to bear the weight of silence. "Okay . . . wow."

Stephen drops his head into his hands and I let out a shuddering sigh. Laurie's eyes meet mine and I realize he can see what's happening to Stephen, that wrenching grief, because it's written on my face too.

"Don't," Laurie says. "Don't freak out."

Stephen still hasn't spoken. I put my arms around him, resting my chin on his shoulder.

Laurie gets up, pacing in front of the sofa. "We'll figure this out."

Stephen looks up, his hands balled into fists. "How? What is there to figure out? I'm invisible because my grandfather was evil. That's it. I am the spawn of evil."

"You're not the spawn of evil," I say, though my stomach is curling into a knot.

"A cursecaster?" Stephen says. "Placing wicked, cruel spells on people is my legacy, and you're trying to say that's not evil. That I'm not somehow inherently evil."

He's shaking and his face has taken on a gray pallor that makes me shiver.

"But you aren't evil," I say. "And neither was your mother. She rejected that legacy."

"And look where it got her." Stephen pulls away from me. He gets up and walks to the window, staring into the distance. "This is who I am. I am invisible."

"No, no, no," Laurie says. He walks to the window, and I'm glad he doesn't bump into Stephen. I'm also touched that he wants to try to be close to someone he can't see. He's trying so hard.

Laurie waves his hands as if trying to clear a foul odor. "We're not doing that. No pity parties, no drowning in despair. Who's for karma?"

"Karma?" I ask.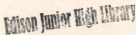

Edison Junior High Library

"I know they say 'no good deed goes unpunished,' but that's crap. Stephen's mother did something amazing. And I think that means something."

"It means she died still being punished for her father being an evil bastard," Stephen says.

"And that sucks, no argument," Laurie tells him. "But that's not the end of the story. It's the beginning . . . maybe the middle."

Laurie reaches out tentatively and I hold my breath. The movement catches Stephen's eye and I watch him tense up. But Laurie manages to lightly touch Stephen's arm. When he feels the muscles flexed under his fingers, he moves his hand up to squeeze Stephen's shoulder.

"You're the story now," Laurie says. "You decide how it's going to end."

I stand up and go to the window. Stephen watches as I take his hand and then take Laurie's hand. We're standing in a circle, facing each other.

Laurie grins. "Your mission, should you choose to accept it—"

Stephen finally cracks a smile. "Nice. Finding an invisible man is as close to impossible as it can get."

"But I found you," I say. Stephen squeezes my fingers.

"And I have an idea," Laurie says. "Be right back."

Laurie winks at me and darts into the hallway, closing the apartment door firmly behind him.

"Why does that make me nervous?" Stephen asks.

"Because while Laurie's enthusiasm can be infectious, infectious things can be very nasty."

Stephen pulls me into his arms. We stand there without speaking. I can see him. I can feel the rise and fall of his chest. Outrage and grief are sloshing around in my gut, hot and volatile as a bubbling cauldron. How could anyone lay a curse on their own child? Or on a baby? Stephen was stolen from this world before he took his first breath. It was a miracle he survived at all. Maybe Laurie had hit on the single truth that we could cling to like a life raft: the story wasn't over. Against all odds, Stephen had made his way in a world that didn't know he existed. Against all odds, I'd moved into a building far away from the home I'd known, the only girl who could see her invisible neighbor.

I want to be in control of my own life. But I can't deny the improbable circumstances that have brought Stephen and me together. And now that I'm here, that I have him, I want to believe impossible things are possible. I'm ready for miracles.

"What are you thinking about?" Stephen asks.

"Saving you," I say. He leans down and presses his face into my neck. I realize he's whispering something. I listen harder.

"I love you," he says again.

My fingers dig into his shoulders.

"I'm back!" Laurie slams the door shut.

It must look so strange: me standing there, clinging to an invisible boy who I love but am terrified for and at times am terrified of.

We let each other go but stay close so our bodies are touching as we turn to face Laurie.

"Don't be mad," Laurie says.

"What did you do?" I ask.

"I had to make a phone call," Laurie says. "We needed a little more help."

"Who did you call?" Stephen takes a step forward, eyes narrowing.

Laurie's cheeks go pink. "Sean."

"What?" Stephen goes rigid, frozen in place as he stares at Laurie.

"Laurie!" I stomp across the room. "You do not use crises to impress your crush. What the hell?!"

Laurie rolls his eyes. "Cut the tantrum, Josie. You splotch when you're angry. It's not attractive."

Stephen's voice is quiet and dangerous. "What did you call Sean for, Laurie?"

"Don't be mad," Laurie says. "I didn't tell him anything. I swear. I just needed to ask him something."

"What?" Stephen walks towards us.

"I remembered something he said when we first met." Laurie's flushed cheeks match the sparkle in his eyes. Whatever it is, he's really excited about it. "I was trying to get to know him and I only knew he loved comics, so I asked him all sorts of questions about them."

"Comics are the cure?" My arms are folded across my chest. I'm about to lose my temper again, splotching or not.

"Not comics, exactly," Laurie says. "When I asked Sean where he usually got his comics, he told me a few places, but there was one he got weird about."

"A weird comic shop?" I ask.

Laurie nods. "He said it's his favorite, but he's kind of afraid to go there."

"Why?" Stephen asks.

"I think he used the expression 'creep show,'" Laurie says. "Going into the shop is like visiting a haunted house or a mad scientist's lair. Sean said kids hang out on the stoop daring each other to stay inside for more than five minutes. He claims none of them can do it."

"Really?" Stephen's expression has grown curious, but his eyes are wary.

"Yep," Laurie says. "Sean said he's never been able to stay longer than fifteen minutes."

"So why does he even go there?" I ask.

"I guess they have a better collection of rare and special edition books than anyone else in the city," Laurie says.

Now I'm curious. "But what does this have to do with our problem?" I ask.

"Not our problem," Laurie says. "Our mission. Let's call it a mission. Or a quest."

"Why does it matter what we call it?" Stephen asks.

"Power of positive thinking. Karma," Laurie says. "Stephen is not a problem. He is a person. Invisibility is not a problem, it is a curse. Our mission is to help Stephen the person. Our quest is to find a way to break the curse."

I love my brother so much I think my heart will burst.

Stephen smiles. "But the shop?"

"Sean says it's not the comics part that gives the place its evil aura," Laurie says. "It's the back room."

I have visions of mafia or drug kingpins. "Illegal stuff?"

"I don't think so," Laurie says. "More like occult stuff. Sean says they have a witch on staff."

"Witches?" I say, frustration building again. "Give me a break."

"Just hear me out." Laurie gives me a hard stare. "Apparently this lady reads fortunes and the usual psychic stuff, but Sean mentioned something about hex breaking."

"Hex breaking?" Stephen's breath catches.

"Yeah," Laurie says. "I think we should check it out."

I balk, worried about wild-goose chases. "But Stephen's dad said we can only break the curse by finding his grandfather."

"That's true," Stephen says.

"And witches, Laurie?" I say, twisting my hands in the hair at my temples, sort of wanting to yank it out. "I mean, witches?"

"Because witches are so much more unbelievable than curse-casters." Laurie glares at me.

"Touché," Stephen murmurs.

"My point is we don't know where to start," Laurie says. "I'm not saying this is the end of our quest. But we need a guide, or a map, or something. We don't know where to start. Maybe we'll get some ideas from this place."

"Can we go with *mission* instead of *quest*?" I say. "I feel like you're trying to be our Dungeon Master or something."

"I'm trying to elevate our experience," Laurie says.

Stephen looks at me and shrugs. "At least we'll get out of the house. I'm feeling trapped in here like I never have before."

I get that. In some ways Stephen's world got a lot smaller, his life limited, by his father's confession.

"All right," I say. "I'm in."

"Where is it?" Stephen asks.

"In the garden level of a brownstone on Eighty-Fourth," Laurie says.

"That's an easy walk," I say, partly wishing it was a bit farther away. I want to drink in fresh air, clear my head. Today is the first sunny day in weeks. I'm hoping there might even be a breeze.

"Yes, it is," Stephen says. He's already heading for the door.

I've done this before, walked the streets with Stephen. I can only think of it now in terms of before and after. The walk was like this before I knew. Now the walk is like that. It's after. After I can see the deft way Stephen weaves through the world. The way he steers clear of the visible ones who would step on his toes, jostle him, or slam right into him. He is forced to constantly adjust, to always move aside. As we pass through the crowds of oblivious pedestrians, I want to yell. Perhaps if I shouted long enough, demanding the attention of enough eyes, forcing them onto Stephen, the sheer force of their stares would break the curse. It's foolish and I know it, but my frustration makes me desperate. I want to solve this problem now. I'm afraid of Laurie's quest. Quests are epic. Quests take forever. We don't have forever. I don't know that we have much time at all. A part of me knows that hearing the truth from his father has broken Stephen. I worry he's in danger of fading away completely, of wishing himself right out of this world. I can't let that happen.

Laurie focuses on the people, the sunlight, and the miraculous breeze as we walk. He can't see the maze Stephen is forced to walk through. A labyrinth of bodies that no one has to navigate but him.

We pass the Museum of Natural History, moving into the busy residential streets of the Upper West Side. We stride past New Yorkers caught up in their own harried lives, ignorant of the questers in their midst.

"It's just before Columbus," Laurie says.

We get to Eighty-Fourth Street, passing small businesses and innocuous-looking apartment buildings.

Laurie hesitates, stopping just short of the intersection to look at a brownstone. "Huh."

"What's wrong?" I ask. Stephen remains silent. I notice how rarely he speaks when we're in public. I understand that choice, but it only adds to my anger. The curse has even stolen his voice.

"This is the address." Laurie points to the brownstone. It doesn't look like any business exists here. There are no signs or advertisements. Passing it on the street, I would have assumed it was solely residential. My stomach drops a little, heavy with disappointment. But Laurie shrugs, heading for the steps that lead down to the garden entrance.

Stephen follows with me trailing. Laurie is staring at the door, which also looks nothing like a business entrance. No hours of operation listed. Not even a welcome mat.

"Do I knock?" Laurie asks.

"Just try the door," Stephen says, making Laurie jump.

He apologizes immediately. "No offense. You still surprise me sometimes."

"It's okay, Laurie. I get that you can't see me."

Laurie nods and turns the doorknob. The door swings open and all I can see is darkness. Laurie pokes his head in and I hear him say, "Whoa."

He disappears into the murky entrance. I see Stephen swallow hard before he goes after Laurie. My heart thuds against my ribs. I can't explain the cool dread that's gripping the back of my neck. I have to force myself to follow Stephen.

The first thing that hits me is the mixture of scents. One is familiar and among my favorites. I'm sure more than one person would call me crazy for claiming to love the smell of comics, but I do. They smell shiny and fresh. That scent would have calmed me if not for the others swirling in the shadowed space. Some I think I recognize: rosemary, melted wax. Others are exotic and so heavy I get a little dizzy.

It's definitely a shop. I can't wrap my head around the welcome sight of bins full of comics that I'd happily spend hours rifling through juxtaposed with the heavy velvet curtains covering the windows and the rows of burning candles on shelves that ring the room.

I lean in to Laurie. "So where's the witch?"

"Sean said there's a back room," Laurie says, pointing to the far end of the store. Behind the service counter I can barely see the outline of a closed door. "But I don't know if it's available to anyone or if you need special access."

"You're just bringing this up now?" I ask.

"Don't worry about it," Stephen says under his breath. "If you two get stalled out here, I can check it out on my own."

"Hey, silver lining," Laurie says.

I shake my head, moving towards the back of the store. At first I think it's empty, but then I notice a hunched figure sitting on a stool behind the counter. His head is bent and I think he's sleeping. But when I get close, he looks up, peering at me through the gloom. I'm glad I stop myself from gasping. He's missing an eye, and a wicked red scar runs from the empty socket down his face and neck until it disappears beneath his shirt collar.

"Help you?" he croaks.

"Uh . . ." I am frozen.

"We heard you have a witch," Laurie says, as if he says such things every day.

The man laughs like gravel crunching under boots. "Did ya now?"

"Laurie." I tug at his hand. If this guy thinks we're a bunch of teen pranksters, we'll get booted from the store with a life ban in hand.

"Why would you need a witch?" He's not looking at Laurie, he's looking at me. My heart thuds against my ribs.

"To help a friend," I say, not sure why I answer.

"Mmmm." The man slides from his stool. He walks past us all the way to the front of the store. When he locks the front door, Laurie grabs my hand.

"Millie!" the man shouts, and then begins hacking like he's about to lose a lung. When the coughing fit passes, he calls again. "You got visitors!"

I hear the sound of someone climbing stairs. The door behind the counter opens. A woman steps into the shop. Behind her I can see stairs leading down to who knows where. She's wearing a

modest flower-print dress that reminds me of a tablecloth. Her silver hair is neatly rolled in the way of ladies who have a once-weekly
appointment at the beauty salon. After eyeing me critically for a
moment, she shakes her head.

"I can't help him," Millie says.

"What?" I stare at her.

She wiggles her fingers and I realize that she's wiggling them
in Stephen's direction. "He's beyond my pay grade. Sorry."

Stephen draws a sharp breath. "You can see me?"

She gives no sign of alarm at the sound of Stephen's voice. The
one-eyed man looks towards Stephen with curiosity but quickly
returns to his usual slouch on the stool.

"No such luck," she says to Stephen. "But I can see the curse."

Then she turns to me. "It took long enough for *you* to find me."

Millie pivots around, tottering towards the staircase. We stare
after her until she throws a glance over her shoulder. "Come on."

CHAPTER 13

"WHO ARE YOU?" ELIZABETH asks as we head into the darkest recesses of the moribund comic store.

"Who I am is immaterial," Millie replies.

"But *what* you are is important," I say.

Millie nods. "You understand perfectly."

I can feel things shifting. My whole relationship to the world is shifting. I thought it was all pretty straightforward, all observable at one point or another. But now it seems that I was wrong. There is a world I didn't know within the world I knew. And Millie, it appears, is its emissary.

The room she takes us to is lined with bookshelves on every wall. A private library . . . but something is off. At first I don't realize what's so disconcerting about it, and then I notice: none of the books have writing on their spines. It's an anonymous library. Or maybe a library I can't read.

"Please sit down," Millie says, gesturing to a table in the middle of the room. Four chairs sit around it, as if she had been waiting for three people.

I find myself hoping for Laurie to interject some humor into the situation, but he's as speechless as the rest of us.

"Why have you been waiting for me?" Elizabeth asks once we've all sat down.

"For the same reason you've come, no doubt."

"I've come because he's invisible."

Millie shakes her head. "No, you've come because you can see him."

"Are you a cursecaster?" I ask.

The old woman looks gravely offended.

"Well, I've never!" she exclaims. "What a horrible thing to say!"

"I'm sorry," I quickly continue. "It's just that—"

"I'll have you know, I am a spellseeker! And"—she looks at Elizabeth—"I know another spellseeker when I sense one!"

"Excuse me?" Elizabeth says.

"A spellseeker. A hexologist. A spellvoyant. Surely someone's told you? You don't just see through invisibility curses with no training!"

"I genuinely have no idea what you're talking about," Elizabeth tells her.

"I'll second that," Laurie chimes in. "I know you're speaking English, but none of it really makes sense."

"Hmpf," Millie says. Then, with a certain acidity, she adds, "So you're a *natural* talent?"

"I assure you, she's had no formal training," Laurie says. "Our town didn't even have a magic club."

"Look," I say, "you clearly know much, much more about all this than we do. I know that my grandfather was a cursecaster, whatever that is. I know that he cursed my mother, so I'd be invisible. And that's about it. That's all I know. We need help. Lots of it."

"Clearly," Millie says, a little less hostile than before. "But you'll have to appreciate that I can't get involved in curses. Especially when it's a family matter."

Part of me wants to weep and part of me wants to grab her by her shoulders and shake hard. To be so close to some kind of answer and to not get it—I liked it so much more when I was oblivious. But there's no going back now.

"You said you could see my curse?" I prompt.

Millie sighs. "Yes. But that's boring, isn't it?"

"I don't think it's boring at all," Laurie volunteers. "Is it like an aura?"

"*'Is it like an aura?'*" Millie mimics. Then she turns to Elizabeth. "Dear, do you want to tell him, or should I?"

Elizabeth looks at her blankly. Millie sighs again.

"It's not like it's a color. Or an aura. I don't literally *see* it. It's like an extra sense."

"A sixth sense," Laurie volunteers.

Millie snorts. "I don't rank them. And if I did, it wouldn't come sixth."

"But I don't sense anything . . ." Elizabeth says.

"Of course you do, dear! That's the only reason I could sense you working at it. I always know when another spellseeker is around. It doesn't happen often enough, but when it does, I know it."

"I haven't sensed anything but Stephen."

"Well, that can't be. This is New York. There are curses and spells *everywhere*. I understand if you're being shy—it's not easy talking about your gift. I was once a girl like you. Although, obviously, I never honed my powers enough to see through an invisibility curse. I promise you, I am not your rival. We are all in this together. So if you would just throw off your, shall we say, reticence, it would be much appreciated."

I can't vouch for her sixth sense, but it appears that at least two of Millie's other senses (sight, hearing) need some work. Because it should be more than obvious that Elizabeth is not being coy here; she's not withholding anything. She genuinely has no idea what Millie is talking about.

Millie goes on. "Your cursecaster was very good at his work. It's impenetrable. Sometimes there are cracks you can see through—that's why people come to me, you see. But there are no cracks in yours. I haven't seen this kind of worksmanship in years."

"His name was Maxwell Arbus," I say.

Millie blinks, then shakes her head. "I don't know him. I take it he wasn't local?"

"No. But are you saying there are other, local cursecasters?"

Now Millie laughs. "That's for me to know and you never to find out! Trade secrets, my dear. And I am nothing if not discreet."

Laurie and I shift in our seats. I look over to Elizabeth and find she's staring at Millie. Staring hard. Millie notices this too and stops laughing.

"What?" she asks, a quiver in her voice.

I have never seen Elizabeth like this. And, judging from his expression, neither has Laurie.

She isn't startled. She isn't in shock. She's concentrating.

"Your mother thought both of you would die," she whispers.

Millie gasps.

Elizabeth continues. "She didn't think both babies would live. So she cast a spell. You lived. Your sister died. And ever since, you've been fascinated by the spells. Because they are both lifegiver and murderer."

"How . . . it's not possible . . . you . . ."

"Elizabeth?" Laurie asks gently.

She turns to him. Blinks. Is back with us.

"Wow," she says. "That was intense."

"What did you do?" I ask.

"I saw the spell. It was right there. I don't know how. But it was—"

Millie stands. "You must leave at once. I will not be attacked in my own hexatorium!"

"What?" Laurie says, grabbing a book off the shelf. "Are these, like, hex books?"

He opens it up, and the minute he looks at the page, he screams out in pain. The book falls from his hands. His eyes burn with tears.

"It's not something you can read," Millie says, picking the book up from the ground. "Clearly, you don't have your girlfriend's talent."

"Girlfriend? That's wrong on so many levels."

"Again, I must ask you to leave."

Laurie and I stand up, but Elizabeth stays put.

She looks directly at Millie. Not staring this time. Beseeching.

"You have to tell me what this means," she says. "I have no idea what I'm doing. None of us does."

Finally, Millie gets it. She looks almost as shocked as she did when Elizabeth saw her spell.

"You really don't, do you?" she says, going over and standing next to Elizabeth's chair. Studying her.

"I swear, before now, I've never done anything like this. I saw Stephen. That's all."

"Well, as far as you know, anyway." Millie sits back down in her chair. Laurie and I remain standing, almost as if we know this is really between the two of them now, and if we interfere, we may lose Millie's help forever. "When I was a girl, I saw things all the time—I just didn't know I was seeing them. That's the talent, really. To know what you're seeing."

"It's just that I have no experience with . . . well, magic, I guess."

Millie groans. "Magic! Now, there's an abused word. What we do is as much a part of a system as physics or chemistry or biology. It's just much less . . . public. It has to be. If you don't understand that now, you soon will." She pauses, sighs again. "I see I will have to start at the most basic level."

"Yes," Elizabeth says. "Please."

"Out in the world, there are spellcasters, cursecasters, and spellseekers. Spellcasters are practitioners who use hexology to influence events, for better or worse. Cursecasters can only do it for the worse. And spellseekers are the only ones who can see what's happening, even if they themselves can't create spells or curses. There aren't many of us, philosophy knows, just as there aren't many spellcasters or cursecasters. It's a dying power, really. But still potent, when used in the right place at the right time."

"And is it, like, hereditary?" Laurie asks.

"Some casters and seekers are made, some are born," Millie replies. "It depends on the situation."

"And can curses be broken?" Elizabeth asks.

"Ah, we're back to that, are we? For your other boyfriend."

"You're much closer this time," Laurie mumbles.

"When was the last time you met another spellseeker?" Elizabeth asks. I don't know why she's digressing from the main topic—namely, my curse—but I trust she knows what she's doing.

Millie looks grumpy again. "I don't see how that's germane," she huffs.

"Ten years? Twenty?"

"Twenty-seven, okay? It's been twenty-seven years!"

"That's quite a long time. You must be very lonely."

"You have no idea!" Millie is near tears now. "A girl like you—so young! You have absolutely no idea."

"Millie, I want to be able to trust you. I want us to be able to talk about things. But I can't do that—I can't come back here—unless you help me break Stephen's curse. Because if I can't do that, I don't really want to be a spellseeker at all."

"But you can't!"

"I can't what? Give it up?"

"No—his curse. You can't break his curse!"

"Surely," Elizabeth says calmly, "in some of the books in your hexatarium—"

"Hexatorium."

"Hexatorium. Surely there must be things in these books that can help us. Or stories of curses that have been broken."

Millie shakes her head. "Yes, but not one . . ." She trails off.

"Not one . . . ?"

"Not one by Maxwell Arbus, okay? Never! Not one!"

"So you *do* know who Stephen's grandfather is."

"You see, that's why I can't be involved. I knew from the moment I saw him. I said to myself, 'That's Maxwell Arbus's work, and you shouldn't get involved. Because if he finds out you tried to break one of his curses, you're doomed.' Those were my exact words."

"But how would he know?" Elizabeth asks.

"Because he's been here! Not in this room, but in the city. I've sensed him at work. But I've never seen him."

"Has he left a body count?" Laurie asks.

Millie looks at him with utter disdain. "Only indirectly. You do know, don't you, that curses can never directly kill someone? That's why they're curses—you have to live with them, in agony, for a very long time."

I can certainly vouch for that. And, I think, my mother could have vouched for it even more.

But I have to block that out for a moment. I can't think of her, or the agony. Millie's other words are sinking in.

"He's been here?" I ask. "You're sure of it?"

"Yes," Millie says. Then she catches herself. "But I said I wasn't going to talk about it, didn't I?"

Elizabeth makes to move out of her chair. "Well, then, I guess we'll leave. And I'll never see you again."

"No!" Millie protests. Then she regains her composure. "Rather, that would be inadvisable. Why don't we do this? Give me a little time to mull this over. Why don't you come back the day after tomorrow at one? We can talk again then."

"Okay," Elizabeth says. But before she can get up, Millie leans over and takes her chin in her hand.

"Look at me," she says. "I can teach you. There are many, many things I can teach you. You will never know what to see until you are taught how to see. Not fully. Don't underestimate that."

Elizabeth waits until Millie takes her hand away. Then she stands.

"I know," she says. "But you're going to have to help me first."

We make our own way out.

We don't speak until we're safely outside, three blocks away.

It's like it suddenly hits Elizabeth. One moment she's walking, and the next she's shaking. We sit her down on a park bench, tell her to take deep breaths.

"Sorry," she says. "I just need to . . ."

"Release it," Laurie says.

We sit down next to her.

"You were brilliant," I say.

"You really saw that stuff, didn't you?" Laurie asks. "About her sister."

Elizabeth nods. "It was so unbelievably strange. It was just . . . there. She was right—it's like a sense. Only I hadn't known to use it before."

"And what you said about her not seeing another spellseeker for twenty years—that was amazing," Laurie says. "You saw that too?"

"No," Elizabeth tells him. "That was just a guess."

"I'm the one who should be sorry," I tell her.

"What? Why?"

"For dragging you into this. I mean, this is a whole lot to deal with. And if you'd never met me, you never would have known."

"I have a feeling this was going to happen sooner or later," Elizabeth tells me. "Maybe I wouldn't have guessed this week, but whatever. What's done is done. And I'm not going to regret meeting you."

"Not yet," I say.

"Never," she swears.

"Lovebirds?" Laurie interjects. "Can we put off the mating call for a sec? Methinks we have some bigger issues on the table. You know, the whole magic-exists-in-the-world thing? Am I the only one who's a little freaked out by that?"

"It's not much of a surprise to me," I admit. "Then again, I *have* been invisible my whole life."

"I'm completely freaked out," Elizabeth says. "To the point that I'm afraid of what I'm going to see, now that I know I'm supposed to be able to see spells and curses. I mean, I imagine it would be more productive to be able to see, like, parking spots. Or people having emergencies I can actually help with."

"I, for one, am feeling a little left out of the magic bandwagon," Laurie proclaims. "Unless, of course, I'm really a spellcaster. I mean, I've cast spells on plenty of boys. But, wait—that wasn't magic. That was just because I'm so damn purty."

Elizabeth swats his shoulder. "I'm so glad you're taking this seriously. Really, I appreciate it."

"I'm just trying to have some quality bonding time with you before they send you off to magic school."

I know I should jump in and banter too—it's definitely improving Elizabeth's mood, and it's making the situation a little less scary than it felt when we were in Millie's hexatorium. But we're also dodging the big question—which is, what should we do next?

I still feel guilt that I've pulled Elizabeth and Laurie into this. Now that I know how it destroyed my mother, I don't want it to destroy anyone else.

When we get back to our floor, Elizabeth lingers in the hallway. Laurie gets the hint and heads back into their apartment, leaving the two of us alone.

"You're allowed to walk away," I tell her.

She smiles. "I know. But in this case, I think I'd rather walk towards."

Still, I can see there's a lot going on inside her. I might not be a spellseeker, but I can certainly read a face.

She's scared. Strong, but scared.

CHAPTER 14

I LIE IN STEPHEN'S ARMS, twining and untwining my fingers with his. I think I've been here an hour, maybe two. I came back to Stephen's apartment the moment I heard Mom leave for work. When Stephen answered my knock at his door, we didn't speak. He took my hand and led me to the couch where we've been curled up ever since. Time seems meaningless—an arbitrary marker in a world that is full of possibilities and problems I'd never dreamed of before today.

We haven't been talking, but the absence of futile words that fail to put together everything we've seen and heard in the past few days is comforting. His eyes meeting mine helps to clear my addled brain. His hands tracing the shape of my body, and his lips on mine, can make me forget everything I've just learned to be afraid of. At least for a little while.

Even so, I'm starting to fidget. The brief wash of calm offered by his touch is giving way to another flood of questions about who I am. I'm realizing, somewhat ashamedly, that all along I've thought of this as all about Stephen. His invisibility. His problem. His curse. His family. My involvement is only a fluke.

But as it happens, this whole mess is about me too. I don't know where to begin. I don't know who I am anymore.

"You okay?" Stephen asks.

"Yeah," I say, but I sound as unconvincing as I feel.

Stephen doesn't try to stop me as I sit up. "You need to be alone again."

I give him a smile, grateful that he can read my moods so easily. "I'm sorry—"

"Don't be." He brushes his hair out of his eyes. Dark hair that only I can see. I reach out to touch it. Wondering why it's me. Wondering why he is visible to my eyes alone. Even another person like me can't see him . . . another spellseeker . . . It's still so strange to have a new category to place myself in. Before, I was Elizabeth . . . Jo . . . daughter . . . sister . . . would-be writer/artist. Now this.

I let my hand drop before my fingers touch Stephen's hair, the impulse borne away by a renewed frenzy of thoughts.

"It's a lot to process," he says, watching me as I begin to shift my weight.

"Yeah," I say again. Great. My new identity has transformed me into an obsessive narcissist. I can't stop thinking about who I am and what it means, but Stephen is still invisible. Still cursed.

"Honestly, I need to sleep for a while longer," he says; the weariness in his eyes lets me know he's passed as restless a night as I had.

I nod, trying to smile at his affection, but remain distracted.

"You know where to find me." He's already wandering out of the room, and it occurs to me that I'm not the only distracted one.

Both of our worlds have been shaken up. He needs time to sort out all the layers of family, magic, and betrayal that I do. We had our time to hold each other. To simply be. But now we're being pulled apart by divergent needs. We each need to figure out what our stories are. Some things we'll be able to do together. Others will leave us on our own.

The moment he's out of sight, I'm regretting saying I needed alone time. My stomach feels hollow, the way it does when I wake up from a nightmare and remember that I'm too old to call out for my mother.

I head back to my apartment and, like Stephen, make a beeline for my room. Laurie isn't in sight, but when I'm walking down the hall, I hear him on the phone. I consider popping my head in to make sure he hasn't decided to share the outcome of our quest with Sean. But I'm just too tired to risk any sort of argument, so I pass his door and go to my room.

I think I'll go back to bed, just like Stephen said he planned to. But a few minutes after flopping onto the mattress, I know sleep is not an option. My mind won't stop. The noise in my head is like a ceaseless drumroll where the cymbal crash never comes. It is maddening.

I roll onto my side, pulling my art supplies out from under the bed. When in doubt: draw. Free sketching is not an option. I need something that will completely absorb me in the work, so I decide to throw myself into the story I've been working on. It's what I hope someday to pitch to Vertigo or Dark Horse to make my way into the world of graphic novels and comics.

Flipping through the sketches—some complete with inks and

dialogue, others only husks of scenes—my hands slow as I'm turning the pages. I'd been calling it *The Shadowbound* because it's a story about people whose steps are dogged by an unseen force that shapes each moment of their existence, usually for the worse. I stare at the page, peering at my own work. My hands begin to shake.

I lied to Millie.

And to myself.

"They're cursed," I whisper. I go back, gazing at each drawing, watching as the unfinished illustrations uncover a world full of people tormented by magics they don't understand and are desperate to be free of.

I *can* see the spells. I've been drawing them all along. That's why I can draw Stephen, while Millie can sense him but not see him.

I've discovered my natural talent. It's been within me, latent, waiting to be recognized for what it is.

I want to scream. I want to cry. I want to perfect a maniacal laugh that will get me checked into a mental institution so I don't accidentally see anything I'm not ready to deal with. Then I wonder if half the people in mental institutions are there *because* of curses.

Pushing the portfolio away like it might burn me, I back towards my bedroom door. Then suddenly I'm whirling around, slamming it behind me as I bolt through the apartment.

"Hey!" Laurie shouts from the couch where he's watching TV. "Where's the fire?"

I don't answer as I throw open the front door and run down the hall. I skip the elevator. I can't wait for anything. I'm running down the stairs.

The fire is in my blood, surging through my veins. I have to know if I'm right.

I don't stop until I'm outside our building. I lean over, resting my hands on my knees, gulping air as I wait for my heart to slow.

Someone is crouching beside me. "Are you okay?"

Laurie's face is scrunched up. It reminds me of the day when he was nine and his pet hamster got sick.

I nod, still trying to catch my breath.

"You see, I don't really accept that answer," he says. "You nearly broke the sound barrier getting out of our apartment."

I straighten. "I just . . . figured something out."

His brows lift.

"I'll just be gone for a little while," I say, starting to walk away. He grabs my arm.

"Uh-uh." Laurie turns me to face him. "What's up?"

"Seriously," I say. "It's okay."

"You're going back to that weirdo shop with bonus library crypt, aren't you?" he says, frowning. "That lady didn't do anything to help us."

"I'm not," I say. "This is something else."

"But something related to our quest." He folds his arms across his chest. "Because I don't think you're running to the store for milk. We're out, by the way."

I look at him for a moment. Part of me thinks this is a solitary quest. But I'm also terrified.

I decided to meet him halfway. "It's my drawings."

"What about them?" he asks.

"My art is all about people who are cursed . . . at least I think it is."

His eyes widen. "Whoa. For real?"

"I'm pretty sure . . . but I need to go for a walk."

"How is a walk going to help?" Laurie tilts his head at me.

"I need to look at people." It sounds really dumb as I say it. But I know it's true. I have to watch them . . . and see.

Laurie rolls his shoulders back. "Okay. Let's go for a walk."

"No," I say. "I'm going. You don't have to."

"Yes, I do," he says. "I'm not letting you wander through magical Manhattan on your own. Spellseeker or not, you're a novice. I don't want any spelltraffickers abducting your naive-ass self for nefarious purposes."

"I really don't think there are spelltraffickers," I say. But I wonder. There could be anything.

He sees the thought flicker over my face. "See. You know I'm right. Think of me as your non-magical wingman."

"Fine," I say, not wanting to sound as relieved as I feel that he's coming along. "But if you distract me, I'll send you packing."

"The non-magical wingman will never distract our heroine!" He pauses and then sighs mournfully. "Oh, man."

"What?" I've taken off down the sidewalk and Laurie keeps pace at my side.

"As non-magical wingman, I am doomed," he says, though he's grinning at me. "The superfluous sidekicks never make it to the end of the story."

I shake my head. "Don't be ridiculous."

"I could make references to oodles of literary and film examples to prove you wrong, but you already know I'm right."

"You aren't doomed," I say, walking faster, "because I'd die before I let anything happen to you."

He looks at his feet because he knows it's true.

"Let's stop here," I say. We're in front of a bodega with a large awning. I pretend to peruse the cartons of fruit, but I'm watching the other customers.

"What do we do?"

I shush him, but when he gives me puppy eyes, I quail. "Fine. You buy something so we look legit and then just let me figure this out."

Happy to have a task, Laurie gets serious with the fruit inspection, fussing over the ripeness of various bananas.

I take a deep breath and try to do again what I did with Millie. I concentrate while I let the world fall away. I can't let the blaring horns on the street or the hardness of the pavement or even the breeze pull me back into the moment. My vision gets slightly blurred. And I go there.

I don't know where it is. Even in the couple of times I've managed to do it, I'm not sure what it is. I've started to think about it as "the background." It's like the regular universe that I live in is still there, but I can see what's going on behind the scenes. And behind the scenes is where the magic lives.

Despite the wavering quality of the scene before me, I worry it's not working. I can't feel or see anything different about the people around me. Then I notice the woman at the curb. At first I sense the energy around her. It's choppy, like static. I draw another slow breath and try to withdraw even further into the background. That's when the static takes shape. It hovers around her like the shadows I sketched, amorphous, always moving, full of a life of their own. Living spells. I can see particles falling around her like bits of straw. And it's not good. I'm beginning to grasp the mechanics of controlling my ability to see curses. I don't think I like it.

"Anything?"

Laurie's voice snaps me back to the bodega.

"What did I say about interruptions?" I glare at him.

"Sorry." He offers me an apple. "But if you stare off into space for too long, it's gonna blow our cover."

He's probably right, and he did manage to find a Granny Smith that looks perfect. I take a bite, enjoying its tartness.

"So what's the deal?" he asks, looking around as if expecting evidence of the new, magical me to be lying around.

"That lady." I nod in her direction. Laurie cranes his head to look at her. She's trying to hail a cab. She's been trying to hail a cab for half an hour. I know this, though I've only been watching her for five minutes. "She can't get a cab," I say, chewing thoughtfully on the apple chunk.

"Sometimes it takes a while," Laurie says.

I smile because as weird as it is, it's still kind of funny. "No. I mean she can't get a cab. She's cursed."

Laurie snorts. "Cursed to not get a cab."

"I know it doesn't really make sense." I shrug. "But that's the curse."

"That's pretty lame," Laurie says.

I'm thinking about the movement of the spell, frenetic and unstable.

"You've got that look." Laurie is peering at me.

"What look?" I compose my face into what I hope is "normal Elizabeth."

He laughs. "The look that you get when you're about to get a forty-point word in Scrabble."

I crack a smile. "I think I might be starting to understand how the spells work."

"Really?" He's still laughing, but his eyes are bright with interest.

"So, it's like what you just said," I say. "The cab thing. She can't get one, which is annoying, but not life and death . . . not like Stephen."

He nods.

"And her curse was . . . wobbly," I say, wishing I could think of a better word. "It felt off balance, like it wouldn't hold together much longer. So what if the way I sense the spell has to do with how strong, or bad, it is?"

"It's a theory," Laurie says. "Why don't you try again?"

I chew my lip. Laurie steps aside, making it obvious that he will no longer distract me. I giggle and it takes me a minute to be able to let go of the world and move into the background. But once I'm there it's only a few seconds before she catches my eyes.

The woman is moving through the crowded street with purpose. She's decked head to toe in designs that are meticulous and refined without being ostentatious. Her cell phone rings. It takes less than two minutes for her to finalize the deal she's been working on all day. It looks like she'd love to skip down the street in celebration, but that wouldn't help the image she so carefully built over the years. As she sweeps past me, I see the spell swirling around her. It surges and shimmers, a snowfall gently pouring over her. The tinkling of bells and a child's laughter chase in her wake.

"Wow," I say, blinking away the giddiness that coursed through me when the spell was near.

Laurie comes to attention. "Another one?"

"A good one this time," I say. "She was surrounded by success."

"How does success look?" he asks.

I cringe a little. "Sparkly. It didn't wobble. It poured."

Laurie pretends to wipe his brow. "Well, it's a relief to know it's not only curses out there. Maybe we can cast a spell that will get Sean to ask me out?"

"Laurie," I groan.

"I was kidding." He holds his hands up pleadingly, but I can see the gears working in his mind.

"No spells." I shake a finger at him before taking another bite of the apple while I ponder our next move.

"Nothing for you?" I ask, noting that he isn't chomping on fruit like me.

He holds up a paper bag. "Mango."

I wipe juice from my chin. "How are you going to eat that while we're walking?"

"I'm saving it for later," he says. "It'll go great with vanilla bean ice cream."

"When did you get ice cream?" I ask as we cross the street. I'm leading, taking us towards the park.

He grins. "I haven't yet. I figure I'll get it at one of our stops along the way."

But the second stop at a store never comes. What I see in the park sets me off in a new direction. We've been walking for half an hour while Laurie drops hints about leaving the greenery for the sake of ice cream hunting when I see him.

He's an artist or he wants to be, and I automatically feel kinship with him. I also like him because he's perched beneath the angel that Stephen brought me to just after I moved to New York. This place calms me. Though the world's been lurching under my feet ever since I found out about Stephen and now me, this spot in the park reminds me that no matter what madness life churns out, Stephen and I still have this place. And each other.

The man is in his twenties, wearing glasses with thick, clear plastic frames and a rambling mishmash of clothes. He's staring at a blank canvas and shuffling brushes in his hand like a deck of cards.

I stop, watching him.

Laurie takes a long look at me. "We gonna be here a while?"

"I think so," I say.

He drops to the ground, rummaging in his bag for the mango.

"Okay, then," I say to myself. Each time I do this it feels new and I'm nervous that it won't work. But a moment later the world has blurred and I'm in the background again. Only the artist remains in focus. I wait, keeping my breath steady. The air around him begins to move, take shape. This isn't like falling straw but appears as threads, weaving around his body. I swear I can hear a low hissing, like angry whispers, chasing around his body as the threads move. I can sense them knotting, tightening.

I pull myself out of the background, a little shaken by what I saw.

Laurie's on his feet. He clasps my wrists, steadying me. His fingers are sticky with mango juice.

"What's wrong?"

"He has no inspiration," I say.

"That painter?"

I shake my head. "His creativity is blocked. That's the curse."

"And it was different than the cab lady's?"

"Yeah," I say. "This one is meant to last. It was tying itself around him. And it had a sound."

Laurie takes a step back. "The curses make sounds."

"His does." I look at the artist.

He's standing up, shoving brushes into a satchel. He kicks the blank canvas over, startling a cluster of pigeons. He doesn't pick it up as he stalks away from the fountain.

"So it's worse," Laurie says, watching him leave.

I don't say anything. I don't need to.

"Well, let's go, then," Laurie says.

"Where?" I ask, still watching the artist. The angry set of his shoulders melts into a slump of despair as he disappears down the path.

Laurie waits until he has my attention. "To see what Stephen's curse feels like."

I can tell he's surprised to see me. And even more surprised that Laurie's at my side.

"Hey." He recovers quickly, leaning in to kiss me.

I resist the urge to try to see his curse right then and there. He deserves fair warning before we do this. Even though as we know there's a curse and kind of know its history, getting me this involved is taking our detective work to the next level.

I'm hugging Stephen hard, tongue-tied by how I've spent the afternoon. Fortunately Laurie has no such troubles.

"She can see them!" He bounces past us into Stephen's apartment.

"I'm sorry?" Stephen keeps his arm around my waist as we follow Laurie into the living room.

Not wanting Laurie to continue speaking for me, I interrupt him, winning myself an eye roll in the process. "The spells. I can see the spells."

"But Millie said—" Stephen is cautious.

"I know." I sit on the couch, tucking my legs beneath me. "But I think that's what she meant when she said I come by this naturally. I can see the spells. They're what I've been drawing."

Stephen sits beside me, leaning back. He doesn't say anything for a while. Laurie makes a get-on-with-it motion, but I ignore him. I don't want to go further without Stephen agreeing.

Finally he lets out a long breath. "What do they look like?"

"They take different forms . . . Some have sounds, both of which seem to correspond with the intent of the spell."

His jaw tightens. "And you're here to see mine."

"Only if you want me to," I say quickly.

"Why wouldn't he want you to?" Laurie asks.

"Why wouldn't I?" Stephen murmurs to himself. And then a moment later, "Go ahead."

"Are you sure?" I don't want to push him.

He nods, closing his eyes.

I want to hold his hand but worry it might interfere with my ability to see the curse. My heart is pounding. I have to draw several deep breaths before I can take myself out of my room. The background is different in the apartment, quieter and closer. I feel a little claustrophobic, like the walls are closing in.

I force myself to stay calm and focus on Stephen. At first he's just there, the way I've always seen him. I pull farther back, trying to separate my feelings for him from the magic I need to see. It stirs reluctantly, slithering up around him. I choke on a scream. These aren't threads. They're tentacles. The thick, squirming appendages all around him. The squelching sound of their suckers latching and unlatching from his body is unbearable, as if they're drawing out the very essence of his being. Stephen is still, settled in the midst of them. He exists within the nest of this curse.

I jerk out of the background. Laurie is staring at me. Stephen begins to tremble when he sees my face. I bolt from the couch and make it into the bathroom just in time to vomit.

CHAPTER 15

THIS WHOLE TIME, I've wanted to know exactly how she saw me. I've hung on to every detail. I've waited for every clue.

Now I'm not so sure.

It is like I am killing her. Just by standing there. Just by having her examining me.

I am killing her.

She runs out of the room, and Laurie follows. I stay in the same spot, afraid.

I don't want her to see me anymore. Not if it does that to her.

Being invisible, I've never had to withstand another person's revulsion before. I've never been the catalyst for such a reaction.

Now I know how it feels.

And it kills me.

Laurie comes back.

"Where are you?" he asks.

"Right here," I say.

He follows my voice. "She's okay. Just a little shaken up. I think maybe we need to call it quits for the day—"

But before he can say anything more, she returns to the room.

"No, it's fine," she says. "Don't worry. I'm fine."

She looks at me. I want to hide. For her sake.

"It's all right," she tells me. "I've turned it off. That part of it."

"What did you see?" I ask.

She shakes her head. "I can't really explain it. I mean, I don't understand it at all. I can see things, but I don't know how to interpret them. All I know is that it's one powerful curse your grandfather's put on you."

"It hurt you to look at it," I say.

"I don't know if *hurt* is the right word. It overpowered me. Almost like it could tell I was looking, and it had to send me away."

"Don't do it again," I say. "Promise me. Not until we know more."

"I promise. Not until we know more."

My father comes home for dinner. I'm not expecting him, but I'm not really surprised, either.

"What did you do today?" he asks, as if I've just come home from soccer practice.

I laugh. I can't even begin to tell him.

"Look," he says. "About last night . . . I hope it's okay that I told you all those things. I've been wandering around the city all day, thinking about it. I never wanted this day to come. I honestly thought that—well, I thought—"

"You thought Mom would be around to tell me. You didn't

think you'd ever have to have the conversation because you knew it would be up to her."

"Exactly."

I call the Italian place down the street and order us dinner, charged to his card, as always. Then I sit back down across from him at the kitchen table.

I have so few memories of him. Sometimes I would make them up. I've seen so many fathers pushing their kids on swings, so many fathers playing catch, so many fathers watching with a mix of nervousness and excitement as their sons took their first sled rides down a steep, snowy hill in Central Park. I could make myself believe that we'd had these things too, in the time before I could remember, in the time before he left. I never needed him to teach me things, or to be my hero. I just wanted him around to carry me on his shoulders when we went to the zoo.

He's talking to me now, telling me about his life in California, telling me about my sisters, trying for once to fill the empty space that he's left in my life. He's filling it with the wrong things, but in some twisted way I appreciate the attempt. I'm not really listening; instead I'm trying to imagine what it was like, to be in love with my mother, to marry her, and then one day to be told about this curse, this threat. He didn't want to believe it was true, and who can blame him? I don't want to believe it's true, and I'm the proof that it's true.

I guess the question I have to ask myself is how much I truly expect my father to bear. What are the responsibilities, really, once things like curses and spells become involved? Can I blame him for not wanting to have anything to do with it?

Well, yes, I can blame him. So I guess the question is whether I *should* blame him.

"Obviously," he's telling me now, "I haven't told them the real reason I'm staying. But I want to be here for you. For as long as it takes to sort this out."

"What?" I say.

"I've told them a business situation has come up. And I think— I hope—my wife knows me well enough to know I'm not having an affair. So I'm going to stay in the city. I don't have to stay here—I respect that you have every right to privacy at this point. But surely there's something I can do."

"It's okay," I say. "You can go."

"No. We'll beat this thing."

He says it emphatically, like I have cancer and he's going to hold my hand for the treatments. *We'll beat this thing.* But there's no treatment that's been devised to beat this thing. There's no need for him to hold my hand.

He starts talking some more about the sisters I'll never meet, the sisters who don't know I exist.

Dinner arrives. As we eat, he asks me about what movies I like. When I name a few he's never heard of, he says we should watch them together. I assume he means this hypothetically. But when dinner's over, he goes straight to the DVD player and puts one in.

He sits in the chair that might have once been his. I sit on the couch. I've seen the movie a hundred times, but this time it's different. We're laughing at the same things. I can feel us both rooting for the main character. I can feel him enjoying it.

It's like one of my fake memories, only real.

Elizabeth, Laurie, and I return to Millie's inner sanctum at the appointed hour the next day.

This time, the door guardian lets us in without a word, simply pointing to the stairs that lead to the hexatorium.

Millie looks calmer and more collected than she did yesterday. She is putting some of the books back on the shelves when we arrive.

"So good to see you again," she says, even though she hasn't looked at us yet.

We sit down in the same places from the day before.

"Now," she says, "before we begin, I must ask your names."

Such an elemental test of trust. It hadn't even occurred to any of us to introduce ourselves last time. I think we assumed she already knew.

We give her our full names. Laurie says he's Elizabeth's brother. I say I'm Elizabeth and Laurie's friend.

"I should have seen the resemblance," Millie says, looking at Laurie and Elizabeth. "I hope you'll pardon me. I was rather . . . distracted."

"Completely understandable," Elizabeth says.

Then we sit for what feels like a minute in silence, waiting for Millie to continue the conversation.

Finally, she tells us she didn't sleep last night.

"So you'll have to pardon me again. There's a lot on my mind, especially considering what I'm about to do. I don't want you to think that what I am about to disclose is being said without any deliberation. This is not easy for me, and I need you to appreciate that."

"We do," Elizabeth tells her. "We appreciate you seeing us again. We appreciate whatever it is you're about to say."

It's like someone's put me and Laurie on mute. There is some connection between Elizabeth and Millie, and, once again, the minute we walked into this room, the story we were acting out became about her, not me. Millie isn't talking to either me or Laurie, even though she clearly doesn't mind if we hear what she has to say. But really, she's only talking to Elizabeth.

"When you came here yesterday, I felt so many different emotions. And those emotions are what kept me awake last night. More than anything else, I felt old. Older than I've felt in a long, long time. I felt the burden of everything I've seen, everything I've learned, and how that burden has made me slower, more hesitant. The older you get, the wiser you are—this is true. But you also question what use this wisdom is.

"When I started sensing your presence, Elizabeth, I assumed you were another relic like me. It never occurred to me that there would be someone with your power who was merely a girl. Untrained. Natural. When you arrived here, I didn't know what to do, how much to tell. I've made a living for so long solving people's two-bit problems, upholding my reputation as the local freak. I've drifted from all the things that I was raised to do."

She pauses for a moment to make sure Elizabeth is following; it's an unnecessary pause, because we're all rapt.

"It may seem like a very strange gift to have—to be able to see spells and curses without being able to do anything about them. That is the paradox that spellseekers live with. It's like being able to hear music but never being able to make it. There are pleasures, but there are also many desires that go unfulfilled. You get used to it, but you're never entirely happy with it. You want to be able to affect the world you see. We all do.

"I've debated how much I should tell you. But I think for you to truly understand, I have to take you back to the beginning, or at least to a long time ago. Don't worry—I'm not *that* old. We're not immortal; we have the same long, short lives as anyone else. But there are histories—many of the last ones are in this very room. So we know what it was like, even a long time ago.

"Nowadays, spellseekers are bystanders. We see things, but there's not much we can do about them. We are, at best, diagnosticians for the damned. We can tell people the cause, but we seem to have lost the cure. Hundreds of years ago, however, this was not entirely so. We were not so helpless. There were more seekers than there were casters, by a large number. And we used our skills to monitor the casters. Some even suspected that a few of the most powerful seekers had the ability to draw out curses and reverse spells, but that was never more than rumor and speculation. Those seekers who may have had that kind of power knew how quickly they'd become targets of the casters. Or maybe they didn't want to shoulder the burden of removing curses when most of us can't. I didn't blame them for wanting to exist in obscurity. We were, to make a crude analogy, both police and judiciary. If a caster was abusing his or her power, we would step in. As a result, cursecasting was extraordinarily rare, and only justified in extreme circumstances. We were, strangely enough, the protectors of free will. And the casters went along with that."

Millie pauses. There is an incurable sadness in her eyes.

"Over time, this changed. There was no single event, no caster revolution. It may have been their plan, to have us die out. I don't know—you'd have to ask them. But whatever the case, there became fewer and fewer seekers. Casters did what they wanted, without repercussions. And, as you know, the world became a much, much bigger place than anyone had known it to be, which meant it was impossible to follow and monitor all of the casters. The rules did not break so much as disintegrate.

"I know I am not the last of the spellseekers, but I know I am certainly one of the last. As the world became smaller again—as technology made us closer—I wondered if there wasn't some way that contact would be resumed. But I've never heard from another spellseeker, even though I've hardly kept my gifts a secret. I imagine it didn't take you very long to find me, did it? That was deliberate."

"All you really need to do is let the comic book geeks know," Laurie says, "and the rest of the world will follow."

"I don't know if that was precisely what I intended, but I can see from years of experience that your hypothesis bears scrutiny. Still, being so open has of course left me somewhat vulnerable. The casters no doubt know what I am."

"Or they think you're a crackpot," Laurie offers.

"Or that. It's always possible. The good thing about casters is that they are unable to seek—they can create spells and curses, but they cannot see the work of others. Nor can they sense seekers in the same way that I can. For example," Millie says, looking at Elizabeth, "I doubt that Maxwell Arbus knows about you. Not yet."

The way she says this makes me shiver; it is as if my grandfather knowing about Elizabeth would be the worst thing in the world.

"Tell us about him," Elizabeth says.

Millie steels herself. Clearly, this was one of the things she debated telling us about. Then she decided that, yes, she should.

"Arbus isn't the most malevolent cursecaster I've ever seen, but he's close. There isn't really such a thing as a benevolent cursecaster—if you for some reason acquire a cursecaster's gifts, the benevolent choice is to never use them. There used to be a few cursecasters who only used their casting punitively—that is, they only cursed murderers and rapists and the like. People who had done evil. But Arbus is hardly like that.

"Arbus is the worst kind of cursecaster: He's clever. And when cleverness meets cursecasting, the result is sadism. For example, he once cursed a man to feel pain whenever he saw the color blue. This seems small at first, no? Then consider the color of the sky, the color of the sea. And how often you see blue in your daily life. Another time he made a woman allergic to the sound of her husband's voice. Every time he spoke to her, her skin would break out into heinous hives. It didn't matter how much they loved each other. It was unendurable.

"Cursecasters don't have an unlimited amount of power. Arbus is genius at making the smallest curse go far. That's why, frankly, I was surprised to see an invisibility curse made in his hand. An invisibility curse will cost a caster a significant amount of power. But if it were in the name of spiting his own kin—well, I can see why he'd expend that much. By and large, cursecasters spend much more energy on people they know."

Hearing all this dark history, my mind goes to a dark place. Yes, invisibility is my curse, forged by malevolent magic. But it seems that this was, at best, a secondary curse. The true curse is much more random, much less magical—the blunt curse of lineage. My mother was cursed the moment she was born to such an evil man. I was cursed the moment I was born to such an evil grandfather. It doesn't take a spellseeker to see that. Everything you need to know is in the blood.

"You said that my grandfather had been in the city. Do you know why? Can you tell what he did?"

"I don't know for sure," Millie replies. There's a sorrowful compassion in her voice. "The curses he made were minor—no doubt aimed at people who displeased him. But there wasn't a single, big curse. He was here for other reasons. Perhaps watching over you and your family."

"There is no other family," I tell her. "Not anymore. It's just me."

Millie nods. "I see. Then maybe he was watching over you."

"But I thought you said cursecasters can't see spells?"

"Not other people's. But they sense their own. I would guess that although you'd be as invisible to him as you are to me, he would certainly be able to sense the curse. But it wouldn't look solid—they can't see curses the way Elizabeth can. You can see it, dear, can't you?"

Elizabeth nods, but something in her eyes must give her away.

"Oh, my," Millie says. "It was rather unpleasant, wasn't it?"

"It was horrible," Elizabeth admits.

I keep reminding myself that I can't take it personally. What my curse looks like has nothing to do with who I am.

But still—the idea of Elizabeth looking at me and seeing something horrible . . . I take it personally.

"You want to break his curse," Millie says, "and I have to warn you again—I'm not sure that can ever happen. The easy, vaguely responsible thing for me to do would be to tell you to give up, to get used to it. He's been dealt the cards he's been dealt, and you just have to use them, live as best you can with the status quo. There is such a grand temptation in that. But what's keeping me up at night isn't the easy, vaguely responsible route. Because, my dear, you're the wild card. You might—*might*—make impossible things possible.

"I don't need to tell you this—I have a feeling you already know—but I'll say it anyway: Even though being a spellseeker is a job like any other job, there's a part of it that becomes an essential part of who you are. And that essential part is linked to the essential part within all of the spellseekers who came before you. I've lived for years—decades—just keeping my nose to the ground, focusing on the smallest pictures possible. But now it's like that essential part is speaking to me, telling me it's time to get back to the big picture. There was a time that spellseekers made sure life was safe for everyone else around them. And maybe it's time for this old spellseeker to remember that."

"So what do you want to do?" Elizabeth asks.

"I want to sharpen your skills. I want to show you the ways. Then I want to find Maxwell Arbus, and I want to take him down.

I want to become the first spellseeker to break an invisibility curse. And I want to do it sooner rather than later, because this broad's not made of time."

"Sign me up!" Laurie cheers.

But it's not Laurie that Millie is staring at.

"Sign me up," Elizabeth says.

"Okay," Millie says, rubbing her hands together. "Boys, you'll have to excuse us. We have some training to do."

CHAPTER 16

MILLIE WASTES NO TIME in shooing Laurie and Stephen out of the hexatorium. She even makes a high-pitched *shoo, shoo* sound, which I don't think I've ever heard a person vocalize before now. Laurie backs out of the room, giving me a thumbs-up as he disappears into the stairwell. Stephen lags, watching me. He's trying to hide a frown, and I throw a smile his way. It's a stronger smile than what I'm feeling, but I know he's worried and I don't want him to be. I'm where I have to be. I need to do this, even if I don't even know what *this* is and I'd rather not be alone with a woman I barely know who says "shoo."

Millie ends up closing the door to the hexatorium in Stephen's face. He'd opened his mouth and I'm left wondering what he was going to say. It was probably just goodbye, but with my world turning end on end with each moment, I don't want to miss anything. Not even a simple farewell. The more I learn of what's at stake, what we're dealing with, curses, magic . . . revenge, the more I'm afraid of what we could lose without any warning.

I push away the chill of suddenly being without the boy I've fallen in love with. The invisible boy.

"Dear, dear, dear." Millie is pinching my cheeks, startling me out of my torpor and sending me back a few shocked steps. "No sallow faces here."

I'm about to snark back, asking what my complexion has to do with spellseeking, but think better of it. I know she's trying to be kind in a weird, grandmotherly way. I'm desperate to stop the rattle of nerves in my bones.

Millie gives me an indulgent smile. "I'll get us some tea and nice cookies."

Yep, 100 percent grandmother.

She vanishes behind a thick velvet wall hanging that I thought was a tapestry but actually conceals a hallway. She must be going to a kitchen, but what else is back there? Does she live below the streets of New York, alone with the hexatorium and the one-eyed bodyguard upstairs?

As much as I'm thrown by her sudden shift in attitude, it's also kind of nice. Between Mom's crazy work schedule and my excuses to be away from home and with Stephen, I've barely seen Mom the past few weeks. As I hear Millie's muffled, out-of-tune humming, it strikes me that this is strange for her too. Her new exuberance for curse breaking was borne not only out of guilt, but also loneliness.

I rub my arms, shivering. The hexatorium feels more like a catacomb than a residence—a place to hide from the world and then be forgotten by it. And Millie's lived in exile here . . . for how many years, I can't be sure.

Certain these sober thoughts are giving me unwelcome sallow cheeks again, I move around the room, searching for distractions.

How can I make this easier? I'm a student. This is school. I know school. I can do school.

I try to pretend it's my first day of class. What would I do?

Before Laurie's hospitalization, I'd been a pretty engaged student, sitting close to the front of class, answering questions. After the attack I'd withdrawn, sullen and resentful of my classmates and even my teachers. My only desire was to be left alone, so I'd migrated to the middle of classrooms. Away from the eager students in the front but equally removed from the troublemakers and jokesters at the back. In the middle I could be present without being noticed. I could sneak comics to read instead of my textbooks. I could work on my sketches instead of taking notes.

I wanted to disappear.

The thought stops me in my tracks. Not only does the idea of invisibility mean something entirely different to me now, but the whole point of being here is because I can't fade away. I have to become whatever it is I'm supposed to be so I can help Stephen.

Squaring my shoulders, I reach for one of the thick books, figuring I might as well get started before Millie brings out the tea. Before I can pull the book down, I'm turned around by the clattering of a tray on the table. Tea sloshes over the edge of the cups but is sopped up quickly by the paper doilies adorning the silver service.

"No, no!" Millie fusses me away from the shelves. I move quickly since I don't want to be shooed.

"Those books are about history," she says. "Our concern is with the present. You need action. The past is for pondering and meditation, and that's for another time. Sit down."

She waits until I obey. I watch as she smilingly sets a cup of tea before me. From the scent I guess it's Earl Grey. Then she pushes a plateful of shortbread towards me. Deciding it's not optional, I select a cookie and munch on it in the hopes that my compliance will get Millie to move along with our training.

She beams at me, takes a sip of her tea, and says, "Now then, let's get down to it. Shall we?"

I'm glad I don't sigh in relief and get away with a nod.

"Like I already told your boys, there wasn't a sudden upheaval that transformed spellseekers from actors into observers," she says. "It was gradual."

She stiffens slightly, lip trembling. "Sometimes I wonder if it wasn't laziness . . . or perhaps apathy."

I see her face shift from doubt to determination. She fixes me in a sharp gaze. "But when I'm having better days, my first instinct is that it was fear."

"Fear?" The tea and cookies are soothing, making me feel like a child being spun a wondrous story. I have to keep reminding myself that I'm living this story, not hearing it. I wonder if I should be taking notes.

Millie sweeps her arm around the room. "You've seen my home. It's a place of wonder, certainly, but it's my refuge. I fear people like Maxwell Arbus. Cursecasters bowed to the judgments of the spellseekers because they had to, but we were always considered a nuisance at best, an enemy at worst. A threat that the cursecasters would come after their perceived persecutors always existed."

"But you don't know?" I cast a sidelong glance at the moldering books.

"Another reason we can't rely on the past." Millie shakes her head. "The histories I have are incomplete. And what I'd be looking for probably wouldn't have made it into the official record. Nasty business that it was."

I raise my eyebrows at her while I take another sip of tea.

She laughs and it lights up her face, taking ten years off. "Black-mail is what I'm suggesting, dear. And of the worst sort. Not the silly fiddle-faddle of these days about someone sleeping with some-one else they shouldn't have. I'm talking about threats to one's fam-ily. To one's own well-being."

As I add *fiddle-faddle* to my new dictionary of Millieisms, sad-ness creeps back into her eyes. "Enough speculation about the past. Let's start with what we do know and what we must yet discover. When did you first gain your sight?"

I stare at her.

"I mean, when did you first sense curses?" Her question is patient.

"But haven't I always been able to sense them?" I ask, frowning. "It was only yesterday that I figured out how to see them."

She nods. "Of course, dear. What I'm referring to is what we call an awakening. Spellseekers are all born with a latent ability to do their work, but he or she doesn't come into that power until the moment of awakening. It's usually an event. A trigger, if you will."

I'm still frowning, confused. "Then I guess it was yesterday."

Now it's Millie's turn to frown. She hasn't lost patience with me yet, but I can tell the conversation is frustrating her. "No, no. Yesterday you learned how to hone in on the curses and see them. That's an ability that's unique to you alone and is tied to your natural talent. What I'm talking about is when you first sensed the curses. It's a shame you were alone because the shift would have affected the way you see the world, but you wouldn't have known why or what was happening."

"I'm sorry." I crumble a cookie beneath my fingers, feeling stupid and helpless.

Fortunately Millie is a good teacher, one who doesn't easily doubt or give up on her pupils. "Then tell me, what made you go out yesterday to look for the curses?"

"Oh!" I sit up straight. "It was my drawings."

"You're an artist?" Millie sounds surprised but pleased.

A hot blush paints my cheeks. "I . . . I want to be. I want to write and illustrate comics."

"How interesting," Millie says, though her face tells me she was hoping I was an artist of the more traditional variety. "So how did your drawings lead you to seek curses?"

"It was the story I've been working on." I speak slowly, thinking about my words as I say them. "It's *The Shadowbound*."

Millie tilts her head, waiting for me to continue.

"And I realized that I've been drawing curses. Cursed people."

"And when did you start working on this story?" she asks.

I have to put my teacup down because my hands are shaking. I know exactly when I started working on *The Shadowbound*. I couldn't sleep. I couldn't eat. I couldn't do anything. So I drew. I drew on recycling-bin-bound paper that the nurses scrounged up for me. I drew for hours while my brother lay unconscious in a shrine of beeping machines and twisting plastic tubes.

I'm staring into my half-empty cup. "My brother was attacked."

Millie draws a sharp breath. "By a cursecaster?"

"No," I say. "By people. Just people."

When I force my eyes up to meet Millie's, she offers me a sad smile. "It's amazing what people can do to each other even without the aid of casters. Amazing and terrible."

I nod, blinking hard so tears won't escape my eyes.

Millie politely pretends not to notice. I am really starting to like her.

"I believe we can safely say that your brother's misfortune awakened your ability," she says. "The awakenings are more often the result of trauma or loss than a happy occurrence."

"Yours was immediate," I say quietly. "Because of your sister. You knew she was missing. You could sense the emptiness that she should have filled."

She takes a deep breath that lifts and lowers her shoulders. "Always. So yes, my case was unique. I sensed curses from the beginning."

I'm feeling unsteady, even a little sick. This is information I'm not certain I'm ready to process. Why do bad things happen to good people? So your superpower can be awakened?

Suddenly I don't care what I might be or how training as a spellseeker could help anyone. What happened to Laurie was unforgivable. A silver lining to that horror is unacceptable. Every cell in my body recoils against that thought.

My reactions must be scrolling over me like a news ticker, because Millie stands up.

"Now, now." She comes around the table to stand beside me, placing her hand over mine. "You mustn't do that."

I think for a moment she's going to comment on my sallow skin again, but she simply squeezes my fingers within her slender bony ones.

"If it wasn't what happened to your brother, it would have been something else," she says. "Your natural talent is greater than any I've known. Its awakening was simply a matter of time."

I manage to squeeze her fingers in return, though I still don't like it. I have to admit that it makes sense. I've never experienced anything so visceral as that siege of emotions that battered me in the wake of Laurie's attack. The world changed around me, becoming brighter, sharper, harder. Full of angles and shapes I'd never seen before.

I'd considered it my initiation into the jaded club, when it turns out I was simply seeing the lingering effects of magic, good and evil, for the first time.

"So we've pinpointed where it began." Millie speaks softly, coaxing me back into the room and out of the dark corners of my past. "Would you like to discuss where it might lead you from here?"

"Yes." I'm surprised by the strength in my voice.

"Let's start simply." She hesitates, withdrawing her hand from mine. "I'm afraid I'll be learning too. It's already obvious that your talent is greater than mine."

I open my mouth to protest, but she shakes her head.

"It's the truth, plain and simple," she says. "I only hope it doesn't hinder our purpose."

She returns to her chair and closes her eyes. "When I was still identifying and analyzing curses as a way of making a living, I could sense the lingering power of magic on the victim. The after-effect of the curse, if you will. It was like looking at the negative image of a photograph, but a blurred negative at best."

"But you said you can't undo curses," I say.

She opens her eyes. "Yes."

"Then why would anyone pay you for your services?"

"Cursecasters are a prideful lot." Her laugh is bitter. "By identifying the curse, spellseekers don't have difficulty tracing steps back to its creator. Many of the cursecasters will take a larger payment than the original fee if they made the curse on behalf of someone else. If the curse is personal, it often only takes groveling on the part of the victim in order for the cursecaster to break their own spell."

"So you helped people find the cursecasters?" I ask.

"It was the most I could do," she says. Then she waves her hand in the air as if batting away a fly. "But my skills only take us so far. You can do more. Tell me what you saw when you discovered the spells."

I rest my forearms on the table, as if I might need the solid wood to steady me. "It's like I fade out of the real world and into . . . I don't know what or where it is. I've been calling it *the back-ground*."

Millie nods, but when she doesn't speak, I keep going.

"When I'm in the background, I can see the spells."

"What do they look like?" she asks in a very soft voice that makes me think she's worried about spooking me.

"I saw three when I was out walking around with Laurie," I say. "Each one was kind of the same, but also different."

"Tell me about them." Millie is folding and unfolding her hands, willing herself to be patient.

"They had specific forms and sometimes a sound," I say. "The first person I saw was a woman trying to get a cab and she couldn't."

She startles me with a chuckle. "Sorry. That's a very common petty curse in the city. And they're usually temporary, set to wear off in a matter of days. What else?"

"The space around her body was filled with moving pieces, like bits of straw falling around her," I say.

"And the sound?" she asks.

I frown. "There wasn't a sound. Well, actually, I think there would have been if I'd waited a little longer. Every time I did it, there was more detail."

"Then tell me about the next one," she says.

"She looked like she was walking through a snow globe that had just been shaken." I pause long enough to roll my eyes. "And it sounded like fairy bells."

"That wasn't a curse," Millie says. "That was a fortune spell."

"I kind of got that," I say. "She was making all kinds of good deals. Work stuff."

Millie purses her lips. "Some spellcasters make profits by offering their services to the public."

"Is that such a bad thing?" I ask. "This woman seemed pretty happy."

"So are people who win the lottery—but usually it just sends them back for more," Millie says. "Magic is tricky, unreliable, and bears unintended consequences. People who rely on it for success are playing a game of Russian roulette. Eventually one of those spells will bring a bullet with it."

I shudder. "Even the good spells?"

"There's no such thing as a good spell," Millie says. "There are spellcasters and cursecasters. Spellcasting may seem benign, but it's still dangerous. People like us guard free will for a purpose; bending nature to your own will carries a price. The more you ask of it, the more it will cost you in the end. Curses are simply the furthest down the spectrum of that danger."

"And someone couldn't just hire a spellcaster to undo a curse?" I'd been keeping that thought in my back pocket.

"No," she says. "One caster can't undo the work of another. Only the originator of the spell or curse can remove it."

I swallow hard. We have no choice but to find Maxwell Arbus. Though it seems like the road we've been walking on has been leading in this direction, I'd been secretly hoping we'd find another route. Or a bypass.

I think about the artist with red threads binding his creativity, making him miserable. Who would do such a thing? Who would he have to beg relief from? What would it cost him?

"I think it's time you told me about Stephen's curse." Millie is looking directly at me. "For me, curses are like silhouettes or shadows, but the details elude me. I need to know what *you* see."

I shudder.

"I know it's horrible," she whispers. "Any curse cast by Arbus is horrible."

Keeping my gaze locked with Millie's, I recall the monstrosity I saw clinging to Stephen in the background. At first she sighs with regret, then as I shiver while describing the tentacles, her breath hitches and she nods.

"Is something wrong?"

She looks away and my blood freezes in my veins.

"I can't help but wonder how he could do it . . . to his own kin," she murmurs. Her already paper-white skin has taken on a gray cast.

"Millie, what did Arbus do to Stephen?" The words feel thick and gummy on my tongue.

I hate the sorrow I see in her eyes. "Do you remember when I told you I was surprised Arbus would cast such a powerful curse on Stephen?"

"Yes," I say. "Because he'd have to give up so much of his own power."

"He wagered that the curse would transfer from mother to child," she says. "But he couldn't control what would happen in that transfer. A curse like that takes on a life and will of its own. It generates its own power."

"What does that mean?" I ask. But I don't want to. I want to cover my ears and close my eyes and hopefully wake up so this nightmare ends.

When she looks at me, her eyes are shining with regret. "It means he will probably end up killing his grandson."

CHAPTER 17

THE WHOLE WAY HOME, Laurie is worried that he's lost me. Because when we're silent, there's no way for him to tell whether I'm next to him or not. He keeps looking over his shoulder, as if that would somehow let him know whether I've fallen behind. After a few minutes of this, I tell him, "Just assume I'm here. I'll let you know if I start to lag."

Neither of us knows what to do. Neither of us knows what Millie is doing to Elizabeth, or if it was a mistake to leave her there.

When we get back to our building, Laurie holds the door open for me, confusing the doorman, who'd been preoccupied with his crossword puzzle. Laurie senses his error but doesn't say a word. He only speaks to me when we're safely alone in the elevator.

"Do you want to go to the roof?" he asks.

I'm not expecting this.

"Sean showed me the way," he goes on. "I'm sure you're up there all the time, right?"

I shake my head, but he doesn't see it.

"If we're at your place or my place, we'll just be waiting for her, you know?"

I know. So I tell him, sure, we can go to the roof.

The door to the roof is heavy, but there isn't an alarm.

Laurie can shove it open easily, but for me it always took a lot of effort.

I only went to the roof when I really needed to.

It's a different kind of daytime on the roof—different from that on the street, different from what comes through a window. We are in the strange borderland between ground and sky—nine stories up, we hover over pedestrians, over cars, over smaller buildings. But there are still-taller buildings hovering over us.

These taller buildings stand quiet, windows closed, expressions glazed. We are in a pocket of city silence, the traffic reduced to a hum, the voices never lifting this high.

Laurie walks over to the railing, looks below. I hesitate. He starts talking, thinking I am there.

"One second," I call out.

It feels like years since I've been up here, even though I know it hasn't been years. I wish there was some personal marker of time, so we didn't have to rely upon days and weeks and months and years. Because each of us has our own unit of measurement, our own relativity. Spaces between loves. Spaces between destinations. Spaces between deaths.

Or just one death. The quickness of time before. The eternity of time after.

"You there?" Laurie asks.

"Yeah," I answer, pulling up by his side, not touching the railing.

He looks out at the park. "Do you come up here a lot? Sean says he hides away here sometimes. I figured it was possible you were up here too. I mean, he thinks he's alone when he does it. But he'd never know, right?"

"I don't really come up here," I murmur.

"Why not? It's beautiful. And it's not like they're going to catch you."

"It's not that," I say.

"Afraid the door will swing shut and you'll get trapped? Sean says there's a way around that."

"No. It's just . . . I don't really like it up here. I never have."

This is a lie, and I know it. I think, *Why can't I tell him?*

"We can go back down," he offers.

I think about everything he's gone through. Not just in the past two days with me and Elizabeth. But before.

"I came up here at a bad time," I tell him. "A really bad time. So it's hard to come back without remembering."

He nods, but doesn't ask anything further. He's leaving it up to me.

I think he might know.

"It was right after my mother died," I say. "I spent about a month in a fog, completely paralyzed. I couldn't believe I was alone. Everything seemed impossible. I knew enough to eat, but that was about it. Dad emailed, offered to come out. But I told him no. I felt that would have been worse, especially because there was no way he was going to stay. I'd just be postponing the abandonment.

"So one night I came up here. I found the strength and pushed open that door.

"For the first time since she died, I felt certainty. It was a flash of certainty: I was going to die. And the reason I was going to die was that I was going to throw myself right over the edge. It was the only solution. It was like all the other options had fallen away and all the walls had closed in, and the only thing that was left in the narrowness was the one exit, the one escape.

"I walked down there." I point to a spot on the railing, even though Laurie can't see me pointing. "I didn't even have to leave a note—I figured eventually my father would notice I was gone. But he'd never really know, would he? I could be anywhere.

"I got one foot on the wall. The certainty was there . . . and then the flash was over. Because I thought to myself that, yeah, there *was* one person I would have to write a note for, and that was my mother. I know it sounds crazy, but I felt that I still owed her that. And as soon as I thought about her, I thought about how sad she would be to see me do this. I imagined my body lying down there, broken on the pavement, and no one would even know I was bleeding. The idea of everyone stepping over me, for days or months or years . . . it was the saddest thing I'd ever thought, and I knew my mother would never, ever want me to do that. It's not like I saw her or heard her speaking to me. I just knew.

"So I guess I learned there's no such thing as a flash of certainty. It's a flash, for sure, but it isn't certainty, even if it feels like cer- tainty. And I haven't been up here since then because I guess it reminds me how close I came. How dark it was. You know?"

Laurie reaches his hand out to me. I move my arm, concentrate there, so he can touch it. So he can give me that comfort, in the way that human beings do.

"I never wanted to die," he tells me. "But I was always aware that it was an option. I felt the other people wanting me to do it, so I worked against it. I never even considered it. That would be my big defiance—I wouldn't go away. Even when I was in the hospital, even when it was pretty dire—I guess I had the opposite of your flash of certainty. The certainty I felt was this foundation, the thing that all of my other thoughts were built on. I would get through it. I would heal. I would get the hell out of that town. They ruined my body, but I wouldn't let them touch my life. I was certain of that. And I still am. Except in the moments when I'm not. But those are the exceptions."

"I guess when it comes down to it," I say, "I don't really under-stand life."

"You haven't had much practice," Laurie says. "But I don't know that practice makes it easier."

"Who needs cursecasters?" I ask. "The amateurs do just as much damage."

Laurie laughs at that—a laugh of recognition, not humor.

"It appears that we've each had a lot of time to contemplate human nature," he says.

"Mostly I found that it gets boring after a while. Contempla-tion never really accomplishes anything."

Laurie nods. "I just wanted to be back on my feet."

"And I decided I wanted to stay on my feet. It's the difference between jumping and leaping, isn't it?"

"What is?"

"When you jump, all you're going to do is fall. But leaping? Leaping is when you think there's something on the other side."

"And you have a sense that we're about to leap?"

"I have a sense that we already have." I pause. "You know you don't have to be a part of it, right? I was born into this. And maybe Elizabeth was too. But this isn't your fight. I can't speak for Elizabeth, but I would completely understand if you didn't want to leap."

"What? And watch the two of you on the other side, not being able to do anything about it? Forget that."

He turns to look over the railings again.

I know my mother wanted to have another child. I heard them talking about it, but I never really understood what the true terms of the argument were. Would the curse have still applied? Did it matter?

I like to think she didn't want me to be alone. That she wanted me to feel like this, like I had someone else on my side.

"I have a question," Laurie says after a minute. "You don't have to answer it if you don't want to."

"That's okay."

"I'm just wondering about the end result of this. It's to break the curse, right? And that means you becoming visible. Do you think you're ready for that? Because being visible makes you really vulnerable."

"I don't know if I'm ready," I say. "But I think I'd like to try."

A noise wedges itself into the silence—the door opening. For a moment I actually think I have to hide. It's as if Laurie has made me forget what I am.

Laurie also looks around for a place to hide, expecting someone from building security. There isn't really anyplace to go, unless he wants to climb the water tower.

But it's not building security. It's Sean, looking bashful and happy.

"I was hoping to find you," he says to Laurie.

"Pretend I'm not here," I whisper. "I'll leave."

Laurie can't say anything back. I wait for Sean to clear the doorway, so I can go back down. But instead he stands there.

"I texted you three times," he says. "And the last two, I felt really stupid doing it."

"I'm sorry," Laurie apologizes. "I've just been busy."

"With what?"

"My sister's been dragging me around."

"And I can't come with?"

"It's just—she has to go to—um—counseling."

Sean's not going to let it go. "What for?"

"You know—adjusting to a new place. She needs a new therapist. So we've been, like, shopping around."

Sean is a New Yorker—this should not sound implausible to him. And, indeed, he buys it.

"My father sent me to a therapist once, when he thought I was spending too much time staring at Aquaman. Like, *too late, Dad.*"

"That must've sucked," Laurie says, and leaves it at that. I realize: Sean doesn't know what happened to him. Sean is part of his new start.

Sean moves closer, clears the door. I know this is my cue to leave.

"Easy things are worthless," Laurie says, and I realize he's talking to both Sean and me. "It's the hard things that matter. Those are the things worth leaping for."

"Like Aquaman?" Sean asks, a little confused.

"Like Aquaman. Or the Wolfman, if you're into that. Or the Invisible Boy. If we don't fight other people's curses, what are we left with? Just a swift fall to the earth, and where's the meaning in that?"

I know I can't answer, not with Sean right there. So I have to rely on silence to send my message. I have to rely on Laurie to know that I wish he had been with me the last time I was on the roof. I have to trust that he knows I'm glad that I stayed.

CHAPTER 18

I AM FROZEN IN my chair.

Killing him. The curse is killing him.

Millie dabs at the corners of her eyes with a lace-trimmed handkerchief. She looks at me as though she expects she'll need to rummage another hankie up for me too. But I don't have tears. My horror is slowly melting into anger, being pushed aside like an iceberg carried on a warm ocean current.

"What do you mean, *probably*?" I ask.

My tone makes Millie jump in her seat. "Excuse me?"

"How can it probably be killing him?"

Millie shifts uncomfortably in her chair. "I'm just trying to warn you. To prepare you for the worst. It's impossible to know for certain . . ."

Her hesitation tells me she's holding something back. "But?"

"Curses have a certain morbid logic to them," she tells me. "A natural course to run. Stephen's curse wasn't a punishment for him, it was a cruel blow to his mother, Arbus's daughter."

"I don't understand." I am frustrated, fidgeting. I want to bolt from Millie's hexatorium so I can find Stephen. It's as if each moment I sit here, waiting for her explanation, it's another moment he's slipping away. He is no longer simply invisible. He's going to disappear forever.

Millie purses her lips. "Arbus designed the curse to render a child invisible, taking his existence—along with all the joy and exuberance that should accompany the arrival of an infant—and keeping him hidden from most of the world, even from his own parents. Arbus is nothing if not careful in his casting—he made sure that Stephen would stay alive, to always haunt his mother. Arbus wouldn't have left anything to chance."

"That's why his clothes disappear. That's why he was solid as a baby. That's why he made it this far."

"Yes, I imagine so."

I can't sit any longer, pushing myself out of my chair and pacing near the hexatorium's door.

Millie watches my frantic procession through the room. "But when Arbus cast the curse, it was laid upon Stephen's mother—not Stephen himself."

She pauses and I force myself to stand still and look directly at her.

"I can only guess." She speaks slowly, deliberately. "But with his mother gone, there's no way of knowing what the effect will be. If the curse was truly meant to span generations, Stephen may be all right. But there's no way to know. As I said, by its own nature and intention, the curse is unstable." Millie sighs. "Thus, it is unpredictable and very, very dangerous. For Stephen . . . and for you."

I meet her gaze, unblinking, as I try to process her words. *Unstable. Unpredictable.* What do those words even mean? I'm looking for a doomsday clock with a precise countdown, but all she's giving me is a sundial on a cloudy day.

Instead I focus on something I can control: myself. "Why would Stephen's curse be dangerous for me?"

"Because you're young and in love." She smiles, but I look away. Love feels distant, while loss feels close.

"That will make you impulsive," Millie goes on. "And less likely to consider risks to yourself."

"I don't care about that. Just tell me what the instability of the curse will do to Stephen." I bring my eyes back up, looking at Millie hard, though my heart is flapping against my ribs like a bird that is falling when it hasn't yet learned to fly.

She takes a quick breath. "You've proven my point. If you want to help Stephen, you must take care of yourself. With your attitude you could do more harm than good."

"But isn't that why I'm here?" I ask sourly. "So you can teach me how to take care of myself?"

"Most definitely." Millie stands up. "And Stephen is safe enough. He's survived the curse this long. He must be a resilient boy."

I almost laugh, but turn my back on her instead. In my mind Millie's claim is as good as someone telling me that we've made it through the earthquake, so there's no danger from the aftershocks. All I can think of is that unpredictable nest of tentacles whipping around Stephen's body. He's not safe if one of them goes rogue and wraps itself around his neck to choke him. As far as I'm concerned,

Stephen is the target of some spectral assassin that could strike at any moment, without any warning. I can't abide Millie's assurances that time is on our side.

I'm about to say so when without any prompting Millie scampers across the room, looping her arm through mine.

"Now, now, don't frown like that," she says as she leads me to the stairwell. "You'll have wrinkles by the time you're twenty."

For a woman of her age, she moves with remarkable speed. I'm working hard not to trip my way up the steps.

"Where are we going?" I ask.

"To finish your training, of course." Millie pulls me into the comic shop. I squint into the darkness.

"Saul, we have work to do," she announces.

The hulking shadow behind the counter slides a curious glance at the tiny woman. "After all this time? You really think that's wise?"

"Tut, tut." She emphasizes her words with short claps. "Unless you're worried you've gotten too rusty."

I gaze at Saul as he unfolds himself from behind the desk. Standing, he's over six feet tall. Despite her age, Millie looks like a child compared to this hulk.

"He's coming with us?" I ask, not having given any thought to the big man who crouched, silently, in the shadows of the comic shop. If anything, I'd assumed he was a bouncer for kids daring each other into the store, wanting to catch a glimpse of the resident "witch."

"Of course," Millie says. "A spellseeker can't work without a safeguard. We'd be much too vulnerable."

She winces. "Though I hardly deserve Saul's allegiance. I've told him many times to seek out someone who's active. Not a has-been like me."

Saul mumbles something under his breath that I don't quite catch.

"You're Millie's protector?" I ask uneasily. He certainly looks the part, but I'm still not getting what sort of protection he's offering.

"Shield," Millie corrects. "Each spellseeker has a shield to watch over him or her while she pursues and rights the wrongs of cursecasters."

With a series of painful-sounding pops and cracks, Saul is methodically stretching his arms, legs, shoulders, and neck. It reminds me of some rarely used machinery groaning back to life, in dire need of oiling.

"What do you need protection from?" I ask Millie.

It's Saul who answers with a snort. "You think I lost this eye peddling comics?"

I'm doubly embarrassed when I not only stare at the scar that cut across his face where his eye should have been, but also shudder. This only makes him laugh.

"Now, now, Saul. Be gentle," Millie chides, but she's smiling fondly at the huge man. "She's just a girl, and this is a frightening business."

"Which is why she can't be coddled," Saul says.

I'm looking back and forth between this odd pair. They continue their banter—and it's clear they've been close to hibernation in this dark Upper West Side shop. As they argue about my readiness for what's ahead, reinvigorated by their new purpose, I feel as invisible as Stephen.

After five minutes of this I clear my throat. "So . . . what is he protecting you from?"

Saul glares at the interruption, but Millie blushes with embarrassment. "Of course, dear. But let me explain as we're on our way."

"Where are we going?" I ask over my shoulder as Millie fusses me towards the door.

"The subway," Millie says. "It's a good place where we can sit and watch without being conspicuous. The number of people getting on and off between Eighty-Sixth and Wall Street should offer a nice variety of curses. I haven't made my way that far south in a while, but as I recall, the Financial District is, as a rule, bursting at the seams with curses."

She's glowing with anticipation while I'm trying to wrap my head around any assortment of curses as "nice" and whether I want to go anywhere near a part of the city that boasts curses in such abundance.

Saul locks the shop door and we're on our way. He takes the lead, each of his long strides forcing Millie and me into double time to keep pace with him.

"Cursecasters are a suspicious lot by nature," Millie says as we hurry down the street. "They move through the world always looking over their shoulders. They harbor a particular dislike for our lot, viewing us as pestering gnats best swatted or squashed."

"Can they do that?" I ask. "Squash us?"

"Not with curses," Millie says as we turn the corner.

"Spellseekers have a natural immunity. Curses can't get a proper hold of us. Of course, you have to build up your immunity—just like all humans do for the more mundane forms of disease. In time the curses will just slide off."

"We've got genetic Teflon for curses?" I laugh.

She wrinkles her nose at me.

"Sorry," I say as we descend the stairs to the subway. "So how are we in danger from them?"

"After I put one cursecaster out of business, she came after me," Millie says. "My poor Saul bears far too many scars on my behalf."

I gasp and Saul throws a thin smile back at me. "Don't worry, little girl. I have a knack for making sure cursecasters' knives end up buried in their own bellies."

Millie's laugh surprises me. "No one is as quick as my Saul."

Saul grins at her.

"He's your bodyguard?" I ask. "Is that how it works?"

Millie nods. "Cursecasters rarely have qualms about keeping their work safe and their identities secret. We're the only ones who can expose them or threaten their livelihood."

We're moving through the turnstile when Saul adds, "It's more than that."

"In my case it's not," Millie says stiffly. "Because I don't have the talent that you do, Elizabeth."

Saul bristles, assuming a watchful stance on the platform while Millie takes my elbow, pulling me close so she can speak in low tones.

"I can identify curses and help victims understand what's

happening to them," she says. "I can offer advice. Usually it's a matter of estimating how long it will take the curse to run its course and how not to exacerbate its effects."

I'm trying to concentrate on her words but finding it difficult. Laurie was right about the smell of the subway. The stifling heat makes the odors, both sour and cloying, pool around us. But it's not just the belly-churning reek of sweat, urine, and refuse. There's a low drone surrounding me, one I can sense but still just barely hear. The noise swells and a wave of dizziness makes me sway. Millie's fingers tighten around my arm.

"Shhh," she says. "I know it isn't pleasant, but try to breathe deeply and steadily. Don't let it overwhelm you."

A train pulls up. Saul stands in front of us as it empties and then shoulders other riders aside. Other than a few muttered complaints, none of the other passengers object as he makes a path for Millie and me to enter the car and shepherds us into seats. I don't blame them, as I'd guess few people outside of professional wrestlers would mess with Saul.

I feel a little better now that I'm sitting down. The buzzing still fills my ears, but it's less intense.

"You'll get used to it." Millie pats my hand.

"I don't think it's the smell," I say.

She laughs. "Of course it's not the smell. It's the curses. You're starting to tune in to them. Soon you'll be able to pick them out without even making an effort."

I look up sharply. The skin around her eyes is crinkled with her sympathetic smile. "You've opened the gate. Now it's a matter of walking through."

"That buzzing . . . the sounds," I say. "It's from curses?"

"From magic in general." Millie nods. "Some curses, some more benign spells. Your body is naturally inclined to seek them out. The sound is pestering you, trying to get your attention. You'll find it's much less intrusive if you don't fight it."

"But . . ." I frown, shaking my head to clear away the drone without success. "I can't see the curses unless I'm in the background." I wince a little at my made-up word for the strange alternaworld where I can clearly see the shape and hear the sound of curses. Millie doesn't miss a beat. She's still smiling.

"From what I've managed to dig up from the older volumes, to break a curse, you'll need to be in that 'background,' as you call it," she says. "But given time and practice, you won't need to leave this plane to identify the magic."

The car begins to move. Saul is standing at one of the poles like a sentinel, eye moving up and down the car.

"The work of shields like Saul is to keep you safe while you're drawing a curse," Millie says. "You're utterly defenseless when you leave this plane to step into the magical one. A shield watches over you, guards against attack."

My skin prickles. Laurie had done that very job when I was experimenting—trying to see the curses. He'd been my shield without either of us knowing it. A surge of gratitude washes over me, following by a hollowing out. I'm suddenly lonely, wishing my brother was with me instead of these two strangers.

"And Saul was assigned to you?" I ask, forcing my attention back to the moment.

"He found me." Millie glances at Saul, and for a few seconds the years melt from her face, revealing a wide-eyed girl hidden beneath layers of age. "The days when shields received official commissions to guard spellseekers are long past. But Saul is from a long line of shields, and he was determined to answer his calling."

I risk a glance at the hulking man, whose eye is on me briefly and then back to scanning the subway car. "Will I need my own shield?" I'm wondering if I could just bribe Laurie with cases of Pop-Tarts to take the job, but on the other hand, I don't exactly want my brother getting into knife fights.

"For certain," she says. "Saul might be able to find someone. He still connects with what is left of the network for his kind. But the simplest solution would be for Saul to serve as your shield. My usefulness in the magical world is limited. Your talent is far more valuable."

Saul doesn't speak, but there's a sudden hitch in his breath, and I know he has no interest in going anywhere that isn't with Millie.

"That's not our concern at the moment," Millie says as we pull in to the next stop, and I'm relieved she's changing the subject.

Millie takes both of my hands, drawing my gaze to hers. "First we need to practice awareness." Her instructions are nearly drowned out by the chaos of passengers jostling on and off the car, but I realize it's a boon to us, offering anonymity amid the noise and crowds. "Go into that plane where you can see the curses. Identify those in this car—there are two I can pinpoint right now— then when you come back to us, try to hang on to that connection. Try to keep seeing the curses on *this* plane."

"Okay." I draw a breath and ease my shoulders back. It's easier now than when I first tried this. I'm sliding away from the waking world and into the strange, sepia tones of the background. Pleased that I can keep my breathing steady, I begin to search the subway car for signs of a curse. The buzzing has vanished, or rather it's become the natural sounds of this plane—the magical plane. It's as if the grating sounds that filled my head on the subway platform were nothing more than the nagging of this strange place, demanding my attention.

The first curse is easy to spot. And I'm aghast that its victim is a man seated opposite Millie and me. My cheeks get hot as I think of how patient she's being with such a novice—someone who can't even see a curse that's right in front of her. I shove aside my embarrassment and focus on the spell. It's different from those I spotted with Laurie. The shape of it is fixed and hard, like a transparent box floating around the man's head. The sound it gives off is a steady pulse accompanied by a strobe-light-style flashing. Forcing myself to relax even more, I push my senses towards the curse, hoping to understand it. Slowly the spell gives up its history.

Like the curse of the artist in the park, this man is suffering mentally. The curse is one of disruption. He's a consultant with a presentation in thirty minutes and he can't focus. The jarring pulse of the curse impedes his memory, forcing the long-practiced hook and pitch out of his mind. It's making him miserable, fraying his confidence with each minute. I wonder if the curse is personal or some sort of corporate sabotage.

Despite my sympathy for the man, I move on, wanting to find the other curse and continue my lesson with Millie. The second curse is harder to spot. It's faint, barely more than wisps circling a teenage girl standing at the far end of the car. The thin lines of smoke dance around her body, not constraining her but doing damage all the same. I grimace. Though this spell is less serious, it's still cruel. My guess is that it's some prank born of a mean spirit alone. The girl is trying to get home and she takes this train every day. But today she's lost. She can't figure out why she's so confused or why the subway map makes no sense. She's getting frantic, but I can tell by watching the curse slip over her limbs that it has little endurance and is fading by the minute.

I'm starting to understand what Millie meant by a nice variety of curses. Even in the short time I've been exposed to this strange, hidden world, I'm astounded by the range of curses that exist. Some are like the one I'm gazing at now—small and petty, wicked jokes that trip up lives but don't do permanent harm; others, like that affecting the man across from us, that could not only ruin his day but have the potential to destroy his career; and yet others—like Stephen's—that are powerful and evil, enough to kill.

Nausea sucker-punches me and I want to reel back from this plane. But I can't. I'm determined to be a good student in this lesson. So instead of jolting back to reality, I inch up little by little, keeping part of my senses in tune with the two curses I've seen. And then I'm back in my body. The colors and sounds of the world I know return. Millie is watching me. Saul continues to patrol the car with his eye.

"Well?" Millie asks.

I nod towards the man across from us when I notice I can still see the strobe light flicker in the air around his head.

"Him." My eyes roam to the girl at the back of the car. She's flicking tears away from the corners of her eyes as they appear, trying to hide her panic. "And her." The wisps are still floating around her body. On this plane I could almost have mistaken them for cigarette smoke.

Millie nods. "Very good. Can you still see the curses?"

"Yes."

"She's a quick learner." Millie smiles up at Saul, who shrugs.

The train halts at the next stop. The cursed man stands up, shaking his head as he leaves the car. A swell of bodies pours into the car, cramming against us, though I notice many try, and fail, to give Saul a wide berth. He angles himself closer so his looming form is directly over Millie and me.

"There's another," Millie says. "A new curse came aboard with this lot. Can you find it?"

I nod, starting to ease myself away from the din of the crowded car. Millie grabs my shoulder and shakes me.

"No, no." She sweeps her hand towards the other passengers. "You have to try to see it on this plane without going into your background."

"Okay." I'm not feeling that confident, but I start by focusing on the girl again. I can barely find her through the press of people in the car. But I glimpse her partially and watch the smoke trails move around her. Taking note of the way it feels to see that curse on this plane, I slowly look over the car's other occupants.

It's the sound that directs my vision. That insistent drone of the background nagging me, drawing my senses. The woman is standing two poles down from Saul. To describe her as bedraggled would be generous. Her hair is a rat's nest of knots and filth. Her eyes are sunken and shadowed by purple dark enough to be bruises, but I can tell it's a symptom of exhaustion. Her thin fingers are trembling even as she grips the pole, struggling to keep her balance. She is a ghost walking through the human world.

The sound that drew me to her sharpens in focus. The buzz of the spell becomes a wail; keening, ceaseless. It's so horrible I want to cover my ears, desperate to shut out its piercing whine. As I watch her, the curse shows itself. Unlike most, this curse is barely moving. It lies over her, dark and heavy, like a cloak meant to smother her, lacking the frenetic quality of so many of the spells I'd witnessed. This thick curse gloms onto her like tar.

"She can't sleep," I murmur. "Or take care of herself. She has no hope."

Millie leans into me. "It's a nasty one."

I'm still gazing at the woman, noticing her unwashed clothes. The dirt under her fingernails. I can sense that these are symptoms of the curse. She isn't without money or a home, but she's lost the ability to be well—physically and mentally.

"Will it kill her?" I ask.

"The curse itself isn't fatal," Millie says. "But it could well do the poor woman in. She's so tired she could walk in front of a bus without ever noticing it was there. Curses of insomnia are very dangerous. And this one has the added twist of self-loathing."

I watch the curse lying corpse-like across the woman's body. Unlike the spell affecting the lost girl, which I could see slipping away, this curse is in its peak, thriving. It isn't going anywhere soon.

"We have to help her."

Millie takes my face in her hands, turning me towards her and away from the wretched woman. "You aren't ready."

"But—"

"The girl," she interrupts. "The lost child at the back of the car. You might be able to help her."

I resist the urge to turn back to the other woman. "How?"

Millie glances up at Saul. He nods.

"We've been talking, putting our heads together," she says. "It's still risky, but I think you should try."

"Try what?" I'm getting impatient. Seeing the curses is exhausting, not physically but emotionally. My mind and spirit are tapped into a darkness that colors the world in brutal shades, shades of vengeance, pettiness, of power fed by pride. It is a world full of ugly truths that once seen can't be unseen, and I am sorry to have seen it.

"As I've said before, my abilities extend only to identification," Millie tells me. Her eyes are pinched with worry. "But according to lore and the few records I've been able to piece together, you might be able to do more."

"Can I break the curses?" I ask.

Saul's voice rumbles towards me. "It's more visceral than that."

I shudder at the word *visceral*, especially coming from this man who I'm guessing has seen his share of guts, given his line of work.

"Your talent may allow you to draw a curse out, like poison." Millie doesn't meet my eyes. "When you do that, the spell will no longer affect its victim."

"Good." I straighten up. "How can I do that?"

She shakes her head. "Listen, child. You don't draw the magic only to let it go. You pull it into your own body. If you're able to do this, you'll need time to establish your resistance to the curse's effects."

I look from Millie to Saul. "What will it do to me?"

Millie is still shaking her head.

"We can't be sure," Saul answers. He bends close. I try not to stare at his missing eye. The scars on his face. "Every spellseeker is different. But your body has the ability—in theory—to fight off curses. To destroy them."

"But there will be side effects at first," Millie finishes. "And we don't know how serious they might be. Or if it will even work."

I pull my eyes off the somber-faced pair and fix my gaze on the girl at the back of the car. She has one hand over her eyes now, having abandoned her attempts to keep her grief concealed.

"I don't care," I lie. The truth is, I'm terrified. But I can't see this other world, these other horrors, and not try to right its wrongs. "Just tell me how."

Saul grunts in what I think might be respect and Millie squeezes my hand.

"Since I can't do it myself, I can only guess," she says. "But I believe your instincts will guide you. You were born to do this."

Her words startle me. I'd never subscribed to the idea of destiny or fate. The world had always seemed too fickle and unfair for such lofty concepts. But if fate was real, it led me to fall in love with an invisible boy. And I would do anything to save him.

I don't say anything, but squeeze her fingers in return and then slide away from her. Away from the world. The background rises up, offering the mysterious plane drained of color. The passengers blocking my view of the cursed girl become no more than shadows. I can see right through their insubstantial bodies.

The girl, in contrast, is a stark outline. The curse is already weakened from the short time ago when I first saw it. I watch her for a minute or two, wondering what my next move should be. The tricky thing about instinct is that it's instinct, not something you generally can call upon at will.

Though impatient, I let myself sit, waiting, watching the curse move. Listening to its rustle. Without prompting, without a conscious decision, I feel a shift in my senses. A stretching, reaching. My spirit gains a focus. Magnet-like strength. And it begins to pull.

I remain very still, breathing evenly. The draw of my spirit continues, creating a link between myself and the spell-ridden girl. The curse stops circling the girl. Wisps of smoke float towards me, leaving her behind. I don't move, though I'm ready to scream. The instincts at work in my body tell me that the curse isn't just going to hover near me. The connection I've wrought will draw the magic inside me, to wreak what havoc it will.

And then it happens. I draw a breath and the smoke slides into my nose and mouth. With a shudder I groan, leaning over. My head throbs.

"Elizabeth! Elizabeth!" Millie is shaking me.

I raise my head and am back in the world. The train is stopped and passengers are entering and exiting as usual. No one casts a glance my way.

"Are you okay?" Saul asks.

My head hurts, but not terribly—a couple of aspirin would

knock out the ache—and otherwise everything seems normal. I sit up, searching for the girl. She's gazing at the subway map in the train. She begins to giggle. Then she laughs out loud, which does draw stares from her fellow passengers. Her face is alight with relief. She dashes out of the car just as the doors begin to close.

"It worked," I whisper.

Millie wraps her arms around me. "You are truly gifted." She plants a dry kiss on my cheek.

Headache or no headache, I feel wonderful. I can do this. I can save Stephen. And maybe I can help countless others.

I stand up, moving towards the pole between Saul and the woman cursed with despair. She needs my help so much more than the lost girl did.

"Elizabeth, sit down." Millie's voice follows me. "You need to rest. We should take this slowly. No matter your talent, you're still very new to this."

"No." I don't look at her. Gripping the metal pole for balance, I slide into the background. It's so easy now, I can switch planes in a second instead of in minutes.

Somewhere, like a distant echo, I think I hear Millie calling me. I ignore the sound, focusing on the woman draped in a curse that could kill her. My spirit stretches out. I'm more aware of it now; it's full of empathy, propelled by the desire to heal. When the connection is made, I shudder, almost losing my footing. I can feel the power of this curse, so much greater than the spell I just drew from the girl. Bracing myself, I beckon the magic. The way it moves is repulsive. While the other curse was floating, this spell slumps from the woman's back and oozes towards me. I'm fighting fear as the dark puddle touches my foot. It slides over my shoe and inside my pant leg. I don't expect the spell to have this much substance, but it is slimy against my skin, leaving a sticky trail as it moves up my body. Still, I keep drawing it until I'm sure I've taken all of it from the woman and onto myself.

I want to step back into the world and see if I've helped her. But I'm feverish. Heat skitters over my body. My skin is on fire. I look down at my arms to see red bumps as large as nickels appearing. They are swelling, bursting open into pus-filled sores. I scream. This is a nightmare. It has to be. I wrench myself out of the background, calling out for Millie.

I think I hear her crying, but my vision is blurry. The sepia of the background is gone, but my world, full of its sounds and colors, is spinning.

My skin is still covered in sores.

"Help me." I choke on the rawness of my throat.

The fever slams through my head, knocking me off my feet and into Saul's arms.

CHAPTER 19

"STEPHEN."

I open my eyes as soon as I hear my father's voice calling through my dream.

"Stephen, are you here?"

He's right in the doorway of my room, and for a moment, I am a child again. With the light behind him, he hasn't aged. He is my father's silhouette, come to wake me up for dinner. My mother is waiting in the kitchen. This is our home.

"I'm here," I say. Not a child's voice at all.

My father turns on the lights. This was the way he'd wake me up as a kid too—the full plunge instead of the gentle emergence.

"Dad!" I yell, turning away from the brightness. There's no way for me to use my hand to shield my eyes.

"Sorry," he mumbles (without turning the light back off). "It's four in the afternoon. You shouldn't be asleep."

"I thought you were working."

"I am. But the rest of my afternoon is email, so I figured I could do it here."

"You really don't need to do that."

"I know."

"I mean, I'm not sure I want you to do that."

"Look, I'll just be in the other bedroom." He starts to leave.

"No," I say, stopping him. "You can't do that either."

"What?"

"You can't dodge the things that I say. You can't just go into another room. Maybe Mom put up with it, but I won't."

It's the way he woke me up. It's the way he called it *the other bedroom*. It's my fear that he is going to try to assert some control over me after all these years. I am not going to let him get away with it. I can't.

"Say what you want to say, Stephen."

I don't want to destroy the bridge between us. I just want it to be a drawbridge, with me choosing when it's up or down.

"You need to give me warning," I say. "You can't just show up."

"Stephen—"

My name hangs in the air for a moment. If he takes this chance to remind me that he pays the bills, I will never forgive him. I am already very aware of that.

But I don't find out what he's going to say, because once my name fades, I hear the reason he's stopped.

Someone is pounding on the door.

I get up on my feet and push past him. It's not a delivery knock. It's urgent.

I look through the peephole and see Elizabeth and Millie and the one-eyed guy from Millie's store.

"Who is it?" my father asks behind me.

I open the door—my father didn't lock it behind him—and see that Elizabeth's leaning a little on Saul. She looks pale and shaken.

"I'm fine," she says. "We just need to come in."

"What happened?" I ask as Saul leads her to the couch.

Millie looks almost as stricken as Elizabeth.

"Baby steps," she says. "I told her baby steps."

"Who are these people?" my father asks.

"Dad, stay out of this."

I've snapped too quickly. He's not going to take that.

"Stephen, I will not have you talk to me that way."

"Dad, now is *not the time*."

Millie walks over to my father and offers her hand. "I am Mildred Lund. I am Elizabeth's . . . teacher. And this is Saul, one of my associates."

It's as if a thought bubble actually appears over my father's head, saying, *What kind of teachers are these people?!?*

"Curses, Dad. They're the ones teaching us about curses." I turn back to Elizabeth. "What did you do?"

"I ate too much. Or had food poisoning. Only, it was curses instead of food. Where's Laurie? We couldn't go to my house, just in case Mom was there."

"Laurie's with Sean. Do you want me to call him?"

"No, it's okay." Then she looks at Millie and Saul. "Really, it's okay. You don't need to watch over me."

Millie shakes her head. "What you did was so foolish. So dangerous. I will not teach you if you are not going to listen to me."

"I want to be alone with her," I say. "Please, can everyone just leave?"

Saul seems eager to take up my invitation, as if he's not used to being in apartments that have windows in them. Millie is more reluctant, tutting over Elizabeth some more. My father doesn't seem to include himself in my request, and remains standing right where he is.

"I would love to rest for a little while," Elizabeth says. She looks at Millie. "I'll see you tomorrow. I promise I won't do anything until then. I've learned my lesson. I went too far."

Millie seems satisfied by this. "No cursewatching," she says. Then she points in my direction. "Especially not with this one."

I think Elizabeth's already learned *that* lesson.

Saul is at the door, and Millie follows, looking back at Elizabeth every two seconds to make sure she's doing the right thing. My father closes the door behind them and makes a show of locking it.

"Dad," I say, "would you mind leaving us alone to talk?"

"Stephen, I'm your father."

"And Dad, Elizabeth's my girlfriend. I want to talk to her. You do not need to be in the room when I do." Elizabeth looks at me like I'm being too harsh; she has no idea what the history is. "Look," I say, tempering my tone, "come back for dinner. We can talk at dinner."

Now my father looks awkward.

"I'm afraid I—well, I have dinner plans tonight."

I don't have any right to be annoyed, but I am. My drawbridge, not his.

"Fine," I say. "I'll see you tomorrow."

"Breakfast," my father says. "I will be by for breakfast."

"It was good to see you, Mr. Swinton," Elizabeth says. Even though she's clearly weak, she has enough strength for niceties.

"Good to see you too, Elizabeth," he says, and I'm surprised he's remembered her name. As he goes into "the other bedroom" to get his laptop, I move to the couch with Elizabeth. Not to the point of crowding her—I know she needs air, space. But I want to be just out of the range of contact, in case she suddenly needs it.

My father says nothing but goodbye before he leaves. Once he's gone, Elizabeth keeps looking at the door, or at everything beyond the door.

"It's just us now," I tell her. "I want to know everything."

She tells me about the subway, about what happened to her.

"You can't push it too far," I say. "Not until you're ready."

"*I know that,*" she snaps. "Please, don't join the chorus on this one. It's already loud enough."

We sit there at an impasse. She's lost in her thoughts, and I'm lost in not being able to know them.

"We have to find him, don't we?" I ask. "That's where this is all leading, isn't it? If he leaves a trail of curses, we have to follow. That's how we'll track him down."

"I'm guessing that's Millie's plan," Elizabeth says. She doesn't seem happy about it. "But I also think she has much more faith in me than I deserve."

"Don't say that," I protest. "You don't know—"

"Stop. I wasn't saying that for your affirmation. Don't treat me like a girlfriend who just asked, 'Does this make me look fat?' You have no idea what my abilities are. None of us do. And to have everything balancing on them . . . that's a lot."

"Look," I say, touching her face, using that touch to ask her to look me in the eye, "nothing is in the balance here. If we don't find him, that's fine. I stay invisible. I've done fine so far. It's enough to have you see me. Nothing truly bad will happen if we don't find him. No one's going to die."

When I say this last sentence—*No one's going to die*—she flinches, turns away.

"What?" I ask. "Has he cursed someone to die? Is there more I don't know?"

Elizabeth shakes her head. "No. It's just . . . Millie makes it sound like what I'm doing is so important. All of these people are cursed—and I'm one of the few people left in the world who can help. I don't know how to deal with that."

I want to tell her how. I want there to be an answer. But the only answer is this:

Our lives are different. Inexplicably, intrinsically joined, but different.

"I was only scared after," she tells me. "During it, I was too overwhelmed. Fear is beside the point when you're faced with the thing you fear. But after, I knew I'd come close to something really bad. Curses aren't passive things. They'll fight back."

I tell her, "Even though I didn't know it was a curse, I thought I could break it." I haven't had these memories in years, and now here they are, waiting to be given. "I thought there was a way for me to fix it. Not just prayers—I tried a lot of praying. But I also tried other things. Harmful things. I heard something on TV about shock therapy. I didn't even know what that meant. But the next time I was alone in my room, I shoved my finger into a socket. I held it in there as long as I could. My parents had no idea. Luckily, it was too much, and I had to pull away. And for a second, I thought the pain was so strong that the next time I blinked, I'd be able to see my hand. I'd be visible. But of course I wasn't. Part of me wonders if death will do it. That when I die, my body will finally be seen. My grandfather's last laugh."

"Don't talk about dying," Elizabeth says, her voice unsteady. "And don't put your finger in any more sockets."

"What happens if we find him?" I ask.

"I don't know. I really don't know."

She looks so tired. Drained.

"It's okay," I tell her. "Sleep here. Just sleep."

I stand up so she can stretch out on the couch.

"I'll call Laurie," I tell her. "I'll let them all know where you are."

"And that I'm safe."

"And that you're safe."

I get her a blanket, turn off the lights. But before I can go, she says, "I want you there with me at Millie's. I want you to be my shield."

I have no idea what she's talking about, but I tell her yes.

When I go with her to Millie's the next morning after a strained breakfast with my father, Millie will not let me in.

"It's too dangerous," she says. "When Elizabeth opens herself up to the curses, you cannot be around. If she happens to look at you when she is that vulnerable—I don't want to say what might happen."

How can I argue? I am banished back to my apartment, banished to pace the floor as I wonder what Elizabeth is doing, and if she is putting herself in harm's way.

Weeks pass like this. My father comes over to tell me that he has to go back to his family, that he's been away too long. He is not going to ask me to go with him—we both know that. He says he'll be back, and that if I need anything at all, I should let him know. I need many things, but none of them are worth him knowing. He doesn't ask me about Elizabeth, about curses, about the "teachers" who appeared in the apartment. He doesn't want to know about any of that, not really. He wants to stay in his own world, the one that most people think is the real one.

Most nights, Laurie comes by after school, and Elizabeth comes by after Millie's. We watch movies. We eat Chinese food. It's all very normal, except for the fact that I'm not visibly there.

The days are the hardest—long stretches of alone time, their loneliness amplified by the sound of the people who are not present. I go to the park. I walk through museums. I suffer in the summer heat like everyone else. But all the while, I am aware of the curses I can't see. I am aware of the problems I can't solve. I see that Ivan the dog walker and Karen the live-in nanny have gotten together. I am happy for them. But I can't feel that happiness inside myself. Not during the day.

One night, after her mother is asleep, Elizabeth slips out to stay with me. She and Laurie have a deal—he'll cover for her if she covers for him on another night so he can go to the roof with Sean. They want to watch the sunrise together.

It's strange to have her over and to know she won't have to leave until morning. We're shyer with each other, but also a little looser, a little freer. When we kiss, it doesn't feel rushed. When we do more than kiss, we only rush when we want to.

Our intimacy stops well short of sex. We're not ready for it yet, and know we won't be for a while. Not because of the circumstances, but because we both need to know each other really well and for a long time before taking that step. Also, in the back of my mind, there *are* the circumstances. I know we would be careful, completely careful. But if something went wrong—would the curse be passed on? Elizabeth and I never talk about this, never mention it. I doubt it even crosses her mind. But it's there on mine. It hovers over the whole future.

It is more than enough to have her sleep in my arms. It is more than enough to be there as her breathing takes on the pace of sleep. It is more than enough to wake up and find she's doing the same thing—watching me, seeing me, marveling at it all.

It starts to feel almost routine. There are a few minutes when I feel dizzy, when I feel a little weak on my feet, but I don't think much of it—I often exhaust myself during the summer, and have never really understood how the sun affects my skin if it can't be seen. Do I get sunburned? Heatstroke? Elizabeth tells me I look fine, but I'm not sure.

When she comes home, it's almost like we're husband and wife, and she's the one who's gone to the office. I ask her how it went. She tells me what she's learned, and I understand about half of it.

Then one day she comes home and tells me something that needs no further explanation.

"He's come back," she tells me. "It's him, Stephen. Maxwell Arbus is here."

CHAPTER 20

I'VE BEEN LYING TO STEPHEN. The lies twist like a restless ball of snakes in my stomach, as if I've earned a curse of my very own. I tell myself that it can't be helped. Repeat over and over that this dishonesty serves a great purpose. But the words are bitter on my tongue, and I know I'm a hypocrite. I know that lying to someone you love is never okay.

But I don't know what else to do.

Things are so much worse than he knows. I think it's worse than even I know.

Sometimes when I'm lying in bed, staring up at the ceiling, I try to remember how it happened.

I push my mind back to that afternoon, to the fever that was burning my body from the inside out, because that's when the memories become a bit clearer. I think it has to do with the way that the fever took me into a place not unlike the strange shores I occupy between dreams and waking.

What happened on the subway comes in jarring flashes that jolt me back to myself before sleep fully takes hold. I can hear gasps from other passengers, followed by shouts to call 911. I feel Saul's arms gripping me and I scream because his touch on my sore-splotched skin is unbearable. Despite my cries, he doesn't let go and doesn't lose his footing when the train slows at the next stop. Through the fog of pain and the fever I sense bodies lurching around me as the train squeals to a halt on the tracks. Millie whispers urgently to Saul. I am lifted, carried from the brightness of the car and plunged into the shadows. People shout after us, pleading with Saul that I need an ambulance, demanding to know where he's taking me.

After that I don't remember anything until a tepid, vile liquid invades my mouth. I imagine gutter water has a similar taste. I choke on the substance, coughing so it runs down my chin.

"There, there," Millie says, patting at my wet skin with a soft cloth. "You need to drink it. Drink it, child."

I start to shake my head, but now Saul is holding my mouth open. The swamp water pours in again and this time Saul clamps my jaw closed, so I can either swallow or drown in a stagnant puddle.

My stomach cramps and I'm sure I'll vomit.

"Breathe." Millie squeezes my hand. And I do breathe, and despite the horrible taste in my mouth, my body begins to unclench. Something cool trickles through my blood and eases through my pores. The fire scorching my skin is smothered and the festering sores that bubbled over my throat, chest, arms, and legs fade to bruises and then disappear altogether.

Saul's grip loosens. "Has she had enough?"

"I think so," Millie answers. My vision isn't blurry anymore and I can see her peering at me. "How do you feel, Elizabeth?"

"Like I'm about to throw up." I hope she doesn't want me to keep talking because if I open my mouth again, I'll be sick for sure.

Millie putters around me in nervous circles. "No, no, no. You can't regurgitate the tonic. Your body needs it to repel the curse. Sit still, be quiet, and I'll go fix you some peppermint tea."

She gives Saul a meaningful look and his huge hands clamp down on my shoulders, making sitting still involuntary. I'm grateful Millie ordered my silence because I wouldn't know what to say to the giant man who's glowering at me. He stands like a statue; I can't even hear him breathing. In the quiet I'm getting fidgety, which I take as a good sign. Instead of feeling nauseated, I'm starting to just feel awkward. When Millie reappears with a teapot, cup, and saucer, I'm ready to try speaking again.

"What was that stuff?" I ask her.

"What stuff?" Millie pours a cup of tea and sets it before me. Only when she nods at him does Saul release my shoulders.

I take a swallow of tea. It scalds my tongue, but even burning peppermint is preferable to the aftertaste of Millie's remedy.

"That stuff you made me drink," I tell her. "It was horrible."

"That horrible 'stuff' saved your life, young lady," Millie huffs.

She looks genuinely hurt, and I backpedal. "I'm sorry . . . I didn't mean . . ."

Millie takes my floundering for the sincere contrition that it is. "I know it doesn't have a pleasant taste, but it's effective."

She watches me like an anxious fairy godmother, and Saul abandons his post at my shoulder to hover over her shoulder.

"The tonic recipes are one of the treasures of the hexatorium's library." Millie waves proudly at the shelves filled with cracked book spines and musty tomes. "I suppose I'm not completely irrelevant after all."

"You could never be irrelevant, Mildred." Saul speaks so softly I barely hear him, but his words paint Millie's paper-white cheeks with a pink hue. Even so, a moment later she's peering at me, eyes sharp as a hawk's.

"Do you realize what you did?" she asks. Her tone makes me fold in on myself. "You're lucky we were able to get you to the hexatorium in time."

Saul glowers at me over her shoulder for emphasis.

"You will never, never draw in a curse without permission again." Millie clasps her hands over her heart as though she's the one who's about to make a solemn vow. "Never."

"But—" I sit up, earning a more menacing look from Saul.

"Not until you're ready." Millie's face is pale again, bearing no trace of the youthful blush that appeared a moment earlier.

I can't back down, though what she's saying is scaring me. The memory of the smell of festering sores on my skin, of the wrenching pain in my stomach, is scaring me. But Stephen. Stephen.

"He could die," I say.

Millie sighs, and without prompting Saul pulls out a chair and Millie sits. Her anger has vanished, and now she looks so, so tired.

"*You* could die," she tells me.

Her weariness is contagious. I slump down. "I know."

"I wish there were an easy way to do this." Millie manages a tiny smile. "But spellseeking runs bone-deep. Your body and spirit need time to adjust to the work."

A shortcut jumps into my head. "What if I always have a tonic with me? I could use it like an EpiPen for curses."

She's shaking her head before I've finished talking. "The tonics are an emergency measure only. Each time you use one, it becomes less effective. You have to build up your own natural resistance to curses. And that will take time."

"What if we don't have time?" I ask. It's a pointless question and I know it.

I know there are epic tales of romance, where love means you're supposed to die. Where it's all about sacrifice. But I don't want to die. I don't want Stephen to die. I'm looking for the scenario where we both get to live. Where we can continue this marvel that is love and discovery and trust. I'm not even asking for happily ever after. Just survival in the meantime so life can keep happening as it will.

There must be another question. Something I could put into words that would magically reveal a path through this minefield. I gaze at Millie, hoping she has the words I don't.

Millie simply puts her hand over mine.

The one concession I wring from Millie is the promise that she won't tell Stephen what really happened on the subway. I stare at Saul until he grunts his oath of secrecy too.

And the lies begin.

Keeping things from Stephen, dangerous things, isn't all that bothers me as one week, then two, and then three pass. The lies force me away from him. And not just in terms of the barriers I have to put up about where my mind and heart live. I'm pushed away from him by necessity. Though I told Millie I wouldn't draw curses without her supervision, I'm unwilling to restrict myself to our daily lessons. I can't tell Stephen what I'm doing. Millie seems happy enough that I'm sticking to our training plan and is taking me at my word. I'm pretty sure Saul suspects I'm cheating because of the way his one-eyed stare bores into me during my lessons at the hexatorium. But if I confided in Stephen, he'd try to stop me. He's not willing to risk me just as I'm not going to risk him.

And I can't tell Laurie for the same reason.

That leaves only me.

I'm going out into the city. Alone. And I'm looking for curses.

I convince myself that I'm not betraying Stephen and Laurie and Millie because I'm not taking risks. Not big risks anyway.

Though I can find curses of all shapes and sizes, laughable to appalling, I only draw the small ones. These are my self-administered inoculations against curses. I should collect a fee from all the people I've saved from taxi-less days. Millie wasn't kidding when she said the cab hex is a common curse in Manhattan.

I try to further mitigate my betrayal by limiting my curse drawing to once a day, after my lessons with Millie, so my body can have the space of hours to recover. If I haven't had too bad a reaction to a curse, I'll rush back to the apartment building to watch *Howl's Moving Castle* or *The Last Unicorn* for the millionth time or continue our epic inventive Scrabble tournament, where all the words are made up but the creator of the word has to provide its definition and all players have to agree that the definition is feasible. We fill the time we share with everything but talk of spellseekers and cursecasters.

Sometimes I can't hide how tired the lying and the curse drawing makes me. When that happens, Stephen will pull me into his bedroom. Into his arms. And I'll sleep curled against him until I feel strong enough to go out into the bustling streets again.

He must know I'm keeping things from him. But he chooses not to ask, not to press about my increased absence from our building. Our safe space. At first I felt the need to construct a mythical purpose, explaining that I needed to learn to navigate the city on my own if I was to conquer Stuy in the fall. Stephen accepted my words at face value, despite their emptiness. I'm certain he's filling that hole with his own narrative of what I'm actually doing. Why I'm spending more time away from him.

But we don't discuss it further. Sometimes I wonder if he's afraid to ask. If he knows that tapping the thin veneer between truth and fiction I've constructed will make it shatter and we'll lose all we've built together. But I don't ask either. It seems almost impossible that we can be so entwined and still hold back.

So we continue our dance of new love, at a close distance.

The morning the pattern breaks, I'm asking myself the same questions I ask every day: Am I getting better at this? Have I built up a resistance? Should I try to draw a stronger curse?

I've developed a regular rotation of curse-spotting locales. The angel fountain. The Apple Store that faces the Plaza. The balloon vendor near the Central Park Zoo. I even return semi-frequently to the 1 train that I took with Millie and Saul, though doing so never fails to give me goose bumps and a stomachache.

I'm at the Frick, which means I'm feeling uneasy. I hunker down in museums when I need a bit of a break. I'm not exactly avoiding curses, because I've spotted a few here, but among these cultural monoliths the Frick is a rather quiet place and I end up here when I don't feel strong enough to encounter a wide range of curses.

Within the halls of the Frick, I don't spend much time looking at the collections. I prefer to gawk at the structure for its original purpose. It was someone's house. Even though I've read that Mr. Frick built the house with the intention that its collections would one day be open to the public, I can't help but feel that the building is seeking redemption for its opulence. That the staircases and walls are self-conscious, aware that so few on this earth will touch the gilt splendor afforded to its founder. I consider the mansion's rebirth as a museum some kind of penance for its previous life as a steel baron's abode: a palace of the Progressive Era that stood a few miles from the withering, over-packed tenements of the Lower East Side.

The Frick, like so many places, reminds me that New York has, and will always have, an identity built on contradictions. It is the perfect reflection of life's imbalances. Maybe that's why I've begun to feel so at home here.

Maybe I come to the Frick because I'm hoping for redemption too. Good deeds of the future to erase my current deceptions.

It so happens that when time begins to speed up, I'm gazing at a clock. Like so many of the clocks at the Frick, this one is gold, but it's a favorite of mine because of the angel swooping across its base. Her arms scoop up a man, and I'm not sure if she's meant to be saving him or if he's running away from the soldier of a vengeful god.

Angels are everywhere in the city. While peering at this one, I wonder if the city's angels whisper to each other about what they see. When they trade their tales, do they laugh at us or weep for us? Probably both.

Since my life has been overtaken by spells and curses, I've been having a lot of thoughts about other supernatural possibilities. It's not a big leap to go from cursecasting to telepathic angels in artwork.

When I start to hear whispers, though, I think my imagination needs reining in. I step back from the clock, but the sound of quiet, urgent voices still slips into my ears. Prickles, sharp and cold, move up my arms. A steady, clear snapping sound joins the murmurs. It must be the clock. What I think are whispers are actually the whir of gears and the snaps it's rendering of the classic ticktock.

I lean in, startled that I can hear the mechanical noises of the clock so clearly. I don't remember having noticed them in any previous visit. With my nose close enough to the clock's face that the security guard clears his throat, making me jump back, it's apparent that the sounds aren't coming from there.

My mouth has gone dry and I can feel my pulse drumming. I force myself to move slowly. I don't know what I'm looking for as I continue to listen. But instinct is commanding me not to make any sudden moves.

Besides the security guard, who continues to eye me with suspicion, there are four people in the Living Hall. A woman and her small child, a boy of three or four; a man in a business suit who looks like he's taking in the museum while he's waiting for a deal to close; and an elderly woman dressed in Chanel whose silver hair shines as if it was just polished by her butler. Nothing about this group strikes me as out of the ordinary.

Then the sudden flicker of a shadow draws my eye. A man is standing in the Garden Court, but he's facing the Living Hall. His focus is on the mother and child. She's crouched down beneath Bellini's *St. Francis in the Desert,* chatting to her son. I guess he's getting an art lesson or the promise of ice cream provided he behaves in the museum.

I quickly look back to the man at the edge of the hall. Something about his skin, or rather the outline of his frame, is off. I can see him against the light of the garden so starkly. When he moves a few steps closer, he leaves an imprint in the air—a shape that looks like a police-chalk body outline drawn in charcoal. Only the image isn't still. The charcoal impression pulses as if it's an electric current. Keeping my eyes averted, I start to make my way closer. Though having my suspicions confirmed makes my skin go even colder, I'm rewarded when the sounds grow more distinct as I approach him. I pretend to examine the vase that flanks the Garden Court door while sneaking glances at the man. Looking at him is hard, and not just because I'm trying to not draw his attention. My eyes slide over him, unable to find a focal point. It's as though I can't look at him, at least not closely. I draw a quick breath and focus, and as I concentrate, I have the sensation that I've pushed through something in order to really examine him. Frightened that whatever I just did might trigger a response, I stare at the vase until its floral facade swims before me. Finally I risk a glance. The man hasn't moved, nor is he paying me notice. His attention remains fixed on the woman and child. The mother has taken up playing a subdued game of patty-cake with her son. The man smiles, but it's a smile full of malice.

I don't have to slide into the background to witness what happens next. The electric quality to the dark outline of his frame strengthens and sparks from within, like a thin cloud alive with lightning. Without breaking his gaze, the man mutters words I can't make out. The black line explodes like a bright camera flash and begins to form a new shape that stretches from the doorway across the room. Small smoke-like ovals build their way towards the oblivious mother, each dark shape overlapping the next.

Links on a chain. A chain that will bind this woman in a curse. I can't breathe.

The casting is so stark, so vivid that I can't believe the other museumgoers wander idly past the chain that links the cursecaster to his victim. The man in the suit brushes against the caster as he pulls out his phone to take a call in the Garden Court. The security guard puffs up and goes after the phone rule breaker but doesn't give the caster a second glance.

I don't know what the curse is meant to do. But those black, ethereal chain links are making the hairs on my arms stand up. They're filled with so much power. I can feel it like a static charge even at a distance. This is the kind of curse Millie was worried about me taking on. Even before it has reached the woman, I can tell it's a curse that would take a greater toll on my body than the subway curse. But maybe all my secret curse drawing, all my inoculations have built up enough that I could take it on.

It doesn't matter. I have to stop it now. I can't let that chain touch her.

I run straight at the caster. He's so pleased with whatever he's about to do to the woman that he doesn't move. Or else he, like most people, wouldn't believe anyone would tackle them in the Garden Court of the Frick.

He's got more bulk than I anticipated. Crashing into him is like hitting a brick wall. Fortunately this wall collapses. He hollers before he hits the ground. I land on top of him but roll away as if he was aflame. I know I have to get out of here. I scramble up, taking a second to make sure the chain isn't there. It's vanished.

The mother in the living hall has scooped up her son. She's staring at me in openmouthed shock. With her son in her arms, she rushes from the room.

I hear a barking voice and see the security guard coming at me. I hop up and bolt for the entrance, forcing my legs to run though my muscles are racked with trembling.

I run and run. I don't know how I'm running because my mind is frozen, stuck in the Frick.

I know who he is.

When I slammed into him, when my arms and legs were tangled with his, I could feel that charcoal line pass through me and I saw *him*. A lonely, angry man. A man who eats food like any other man but whose nourishment is the anguish of others. A man who wants others to fear him. A man who lives to control. A man who shares the blood of an invisible boy.

I knew, beyond a doubt, that I'd just tackled Maxwell Arbus.

I collapse at the angel fountain like a supplicant. Tourists gawk at me, and a man wearing an I ♥ NY visor comments loudly that New Yorkers are all crazy. I ignore the stares and sit down with my back against the fountain's base. Part of me wonders if Arbus got beyond the shock of someone plowing him over in time to memorize my face. I can't help but be terrified that he might have followed me and will appear from between the columns of the terrace to wreak vengeance on me.

But the terrace remains peaceful, if busy with sightseers and park regulars, and the angel benevolent as she looks down on me.

When I manage to catch my breath, I'm surprised at my first clear thought.

He wasn't what I was expecting.

Then I laugh out loud when I realize that Stephen's grandfather wouldn't be Lord Voldemort's identical twin. My sudden high-strung giggles earn me more wary looks from the tourists.

I lever myself against the fountain until I'm standing. My legs tremble like jelly, but I have to get home. Millie's face and reproving frown flit through my mind, but I can't go to her. Not first.

Stephen deserves to know first. He needs to know.

Maxwell Arbus is here. In Manhattan. And I don't think it's a coincidence. Maybe he's somehow learned of his daughter's death and has come to look at her final place of residence. He might even be searching for an invisible grandchild. If he even knows that Stephen was born.

The implications of Arbus's appearance in New York rain down on me in a torrent. I may not be ready to face him, but it doesn't matter. I have to hope that I'm strong enough, that I've built up enough of a curse immunity to survive his.

Though the steamy air and scorching concrete proclaim it's still summer, I know that these days of freedom are numbered. Mom has begun peppering me with back–to-school questions. I have to pick my classes for the fall. When I'm confined in class, Stephen will be alone. Vulnerable. What if Arbus finds him and I'm not there? I can't wait. We have to find Stephen's grandfather before he finds us. I have to tell Stephen that the man who made him invisible has returned, that, despite the risk and Millie's warnings, we're out of time.

I'm running a race where winning means losing, and I've just spotted the finish line.

CHAPTER 21

MY ENEMY.

My grandfather.

I don't know how to think of him.

If I am the invisible boy, is he the invisible man?

But not invisible. Only invisible to me. To the boy he cursed.

He is visible to Elizabeth.

He is visible, and he is here, and he has done something to her.

I make Elizabeth tell me the story again and again. I devour every detail, hoping that once I consume them, I will know more. I want a picture to emerge. I want to put a face to the name, so I can blame it for everything.

"We have to tell Millie," I say. It seems obvious to me. But Elizabeth is hesitant.

"She's going to say I'm not ready. She's going to say I was foolish to interfere."

"What you did was brave. She'll know that."

I say it, and then I realize: if Millie is in fact going to see

Elizabeth as brave, Elizabeth's going to have to be much more convincing than she is now. She doesn't look brave at all. She looks guilty.

"Is there something else?" I ask gently. "Something you're not telling me?"

We are in our usual position, next to each other on the couch. *Our comfort zone,* she called it one night as we nestled in to watch a movie. But right now, she doesn't curl into me. She doesn't smile. She's heard my words and she's trying to rearrange them into an answer, but it's not working.

I feel like a jerk. She's just confronted my grandfather, my enemy, and I am not giving her the space to recover. I want her to relive the moment over and over again so I can somehow be there with her. So I can encounter this man, this mystery, who has haunted my life in ways I can't even begin to understand. But however much I desire that insight, that connection, it's not fair to her, because it isn't letting her step outside of it, to see it for what it might be once the heat of the moment cools into perspective.

I think, not for the first time, *What have I done to your life?*

I wish I could simply be her boyfriend. I wish we didn't have all of these shadows swirling around us. But even if they weren't there, I'd still face the everyday, extraordinary challenge of being a boyfriend. A good boyfriend. There are times—times like now—when I wonder if being invisible is the only thing I'm good at. It feels like there's too much to catch up on, too much that everyone else already knows. If we build our current relationships from the relics of old relationships, I am starting without any material.

I see that something in her has been twisted, that something in her was touched by his poison. *My grandfather. My enemy.* He tore my mother's world apart. He doomed my parents' marriage. He determined my life. And even now, he's dictating the moment. He is standing in the way of me and Elizabeth, just as he's stood in the way of everything else.

There's a knock on the door, followed closely by Laurie shouting out, "Hey, lovebirds—are you mating?"

Elizabeth looks relieved by the interruption, which I take as a rebuke of my relentless curiosity.

"I'll get it," she says.

As soon as the door is opened, Laurie bounds in. He takes one look at her and says, "Definitely not mating. What's going on?"

Elizabeth doesn't answer.

"Your sister had something of a run-in today," I say.

"Anyone I know?" Laurie asks flippantly. Then, when he really looks at Elizabeth, he gets serious. "Was it someone from home?"

She shakes her head. "No. Not that."

"Oh God. For a second, I thought . . ."

"It was Stephen's grandfather. Maxwell Arbus."

Laurie stays serious. "That's not good."

"We needed to find him," I point out.

"Was he nasty?" Laurie asks.

Elizabeth nods. I expect her to launch into the full story, but she stays silent.

"I think I've exhausted her," I tell Laurie.

"It's *fine*," Elizabeth says, but there's a testiness in her tone that isn't fine at all. "I just need to think."

"We all need to think," I say. "Together."

The words feel worthless. I'm not certain why. I look hard at her face. She is pale, preoccupied. There's a traffic jam of thoughts going on in her head, but I'm not in the car with her.

He's done something to her. Seeing him—fighting him—has done something to her.

And by not telling me what it is, she is making me feel like she wants it to happen again.

I want to stop it. Right now, I want to turn it all back. Forward feels dangerous, and I'm no longer the one who's most at risk.

"Elizabeth," I say. I want the understanding to be there in my voice, for her to hear it.

She looks at me. Straight at me, taking everything in. Even now, it's still unsettling, to be seen that much.

"Who wants pizza?" Laurie asks. "I know *I* want pizza."

"At least now I'm sure," Elizabeth says. "If he's anywhere near us, I'll know."

"And then you'll kick his butt," Laurie tells her.

"My dear brother," she replies, "it's not going to be that easy. It's not going to be easy at all."

Millie is horrified. She is horrified that Maxwell Arbus is so close. She is horrified that Elizabeth saw him. She is horrified that Elizabeth didn't run the moment she knew who he was.

"Have I taught you *anything*?" she cries, sitting down in her usual chair in the hexatorium. It's the first time we've been here so late at night, but the circumstances seemed to call for an immediate visit, a banging on the door. "Your lack of caution will destroy everything."

I don't think this is fair.

"What else was she supposed to do?" I ask. "Just let him hurt people?"

"Sometimes there is a greater safety than the one at hand," Millie replies, turning back to Elizabeth. "Do you understand what you've done? He knows you now. He knows you can see. And if you think for a second that he'll forget that, then you are thoroughly unworthy of your gifts."

"It happened so fast," Elizabeth argues. "I'm not even sure he got a chance to really look at me."

"Do you remember what he looks like? Do you remember every aspect of what you saw?"

"Yes, but—"

"Then you must assume he remembers everything just as clearly. Probably more so. You are a pawn and he is a king in this game. For all we know, it was a trap."

Elizabeth doesn't respond to this, so Laurie asks, "What kind of trap?"

Millie sighs. My presence and Laurie's presence are clearly an imposition, but from her tone, we were right to have come along.

"You have no idea what Arbus has been up to," Millie says. "Even if he doesn't see Stephen, he may still be drawn to him. It might be irresistible. He wants the power that will come when the curse is done."

"What do you mean, 'the curse is done'?" I ask.

"She means that he wants to check on his handiwork," Elizabeth tells me. "Every curse is a story, and every cursecaster is naturally curious about how the story turns out."

Millie gives her a hard look. "That's one way of looking at it," she says.

"Are you saying that he knows where Stephen is?" Laurie asks.

"I am saying it's possible. And I am saying it is also possible that he would know that Elizabeth is a spellseeker who is close to Stephen. It is, in fact, possible that everything Elizabeth witnessed was meant to draw her out. And that's exactly what he's done. Arbus might not know of Elizabeth's connection to his grandson, but he certainly knows there is a girl in Manhattan who can see— what did you call it? Oh, yes. His *handiwork*."

"You think it was a setup?" Elizabeth asks. It's clear this option is not one she's considered until now, and she feels stupid for it.

"I think that a man as experienced as Arbus would need a reason to make such a public display," Millie says. "And how *convenient* that you should be there to witness it. But what do I know? Maybe he's too old to care anymore. That's possible. The question is whether it's *probable*."

I look around the hexatorium for answers. But Millie is saying she doesn't know, and neither do we. I look at all the volumes on the shelves. We are surrounded by so many books, so many words, so many thoughts . . . and not a single one can help us. I think, *What's the point of all this magic, if no one really knows how to use it?* But I guess the same could be said about life. Which is another form of magic, only less showy.

Millie starts asking very pointed questions about my grandfather, and I wonder if my inquisition sounded as fierce to Elizabeth. She answers dully—maybe because she's already been through it with me, or maybe because the idea of a trap has sprung full force in her head, and suddenly she's regretting some of her bravery. I don't want her to do that. No matter what Millie says, saving others is always more important than saving yourself. It has to be, or none of us would do any good.

As Elizabeth explains further, I look around the hexatorium again. This fortress of books. And I think, perversely, of the Three Little Pigs. I wonder if we are the pig who built his house out of books and words and thoughts. What happens when the Big Bad Wolf arrives there? Does the house hold up? Or does it all fall down?

"It was so . . . powerful," Elizabeth says. "Intense. You can talk as much as you like about it, but when it's there, there's no way to explain it. It just is. And you have to respond."

"You're not ready," Millie says.

"But what does *ready* matter, when it's happening?" Elizabeth counters.

"You can't do anything like this again," Millie insists. "You must promise you won't."

"I promise," Elizabeth says.

I look at Millie's reaction, then Laurie's. I gauge my own.

We all know she's lying.

Laurie does most of the talking on the way home, fantasizing out loud about giving Millie a makeover and getting her a reality show on Bravo. It's a verbal blowing of bubbles—weightless words to make us smile despite ourselves. I admire the attempt. Elizabeth doesn't appear to be listening.

When we get back to our floor, there's a tense moment when we each realize that we don't know what Elizabeth's next step will be. Is she coming back to my apartment or going home with Laurie?

She looks at me apologetically. "Mom should be home soon," she says. "So . . ."

"Can I just borrow you a little longer?" I don't want to leave her yet, not like this. "I promise I'll give you back."

"Go ahead," Laurie says. "I'm going to run up to Sean for a sec anyway. And family bonding is never the same when I'm not around."

"Sure," Elizabeth replies. But then she doesn't say another word until we're in my apartment.

Again, I think there have to be boyfriend rules about how to handle these things, and then I think that there's no way that boyfriend rules cover this kind of problem.

"What's going on?" I ask. Because I want to know. Because it feels like I have to know, to help her. I can't be there for her until I know where *there* is.

I mean it sincerely, but from her reaction, you would think I'm asking about a sports team, or the weather.

"Not much," she tells me. "And yourself?"

I know I should just leave her alone. I should let her talk when she wants to talk. But I am not reacting to the things I know I should do. I am reacting to the emptiness, the loneliness I feel when she's standing right in front of me and feels as far away as the ends of the world.

"Talk to me," I plead.

She shakes her head, and I know: she's regretting that she followed me here. She's regretting that she agreed to come.

"You have to listen to Millie," I go on. "If she says this is dangerous, you have to listen to her."

"I don't *have to* do anything. I understand that Millie's been doing this a lot longer than I have. I get it. But you have to understand that she's basically locked herself away from the world. She's given up. And it's fine if she can sit there and watch people get hurt. I can't. I'm not like that. Besides, I have more power than she does. I can do more."

"I know," I say. "But you have to be careful."

"*Careful*. I don't even know what that means anymore. It's not like I search these things out. It's not like I walked into the Frick and thought, 'Gee, I wonder if Arbus will be here.' I don't get to choose what I see, what I sense. Not anymore. These people just sit there like burning buildings, Stephen. And the choice is whether you walk on by or whether you do something about it. *Careful* isn't part of it."

"But you have to know your limits. You can't take everything on. Especially not with someone like Arbus."

"Give me a little credit, will you? Just for one moment, I would love to be given a little credit."

The look she gives me is withering. The sound of her voice is both critical and disbelieving.

Every relationship hits this moment: the first time it stops coming together and starts coming apart. Often it's just a brief glimpse, but this lasts longer.

"Let's stop," I say. "This is ridiculous."

"What's ridiculous?"

I try to make the air less heavy. I try to ease us back on track. I say, "Most couples have their first fight about what movie to see, or about whether or not they should, like, split the check. We're having our first fight over how to best use your spellseeking powers. You have to find that at least a little bit funny."

But she doesn't. Not in the least bit.

"You weren't there," she says. "None of you were there. None of you saw what it looks like. None of you felt what it feels like."

"True," I say—and then I don't know where to go from there. I could ask her to tell me what it was like—but I already have, and she already hasn't.

We haven't even sat down. We're hovering by the door.

"Even if I don't know what I'm doing," she says, "I still know more about it than anyone else."

"But Millie's been doing this much, much longer than you have. And even if she seems like a shut-in now, she's been out in the world. If she says you're in danger, you have to believe her. Arbus destroyed my family. I have to carry that. It's as much a part of my life as any other part. So I do get it, at least a little bit, because I have been living with it for my whole life. I may not see what you see or feel what you feel, but I'm the one who's hostage to his cruelty here, and it doesn't help me any if you get taken hostage too. There's no reason for you to be in danger. Not for me."

"What do you mean, not for you?"

"I mean, I'm the reason we want to find Arbus. I'm the reason all this started. You're out there because I can't be. And I don't want you getting hurt because of that. Ever."

I put my hand on her shoulder. I will my hand to be there, for her to feel it.

She pulls away.

"This isn't all about you, Stephen," she says. "Not anymore."

CHAPTER 22

AFTER YOU'VE SPENT ENOUGH time drawing people, especially their faces, you learn the trick of creating your own mask. I've constructed mine with the utmost care this evening. I wear it without doubt or regret.

Mom has insisted that we have a more "engaged" family night, so our movie has been usurped by Scrabble. I'm surprised she picked this game, and even more surprised that Laurie agreed to play it. Our family history would witness that I'm a champion at Scrabble. Mom and Laurie—and, once upon a time, my dad—live in fear of my triple word scores. Tonight I don't have it, though. That spark, that clarity of linguistic architecture through which I dominate the board, is absent.

Mom plays with a furrowed brow. Placing her wooden squares, but casting inquisitive glances my way. She's sensed something is off tonight. Even before we began the game. I realize that's why she offered up Scrabble, hoping triumph would fix whatever ails me. But her plan is failing, and now she's searching for answers in my face. Hence the mask.

Laurie takes a different tack, filling the board with bawdiness that makes our mother cover her mouth and giggle as her cheeks flush like cherry ChapStick. Mom tried to soothe whatever hidden wound pains me. Laurie's plan of attack: provocation by humor, or shock, into the revelation of real emotion. Once the mask is cracked, Laurie knows it's only a matter of time till it all falls away. He's working hard to speed up that process. The look he's giving me might as well be a chisel, chipping away at the plaster cast with which I've covered my true face.

I excuse myself while Mom and Laurie are arguing about whether *French* can serve as a verb rather than a proper adjective when used in certain contexts. In the sanctuary of my room I pull out my sketch pad. Drawing helps me think, and what I need now is a plan.

The sketch taking shape on the white page puzzles me. It's a map, and I'm not usually a cartographer. I prefer figures and action. Yet I can see why my fingers create these lines and shadows. The Frick is immediately recognizable. Soon hazy shapes form around it. Fifth Avenue. The eastern edge of the park. My other nearby haunts.

I'm musing as I draw, feeling that my brain somehow remains disconnected from the action of my hands. Familiar places are still materializing under my gaze. The usual suspects that I visit, all within walking distance of our apartment. Squinting at the hazy building outlines, smudged streets, and park pathways, I can see what my fingers wanted me to comprehend.

I haven't drawn a map. What lies on the page is a perimeter—a perimeter born of the question that I've been ignoring but hasn't stopped catching me off guard when it springs into my thoughts.

What if it was a setup? What if Arbus was hunting, not only for Stephen but also for me?

Even if the cursecaster only had a suspicion of me, throwing myself onto him mid-curse definitely confirmed those suspicions. Pursuing this line of thought is a challenge. It makes me feel like a narcissist. Stephen is still the one who's invisible. Who has to make an enormous effort to engage even in the slightest physical contact with the material world.

Stephen is who I'm supposed to be helping.

But even though I was angry with him when I said it, my words didn't lack conviction. What's happening is no longer just about him. And I didn't just mean it's also about me. The invisible world that Stephen lives within, the world of curses and magic, is just beginning to reveal itself. I refuse to let it remain a mystery.

I continue to sketch. Muddled shapes become concrete. My eyes fly over the pages, searching for patterns, clues. I stare at what I've drawn for so long my eyes begin to blur. I rub my weary eyes and return to the hunt.

Had Arbus cast a wide net, hoping to snare me? Was the Frick his first stop, or were his curses plaguing others he'd chosen before he drew me out?

What if he'd purposefully targeted that mother and her young son, guessing that anyone who knew about Stephen wouldn't be able to let harm come to a similar pair of innocents?

Or am I overthinking this encounter? Is Stephen's grandfather so twisted that randomly casting curses on people is a way for him to pass the time?

Grinding my teeth, I dismiss the last question because my gut tells me to. Not that I don't believe Arbus is capable of such a loathsome habit but because somehow I know he was looking for me. Not me specifically, but a spellseeker.

I wonder what that means. What this potential trap should be telling me. Remembering Millie's anger, her warning, I also recall the way her face paled. The trembling of her hands. How angry she became—a kind of fury only unleashed by panic, by the unraveling of one's carefully constructed existence. Knowing that Maxwell Arbus had returned to New York frightened her more than anything else. I can tell that she's afraid for herself. But she's more afraid for me.

There's a knock, but without waiting for an answer, Laurie comes into my room and shuts the door behind him. When he sees my face, he grimaces.

"I know kohl worked wonders for Cleopatra, but I think you overdid it. Next time, visualize smoky, not raccoon."

"Shut up and hand me a Kleenex." I lift my hand until he deposits one in my palm.

While I'm wiping charcoal from my face and fingers, Laurie wanders through my room. It's an impressive feat, given that wandering doesn't normally lend itself to a nine-by-ten space. He tries to sneak glances at my sketch. I don't bother to hide it, seeing no reason to cover up my blurry quasi-map of the space between our apartment and the Upper East Side.

Realizing I'm not going to spill my guts after a few moments of silence and his awkward staring, he goes for faux casual.

"So whatcha drawing?"

"The neighborhood."

Laurie cranes his neck, hoping to catch me in a lie. But the neighborhood, plus a bit more, it is.

"New storyline?" he asks.

I make a noncommittal sound.

"Josie!" Laurie shouts my name in a whiny growl. He grabs fistfuls of his hair and tugs on it till it stands up in all directions. That gets my attention. He used to do it all the time when he was little and really frustrated with me. I'm particularly alarmed because the hair thing was usually followed by an all-out, tomato-faced, shrieking tantrum.

"Laurie . . ." I start.

"No." He interrupts me, forcing himself to take deep breaths while I gaze in amazement at his purpling face.

"Listen . . . to . . . me . . ." Laurie's intimidating gaze becomes a lot more convincing.

I nod, a little worried that he might pass out.

"You're going to tell me what's going on," he says. "I was trying to be unintrusive about it, but you're forcing me to go all intrusive on you."

"Ummm." I have no answer for him, but his face is pastel pink now instead of purple. I take that as a good sign.

"Despite all of this insanity that is in fact reality, you are still my sister and I love you."

A couple beats pass and I say, "Okay."

"And you know what that means."

"I do?" I'm not sure I do.

Laurie nods. "It means that I am in this with you. And you are going to tell me what's going on with you, what you're plotting, and how I can help. Because I'm going to help. Don't make me hold your art supplies hostage. We know how ugly that can get."

I crack a smile, to which he responds, "Good. So talk."

"I think Millie was right," I tell him, conceding victory. Holding up my rough sketch so he can get a better look, I explain. "She said that Arbus might have been trying to draw me out. I don't know if he was looking for me in particular, but I have a feeling he was after a spellseeker."

"Your spidey sense is tingling?"

"Yup." I set the page aside. "That was just me thinking on paper. Trying to sort out where else he might have gone."

Laurie glances at the sketch again. "You think he's hanging out in our neighborhood?"

"I don't know," I say. "But maybe that's not a bad thing."

"How in any possible way is that not a bad thing?" Laurie asks.

I run my fingers over the paper, smudging the lines, crisscrossing Central Park with a spiderweb of shadows. "Because it means I might be able to draw *him* out."

Laurie's face pinches. "And why would you want to do that?"

"So I can get a better handle on what I'm dealing with," I say with more confidence than I feel.

"But what about everything Millie's said about him?" Laurie

stands up, shaking his head. "You don't go toe to toe with a guy like Maxwell Arbus."

"I don't think there is any other way to deal with him. He's the big bad. We man up and take him out."

"First of all, I'm going to pretend you didn't say 'man up.' Second . . . okay, I have no second. Everything you've just said is crazy. That's all."

"Just listen." I'm suddenly eager to try out my theories on Laurie. "What you said before—I think you're right."

"About 'man up'?" Laurie lifts his eyebrows. "Of course I'm right. No one should say that. It's not only gender injustice. It's lame as hell."

"No," I tell him. "I mean about Millie's warnings about Arbus. I don't think she's shown all her cards. She's holding something— maybe something vital—back. Definitely about Stephen's grandfather. Possibly about spellseeking."

"Where are you heading with this?" Laurie frowns.

"I don't know," I tell him. "I'm thinking about going head to head. About fighting back. If I can dismantle curses after they've been made, who's to say I can't stop them at their source?"

"Elizabeth, come on." Laurie's face becomes lines and curves of anxiety and love.

"If you want to be part of this, it means we find him," I tell Laurie.

My brother drops onto the bed beside me. Now he's the one who looks defeated. "I can't begin to tell you what a bad feeling I have about this."

"I'm the magically inclined sibling." I elbow him. "When it comes to feelings and hunches, we go with my spidey sense."

"Fine," he says, but he sounds distracted, and I know he's thinking about something else. Guessing what that something else is comes easily.

"You have to promise me," I tell him, summoning words like *stern* and *flinty* while I wait for him to look at me.

He meets my gaze and groans, knowing he's caught. "Promise you what?"

"That you won't tell Stephen." It's not at all easy to say, but I have to say it. "He's too close to this. We have to find out what I can do to stop Arbus without him—at least for now."

Laurie answers much too quickly. "Fine. As long as you promise to really let me help you. No more secrets. And asking me to cover for you with Mom does not count as help."

"Fine," I tell him, even though I saw him quickly tuck his left hand behind his back and know that no doubt he's crossed his fingers to permit his lie. Laurie is a sucker for traditional loopholes.

I'll have to pretend I didn't see it, though. Even without breaking his promise in what he considers a fair way, I know Laurie would have cracked and spilled all my plans to Stephen. I don't blame him.

All it means is that I have to work fast. It means I have to find Arbus before Stephen figures out a way to stop me. Or worse.

CHAPTER 23

JUST AS A FEVER makes cold feel colder, love can make loneliness feel lonelier.

She has not disappeared. She is still here with me. But there's a part of her that's disconnected. There's a part of us that has retreated into her. We don't talk about it, because every time I bring it up, it retreats a little farther.

We haven't fought. But still it feels like we're living in a truce time. Our happiness right now can only exist in a bubble of questionlessness, and I keep thinking of the questions that will cause the puncture, will ground us back into awkwardness, if not argument.

She doesn't acknowledge any of this. To ask her, we are doing great. To ask her, Arbus is something that happened and is no longer happening. To ask her, we are in this together.

But still, I feel the loneliness. I feel the absence in the presence. She notices. She has to notice. In her way—a way I am still learning—she tries to make amends. Not through disclosure, but trying to compensate for the lack of it. She brings flowers to my apartment, and instead of putting the whole bouquet in one vase, she leaves a flower in each room. We watch movies together. She stays over some nights. And in that intimacy, I can often forget. I can often lose the loneliness. But then I will wake up in the middle of the night. I will stare at her sleeping in the blue-dark. I will feel such tenderness . . . and I will also feel the pinpricks of all the things I am not saying.

She suggests we go to the park. She has to be at Millie's in an hour, but there is still time for the park. I ask if she wants to invite Laurie along and she says no, this time is just for the two of us. I wonder if this means there's something she wants to tell me. I wonder if she's seen or learned anything more.

But maybe it's the simple togetherness she wants, which is still a meaningful prize. She holds my hand as we make our way to Sheep Meadow—she holds it close to her side, against her hip, so it doesn't look unnatural to people passing by. She's also gotten a headset for her phone, so she can talk to me without getting stares. But today, we just walk. I am worried we've run out of words, and am hoping she is just saving them for later.

There are hundreds of people around us, most on blankets or towels, a few on lawn chairs. In summer, Sheep Meadow becomes something like the town square of Central Park—a place to gather, a place to picnic, a place to slip away from the tall buildings and expose yourself to the sun. To sit in the sun—a desire I am sure is as old as time. My mother had no idea what effect the sun would have on me, if any. Looking back, I realize she had no idea what the parameters of the curse were—was I invisible just to other people or invisible to the elements as well? Since sunscreen wouldn't necessarily work, she kept me to the shadows, the shade.

Now I decide to risk it. Because this I know: I can feel the sun. I know what it's like to bathe in it, to hold your face into it and feel the radiance settle lightly on your skin.

Elizabeth lays out a blanket, and I sit alongside her. To any observer, it will look like she's waiting for her boyfriend to show up. Nobody will question this.

"Have you ever been to Shakespeare in the Park?" she asks me.

"No," I murmur, shaking my head. I still haven't gotten used to the fact that I don't need to say "no" out loud when I'm shaking my head, not with her.

"We should go before the summer's over. I'll wake up at dawn and get two seats. It'll look like you've stood me up."

"You could give Laurie the seat. I can just sneak in behind you and stand on the sides."

"No." Elizabeth smiles at me. "I want to go with you. I want you sitting next to me."

"I won't argue with that. We better not tell Laurie, though."

"If he wants to go, he can get up at dawn too."

"What are the odds of that?" I ask.

"About the same odds as your grandfather treating us to dinner afterwards."

There. She's mentioned him. I wait for more, for this to be a transition into another conversation. But I wait for a few beats too long. By the time I realize it's a dead end, it's too late for me to construct a road.

"I was once Viola in *Twelfth Night*," Elizabeth says. "We had a major shortage of boys interested in drama, so the boy cast as Sebastian was Korean. Everyone was *very* surprised when we ended up being twins in the end."

"Why didn't Laurie play your brother?"

"Ha! When Laurie was a freshman, he had these legendary fights with our drama teacher over the school musical. She wanted to do *Annie Get Your Gun*. He wanted to do this musical based on the life of this huge gay kid. She said *tomato*, he said *to-mah-to-you-bitch*, and as a result he was blacklisted from all future productions. The only role she would have given him in *Twelfth Night* was the role of the storm that caused everything in the first place."

Elizabeth closes her eyes, leans back. "That feels like another time, another country. You think it will take you forever to break free, and then you break free, and there you are. Free."

She turns her face away from me, towards the sun. I remain sitting up, looking at all the people around us, caught as they are in their own stories. As Elizabeth drifts off, I try to glimpse lines or paragraphs of what's going on. I lose myself in others because I can never lose myself in myself.

"It's nice," Elizabeth murmurs.

"It is," I agree.

She sleeps. In the middle of the park in the middle of the city, she sleeps. Like a child, napping during the day. Quieting herself. Resting.

It's only as the hour turns, only as her time with Millie nears, that I have the heart to wake her.

"Wow, how long was I out?" she asks once I nestle her into consciousness.

I tell her.

"Sorry," she says. "I guess I really needed that."

She stretches out and looks around at the people around us. I find myself wondering if she's seeing what I see. Or if there's another element layered on top of it. What spells could all these people be under? What curses will destroy them?

If she sees any of this, it doesn't show. She stands as any other girl would stand, gathers her things as any other girl would gather them. Her expression does not betray any sign of noticing spells or curses.

"I think I'm going to stay here a little while longer," I tell her. It's not like there's anywhere else I have to be.

"Cool," she says. "I'd leave you the blanket, but, you know, you're invisible."

"Thanks for that reminder. I'd almost forgotten."

The smile on her face is still a little sleepy, even under so much daylight.

"I am kissing you goodbye," she says into her phone mike.

"I am happily receiving your kiss goodbye," I tell her. This is the best we can do in public. People in New York are forgiving of conversations with the air, but they tend to get worried when you start kissing it.

I watch her go. As I do, I realize we've managed to stave off the loneliness for almost an hour.

But I only realize that because I feel its return.

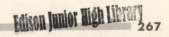

Edison Junior High Library

I sit on the grass, but I don't really feel the grass. I sit in the park, but the park doesn't recognize that I'm there. Children play around me. Lovers have no sense that I'm close. A cloud passes over the sun, but it has no idea that I feel the shadow it leaves.

I used to do this a lot, especially in the summer.

It feels different now.

Ivan, my favorite dog walker, comes into view. He is leashless, dogless. Instead, Karen the nanny is by his side. She has been unmoored from children for the day. It is just the two of them, and they would seem like just about any other young couple, only I can't take away what I already know about them, can't help but picture the dogs and kids that aren't there.

I shiver, even though the sun has returned. The woman sitting alone on the blanket next to me has started to itch her face. I notice it out of the corner of my eye. Politeness decrees that I look the other way, but there's something about her that makes me look more. The itching has turned to scratching. She is starting to claw at her face, her fingernails drawing blood. I want someone else to notice. I am invisible; I can't help.

I hear a scream. I assume someone has seen what this woman is doing. But it's coming from the other side of me. I turn and see a man has set his blanket on fire. "I'm so cold!" he is shouting as his wife pulls their child from the blanket. She keeps screaming.

People are starting to look over. People are wondering what's going on.

A man runs over to help. He looks like an off-duty cop or fireman. He stomps on the blanket . . . even as the father reaches again for his matches and starts to set his own clothing on fire. The cop yells at him to stop—but no words come out of his mouth. He is shocked by this. He goes to scream again. But nothing comes out. The mother is wrestling the matches away from her husband. The woman on the other side of me has blood running in trails down her face, and she is about to go for her eyes. People are starting to run away. They saw the fire and are running away. But one girl—she can't be older than me—goes to run and she can't move her legs. I see her trying. But her legs won't work. She's lost control of them.

I feel faint. The shivers are rocking my body. I can't explain it—I feel weak. And at the same time, I feel like I am responsible. I feel that something coming from me is becoming *this*.

It is the child who tips me off. The boy who was saved from the burning blanket. As people run and scream and try to help, he is looking at a fixed spot. He is looking at someone who is there to him but isn't there to me. And that's how I know my grandfather is here.

Someone has wrestled the woman to the ground before she can scratch out her eyes. But she is putting up a mighty fight, screaming that they must come out, that her face must come off. The girl who can't run is crying; the man who can't speak is stuck still.

Ivan is running over to help. As he does, a woman he passes drops to the ground and starts eating the dirt.

"RUN!" I shout. I don't know what else to do. "RUN! RUN!" I scream it over and over again—this voice that isn't attached to any body. I make it over to Ivan and push him away, push him back to Karen. "GO!" I tell him. "GET OUT OF HERE!" He does.

My grandfather can hear me now. My grandfather knows I am

here. But of course he's known that all along. My curse has tipped him off.

He can't see me. I can't see him. But here we are.

The woman drawing blood. The man who feels he's so cold that he's setting himself on fire. The man who can't speak. The girl who can't move. The woman eating dirt. How can he be doing all of these curses at once?

I feel it draining from me. The energy. It's not that the curse is lessening—I am no more visible than I've ever been. But he's feeding off of me. I know this. And because of that, I know that I'm the one who has to run.

I am careful not to bump into anyone. I am careful not to leave any kind of trail. I don't want him to know which way I've gone. Although, if I'm right about him sensing me, then he will certainly know I've left—and where I'm going.

I can't go back home. I don't want to draw him there. And I can't go to Millie's, for the same reason. So I plunge north, deeper into the park, as far away from anyone else as I can go. I push through the Ramble, skirting past any people I encounter. I allow myself to be a purely invisible boy once more. I untie myself from the city and become its watchful ghost. I glide through and hold on to the illusion that nothing I do can touch anyone. I am a cause with no effects. I am footsteps without a sound. I am nothing but air—noticeable in motion, but gone even as it arrives.

The screams follow me through the air.

CHAPTER 24

I'VE NEVER THOUGHT to care about tea one way or another, but sitting in the hexatorium while Millie pours me the zillionth cup I've had since I met her, I decide I hate it. I hate everything about this place. This bunker of secrets that has proven utterly useless. Like the tea, it's meant for sitting and steeping, but with neglect inevitably comes bitterness.

I haven't put milk or sugar in my cup. Nonetheless, I stir my ridiculously tiny spoon in the amber liquid, letting the silver scrape against porcelain, the rasping noise echoing my irritation.

I'm ready to share all of my discontents with her, lest I suffer alone, but I wait for my moment.

Millie clasps her delicate, wrinkled hands in front of her chest.

"Let's begin." She smiles and I grimace, but she ignores my sour look. "Tell me the code of the spellseeker."

Recitation is Millie's education tool of choice.

"A spellseeker identifies the presence of magic in the world."

"To what end?"

"To sanction just practice and eradicate the malicious."

Millie smiles at me. "Very good."

"So how do we eradicate anyway?" I ask, not waiting for the next prompt. "I would like to get to the eradicating ASAP."

With a brief, chiding glance, she circles the table, continuing the lesson and letting my question vanish in the air like the steam from my cup.

"What are the spellseekers' tools?" she asks.

I manage not to groan. "Knowledge, patience, and will."

"And how does one gain knowledge?"

"Through study and observation." I look at the cobwebs linking the top shelf of thick tomes to the ceiling, thick enough to mimic lace. "When was the last time *you* studied?" I point at the dust-covered books.

Millie's hands fly to her hips and I'm surprised that she almost looks ferocious. "Young lady, must you waste our time with this selfish, rude behavior?"

"I'm not the one who's wasting time," I mutter.

Her fingers whip out before I can move, and she's grasping my chin. "Elizabeth, I am deadly serious. The time we spend in these sessions is precious, and if you want to help your friend, you must take me seriously. This is the way it is done. The way it's always been done."

I jerk my face away from her. My eyes burn, and I blink as quickly as I can. Her words haven't provoked tears; my frustration has. No matter how many years of experience or how much tradition Millie brings to the table, it doesn't sway me. I can't sit here anymore. Not with Arbus out there, plotting who knows what. Why can't Millie understand that?

Millie pulls a chair close, sitting beside me. I resist the urge to flinch when she pats my hair, knowing she means well.

"There, there, dear," she says. "I know this must be difficult. I'm simply trying to protect you."

I stiffen. "I'm not the one who needs protecting, Millie. Stephen—"

Before I can go on, a ruckus erupts above our heads. I hear a muffled shout and the rapid beat of shoes on floorboards, immediately followed by the clomping of heavy boots. A door bangs open out of sight. The flurry of footsteps grows louder as they descend the stairs.

Stephen flings himself into the room. I've never seen him like this. His hair sticks to his forehead. He's out of breath but obviously desperate to speak.

I stand up when he says, "Elizabeth." Hidden in the way he's said my name is a story that I'm afraid to hear.

"Why are you here?" Millie asks the general space from which Stephen's voice came.

From the sound that erupts out of the stairwell I expect a boulder to appear, but it's Saul. He's wielding a crowbar.

"Where is he?" Saul menaces the room.

Catching sight of the crowbar, Stephen wisely remains silent. Still, I edge my way between him and Saul.

Millie wags her finger at the huge man. "Put that down. It's just the boy."

"No one comes in without being cleared by me!" Saul shouts. The veins in his neck are bulging. "I don't care who it is. Them's the rules!"

As if she's speaking to a raging beast, Millie coos, "It's fine, Saul. There's no danger. Stephen didn't know any better."

She glances at me for help.

"Something's happened," I say quickly. "Hasn't it?"

Making sure he's out of striking distance, Stephen speaks. "The park."

He begins to cough, a violent racking through his limbs, and I realize he's dry heaving.

"Is he ill?" Millie asks me, squinting at the rough sounds coming from Stephen's throat.

"I don't know." Fear leaves a raw tang in my mouth. "Stephen . . ."

"I'm okay." He rights himself, but his face has been robbed of its color.

Saul leans in Stephen's direction. "You listen to me, boy—"

"Shut up!" I snap at Saul. "If you could see him . . ."

I approach Stephen carefully, lifting my hands to touch his cheeks with my fingertips. He lays his palms over my fingers. His skin is cold.

"Tell me." I look directly into his eyes, hoping that our connection will help him get through whatever this is.

Without breaking our gaze, Stephen nods. "He was there, Elizabeth, after you left. I couldn't see him. But he was there."

"Your grandfather?" Horror snatches my breath, and the phrase comes out in a whisper. This isn't how it was supposed to happen. I was going to keep Arbus away from Stephen. I'm the spellseeker. I'm the one who can save Stephen. But Arbus got there first. I've failed before I began.

Stephen is still talking, his words fevered. "He unleashed curses. Not just one. People all around me."

"Multiple curses?" I turn to Millie. "Can he do that?"

Millie doesn't answer me, instead asking Stephen, "What curses?"

He shudders. "Curses meant to kill. Kill horribly. A man . . . set himself on fire."

I've stopped breathing. Nothing I've seen—what I've thought to be the worst kind of torment in curses—nothing comes close to that.

But it isn't over. "He made a woman eat dirt. And another woman . . . she was going to claw her own eyes out."

I must have gasped because Stephen says, "People stopped her. But she was still fighting them, trying to tear her own skin off."

Millie puts her hands over her mouth, but her eyes have moved from Stephen to Saul. I follow her gaze quickly enough to catch the twitching of his face. A spasm within the cluster of muscles in which an eyeball used to nest.

Still trapped in his memories, Stephen doesn't see it. "I couldn't do anything to stop it." He pauses, drawing a ragged breath. "And I felt like he was able to do it because of me."

"What are you talking about?" I move my hands from his face to grip his shoulders.

"When the curses manifested, I didn't just see what they did. Something physical happened. Like he was siphoning power from me."

I run my thumbs over the backs of his hands, hoping to transfer some warmth from my skin to his. To give back some of the life that his grandfather just stole.

"None of this is your fault," I say. "It never has been and it never will be."

Stephen falls silent. I keep his hands in mine but look at Millie.

"Is it him? Is it Arbus?"

"Those curses," she says slowly, sinking into a chair, "are a few of Maxwell's signatures."

"And was it—" I turn to Saul, not sure if I should ask the question I'm considering, but find that his hulking shape is already disappearing up the stairwell. Anger spent, he'd apparently had enough of us. Or perhaps the hexatorium had filled with too many painful memories for him to abide.

With Saul out of earshot, I finish my thought. "Maxwell Arbus is the reason Saul lost an eye?"

"Yes," Millie answers stiffly. "But that was a long time ago. Saul has moved on. So have I."

Whatever checks I'd held on my emotions shatter.

"Moved on?!" Whirling around, I storm at Millie, waving my arms like a maniacal marionette. "I don't care if it was so long ago we could only get there with a TARDIS! There is no moving on because it's happening right now!"

Millie scampers from her chair, putting more distance between us. I continue to advance on her.

"Don't you see!" Grabbing a book off the shelf, I shake a cloud of dust from its pages. "These aren't helping. I can't be a student in your school when Central Park has become a war zone. I won't keep hiding here with you. We have to do something!"

I've badgered the little woman across the room to the point where she's quailing against the far wall.

"Elizabeth." Stephen's voice is quiet, but right behind me. The bubble of my outburst pops.

I look at Millie's hunched body, her wide, fearful eyes, and I'm ashamed.

Taking several steps back, I don't look at her when I say, "I'm sorry. I shouldn't have . . ."

"We're all afraid." Stephen's words fill the void. The truth in them makes me feel very small.

The soft shuffle of Millie's house slippers on the wood floor alerts me that she's approaching. I'm frozen in place, not knowing whether to cry, pretend I'm okay, or ask for a hug.

Millie clasps my elbow, her palm powdery against my skin. She's recovered her dignity, and offers a wistful smile.

"I've only seen that kind of spitfire a few times in my life." She points to her mouth. "And it was spewing from these lips."

With a bit of disbelief, I try to smile back at her.

"While I don't appreciate being screamed at by a banshee," Millie continues, "it's time for me to admit that you're right. We can't wait while Arbus spreads his disease through this city. To do so would be to fail in our duty as spellseekers."

"To eradicate the malicious?" My smile grows bolder.

She beams and I can see a young woman beneath the layers of age. A woman full of force and fight.

I'm ready to grasp the branch of hope she's offered when we both jump, startled by the rumbling and screeching one floor up. The sound moves, heavy groans marked by sharp whines, like something unwieldy is being dragged across the comic book shop.

Millie starts for the stairs, but without explanation Stephen begins to run. I hurry after him. He's taking the steps three at a time. I'm halfway up and Millie's at the bottom of the staircase when Stephen tries to open the door to the shop. He turns the knob, pushing the door, which opens out, and it moves less than an inch. He shoves the door again. It doesn't open.

"Saul!" Stephen shouts. "Open the door! Saul!"

No answer.

I stare at Stephen and the unopenable door. "He trapped us here?"

Stephen clenches his jaw and throws his shoulder into the door.

"What the hell is he doing?" The door rattles in its frame as Stephen wrestles with it in vain. To Millie it probably looks like a restless spirit is banging around in the stairwell, desperate for attention from the living.

Millie is winded when she reaches the landing. She looks at the door, then closes her eyes.

"No," she whispers, folding her hands before her face as if in prayer.

Exasperated, Stephen gives up on the door and turns to her. Even though she can't see how insistent his blue eyes are when they fix on her, I'm sure she can feel their intensity.

"Why did he leave us here?" Stephen demands.

Tight-lipped, Millie shakes her head. Her hands tremble and stones fill my belly when I see tears brim in her eyes.

Stephen continues to glare at her, but I hold up a hand, warding off any further interrogation.

In a voice so gentle I barely recognize it as my own, I say, "Millie, where did Saul go?"

"He's going after Arbus," Millie whispered.

The anger in Stephen's voice is replace by shock. "Are you sure?"

"Yes," she answers. She tilts as if her legs are about to give out and I jump forward, catching her around the waist so she can lean on me.

"Why?" I ask her.

Millie begins to cry, but I can make out words through the tangle of grief. "Because Saul knows Maxwell Arbus won't leave New York without trying to kill me. And this time he'll succeed."

CHAPTER 25

"I'VE BEEN SO FOOLISH," Millie says. "So very foolish."

I've stopped pummeling the door and am now feeling through the small opening I've created, to figure out what's preventing the door from opening farther. Meanwhile, Elizabeth has guided Millie to sit down next to her on the stairs.

"Why have you been foolish?" Elizabeth asks.

"Saul told me this would happen. The moment you left, that first day, he said to leave it alone. He knew you'd bring Arbus here, one way or the other."

"But why would Arbus want to kill you?"

"Because I am a spellseeker. Because I am one of the last. Because many years ago, our paths crossed."

"Why didn't you tell us this up front?" Elizabeth is incensed. "You lied to us."

Millie sits up straight. "I don't think you should be the one teaching the lesson on lying, young lady."

I stop what I'm doing and study their faces. Both stubborn. Both angry. Both guilty.

"What's going on?" I ask. I can't get more specific than that, because I'm not the one in the room with access to the specifics.

"Tell us what happened," Elizabeth says to Millie, as if my question hadn't applied to her.

Millie sighs. "It was twenty years ago. I had a modest spellseeking practice. Private clients. Nothing advertised—everything by referral. It wasn't much, but it paid the bills. And I felt I was doing a service. Strictly diagnostic, but you'd be surprised how much that meant to people. To know it wasn't their fault. To know they weren't crazy.

"I'd had some encounters with cursecasters—in a city this big, that's inevitable. If they don't live here, they're always passing through. But it was rare for me to encounter them face-to-face. Mostly, I knew them through their work.

"All of a sudden, these intricate curses began to appear. I didn't know what to make of them. I had heard of Arbus's curse patterns, but I'd never seen them myself."

"Who'd told you about him?" I asked.

"Other spellseekers. Dead now." Millie shakes her head. "There once was a network. Now there are only outposts. It used to be, if someone like Arbus showed up, there would be a dozen people to call. Now I don't know what to do."

"So what happened after you started to see people with his curses?" Elizabeth asks, trying to get Millie back on track.

"I did the best I could. I couldn't make sense of some of them.

And others scared me deeply. I started wandering the streets, looking for traces of him. I was so naive—not young anymore, but still naive. I didn't realize that he was after us. He wanted to destroy all spellseekers, so cursecasters could reign unhindered."

"But how did he know you were a spellseeker?"

"I imagine he used a lure. It's one of the oldest tricks in the book. A caster curses someone, knowing he will run to the nearest spellseeker. Then once the cursed individual discovers that the spellseeker cannot in fact cure him of the curse, the cursecaster returns, offering to end the curse in return for information. Who could resist such an offer?"

"So someone ratted you out," Elizabeth says.

"I have to imagine so. Or maybe Arbus sensed me—I have no way of knowing for sure. I often wondered what brought him to New York, but now I imagine he was looking for your mother, Stephen. I'd like to think that it wasn't entirely random."

"So what happened?" I ask. "Did he track you down?"

Tears start to form again in Millie's eyes as she remembers.

"It was an ambush. I was just locking up for the night. It was late, and I wasn't paying attention. So it was as if he just appeared there, out of the air. He didn't say a word, but I knew who he was. I tried to shout for help, but his hand was too fast—he went right for my windpipe. I dropped my keys, kicked with all I had. And Saul—somehow Saul knew something was wrong. Just as I was about to black out, he came in and saved me, at a great cost to himself. It caused such a commotion that other people came running too. Arbus tried to curse them away, one by one, but he could only handle so many people at one time. So he fled. And I lived. But he's not the kind of man to forget his unfinished business, is he? The only way to rid yourself of a spellseeker is to kill her. I'm sure Arbus knows that."

I look at Elizabeth, to see if this registers. I look at Elizabeth, expecting her to crack, if only a hairline. I want her to feel the fear I am feeling.

But if Millie's a wreck and I'm afraid, Elizabeth keeps a look of calm determination. She is taking everything in, but it is not disturbing her. It is only information. It is not a death threat, because she won't let it be one.

I wish I knew why.

"Any luck with the door?" she asks.

I've forgotten completely about the door.

"Here," she says, standing up. "My arms are thinner. Let me try."

She presses against the door and reaches around.

"It looks like he put all the furniture in the room against it," she reports. Then she takes out her phone. "I'm calling for backup."

It takes Laurie about twenty minutes to get there, and another ten minutes for him to push away enough of the furniture to clear us out.

While we wait for this to be done, I try to get more out of Millie.

"Is there any way he can be stopped?" I ask her. "I mean, what is Saul trying to do right now?"

"I don't know what Saul thinks he can do. He's not a murderer. None of us are murderers. But that's what it would take. Cursecasters are humans just like the rest of us. Stab them and they will bleed. You just have to get to them first. Catch them unaware. Which is an extremely hard thing to do."

"But it can be done," Elizabeth says. I hadn't even realized she was listening to our conversation.

"Yes," Millie says. "It can be done."

This fact doesn't seem very encouraging to her. She says the words, but her tone is laced with doubt.

"Almost there!" Laurie calls out.

I move close to Elizabeth, so Millie won't hear.

"Let's go home after this," I say. "Or let's go with Laurie to a movie. Something normal."

Elizabeth pulls away from me. Not dramatically, but enough that I notice.

"Arbus is out there," she says. "Saul is out there. I need to help Millie find them. I know you can't, but I can. It's what I have to do."

There's no discussion in her voice, no desire for my opinion.

This is bigger than the two of you, I remind myself.

But I don't want it to be. I want to narrow the world back down to the two of us, just for a little while. I want her to be able to retreat into me, and I want to be able to retreat into her.

When Laurie breaks through, Elizabeth gives him a big hug, even though he's a sweaty mess. I want to hug him as well, but I suspect that will only freak him out. People like to see the people they're hugging.

"Why is it that old furniture always weighs more?" Laurie asks.

"Time makes everything heavier and slower," Millie replies. "Believe me."

Still, there isn't much heaviness in her movements once we're free.

"I have to go find him," she says. Meaning Saul.

"I'll help you track him down," Elizabeth says. Meaning Arbus.

Millie knows this. "You are to leave Arbus alone," she warns. "No good can come of another run-in."

"I won't do anything," Elizabeth promises. "He has to have a home base. I want to find it, so we can watch where he goes, see what he's doing."

"No," Millie says. "I don't trust you."

Laurie looks as surprised as I feel. "Whoa," he says. "That's a little strong, isn't it? We're all on the same side."

Millie isn't backing down. "We are. But I think we have different interpretations of what this means. Don't we, Elizabeth?"

"If I say I won't do something, I won't do it."

"Can someone please tell me what's going on?" Laurie asks.

I tell him about Saul and about Arbus, including my own run-in.

"All right," he says, "this is what we're going to do. Let's focus on getting Saul back before he does something stupid and ends up being cursed into oblivion, okay? And we'll also keep on the lookout for Arbus, but we will *not* search him out. Understood?"

He looks at Elizabeth when he says this. Instead of nodding, she glares at him. The meaning is clear: *Who put my brother in charge?*

Laurie is undeterred.

"Millie, you know Saul better than the rest of us. So Elizabeth, Stephen, and I will follow your lead."

Millie mulls it over. I can tell she wants to go searching on her own. But she also realizes she can't do it alone, not with Arbus on the loose.

"You and Elizabeth, yes," she says. "Stephen, no."

"Why not?" I ask.

"It's too dangerous. It's clear that Arbus can feed off your power. So if we happen to encounter him, you will only hurt us, not help. And you can't see him. So if he attacks, you won't be able to warn us."

"But I can see Saul, can't I?"

Millie is on her feet, moving to the door. "We're wasting time, and that's a luxury we can't afford. Stephen, listen to me— you cannot help us. You can only make things worse. This is not at all your fault. It is entirely the fault of your curse. I can't deny your harmfulness just to spare your feelings. Not right now. I hope you understand. But even if you don't, you must go home. Immediately."

I look to Elizabeth for help, for support. But she is equally unyielding.

"I will come by the minute we get back," she says. "I promise."

Only Laurie seems to understand how left behind I feel.

"We need you," he tells me. "Just not for this."

I don't think it's fair that he gets to go and I don't. But I would feel childish saying so. This isn't a trip to a baseball game.

Millie is writing Saul a note, just in case he comes back and we're gone. I almost offer to stay here and wait for him. But if I'm going to be stuck alone, this is the last place I want to be. There is no welcome here, only the specters of risk and casualty.

"Fine," I say.

"I'll see you soon," Elizabeth says, softening a little.

I can only hope this is true.

Coming back to my apartment, I feel worthless. While they go forward, I must retreat. I understand why, but it's a comfortless knowledge.

If she's in harm's way, I should be in harm's way too. I should not have the refuge of home.

My thoughts are loud as I go inside. I cannot stop berating myself, thinking if I'd said something different, done something different, I wouldn't be on my own, forced to wonder what's happening. It isn't until I'm in my bedroom that I allow myself to stop for a moment. I can't stop the concern, but the running commentary of concern stops. Just for a second. Two seconds. I look at my computer and think about turning it on. Then I pause again.

I have spent most of my life in this apartment. I know every inch of it, every corner. I know which books belong on which bookshelf, and in what order. But most of all, I know how the apartment sounds. The hiss of heat in winter. The thrum of air-conditioning in summer. The muffle of traffic as heard through glass. The refrigerator shifting in its seat. The breathing of the floorboards.

I can't pinpoint why, but something is off. As faint as the ticking of the clock in my parents' bedroom, there is a new presence.

"Dad?" I call out, thinking maybe he's come back. Maybe he's asleep in his old bed.

But when I look in that room, he's not there. I call out again, but there's no answer.

This, I think, *is what happens when fear metastasizes.* My concern for Elizabeth—my concern for all of us—is spreading through all of my perceptions, curling their edges.

This is what I should have told Elizabeth and Millie: I need to be doing something, because doing nothing is just as harmful as facing danger head-on.

I think about calling my father, because I have to admit, it might be better if he were here. I don't think it would make me any less restless, but it would at least divide my attention a fraction.

I head into the living room, figuring that if I can't have actual human interaction, I can at least drown myself in some television. I concentrate and pick up the remote control, watching it hover in the air for a second.

"You really shouldn't leave your key outside," a voice says. "You never know who might let himself in."

The remote falls from my hand. I turn to look and see where the voice is coming from.

Nobody's there.

"Stephen," the voice continues. "I thought it was time for us to meet."

The voice is old, but not weak. It is deep and rough and devoid of any trace of kindness.

I remain silent. To say anything would be to acknowledge him. I refuse to do that.

"The apartment is not as I pictured it," my grandfather tells me. "For all these years, I don't know what I was thinking."

The voice is just as any voice would be. But the body is not there. This is what hits me, what hurts me. This, I now know, is how I appear to other people. This is what it must be like to be in a room with me.

How fitting that Maxwell Arbus should be my first person who isn't there.

"I know you're here," he says. "I can feel you. That is part of it, you see. A person who paints a picture does not experience it in the same way as a stranger—there is an element of experience in every encounter, and that experience manifests itself not in sight but in feeling. So it is with what I do. I know you are there because I created you."

He is standing in front of the door. He wants me to know precisely where he is. Blocking my escape.

I don't say a word.

"There's no need to be afraid of me. What's past is past. Since you have been keeping the company of spellseekers, I imagine you have some idea of what's happened. Perhaps your mother told you. Or your father."

He is waiting for something from me. I will not give it to him.

He tries to sound patient, but he's not good at masking his displeasure. "I'm old, Stephen. I'm tired. I can only imagine what your mother told you, but believe me, there were two sides to that story. She wasn't a strong woman, your mother. She didn't want the power I could give her. But you, Stephen—you're strong."

This time, he pretends I've responded.

"How do I know you're strong? Because I know your curse. I know what it must have taken to live with it. You have to be strong. If you weren't, you wouldn't be alive."

"What do you want?" I ask quietly.

"There you go. It's good that we're talking. I don't want anything for myself, Stephen. Not really. What I want is for you to accept your birthright. As my time grows short, I want to give what's left to you. It's a powerful legacy—you must realize that. And I have no one else to give it to. No one deserves it more than you."

I fall silent again. He sounds reasonable, not malevolent. But he's still the wolf at the door.

"It's easy to remove the curse," he says. "Once you agree to it, I can do it in a matter of minutes. You will be visible to everyone. Think about it. What a life you'd have."

There's a hitch. There has to be a hitch.

"Say the word, Stephen. Tell me you don't want to be invisible any longer."

I don't trust you. Millie's words are there. Even as my hopes want to take charge, want to make a deal with him, I know I don't trust him. He's not offering this out of the goodness of his heart, because there is no goodness in his heart.

He laughs mirthlessly. "I should have known—you're just like your mother."

This is not meant as a compliment.

I want to yell at him. I want to tell him that he doesn't even know the meaning of strength if he thinks my mother was weak. He can't possibly imagine the hell he put her through, and what it took to navigate that. Especially with me. Especially with her invisible son, who she cared for every single day of her life. And, yes, ultimately it defeated her. Ultimately her body gave way. But she lasted long enough for me to become a person. She lasted long enough to know I'd survive.

I don't tell him any of this, though. I don't yell. I don't attack. Because I don't want him to think I'm his enemy . . . even though I am.

"Do you really mean it when you say I could be a cursecaster too?" I ask in a breathless whisper, as if he's Santa granting my biggest, best wish.

"Of course," he intones. "You're an Arbus, after all."

"You'd teach me?"

I am guessing he nods, then realizes I can't see it. There's a pause, followed by him saying, "Yes. I would."

Right now, I could undo it. All I need is to tell him I want it, and he can end what I thought was a life sentence.

But if I do that, he could put a new, different curse on me. And the energy from my old curse returning to him could make him even more powerful than before.

I can't risk it. But I also can't risk him knowing I'm on to him.

"I need time," I say. "Not that much time, but a little. Because it will change everything. And I want to prepare for that."

"This isn't something you need to think about," he says, angry.

"I am offering you what I imagine you've wanted your entire life. I may never offer it again. I'd advise you to accept."

I match his angry tone. "I didn't get this far by making snap judgments. You say you want me to join the family business? Well, do you want a worker who's impulsive, or do you want one who sees every angle? If you're looking for someone stupid, there are millions of other people in this city you can choose."

This time, he's the one who's silent. *I've pushed it too far,* I think.

Finally, he says, "I will give you twenty-four hours. And that, you'll find, is very generous of me. You've seen what I can do to people. Don't make the wrong decision, or a lot of people will pay for it."

The door opens and closes. I assume he's left. But for all I know, he's still here. Watching. Haunting. Knowing.

He hasn't told me how he'll find me twenty-four hours from now.

But I don't imagine that's going to be a problem.

Not for him.

CHAPTER 26

I'M SO ACCUSTOMED to Millie's gentle shuffling back and forth within the confines of the hexatorium that I'm stunned by how quickly she moves now. With her silver hair flashing as it catches the afternoon sunlight, she flows into the swift current of Manhattan's streets without pause and I'm rushing to catch her.

Laurie's noticed too. "What the hell does she put in her tea?" he huffs, running beside me as we find ourselves working to keep pace with Millie.

"One lump of sugar and some milk," I say with a groan when I lose sight of Millie in the crowd heading towards the Museum of Natural History. "Maybe she speed walks at malls with the other seniors."

"News flash, Josie," Laurie returns. "We're in Manhattan now. Mall-free zone. Malls are of our Minnesotan past."

I grab his hand, tugging him forward as I catch sight of Millie's carefully pinned hairstyle bobbing in the sea of tourists.

Laurie squeezes my fingers tight. "Is she trying to lose us?" He sounds a little hurt and a lot afraid.

I understand. That's how I'm feeling too.

But not because Millie seems more intent on getting to her destination than making sure her sole pupil, and maybe the only other spellseeker still alive, is along for the trip. I can't help but notice that the distance between us is growing. Where people keep stepping in front of me and Laurie, slowing us even more, the crowd adjusts itself to accommodate Millie's determined stride.

Part of me doesn't blame her for not caring if I get left behind now. I haven't exactly been a model student. Instead of letting the people who could help me get close, I've been pushing them out. As much as I've justified my choices and rogue spellseeking as necessities, as part of trying to solve the puzzle that is Stephen's curse, I know that's a lie too. Just another excuse to avoid the thing more frightening than magic or curses: trusting someone else. Loving someone else. Needing someone else.

The lies we tell ourselves are the worst ones.

The mass of bodies inhabiting Central Park West's sidewalk has become a gridlock. Everywhere around me people are stopping, gawking across the street. Phones come out of pockets to shoot out a rapid fire of texts or take videos. Alarm throws an electric charge into the air, so palpable I can almost see it. I wonder if it means we're all cursed now.

"Keep your eye on Millie," I tell Laurie. "Don't lose sight of her."

Trusting that he's heard me, I lift to my tiptoes, peering over the crowd—and I don't blame them for staring.

I must tense up, because Laurie gives my hand a gentle tug.

"Still watching the target, I swear," he says. "But what's wrong?"

"They're closing the park." I'm watching squad cars line up, lights flashing. The NYPD is setting up barricades, cutting off all traffic—including pedestrian—into Central Park. The iron-clad hoofbeats of police mounts clatter on the pavement as more officers arrive, blocking the paths of any observers whose curiosity brings them too close.

Laurie is guiding me forward. My ears are open, my chest cramping as I hear the rising tide of panic in the voices of the other watchers.

"The whole park? No. That can't be right. Seriously? The whole thing?"

"Six people? I heard twenty!"

"Please, not another attack. Not another."

"Damn right they should shut her down. Can't let the bastards get out of there. Probably hiding in the woods."

"Bioterrorism? Oh my God. Should we get out of the city?"

"Is it over? Did they get everyone out?"

A much closer voice pulls me from the din. "Thank God."

"Thank God for what?" I ask Laurie, who's pulling me sharply left.

"Millie turned," he answers. "I couldn't handle that sidewalk a second longer."

I don't know if he means the tangle of bodies that impede our progress or the infectious terror that's infusing the crowd. My stomach is a hornet's nest, alive and stinging me.

Me and Stephen. Me and Stephen.

Since I met him, even before I learned he was the invisible, cursed boy, this summer had been about us. Nothing else. We two. As if we existed outside of the rest of the world. Exceptional. Enviable for the space we'd been given to discover each other.

When Mr. Swinton explained the cause of the curse and Millie explained curses to me, I'd been drawn back into the world—albeit a somewhat altered one. But deep down all that happened still meant one plus one equals us. Other details remained peripheral.

Maxwell Arbus has in the space of hours relocated the periphery to center stage. And he's bringing Manhattan—and once the news hits the national wires, likely the whole country—along for the ride. He doesn't mind tormenting strangers to advance his petty agenda. Maybe terrorist *is* a fitting label.

Laurie is thinking about it too. "He's crazy. Shutting down Central Park. Who does that?"

"The bad guy," I mutter.

Free of the still-growing mob on Central Park West, Laurie drops my hand as we break into a run. I follow his gaze and see Millie waiting to cross Columbus again.

The light changes and Millie hurries into the street. Laurie and I sprint to make the light.

We get to the other side of Columbus with only one taxi blaring its horn at us, and I call it a win. Millie walks just a few yards ahead now. She pauses to look up at a blue awning. Her shoulders rise and fall, as though she's taken a deep breath. Then she returns and enters the blue-awninged business.

"It's a coffee shop," Laurie tells me when we reach the door.

"I can read," I snap, but don't object when he flicks my forehead in punishment. He hasn't earned my irritation, so I say, "Sorry."

"Forgiven."

I lead the way into the café. It's a space that even the best real estate agent would have a hard time selling as cozy, since it's crammed with four tables that barely afford walking space to the counter. It doesn't help that one of the tables is occupied by a giant man whose bulk spills onto two dainty chairs. Millie is standing beside Saul, who sits staring straight ahead. His large hands are wrapped around a white mug, filled to the brim with black coffee.

"Approach with caution," Laurie murmurs from behind me.

"Duly noted," I answer.

When I get closer, I notice there isn't steam rising from Saul's cup. I wonder if he's been here the whole time. Sitting. Waiting. For what?

Millie's voice rattles at Saul. "You don't know that he'll come here. Stop being such a mule about it."

Rather than answer her, Saul looks at my brother. "So that's how you got out."

Millie glances at us, pursing her lips and giving me a short nod.

"It was wrong of you to trap us, Saul." Millie returns her attention to him, speaking as though she's scolding a toddler. "You should apologize to me and to Elizabeth."

"I know my business," Saul tells her. "It's going to happen here. And here's the last place you should be."

"Why are we here, anyway?" I ask Millie.

"This establishment was my office and my home." Millie takes a seat, her back straight with pride as she speaks. "Before Arbus found me here and drove me underground. The hexatorium once showed its face to the public."

Laurie snorts. "What did you put on the sign?"

"We had no sign," Millie answers. "Those who had need knew where to find me."

Smoothing a few silver flyaways that escaped their bobby pins, Millie sighs. "This space has had many lives since then. First it was a greasy spoon. Then a pastry shop. Then a wine bar. Then a cheaper-than-the-wine-bar bar. Now it serves coffee and the World Wide Web."

I glance around the café. Even in this tiny space, the few occupants are hunkered over their laptops. Or frantically texting. The staff are huddled near the espresso machine. Each face in the coffee shop is blanched with fear. No one is certain what's happened.

"What's coming next?" I ask.

"He's hunting Millie," Saul says.

Millie reaches for him. Her hand, the tone and texture of an ancient peach, disappears in his grasp. "We can't be sure of that."

"Arbus doesn't hold grudges," Saul barks. "He lives for them. Don't be foolish about this, Mildred."

Millie blushes when he says her full name. "I didn't think I would matter anymore. It's been so many years."

Laurie coughs. "I don't mean to belittle your, um, history, but I think you're missing the point."

"What do you mean?" I ask.

Teetering back a few steps when Saul scoffs at him, Laurie tells us, "It's not that you're wrong. I get it. Arbus lives for grudges."

"Don't need my own words repeated to me, boy." Saul's one eye has mastered the skill of intimidating glares.

"No question there, friend. Er, sir. Er." Laurie gulps, waving his hands at his sides as if he's working hard to stay afloat. "How to put this delicately . . ."

Saul half rises, but Millie clucks her tongue and he sits again.

With a sudden gasp, I clap my hand over my mouth.

Laurie points at me. "Yes! Thank you. She gets it! Please help me out here, sis."

"He might come after you eventually." I speak slowly, having to remember to take each breath. "But you're not his most elusive prey. You're not the one he's hunting."

"You don't know what you're talking about," Saul growls at me. "You're nothing more than a baby, learning to crawl in all of this."

"A baby is all this is about," Laurie says quietly.

Millie draws a sharp breath. "Oh."

"You said it yourself." I hold Saul's unfriendly gaze. "Arbus lives for grudges."

I look away from him so I can catch Millie's eye. "You know there's a grudge he holds that's bigger than a professional one."

"His family," Millie answers.

"Stephen." My voice cracks and all I can do is look at the floor.

"And we just left him alone," Laurie finishes for me.

The four of us fall silent. The coffee shop remains abuzz with the clack of keyboards and the worried voices of the baristas.

I sneak a glance at Saul. He's shaking his head, but his grip on the coffee mug has gone slack. It's not hard to understand why he so bullishly struck out on his own. Why he ended up here, the site of his last encounter with Maxwell Arbus. This place must teem with memories, both hard and sweet, of his life protecting Millie.

In crises we fixate on keeping the things we love safe. I don't think it was his work ethic that rendered Saul willing to fight on, half-blind because of a curse, until Millie was out of harm's way.

What gave Saul resolve is the same thing that has me backing away from the others. Then I'm out the door and I'm running. I'm halfway down the block when I hear Laurie shouting my name, but his voice fades quickly. My feet strike the pavement as fast as I can will them to. If the NYPD wasn't already fully occupied by Arbus's attack on Central Park, there's no way I wouldn't have been tackled by an officer. I knock over half a dozen hapless pedestrians and almost overturn a stroller in my reckless flight. I don't stop to apologize. Not once do I look back. I'm chased by every epithet in the dictionary and a few threats of violence.

When I finally reach our building and blow past the doorman, my lungs are on fire and my thighs feel like rubber.

The doorman follows me towards the elevator. "Are you all right, miss?"

I'm bent over, gulping air, but I nod and wave him off. He gives me a dubious look, but fortunately the elevator arrives and I stumble inside, hitting the button for the third floor until the doors close.

Despite my best attempts to breathe normally, I'm still seeing black spots when I reach Stephen's door. I begin banging on the wood with both fists like a wild thing, aware that I'm dancing an uncomfortably close two-step with madness.

Both my fists are lifted, about to strike the door again, when it opens. Caught off balance, I fall into the apartment. Though I can see Stephen is there, startled and looking as bone-tired as I feel blood-crazed, I don't know if he'll catch me. He's told me about the effort it takes to become material. That knowledge is little help, as I can't stop myself from falling now. I'd been flinging myself against his door with all the strength I had left.

I close my eyes. Not wanting to see the floor when I hit it. I can take the bruised elbows and knees, but I can't bear the idea of falling through him. I don't want to see myself pass through like he isn't standing in front of me. I need him to be there. To be real.

He is.

He catches me.

And I can breathe again.

But with my breath comes tears. Tears that have been trapped inside for months. Tears I'd convinced myself weren't there.

Now free, they flood my eyes. There are so many, for so long, I think I'll probably drown in them.

Stephen doesn't say anything. He just holds on to me.

CHAPTER 27

TWENTY-FOUR HOURS.

But not even that. Now, twenty-three. Less.

People say that time slips through our fingers like sand. What they don't acknowledge is that some of the sand sticks to the skin. These are the memories that will remain, memories of the time when there was still time left.

Three minutes.

I hold her for three minutes. I am strong enough for three minutes. We haven't really gone anywhere, but it feels like we're returning to each other. The assumption of the word *reunion* is that, once you're together again, you are united. Two as one. Pulling close to someone is only a temporary symbol. It's the way you breathe with each other that's the telltale sign.

Thirty-seven thoughts, all present in three minutes.

You are here.

Something's happened.

All I've wanted is for you to be here.

He's been here.

I'm scared.

The fact that I'm scared is scaring me.

I need you.

Don't cry.

I just want to stay like this, like this, like this.

You see me.

He is going to destroy us.

I should have never led you to this.

You would be so much better off without me.

I have done this to you.

He has done this to me.

Hold me.

Hold.

Hold on.

What's happened?

I need to tell you.

I don't need anything else besides this, this, this.

Not true. There is so much more to the world than two people.

I am cursed.

Loving me is what curses you.

I need to let you go.

Hold on.

We need to kill him, but if he dies, I will be like this forever.

If we try to kill him, he will kill us instead.

I am okay with dying, but you have to live.

I should not be thinking these thoughts.

I should just hold you.

Like this, like this.

I want this to be the sand that stays on my fingers.

You. When everything else is gone, I want to remember you.

I have to stop thinking like it's over.

Twenty-three hours.

I wish we could stay like this until then.

Four knocks in quick succession on the door.

Laurie calls out from the other side. I let go, dissolve back into the room. Elizabeth answers the door, letting in not just Laurie, but Millie and Saul as well.

"The gang's all here," I say. "Even our favorite mover of furniture." Although it seems like Elizabeth and Millie have forgiven him, I'm not entirely ready to let Saul off the hook for barricading us in the hexatorium.

Saul is unapologetic. "You would've been better off staying there," he says.

"Are you safe?" Millie asks, looking around the room.

This is one of the good things about having them here: If Arbus were still around, they'd see him.

I explain what happened, and the four of them go through the whole apartment, just to make sure we're alone. I feel like a kid who's sent his parents off to banish a ghost in the middle of the night, one he is sure is just out of view, hovering in the deadly shadow zone where specters and monsters reside.

When they're certain he's gone, we regroup. Elizabeth and

Laurie fill me in on why Saul did what he did, and I'm almost amused that Arbus can make so many people feel so vulnerable at once.

Say what you want about my grandfather, at least he leaves a mark.

"So," Laurie says, looking at the clock on his phone, "we know he's going to be back in twenty-two hours and forty minutes. That's enough time to spring a trap, right?"

"If it were that easy," Saul replies gruffly, "I think it would've been done by now."

"We need to think," Millie says, as if we'd been planning otherwise.

"We need to *kill him*," Saul asserts.

"No!" Elizabeth says. "If we kill him, all the curses remain out there in the world."

"And here in this room," Laurie points out.

Saul shakes his head. "You children don't understand. You're not going to get Arbus to take back his curses. Never. The best you can hope for is that he revokes one curse in order to put on another—and you kill him in the space between. But even then, he can only revoke one curse at a time. So you've got one shot. And all the other curses will remain. You don't kill him in order to kill the curses of the past. You kill him to prevent the curses of the future."

I know Saul is unyielding in his convictions, so I turn to Millie. "Isn't there another way?" I ask her. "Short of murder. Isn't there some way of draining his power, turning him into someone ordinary?"

Millie shakes her head. "If there is, I've never come across it. I've looked. Believe me, I've looked. But death seems to be the only way to stop a cursecaster. In the old days, there was banishment or confinement. But that's not how our world works anymore. You can't just banish someone. They'll only end up somewhere else."

"So basically I have the choice between killing my grandfather and joining him?"

Millie looks alarmed. "It's not really a choice, is it?"

I tell her no. But still, I'm thinking there has to be another way.

Saul is restless. He keeps looking at the door, shifting from foot to foot.

Finally, Millie says, "What?"

"If Arbus broke in here once, there's nothing to stop him from coming in again," Saul says. "I've got to get you out of here."

Not all of us. Just her.

Millie notices this too.

"It's not about me," she gently chides. "We must look at the overall picture."

"Well, let's look at the overall picture from back home," he says. "We can protect ourselves there."

I can see Millie's going to protest further, but the truth is that I want her and Saul gone. I am not going to figure this out with them around, especially if I know that Saul will throw me headfirst into Arbus's clutches if it means saving Millie.

"How about this?" Elizabeth says. "Why don't the two of you go back to the hexatorium for now? Laurie and I will stay with

Stephen—we can even smuggle him into our apartment. If he's with me, I'll be able to see Arbus coming. And in the meantime, we can try to come up with a plan for tomorrow. Because there has to be a plan."

Millie nods. "Come by at eight," she says. "There are a few things I want to look into. Then we can figure out what to do next."

We all cling to the illusion that we're a team. But I think we all know: Arbus could break us apart in a second. Some of our loyalties are thinner than others.

When it's just me, Elizabeth, and Laurie, I can let my guard down a little more. We might not have any answers, but at least I don't have Saul glaring at me like I'm the Trojan who opened the gate for the horse.

"Why is it that there are five of us and only one of him, and I *still* feel like we're outnumbered?" Laurie asks.

"Because he wants it more than we do," Elizabeth responds.

"Wants what?"

"To destroy us. That's the problem, isn't it? He wants to destroy us more than we want to destroy him. Because we have a moral code and he doesn't. In a fair world, this would give us an advantage. But now? Not so much."

She's denying her own fury, and I wonder why.

"We can't let the jerks win," Laurie says. "I mean, that's what this is about, isn't it? That's what it's always about. Look—do I want to chop off his head and hoist it in the air as a trophy? Not even a little bit. But I don't want him to win, either. There's no way we can let him win."

"That's the problem with having a moral code," I say. "We want to destroy the jerkish part of the jerks, but we want to save the human being underneath."

"And do you think that's possible?" Elizabeth asks. "He's an old man. You're his only family. Is there any chance of persuading him to change?"

I wish I could believe it was an option. But I can't.

"No," I say. "If I turn him down, that's it. It's all over. He's not going to back down."

"So he has to die," Laurie says.

"No," I say.

"Then he lives."

"No."

We hang there for a moment, in the uncertain gap between each no.

Then Elizabeth says, "Exactly. My point *exactly*."

I step away from them. I say I'll be back in a second. I just need to be in another room. I need to think about this without them in front of me, without seeing the consequences playing across their lives.

I retreat to my bedroom, as I have for as long as I can remember. Surrounded by all the touchstones of my youth, I wonder if I am strong enough to walk away from it all. Because that's the question in my mind now—if I left, would Arbus follow me? What would happen if the invisible boy vanished? If I left this small, small world I've constructed, would it remain safe?

I think of my father, of his life in California. What if I

started there? Even if he doesn't want me around, I know he would help me.

It's possible. Entirely possible. Emptily possible. Because even as I consider it, I know there's no way I will leave. I want to escape, yes. But it's not the future I want to escape into. I want to take the path that leads back to us, not away from us. It's selfish, I know. Perhaps destructively selfish. But I can't be selfless enough to erase everything I've found in these past few weeks.

My mother stayed. She is here with me now because she stayed with me then. I'm sure she thought about running too. She ran once, when there was truly nothing to live for. But then she stayed, when she found something, and that something was me.

"What should I do?" I ask her now, knowing the silence I will get in return. Even though I know she can't answer, I still like to think she's listening.

I hear Elizabeth's footsteps approaching down the hall. She calls out my name, giving me warning, the chance to tell her I want her to stay away.

"In here," I tell her.

We wear our concern so nakedly with each other. I see it on her face and know she must see it on mine.

She doesn't ask me if I'm okay. She knows. Instead she asks, "Is there anything I can do?"

"Millie hasn't taught you how to turn back time, has she?"

Elizabeth shakes her head. "She's keeping that one to herself."

"That's too bad," I say, "because what I'd really love right now is for us to exist in the world as we knew it five weeks ago. I want us to be there, to be like that again. No Arbus. No Millie. Just the two of us meeting each other and having the world be so purely ours."

"All couples get nostalgic about the start of their story," Elizabeth tells me, coming closer. "There's nothing wrong with that."

"But not all couples are going to have the next day that we're going to have."

She wraps her arms around me. I make myself there for her.

"We can't do this alone," she whispers. "You know that, right? It has to be both of us. Together. There's no other way."

This isn't true. There are plenty of other ways.

But it's also true, because neither of us is going to take another option.

Protection. For so many other couples, this is a metaphorical vow. It is the emergency form of caring, the defense mechanism against the unexpected. But Elizabeth and I have woven it into the fabric of who we are together. So I must not try to separate it, or separate us. I must wear it all.

We walk back into the living room and find Laurie lying back on the couch, staring at the ceiling.

"Any revelations?" Elizabeth asks.

"No," he says. "But you could probably use a new coat of paint."

I look up and see the chips and cracks he's talking about.

"Not a priority right now," Elizabeth tells him.

"Well, we can just add it to the list of things we'll do when we're through with this, right?" Laurie says, undeterred.

"Sounds like a plan to me," I say.

Every fight for survival is really a fight to return to the inconsequential concerns of the mundane. I can picture us in this room—sheets over the furniture, paint dripping off rollers, paint splattered all over our clothes. We are happy in the hypothetical future. I cling to that.

"We really need to head back," Laurie says. "Mom is going to be worried soon."

"You're coming with us," Elizabeth tells me. "I wasn't lying to Millie—we're keeping an eye on you, and an eye out for Arbus. I don't want you alone here, just in case he decides to come back early. Laurie and I will make an excuse to leave at eight, and you'll come with us. But in the meantime, you can be witness to a good, old-fashioned family dinner."

This sounds great to me.

Elizabeth and Laurie's mom must hear us coming down the hall. She opens the door before either Elizabeth or Laurie can get out a key.

"You're late," she says to Laurie.

Then she turns to Elizabeth.

"Sorry," she says. "That was rude." She offers Elizabeth her hand. "You must be one of Laurie's friends from school. I'm his mother. Would you like to join us for dinner?"

CHAPTER 28

I GET THAT MY MOM doesn't know I have an invisible boy-friend whose grandfather is a maniacal black magic user. I get that she doesn't know said crazy evildoer is in town, was in our build-ing, is the reason Central Park is shut down. But I don't have the patience for this.

"Ha, ha," I say. "I know I've been out a lot, but come on."

"I'm sorry?" Mom frowns; she's looking at me like she's trying to figure something out.

Laurie, ever the mediator, steps between me and Mom. "So what's on the menu? Chinese? Italiano? Or perhaps the elusive, yet scrumptious, homemade mac and cheese?"

Mom's face falls a bit. "Oh." She glances at me with an "I'm a bad mother and hostess" face. "If I'd known you were bringing a guest, I would have . . . but work."

"Mom!" I break in. "Please. You know we don't expect you to cook. This is the twenty-first century. You're supporting our family in Manhattan by yourself. Forget the mac and cheese."

"Ummm." Mom looks at me like she doesn't know if she should laugh or scold me. Her gaze turns pleadingly to Laurie.

"Introductions?" she asks, and she forces a smile in my direction. Her eyes are on me, curious, confused. Unknowing.

It doesn't sink in until I feel Stephen's hands on my shoulders. The trembling begins in my own hands but quickly overtakes my arms, legs. I managed to keep it out of my face, knowing a trembling lip is a two-second prelude to tears.

Mom doesn't know who I am. She looks at me and sees a stranger.

For Mom's memory to be erased, there must have been an eraser. Here. In our home.

Maxwell Arbus didn't only visit his grandson. He took the time to stop by my apartment and leave a parting gift.

I stare at Mom, knowing that to her it must be awkward and inappropriate, but I can't help believing that if I gaze at her long enough, she'll know who I am. She *has* to know me.

Please, Mom. Please.

Mom manages to hold on to her smile, though it's become uncertain. I can no longer bear looking at her, so I look at my shoes.

Laurie doesn't miss a beat. "Come on, Mom." He speaks in an exaggerated, game-show host voice. "It's family dinner."

"Oh!" Mom gives Laurie a huge, approving smile. "You're acting—this is a homework exercise, right? Are you two siblings in a scene that you have to perform?"

Touching his finger to his nose, Laurie grins at her. He quickly shoots me an I'm-so-sorry-but-what-the-hell-else-can-we-do glance. Beneath his white flash of teeth, I see the twitch of panic in his face.

Mom laughs, clapping in delight. "What fun! Now I have a son and a daughter. Whose name is . . ."

"Elizabeth," Laurie offers.

"What a lovely name."

I force myself to look up.

Mom smiles at me, then glances over her shoulder into the waiting apartment. "I hope I remembered correctly that you love your Chinese takeout spicy and vegetarian."

"That's me." Returning her smile is painful. I want to scream, *It's me!* I want to hug her and shake her and plead until she can recall that my favorite ice cream is peppermint bonbon, that the only time I sing is along with the radio on road trips, and that I've pledged myself to a career that will likely mean she's forever underwriting my life.

But Mom can only look on me with the kind, polite reserve of a stranger.

Stephen leans in, whispering, "I'm right here. I'll be right here the whole time."

That's when I realize I can't do what I want. I can't run from the building, not stopping until I get to Millie's and demand that she fix my mom, my life. Instead I have to sit in an apartment that belongs to my family and be treated like I'm a stranger passing through because of Laurie's homework assignment.

I wish I could stop seeing the curse. Once I knew it was there I can't shut my awareness of it off. Bursts of light appear in a steady pulse, hovering before my mother's eyes. Blinding her like an unending camera flash. I know I could draw the curse, but I can see it's been created to last—which means it would take a serious toll on me. Or kill me. Knowing that a confrontation with Arbus could happen at any time, without warning, I can't afford to be weakened by attempting to free my mom's mind. Soon I can't look at my mother. The flashes make my eyes burn and my head ache.

Mom waves us in. Laurie gives my hand an encouraging squeeze before following her. My shoes feel like cinder blocks as I force one foot to follow the other through the door. Stephen wraps his arms around my waist, taking each step with me. I wonder if he's afraid I'll collapse or if he's just as unsettled by this new twist in our mis-adventures as I am.

I grit my teeth when I see the table. Boxes of takeout Chinese are already open, waiting, steam rising from within. Two places have been set. Mom hurries to add a plate for me, her unexpected daughter.

Robotically, I settle into the chair in front of the hastily arranged place setting. Stephen remains beside me. It's a good thing Laurie has acting chops. He keeps Mom occupied, regaling her with stories about school and teen hijinks across Manhattan. I try to throw on the actor's mantle too. Supplying nods, forcing laughs, and adding short embellishments to Laurie's tales, I keep up with the ruse. I focus on Laurie and not Mom.

Until Mom beams at me and says, "I'm sorry to break charac-ter, but I have to tell you how lovely this is. I always wondered what it would be like to have a daughter."

I become a statue, feeling blood drain from my face and my fingers go icy. Even Laurie flinches, strangling on words he can't get out. Stephen kneels beside me, folding my hand in both of his. He can't speak, not without Mom hearing, but he kneads my fingers, coaxing life back into my frozen limbs.

Finally, Laurie blurts, "As if I'm not enough!"

Mom, whose brow had begun to furrow in concern as she watched me, quickly turns to Laurie with a laugh. "Oh, sweetie, you know that's not what I meant."

Laurie faux pouts and Mom clucks affection at him.

"May I use the restroom?" My smile is so brittle I think my face will crack.

"Of course," Mom answers. "Down the hall to the left."

I nod, as if I need directions, and duck out of the room. My intention was to make a break for the bathroom so I could splash water on my face and clear my head. I get past Laurie's room, but when I reach my bedroom door, I pause. I don't know what I expect to see when I peek in, but it's not what's there. Everything is as I left it: kind of messy, evidence of my artwork scattered on the bed and my desk, laundry waiting to be folded.

Footsteps approach from behind and I know it's Stephen.

"What do you think she sees?" I ask him. "A storage space? Her home office? A guest room?"

Because I know the curse affects everything my mom sees. There are still pictures of me, Laurie, and Mom hanging on the hallway walls and sitting in frames on the living room end tables. Mom can't see any of them.

I've become invisible to my mother. My entire life has disappeared for her.

Stephen takes my elbow, turning me from the room. "I'm so sorry."

"It's not your fault," I respond as a reflex.

He shakes his head, not voicing an argument. But I see the weight of guilt settling on his features.

My lip is threatening to quiver again, so I bite it. "What are we going to do?"

Stephen reaches out. He cups my chin in his fingers; his thumb draws my lip from my teeth. He leans down, kissing me gently, offering an apology I don't want but also the warmth of his touch that I need.

The kiss ends, but he keeps his forehead pressed to mine. "I'm going to fix this."

I shake my head without breaking contact. "We. We're going to fix this."

Stephen doesn't answer and I go very still.

"I don't want to see you hurt," he murmurs. "My grandfather is punishing you now. Because you love me."

I don't know what to say. Anger and grief have clogged my throat.

"Ah! Hallway party." Laurie appears beside us. "Good times. You should get back to the table. Mom is worried you have food poisoning. She's starting to eye the takeout boxes like they're murder suspects."

His gaze slides past us to my room. "Huh. It's the same as always."

"The curse only affects your mother." Stephen steps away from me.

There's a sudden distance in his voice, a resolve that frightens me.

Stephen looks from me to Laurie. "You two should stay here. Finish dinner. Then Elizabeth can draw the curse from your mother."

"Have you looked at the curse?" Laurie asks me, frowning.

"Yes," I answer. "And if I do anything about it, I'll be benched for the rest of the game. Or worse."

"That's probably what Arbus wants." Laurie sighs. "He's a smart evil dude, isn't he? Dammit."

"I'll go to Millie's," Stephen continues. "But you have to take care of this first."

Laurie begins to nod.

"I already told you I can't draw the curse," I tell them, cutting a sidelong glance at Stephen. He's trying to keep me and Laurie away from what promises to be a final confrontation with his grandfather. While a part of it I'm sure is about keeping us out of harm's way, there's something more behind the steel edge that's crept into his blue yes. It frightens me.

"I'll excuse myself so Stephen and I can go to Millie's," I say before Stephen says anything else. "Laurie, help Mom clean up and then tell her you have plans with friends tonight. Meet us at the hexatorium."

Laurie's shoulders sag. He doesn't want to be left behind.

"I just want to be sure that Mom hasn't been affected in any other way," I tell him with a thin smile. "And you should talk about how great I am."

"What?" Laurie frowns.

"If all else fails," I say drily, "you're going to have to convince her to adopt me."

Laurie snorts, but his eyes are shining a little too brightly. "Yeah, right. Like I'd want a pain like you around when I can have this place all to myself."

He darts forward and wraps me in a hug so tight I can't breathe. That's good because if I could draw breath, I'd probably start sobbing.

We return to the kitchen, and this time Stephen isn't holding my hand or touching my shoulder. He's lost in his own thoughts, withdrawing in a way I can't stand but don't know how to stop.

"Are you okay, dear?" Mom asks me.

"I'm fine," I say. "Thanks for the awesome dinner."

"You won't stay?" She gestures towards the living room. "We usually do popcorn and movie night after family dinner."

I want to say, *I know,* but I shake my head. "Thank you. Another time, maybe."

The corners of my eyes begin to sting, so I shout, "Bye, Laurie!" and rush for the door.

I don't stop until I'm at the elevator, punching the down button over and over. Stephen's hand closes on my wrist, pulling it away. I'm glad he's touching me again, but I can still sense the rigidity that's taken hold of him.

The elevator arrives and we step inside.

When the doors close, I say, "Whatever you're thinking of doing, don't."

He doesn't answer.

"Stephen." I turn to face him. "We said together. We promised. Remember?"

If time wasn't working against us, I'd stop the elevator,

holding us hostage until Stephen confesses to whatever secret plan he's settled on since encountering my mom's curse. But we have so little time as it is. I can't risk a delay.

We don't talk as we make our way through the Upper West Side to Millie's shop, but this time it isn't to avoid strange looks from other pedestrians who think I'm talking to myself. This silence is new, unfamiliar, guarded. I don't like it.

When we reach the brownstone, a sign hanging on the shop door reads *Closed*. I turn the doorknob and find it unlocked. The shop floor is dark.

"Saul?" I peer into the shadows, waiting for an answer. There is none.

The odors of must and ink are familiar, but my skin feels tight and itchy as if reacting to something strange and unpleasant in the shop.

"Elizabeth." I hear the warning note in Stephen's voice, but I turn to shush him. What choice do we have other than to continue to the hexatorium?

"Oof!" I'm still half facing Stephen when I stumble over something.

"What happened?" Stephen asks. "Are you okay?"

"Yeah." I look down to see what's been left in the aisle.

It's not a what. It's a who.

Saul lies prone on the floor. In the dark I can't see if he's wounded. I don't know if he's dead or unconscious. I don't wait to find out.

With a cry of alarm, I bolt for the door to the hexatorium.

"Elizabeth, wait!"

I ignore Stephen, barreling down the stairs.

"Millie!"

Millie is seated at the table with a teacup and saucer before her. Her face is chalk white with fear, but her mouth is a razor slash of fury. Beside her a tall, lanky man pours tea into her cup. I've seen him once before.

Without looking at me, Maxwell Arbus says to Millie, "Why, if it isn't your protégé, Mildred. How lovely of her to join us."

Maxwell tilts his head slightly, as if listening to something. "And you've brought my grandson. Stephen, I'm disappointed with your impatience. Our meeting isn't scheduled until tomorrow. As you can see, I have other business to attend to. No sense wasting precious hours in this sleepless city."

I didn't hear Stephen come down the stairs, but now he is standing beside me. I reach for his hand. When I close my fingers over his, he remains still.

"Together." I breathe the word so quietly I don't know if he hears me.

"Go back to your home and wait for me," Arbus tells Stephen without turning around. "I'll come to you at the appointed hour as we agreed."

"No." Stephen's reply is quiet but unwavering.

I'm clasping his fingers so tight my knuckles are bloodless. Nevertheless, Stephen takes a step forward and pulls free of my grasp. I grab for his hand, wanting to draw him back and hold him beside me. But he's determined to move without me because when my fingers reach Stephen, they pass right through his skin.

CHAPTER 29

SAUL IS DEAD, and I have no doubt that Millie will be next if we leave this room.

I cannot see my grandfather, but I can trace Millie's stare.

She knows.

I lunge forward. Arbus is not expecting this. But he senses me, dodges slightly so I end up barreling into his side. I knock him over, but he's eluded my grasp.

"Damn you!" he shouts, kicking out at me.

I cannot see what he does next, but from the reactions in the room, it's clear enough. He gets to his feet and pushes towards Millie. In a split second, Millie snaps out of her grief—as Arbus gets within range, she picks up her cup and throws the hot tea in his face. He cries out and stumbles back. I follow the voice, and tackle him down. Millie rushes around to help me, but Arbus releases himself in a surge of strength—it is hard for me to manifest my body into solidity and hold him at the same time.

Arbus reaches into his pocket and takes out a bloody knife—the same knife, I have no doubt, that stabbed Saul in the back.

Elizabeth and Millie step away from him. I try to quiet my breathing, make myself as invisible as possible.

"So it has come to this," he says, trying to find me even though he can't see me.

I know better than to say a word.

"Stubborn like your mother and stupid like your father. You were born to suffer like them both, and so you shall."

Everything that has gone wrong in my life can be traced to this man. This one man.

He is starting to back his way to the door. Then there's a sound from the stairs.

"Elizabeth!" Laurie calls out. "Stephen!"

"No, Laurie!" I yell. "Run!"

I think Arbus will come for me now, but instead he turns towards the stairway and starts to murmur a curse.

"Don't you dare!" Elizabeth shouts. I can feel Arbus harnessing the energy of my curse, drawing me closer. At the same time, Elizabeth is making a motion with her hands, and as Arbus releases what he has—I can feel him do it—she draws it to her, takes enough of it in for it to fail.

Furious, Arbus tries to turn his curse on Elizabeth, but it won't work.

The knife, however, will. When it's clear that he cannot rely on magic, he brandishes the weapon. I watch it rise in the air, safe in his invisible hand. He doesn't care how he draws blood, how he causes harm. Magic and violence are the same to him.

As he moves forward, Millie tips over the desk to stop him. I reach forward to block him.

All I can see is the knife, so I go for the knife.

Out of the corner of my eye, I can tell that Elizabeth is faltering—absorbing the curse has cost her. But I can't focus on that. I focus on where Arbus's arm must be. I throw my body into that space and hit bone. Arbus cries out, turns the knife towards me. But in that moment, I pass right through. He spins, off-kilter, then recovers.

I expect him to go straight for me. But he takes advantage of this and jumps for the door. I stop to block him, but I'm too late.

I can feel him leave the room. I can feel my curse bend after him, his body desperate to keep the curse's energy.

"Laurie!" Elizabeth cries, her face all panic.

I want to rush after Arbus, but I need someone who can see him to take the lead. For all I know, he's at the top of the stairway, waiting with his knife ready.

Millie charges ahead. I warn her to be careful, but she doesn't care.

I follow, with a shaky Elizabeth behind me.

Arbus is not waiting for us at the top of the stairs. But there is Saul, right where I left him, turned over so his wound is visible. Millie falls to her knees beside him, cradles him in her arms. I know she will not leave him, so all I can say is, "I'm so sorry." Because haven't I brought this upon her? My curse is the beacon that brought him to this city.

As I find myself lost in this moment of guilt, Elizabeth takes charge. "Lock the door," she says. "Just in case he comes back." Millie doesn't even seem to be listening. She starts to howl—a raw, guttural release of grief, the most painful sound that doesn't exist in any language. I want to comfort her, but what comfort can I give her? The only comfort will come when Arbus is dead.

I can't kill him, though. Not before he undoes all the curses, including mine.

Elizabeth is already out the door. *Laurie,* I remember. He probably has a two-minute lead on Arbus. Not enough.

We have to assume he's headed home. Elizabeth is trying to call his phone, but he's not picking up. Hopefully because he's too busy running.

Arbus's malevolence cannot contain itself. The adrenaline of our confrontation must be manifesting itself in spite. Because he's left us a trail. A horrible trail.

These poor people thought that they were taking a walk on a nice summer evening. They may have been coming home from dinner or a late night at work.

Now they are victims.

A man in a suit lies on the sidewalk, screaming, "Where are my legs? What have you done with my legs?" An eleven-year-old girl is tearing off her clothes as if they're covered with scorpions. The boy beside her is tearing out his hair in clumps, not recognizing the blood on his fingers.

A block later, two lovers who went for a stroll are now beating each other to a pulp. A man who's taken his dog out for a walk is now trying to hang it by its leash. Not hesitating for a moment, Elizabeth runs over and punches the man in the chest; startled, he drops the leash, and the dog runs safely away into the park.

It's an awful choice—do we stay and help these people, or do we rush past them and try to stop Arbus?

"Come on," Elizabeth says, running ahead. She's got her phone out again and is calling the police.

Let them handle this. We have to cut right to the cause.

"He's using up so much energy," Elizabeth says to me once she's off the phone.

"He wants us to find him," I say. "This is it. Checkmate."

We get to our building and find that the doorman is throwing himself back and forth through the plate glass window, knocking shard after shard with his body. I don't want to touch him, because there is glass all through his skin, but how else can I stop him? Elizabeth moves to block him and I move to catch him, but he dodges us, kneels to the ground, and starts to pick up the glass, moving it to his lips. Elizabeth kicks it out of his grasp; he howls.

Another tenant approaches the building—Alex, the preppy jerk from 7A.

"What's going on?" he says, shocked.

"Hold him and don't let go until the police come," Elizabeth orders.

Alex goes into a wrestler pose, grabs the doorman, and nods.

"I've got him," he says, unyielding and unquestioning.

We sprint for the elevators.

"My apartment or your apartment?" Elizabeth asks.

I shake my head and point to where the elevators have gone. Both of them sit on the top floor.

"The roof," I tell her. "It has to be the roof."

CHAPTER 30

I'M RUNNING FOR THE stairs. I take them two at a time, flinging myself from landing to landing. I don't look at the floor numbers. I can't think about the climb or the precious minutes stolen by each flight or the way my lungs are burning. All I know is that *I will not stop running* until I am on the roof.

Stephen is behind me, but he doesn't speak. There is no pausing to collect our thoughts. There is no strategy. No plan.

And then I am facing the door to the roof. It is a gateway of thick, imposing gray metal. I shove through.

Our squat, nine-story apartment building isn't one of those with an on-trend, sexy rooftop garden. The space I stumble into, squinting in the sudden, harsh daylight, is a bleak, open square of cement ringed by a low brick edge.

I see my brother first.

"Laurie!"

I start towards him, but a chillingly calm voice brings me up a few yards short of him.

"I wouldn't get any closer if I were you." Maxwell Arbus stands with his hands clasped at his back. His gaze is speculative and practiced, like he's assessing the worth of some antiquity.

Without taking his eyes from me, Arbus tilts his head in Laurie's direction. "Your brother is entertaining some unusual ideas at the moment."

I risk looking away from him so I can focus on Laurie. My brother's eyes are glassy, his expression grossly serene.

"I haven't decided yet what Laurie most wants to do," Stephen's grandfather tells me. "Fly or jump to the next building."

"Don't." My voice almost cracks. I don't want to break for this man, and I know I'm on the verge.

"The jump would be more sporting, don't you think?" Arbus continues. "He might make it."

I attempt negotiation. "Please let him go. My brother has nothing to do with this."

Arbus's laugh is like a sharp bark. "He's here, isn't he? I think that makes your brother very much a part of this."

"And my mother?" I don't want to do this. I'm letting him bait me, but I can't stop. Rage and fear are driving my thoughts, my words.

"A lovely woman, I'm sure," Arbus answers. "Such a shame that single mothers can't discipline their children as needed. If you had a proper father, I'm certain we wouldn't be in this unpleasant predicament."

I'm withering beneath his cruelty and he can tell. A smile slides up one side of his thin mouth.

"In fact." His voice becomes dangerously quiet. "I'd hate for her to miss the finer points of my instruction."

After shifting his weight slightly and uttering a few words I can't hear, Arbus says, "The curse on your mother is lifted."

I know better than to feel relief, an instinct that's confirmed when he tells me, "Soon she'll fully grasp what a mistake it is to leave her children alone for so many hours of the working day, all too free to meddle in the lives of others. Consequences are best realized in a stark and brutal manner. Else the lesson may not be learned."

His gaze shifts to Laurie. My brother, wearing a bemused smile, begins to walk to the edge of the roof.

"No!" The shout isn't mine. It comes from Stephen.

Laurie stops just shy of the two-foot brick ledge that rings the building.

I understand why Stephen hasn't spoken before now. He can't see his grandfather, but Arbus has been chatting so freely with me that Stephen knows precisely where the cursecaster is standing.

Arbus's eyes narrow, focusing on the space behind me. "I was wondering when you'd join the conversation, Stephen."

Stephen doesn't answer. Arbus continues to look over my shoulder, but in my peripheral vision I can see Stephen quickly sidestepping. I don't let my gaze follow him. Stephen's grandfather is unconcerned that his voice continues to pinpoint his location. He rocks back on his heels, pleased with the way this rooftop scene is playing out.

"I want to give you one more chance," Arbus tells the empty space where Stephen used to be. "Understand this is who you are."

He gestures towards me and Laurie. Why motion with his hands when Stephen can't see it? Then I realize it's for my benefit.

Wherever Arbus is going with this, he's betting on me to help him get there.

My suspicion is confirmed when he continues to address Stephen but keeps his eyes on me.

"What can you offer these people?" Arbus asks. "Your inheritance is pain. Whether you like it or not, suffering will spread around you like a disease. Are the last few days not demonstration enough of that truth?"

"That was you!" I shriek at Arbus. "Stephen has nothing to do with your curses!"

His eyes narrow at me and I see Laurie put one foot on the building ledge. I can't risk speaking again. My brother's head and shoulders are surrounded by a swarm of silver and gold winged creatures that fill the air with a chiming, playful melody. They're moving so fast I can't tell if they're fairies or birds. They dip and swirl around my brother like a glimmering tornado, their sweet music and light luring him to towards his doom.

I have never hated anyone like I hate Maxwell Arbus in this moment. Every one of his curses is stronger than I am. I've always been a fighter. Plucky. Defiant. Sometimes obstinate. But any grit or earnestness I could supply is outflanked by the years of experience Arbus brings to the game. I'm still a rookie, while he's a Hall of Famer. By working a curse upon my brother, Arbus has rendered me helpless.

An entire reel of emotions plays out in the blink of an eye. I see images of myself: sobbing, screaming, howling, vomiting, fainting. Not one of those reactions will help me or Laurie or Stephen.

An already-horrible scenario is made even worse by Maxwell Arbus's obvious enjoyment of our plight.

"I'm waiting, Stephen." Arbus flicks his wrist and Laurie steps onto the ledge.

I am on my knees. Mute and desperate.

Though that hook-like smile still graces his lips, Arbus glances at me, and in his eyes I catch something. A flicker of wariness. I can't breathe, but fear isn't the culprit. Arbus needs me off balance, and not only as a ploy to get what he wants from Stephen.

The cursecaster went after Millie. Settling an old grudge was part of his motivation, but there was more to it. As a spellseeker, Millie remains a threat to Maxwell Arbus. And I'm a threat too.

I stay where I am. Low. Submissive. But sparks are firing in my brain, charging my body until my blood is electric. I am not a cowering girl. The sliver of Stephen's grandfather that fears me poked through his facade of unwavering confidence. I recognized it, and now I grasp the hope it offers. My only way of protecting Laurie is to exploit the cursecaster's elusive vulnerability.

I know what I have to do.

It takes more will than I know I have to look away from Laurie. In doing so I'm giving away Stephen's location, but I have no choice. I am a spellseeker. I can cut through the knots of pain and suffering that monsters like Maxwell Arbus tie in the lives of others.

Placing my hands on the sun-heated roof to ground myself, I take a deep breath. Stephen's curse is already hovering around him. Its dark tentacles, ephemeral as mist, become solid as I watch Stephen. The squelching sound of the curse fills my ears.

Before I begin, I tell myself it's not suicide. I've been training. My resistance has grown. Taking on this cursecaster's masterpiece will not kill me. I am comfortable enough with this lie to believe it for Laurie's sake. For Stephen's sake. I must cut off as much of Arbus's power as possible.

Stephen is watching his grandfather as he takes careful side-steps across the roof. He stops suddenly, pivoting to face me the moment my mind connects with the curse, as if I'd physically touched him. His eyes widen in alarm. He begins to shake his head.

It doesn't matter. This has to be done. And then I am drawing the dark into my veins.

CHAPTER 31

WHATEVER IT IS THAT she's doing, it's too much for her.

One moment, she is the picture of concentration.

I cannot do anything. I cannot stop her.

The next moment, she starts to break.

It is there first in her eyes. The shock. Her body falls back, as if it's been pushed in the middle. She can barely stay upright.

Then her nose starts to bleed. A single rivulet of blood at first. Then more. And more. Blood running down her face. And the scariest part is that she doesn't seem to notice.

She cannot steady her hand. Once she opened herself up, she stopped being in control.

My grandfather starts to flicker. There, in front of my eyes, he appears, then disappears. I look down at my hands. For the first time, I look down at my hands and I see them. It almost doesn't register at first. These must be someone else's hands, I think. They flicker into being, then flicker back away.

Elizabeth collapses.

I run over to her, try to use my voice, my hands, my will to revive her. She is writing. The blood won't stop pouring out of her nose. I see it on my hands, then I stop seeing my hands again.

He's killing her.

Just as I see him flickering, he sees me flickering. I do not feel him drawing on my curse, like he did before. No, this is something else.

Laurie is calling out Elizabeth's name. He is off the ledge and running to us.

My grandfather looks me in the eye, then disappears.

I do not feel any of this.

It is Elizabeth who feels it. Elizabeth who suffers.

Elizabeth who is dying.

My grandfather is winning. He knows it, and the next time he's visible, I can see the smile on his lips. The satisfaction.

I must stop him.

Laurie is cradling Elizabeth's head in his lap. He's crying out to me, asking me what's happening, what's happening. He's telling me to make it stop.

I have to make it stop.

There's a gurgle in Elizabeth's throat. More blood coming up. Coming out.

I cannot ask my grandfather to stop. I know he will not stop. He will never stop. I cannot take his powers away from him. I am not that strong. None of us can be that strong.

If he does not die, she will die.

I would like to kill within a rage. I would like to kill without thinking.

But that is not what this is.

I know I am making a choice.

As Laurie watches over the only girl I will ever love, I ram my body into my grandfather, summoning all of the strength that I have. As we flicker, we are not quite human, not quite magic. The only thing we are is kin. He wields his knife, but I grab him by the throat. It jolts him, loosens his grip. I twist his wrist and the knife falls.

"Stephen," he gasps. But all I can think is that he doesn't have the right to know my name.

We are invisible again, but I hold on. I am pushing him back, back.

Elizabeth is convulsing. Laurie can't stop crying out.

I need to finish this.

As I push my grandfather to the ledge, I am apologizing to my mother. She would not want me to do this, although I hope she would understand. I am apologizing to Elizabeth because I should have never met her, should have never let her love me. I am apologizing to myself because if I do this, the curse will never end. But the only alternative is for it to continue filling Elizabeth until she is dead.

I will not lose her. Not for anything.

We are at the edge. My grandfather is struggling but losing power. As we flicker, I see the hatred in his eyes. The disgust for me. For us all.

With one hand, I hold his throat.

With the other hand, I push.

As I do, a surge of power fills him. With a strength I didn't know he still possessed, he grabs hold of me. If he's going to fall to his death, he is going to take me with him.

For a moment, we are strangely balanced. I lean away, he leans back, and we hover there in the air, visible and invisible, about to die and still alive, grandfather and grandson, the curser and the cursed.

Then his hold grows even stronger, and I feel myself moving in his direction.

There's a scream. My grandfather's scream. And an arm around me. Laurie's arm.

My grandfather has a knife in his side. He doesn't have the strength to hold on to me anymore.

He falls.

And as he falls, he disappears.

And as he falls, I disappear.

Laurie holds on to me.

Laurie holds on.

And I must make myself solid to him. Until I see that knife hit the ground. Until I know it is now over, and my grandfather is dead.

I am safe, and I will always be invisible, and Elizabeth will die anyway.

Laurie lets go of me, runs back to her. I am right behind him. She has risked everything to save me. Everything. And I don't believe enough in a fair world to think she'll be okay now.

Both of us call out her name. We see the slight rise and fall of the breath moving through her body, and we are infinitely grateful for it. It's hard to tell if the blood has stopped. There is so much of it, everywhere.

"We need to get her to a hospital," Laurie says.

I stand up, as if there's something I can do.

But what can I do? Nobody outside this roof will ever see me or know me or even know I exist.

I kneel back down beside her.

It is the most horrible feeling in the world, to be willing to give anything and to know it's not enough.

I reach out for her hand and put everything I am into that touch. Every desire I have ever had, any ounce of love I have ever received. I borrow every piece of the future and pull them into the present, bring them here for her to sense, to feel, to know.

"Please, Elizabeth," I tell her. "Please be okay."

Miraculously, her eyes startle open.

CHAPTER 32

"IT WORKED." I look up at Stephen, visible Stephen, and try to smile through my exhaustion, not knowing why those two small words made him wince.

I try to sit up, but my arms and legs are boneless. Looking down, I see all the blood. Crimson soaks the cotton of my shirt, making the fabric warm and heavy on my skin. It takes a moment, and the salt-copper taste on my lips, for me to realize the blood is mine. Stephen begins to carefully leverage his arms under my back, but Laurie appears beside him.

"You can't carry her," my brother tells Stephen.

"Laurie!" What I intended to be a joyful shout comes out as a pathetic croak.

Laurie kneels and takes my hand. "Yeah, Josie. I'm here. It's all going to be okay."

While Stephen reluctantly pulls away, Laurie gathers me in his arms.

"Are you sure we should move her?" Stephen asks, notwithstanding the fact that he'd just been about to pick me up himself.

Laurie nods. "It's not her bones I'm worried about. She's lost a lot of blood."

Now that Laurie's lifting me, those words come to life in my body. With each movement spots float across my vision and my skull feels like it's been jammed full of cotton.

Though my brother is carrying me towards the door, I try to look around. Moving my head makes me feel sick and my sight becomes increasingly blurry. Closing my eyes against the spots and the nausea, I ask:

"Arbus?"

"Gone," Laurie says.

I keep my eyes closed. "Gone or dead?"

"Dead." Stephen's voice is close. "Off the roof."

My numb fingers manage to grasp Laurie's shirt. It was much too close to being my brother who went over the ledge instead of Stephen's grandfather.

"I think you should try not talking, Elizabeth," Laurie tells me. His voice is gentle, so I know it's not a joke.

Normally I'm allergic to obedience, but I'm so, so tired. I lean my head on Laurie's shoulder, letting the spots expand from little points of darkness to large globules that blot out all the light.

I experience the next few hours in a bizarre, episodic fashion.

Episode one:

My brother and Stephen wait for the elevator and have a conversation I don't understand.

"You didn't kill him," Stephen murmurs.

Laurie's arms tighten around me. "Don't talk about it. Just don't."

Stephen glances at me, sees that I'm frowning but looks away. "I have to say it. You saved me. Nothing else happened."

"I stabbed him," Laurie answers. "I think that counts as something else."

I force my chin up so I can see Laurie's face. He's wearing a bleak expression that makes him seem so much older than he is.

"You had to," Stephen says quietly.

Laurie replies, "We both had to."

I remember the elevator doors opening and then nothing.

Episode two:

The blaring sirens bring me back to consciousness. The Upper West Side has been invaded by triage units: the result of Maxwell Arbus's cursing spree through our neighborhood. The upside of this horror is that my condition doesn't strike the EMTs as strange. I'm just one of a dozen or more victims. The downside is, well, obvious.

As I'm transferred from Laurie's arms to a gurney, I lift a hand towards Stephen, who is hanging back.

"I need him," I say to the EMT who is pushing the gurney to a waiting ambulance, which also takes me away from Stephen.

The EMT glances at Laurie. "He's right here."

Laurie bends down, whispering, "The ambulance is too crowded. He can't get in without bumping up against somebody. It's too risky."

I shake my head and Laurie says, "I told him which hospital. He'll meet us there."

The ambulance doors slam shut and the wail of its siren sends a new wave of darkness to swallow me.

Episode three:

The room is too bright and I'm covered in a sheet that's too scratchy. The itch concentrates in the crook of my right arm, but when I attempt to relieve it by rubbing the culprit spot with the heel of my hand, I'm rewarding by a sharp pain.

"Oh!" The needle joining my vein to the IV drip punishes me for disturbing it.

My cry brings someone rushing to the bedside.

My mom presses her palm to my cheek like I'm three. "Sweetheart, you're awake."

"You know who I am," I say. My eyes sting with sudden tears.

"Of course, Elizabeth." Mom glances at the IV. She must think that the medicine has skewed my mind towards looniness. "How are you feeling?" she asks.

"Weird," I say. Vague, I know. But I don't really want to say that my body feels like a million overstretched rubber bands and that I still taste blood.

"You'll probably feel weird for a while." Mom smiles and looks across the room. Following her glance, I see Laurie seated in one of the hospital room's chairs. Stephen is sitting beside him in the other chair. Without looking at Stephen, Laurie gets up and comes to join Mom.

"Hey there," Laurie says. That withered effect from earlier is still touching his eyes.

"You okay?" I ask him. When I stretch out my hand, he catches my trembling fingers in his.

"Let's not worry about me," he answers. "I didn't try to donate four gallons of blood to the pavement."

"What happened?" I ask Laurie, knowing he'll understand that I mean, What does Mom think happened?

It's Mom who answers. "They just don't know, honey. So many people were affected. And after what happened in the park, they think it's some kind of neurotoxin."

I groan. Even dead, Maxwell Arbus leaves us a legacy of his curses: a paranoid city, hunting for a culprit they'll never find, but always fear. It would be so much better if I could tell Homeland Security and the NYPD that they can stop their investigation right now. That this mess was made by a cursecaster run rampant, but he's gone and we can all get on with our lives. But that won't happen. I don't want to be transferred to the psych ward.

Stephen is still sitting. Mustering what sass I can, I smile in his direction. "You shy in front of the family or what?"

Laurie coughs. "You know I'm never shy. Mom has been watching the news, so she knows more."

I cast an irritated glance at Laurie, still speaking to Stephen. "Glad you found the hospital."

Mom's hand moves from my cheek to my forehead. "Are you feeling all right, Elizabeth?"

"What do they have you on anyway?" Laurie pretends to fiddle with the IV bag, but his eyes shoot me a warning.

I go silent. What else can I do? Stephen stares at me, remaining perfectly still. He is here. With me. And nothing has changed.

I am the only person who can see him.

Pain flares through my limbs as my body tenses, straining against all the questions I can't ask with my mom here. What the hell happened? Why was I covered with blood and half-conscious if Stephen is still invisible? What does it mean that he's invisible and his grandfather is dead?

"Elizabeth?" Mom murmurs, but I hear the worry in her voice. "Should I call the nurse?"

I am shaking my head, grateful, when her attention turns to a knock at the door.

"May I come in?"

I'm sure I've imagined the sound of Millie's voice, but a moment later I see her papery white skin and familiar face marked by wrinkles that seem to have worn deeper since I last saw her. Millie is wearing a black dress and black gloves. My stomach knots up when I remember why.

"How are you, dear?" Millie questions me before she's introduced herself to my mother.

I'm fumbling for an explanation of her arrival, but Mom speaks first.

"I think the meds are making her a bit fuzzy," she tells Millie. "But the doctors say no permanent harm was done."

"Thank goodness." Millie offers my mother a reassuring smile.

"Do you two know each other?" I am imagining some covert meeting that Millie arranged with my mother, all the better to regulate my activities.

Laurie pipes up. "I called Millie. I thought she'd want to be here."

"And he was right." Millie nods.

"I'm glad Laurie had the sense to introduce us." Mom gives me a pointed look. "The next time you get a job, I expect to be consulted about it."

"A job . . ." I glance at Laurie, who picks up where I left off.

"At the comic book shop," Laurie says. "I know it's only part time, but you've talked so much about Millie. I figured I should let her know what happened." He forces a laugh. "Didn't want you to get fired for missing work."

"Laurie," Mom chides.

"Too soon for jokes?" Laurie mock-slaps the back of his hand. Mom sighs.

Stephen is still in the chair. Silent.

"Mom, could you get me some juice?" I ask.

"There's water." Mom picks up a glass. "I don't know if you can have anything else yet."

"Can you ask the nurse?"

Mom hesitates, but then says, "Okay."

I wait until she's out of the room.

"Stephen." My voice breaks.

He is out of the chair and at my side, opposite Laurie and Millie.

"Tell me the truth," he says, stroking my hair. "Are you okay?"

Tears are clogging my throat, but I manage to choke out, "Why can't they see you?"

Stephen doesn't answer. I can still feel the touch of his fingers at my temple. Reaching up, I cover his hand with mine and look at Millie and my brother.

"Why can't you see him?" I ask accusingly, as if Stephen's invisibility is somehow the result of their collusion.

"Dear Elizabeth," Millie says quietly, "of course it's the curse. Just as it's always been."

I shake my head. "But I drew the curse from him. I felt it inside me."

When I say it, I can't stop the shudder. My limbs convulse at the memory. Blood poisoning. That's the only way I can think to describe it. I once saw a movie set sometime in the past when medicine sucked and a character died of blood poisoning after his wound became infected. I remember the gruesome close-up of the fatal gash. Black veins spidered out from the wound, evidence of the way his body had turned against itself.

That's how Stephen's curse felt when I drew it out of his body and into mine. Dark squiggles of resentment and malice that wormed through my veins, sickening and painful.

"I had to stop it," Stephen finally says. "It was killing you."

My voice is flat. "I'm not dead."

"You would have been," Stephen insists. He turns pleading eyes on Millie.

"It's the strongest curse I've ever seen," Millie tells me. "You wouldn't have survived it."

Anger is pummeling my chest, making me ache all the more. "You don't know that."

Her silence tells me that she doesn't.

"Josie." Laurie takes my hand. "How could he risk it?"

"I couldn't." Stephen leans down and presses his forehead to mine.

"You couldn't," I whisper, closing my eyes so I can just feel the warmth of his skin. I try to tell myself that this is somehow okay. That what I can feel, what I can see, is enough.

"Juice!" Mom announces from the doorway. At the sound of her voice, Stephen backs away. I open my eyes.

Mom presents a cup of apple juice to me with a flourish.

"Who's the superhero now?" She grins and winks at Millie as if she's just established some sort of comic-book-shop solidarity.

I try to smile, but I feel my lips wobbling. Laurie and Millie look at me with sympathy that verges on pity. I want to throw the apple juice across the room.

CHAPTER 33

I KEEP VIGIL. THE doctors and nurses parade in and out. Elizabeth's mother visits with Laurie. Elizabeth sleeps and wakes. The whole time, I stand in the corner, waiting for the moments when she and I are alone together, when I can keep her company. Even when she sleeps, I try to hold her hand. When she is well enough, she asks me to climb into the bed with her, to hold her there. We lie like that for hours, nothing but bodies and breath, wondering what will happen next.

As I keep vigil, the police remove my grandfather's shattered, bloody body from the pavement in front of my building. He is the day's only fatality, and the story goes that he was a man so severely affected by whatever struck those few blocks in Manhattan that he stabbed himself and jumped from the roof. His body will lie in the morgue for weeks, unclaimed. Finally, he will be given a mournerless funeral, a pauper's grave, an anonymous death.

I do not need to read the coroner's report to know: The knife may have surprised him, but he died from the fall.

I feel that remorse should bloom into its own kind of curse within me. But it hasn't done so yet.

My father leaves messages.

I don't know this until I stop off at home, three days after Elizabeth is taken to the hospital. Even though I am invisible, I need a shower and a change of clothes.

It is strange to hear my father's voice, because he has no idea what's happened. It is like the past is calling me, and doesn't realize I am already in the future. He attempts a casual tone, as if he's calling me up at college, wondering how my classes are going. He even asks me about Elizabeth, and tells me that he liked her, for the brief time they were in the same room. The sincerity of this makes me unsteady; the weight of all the things he doesn't know fills me. I sit down on the floor, close my eyes, regain myself. I listen to his other messages—each one growing more urgent with my lack of response.

When I call him back, there is actual relief in his voice. He asks me where I've been, and I tell him that Maxwell Arbus is dead. This, I've decided, is all he needs to know.

Immediately—eagerly—he asks me if the curse has been broken.

I tell him that it hasn't. Silently, I hope he will find a way to love me anyway.

I cannot return right away to Elizabeth. This is not the time for her to see my vulnerable need, my naked want.

I call Laurie and find that he's up in Sean's apartment. I tell him

I'm sorry to interrupt, but he assures me I'm not interrupting. He asks me if everything's all right with Elizabeth. I explain to him that I've come home for a short time. He says he'll be right down, and I don't try to persuade him to stay with Sean. I want to talk, even if I'm not sure what I want to say.

We don't go to the roof. We may never go to the roof again. Instead he lies down on the floor of my living room, face to the ceiling. I position myself next to him, also staring up. I make noise as I do, so he knows precisely where I am.

"I like Sean," he says. "But it feels a little different now. The possibility that he'll know me—that he'll know me *completely*—is gone. I was working up to telling him what happened in Minnesota. But this? We're the only ones who are ever really going to know about it, aren't we?"

"We are," I tell him. "For better or worse, it's ours."

He turns to me and says, "Promise me something."

"What?"

"Promise me that we're not going to stop knowing each other. The last thing I went through, I went through alone. I don't ever want to do that again."

I look right into his eyes. "We will never stop knowing each other," I promise.

Even though he can't see me, he looks like he does. He looks like he sees me perfectly.

"Good," he says.

The doctors don't know what's wrong with Elizabeth, but Millie does. Even though it horrifies her, she can see Arbus's presence within her, the last tendrils of dark cursework that have gripped her in spaces that are neither blood nor tissue, muscle nor bone.

"Will it go away?" I ask. Elizabeth is safely sleeping. Millie does not have to pretend that everything is all right.

"Over time, I believe so," she tells me. But I can see she's not sure. "It is a miracle that she survived. But just as you remain invisible, the power that she absorbed from him doesn't go away when he dies. We're basically relying on a magical immune system to break down what she's taken in—the hope is she's built up enough resistance to fight it off. Especially since she's young and innately powerful. More so than most."

"But there's no precedent?" I ask. "Nothing like this has ever happened to you, or to any other spellseeker?"

Millie shakes her head. "None that I know about. None who lived."

"And there's nothing you can do?"

"I can see it. That's all."

"So she'll live with it inside of her?"

"Yes. Her body will recover from the shock of it. But it will be there, until it isn't. But when that will be—I don't know."

The doctors think it's a speedy recovery. But Millie and I know better. And I suspect that Elizabeth knows better too.

I watch her asleep in her hospital bed. She is bruised. Her hair is greasy, dank. There are dark patches under her eyes and blotches on her neck. Her breathing sometimes comes in clots. A line of drool creeps from her mouth.

I have never loved her more.

She becomes well enough to leave the hospital.

I accompany Laurie and their mother as they wheel her home. This is her request—that if she's going to have to go back in a wheelchair (the doctors are worried she's still too weak, too drained) that they will not be taking a cab or an ambulance. She wants to be in the air again. She wants to see the city that we saved. She wants me there beside her, an invisible participant in the home-coming parade.

It is a beautiful summer day. Even though the city still hovers under the fears that Arbus's attack unleashed, the weather eases people's minds somewhat, because we all treasure the innate illusion that nothing bad can happen on a beautiful summer day.

Elizabeth smiles under the sun.

It is hard to get Elizabeth's mother to leave her side, but a few hours after the grand return, Laurie manages to convince her to go grocery shopping with him, leaving me and Elizabeth alone together.

"How are you doing?" I ask her. "Do you need anything?"

She's sitting on the couch. She pats the space next to her.

"Come here," she says.

I make my shoulder solid so she can lean on it.

"I still don't remember most of it," she tells me. "I wonder if that will come back to me, or if it's lost."

"You don't need to remember it."

"But I want to. I don't like having this gap in my past."

"You were brave."

"That's not what I'm asking."

"You were astonishing."

"Stop it."

"You were strong."

"But not strong enough."

"Definitely strong enough. Because he's not here anymore, is he? You did what you had to do."

She closes her eyes, tired.

"It's over," I tell her. "Now we go back to normal."

She lets out a breath that's part laugh, part sigh. "You have a very strange conception of normal."

"You know what I mean. In a few weeks, you and Laurie will go to school. I will stay at home and wait for you to come back. It's not a normal life for anyone else, but it will be a normal life for us. That's what matters. Not that it's normal to anyone else. But that it's normal to us."

Her hand finds my hand. She squeezes.

"You're right," she says. "That's how it will be. Only, it's not over. I still have many, many things to learn."

"We all do. And we'll learn them."

She nods, and I can see I need to let her rest.

I kiss her a temporary goodbye.

"We're safe," I tell her. "That's what matters."

"Yes," she says. "We're safe."

Then she drifts off into dreams.

I return to my apartment. All the familiar, quiet sounds. All the familiar furniture, all the familiar history.

For a moment, I feel alone again. Entirely alone. I can believe in a life that exists only in this apartment, only on its own. My old life. The life I thought I would always have.

Then I imagine Laurie and his mother returning to the apartment. I imagine Elizabeth on her couch. I even imagine Millie alone in her hexatorium and hope that she, in turn, is imagining us.

This is more than I ever could have wanted. This is more than I ever thought I'd have.

CHAPTER 34

IN THE AFTERMATH OF it all, when I am sick and broken and so very, very tired, I finally understand that I am not a superhero. I've discovered my fragility, my humanity.

In meeting Stephen—in seeing Stephen—I stumbled upon an extra set of senses. Millie claimed me as part of her magical heritage, which I've barely begun to understand. She named me a spell-seeker.

What little seeking can accomplish.

I see curses. Identify them. But when it's life and death at stake, I fold.

I thought I could help Stephen, that I could embrace this new, magical me and change the world. But nothing has changed for Stephen since I first discovered he was invisible. I am still the only one who can see him. His passing through the world draws less notice than a flicker of shadow.

It is not fair.

But life is not fair.

How quickly we forget that lesson only to learn it again.

Sometime soon I will go back to Millie's basement, which smells of tea and musty books. Under the guise of working part time as a purveyor of the comic books I adore, I will train with her. I will be the earnest pupil she deserves. I will try to fill the void that Saul has left. I will get stronger, better . . . deadlier.

But not yet.

I have enough self-awareness to know that I can't just bounce back from what happened on the roof of this building. None of us can. It's more than a vague notion of the events that occurred between my attempt to draw Stephen's curse and opening my eyes to find myself looking up at the sky. Only it wasn't the sky, but the vivid blue of Stephen's gaze.

I don't know how Maxwell Arbus died. Of course I know hitting the pavement after a nine-story fall took his life. But I have no memory of how Arbus took Laurie's place on the ledge. Or what made him fall.

The way that Stephen and my brother steer me sharply away from the subject anytime I get near it makes me think I probably don't want to know. Maybe it's better this way—that we keep our darknesses close, hidden in our minds, protected by our hearts.

We're each coping in our own ways.

Laurie is hinting that he's going to bring Sean to dinner so he can meet Mom. This will be new territory for Laurie. For all of us. We are looking forward to our pioneer days.

Stephen is slowly rebuilding ties with his father. They speak often and Stephen relays the conversations to me. This is his frontier. I can see the sparks of hope in his easy smiles, in the gradual melting of the cold edge that his voice carries whenever he mentions his father.

My solace comes from a familiar place. I counter the sluggish recovery of my body with the sharpness of my mind and force the fever that lingers in my blood to become one of spirit. My hands are steadiest when they hold a pencil, pastel, or charcoal. My vision is clearest when a blank page fills my sight.

I have a story to tell that I've been holding on to, thinking it was mine alone.

But I was wrong.

It is after midnight when Mom finally goes to bed. She's been taking a couple days each week to work from home so she can spend more time with me. That also means she stays up late to get hours in at the virtual office to compensate for the lengthy Scrabble games we play. I love the time with her; I want very much to reassure her that I am okay—even if that okay is heavily qualified. But it makes finding time with Stephen more of a challenge. When I don't find that time, I am lost.

Stephen is at his door a moment after I knock.

"Hey."

"Hey."

We share a smile. He takes my free hand while his glance takes note of the portfolio under my arm.

Stephen leads me to his room. He sits on the edge of his bed while I empty the portfolio. He has to stand to create enough space for all the pages. I've arranged them for him to view. His quilt is papered with sketches. Some are brightly hued. Others resemble little more than a jumble of shadows.

I step back, watching as he leans forward. His eyes widen, then narrow. He knows this story. It is our story.

Yellow and blue shopping bags in disarray.

A room full of unopened boxes.

Two glasses of lemonade.

The angel watching over us.

A door left open to an empty hallway.

A dark, velvet-draped shop and a man with an eye patch.

Wrinkled hands, holding a teakettle.

A woman cradling an infant in her arms. An infant that cannot be seen.

The outline of a small boy and the long, cruel shadow of a man falling over him.

A riot of shapes and colors: my collage of curses.

A different mother and a different boy. A museum. The same shadow.

My room in the daylight.

Stephen's room in moonlight.

An Upper West Side block, rendered in jagged pieces.

The roof.

The sky.

Blue eyes and dark hair.

A hospital bed with two occupants.

A close-up of fingers entwined.

The long, cruel shadow turned to ash. Scattered by the wind.

Stephen looks at the sketches for a long time.

"It has a beginning and an end," he says, touching the edge of the last page.

"Yes."

He turns to face me. "And after the end?"

"Another beginning." I rise on my tiptoes and kiss him.

I don't say that I haven't given up.

I don't swear that I will someday free him of this curse.

I have already sworn that to myself.

But I don't know when that day will arrive, and it would be too easy to forget to marvel at the beauty in this moment. In every moment.

I am touching Stephen's cheek and looking into his sky-blue eyes. He is looking back at me. His hand mirrors mine. His fingers are warm on my skin.

We see each other, and it is enough.

For today.

Turn the page to sample the first book in
Andrea Cremer's bestselling series.

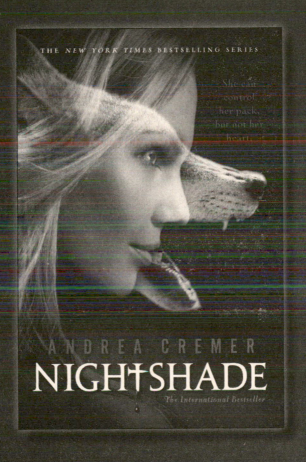

I'D ALWAYS WELCOMED WAR, BUT IN BATTLE

my passion rose unbidden.

The bear's roar filled my ears. Its hot breath assaulted my nostrils, fueling my bloodlust. Behind me I could hear the boy's ragged gasp. The desperate sound made my nails dig into the earth. I snarled at the larger predator again, daring it to try to get past me.

What the hell am I doing?

I risked a glance at the boy and my pulse raced. His right hand pressed against the gashes in his thigh. Blood surged between his fingers, darkening his jeans until they looked streaked by black paint. Slashes in his shirt barely covered the red lacerations that marred his chest. A growl rose in my throat.

I crouched low, muscles tensed, ready to strike. The grizzly rose onto its hind legs. I held my ground.

Calla!

Bryn's cry sounded in my mind. A lithe brown wolf darted from the forest and tore into the bear's unguarded flank. The grizzly turned, landing on all fours. Spit flew from its mouth as it searched for the unseen attacker. But Bryn, lightning fast, dodged the bear's lunge. With each swipe of the grizzly's trunk-thick arms, she avoided its reach, always moving a split second faster than the bear. She seized her advantage, inflicting another taunting bite. When the bear's back was turned, I leapt forward and ripped a chunk from its heel. The bear swung around to face me, its eyes rolling, filled with pain.

Bryn and I slunk along the ground, circling the huge animal. The bear's blood made my mouth hot. My body tensed. We continued our ever-tightening dance. The bear's eyes tracked us. I could smell its doubt, its rising fear. I let out a short, harsh bark and flashed my fangs. The grizzly snorted as it turned away and lumbered into the forest.

I raised my muzzle and howled in triumph. A moan brought me back to earth. The hiker stared at us, eyes wide. Curiosity pulled me toward him. I'd betrayed my masters, broken their laws. All for him.

Why?

My head dropped low and I tested the air. The hiker's blood streamed over his skin and onto the ground, the sharp, coppery odor creating an intoxicating fog in my conscience. I fought the temptation to taste it.

Calla? Bryn's alarm pulled my gaze from the fallen hiker.

Get out of here. I bared my teeth at the smaller wolf. She dropped low and bellied along the ground toward me. Then she raised her muzzle and licked the underside of my jaw.

What are you going to do? her blue eyes asked me.

She looked terrified. I wondered if she thought I'd kill the boy for my own pleasure. Guilt and shame trickled through my veins.

Bryn, you can't be here. Go. Now.

She whined but slunk away, slipping beneath the cover of pine trees.

I stalked toward the hiker. My ears flicked back and forth. He struggled for breath, pain and terror filling his face. Deep gashes remained where the grizzly's claws had torn at his thigh and chest. Blood still flowed from the wounds. I knew it wouldn't stop. I growled, frustrated by the fragility of his human body.

He was a boy who looked about my age: seventeen, maybe

eighteen. Brown hair with a slight shimmer of gold fell in a mess around his face. Sweat had caked strands of it to his forehead and cheeks. He was lean, strong—someone who could find his way around a mountain, as he clearly had. This part of the territory was only accessible through a steep, unwelcoming trail.

The scent of fear covered him, taunting my predatory instincts, but beneath it lay something else—the smell of spring, of nascent leaves and thawing earth. A scent full of hope. Possibility. Subtle and tempting.

I took another step toward him. I knew what I wanted to do, but it would mean a second, much-greater violation of the Keepers' Laws. He tried to move back but gasped in pain and collapsed onto his elbows. My eyes moved over his face. His chiseled jaw and high cheekbones twisted in agony. Even writhing he was beautiful, muscles clenching and unclenching, revealing his strength, his body's fight against its impending collapse, rendering his torture sublime. Desire to help him consumed me.

I can't watch him die.

I shifted forms before I realized I'd made the decision. The boy's eyes widened when the white wolf who'd been eyeing him was no longer an animal, but a girl with the wolf's golden eyes and platinum blond hair. I walked to his side and dropped to my knees. His entire body shook. I began to reach for him but hesitated, surprised to feel my own limbs trembling. I'd never been so afraid.

A rasping breath pulled me out of my thoughts.

"Who are you?" The boy stared at me. His eyes were the color of winter moss, a delicate shade that hovered between green and gray. I was caught there for a moment. Lost in the questions that pushed through his pain and into his gaze.

I raised the soft flesh of my inner forearm to my mouth. Willing my canines to sharpen, I bit down hard and waited until my own blood touched my tongue. Then I extended my arm toward him.

"Drink. It's the only thing that can save you." My voice was low but firm.

The trembling in his limbs grew more pronounced. He shook his head.

"You have to," I growled, showing him canines still razor sharp from opening the wound in my arm. I hoped the memory of my wolf form would terrorize him into submission. But the look on his face wasn't one of horror. The boy's eyes were full of wonder. I blinked at him and fought to remain still. Blood ran along my arm, falling in crimson drops onto the leaf-lined soil.

His eyes snapped shut as he grimaced from a surge of renewed pain. I pressed my bleeding forearm against his parted lips. His touch was electric, searing my skin, racing through my blood. I bit back a gasp, full of wonder and fear at the alien sensations that rolled through my limbs.

He flinched, but my other arm whipped around his back, holding him still while my blood flowed into his mouth. Grasping him, pulling him close only made my blood run hotter.

I could tell he wanted to resist, but he had no strength left. A smile pulled at the corners of my mouth. Even if my own body was reacting unpredictably, I knew I could control his. I shivered when his hands came up to grasp my arm, pressing into my skin. The hiker's breath came easily now. Slow, steady.

An ache deep within me made my fingers tremble. I wanted to run them over his skin. To skim the healing wounds and learn the contours of his muscles.

I bit my lip, fighting temptation. *Come on, Cal, you know better. This isn't like you.*

I pulled my arm from his grasp. A whimper of disappointment emerged from the boy's throat. I didn't know how to grapple with my own sense of loss now that I wasn't touching him. *Find your strength, use the wolf. That's who you are.*

With a warning growl I shook my head, ripping a length of fabric from the hiker's torn shirt to bind up my own wound. His moss-colored eyes followed my every movement.

I scrambled to my feet and was startled when he mimicked the action, faltering only slightly. I frowned and took two steps back. He watched my retreat, then looked down at his ripped clothing. His fingers gingerly picked at the shreds of his shirt. When his eyes lifted to meet mine, I was hit with an unexpected swell of dizziness. His lips parted. I couldn't stop looking at them. Full, curving with interest, lacking the terror I'd expected. Too many questions flickered in his gaze.

I have to get out of here. "You'll be fine. Get off the mountain. Don't come near this place again," I said, turning away.

A shock sparked through my body when the boy gripped my shoulder. He looked surprised but not at all afraid. That wasn't good. Heat flared along my skin where his fingers held me fast. I waited a moment too long, watching him, memorizing his features before I snarled and shrugged off his hand.

"Wait—" he said, and took another step toward me.

What if I could wait, putting my life on hold in this moment? What if I stole a little more time and caught a taste of what had been so long forbidden? Would it be so wrong? I would never see this stranger again. What harm could come from lingering here, from holding still and learning whether he would try to touch me the way I wanted to him to?

His scent told me my thoughts weren't far off the mark, his skin snapping with adrenaline and the musk that belied desire. I'd let this encounter last much too long, stepped well beyond the line of safe conduct. With regret nipping at me, I balled my fist. My eyes moved up and down his body, assessing, remembering the feeling of his lips on my skin. He smiled hesitantly.

Enough.

I caught him across the jaw with a single blow. He dropped to the ground and didn't move again. I bent down and gathered the boy in my arms, slinging his backpack over my shoulder. The scent of green meadows and dew-kissed tree limbs flowed around me, flooding me with that strange ache that coiled low in my body, a physical reminder of my brush with treachery. Twilight shadows stretched farther up the mountain, but I'd have him at the base by dusk.

A lone, battered pickup was parked near the rippling waterway that marked the boundary of the sacred site. Black signs with bright orange lettering were posted along the creek bank:

NO TRESPASSING. PRIVATE PROPERTY.

The Ford Ranger was unlocked. I flung open the door, almost pulling it from the rust-bitten vehicle. I draped the boy's limp form across the driver's seat. His head slumped forward and I caught the stark outline of a tattoo on the back of his neck. A dark, bizarrely inked cross.

A trespasser and trend hound. Thank God I found something not to like about him.

I hurled his pack onto the passenger seat and slammed the door. The truck's steel frame groaned. Still trembling with frustration, I shifted into wolf form and darted back into the forest. His scent clung to me, blurring my sense of purpose. I sniffed the air and cringed, a new scent bringing my treachery into stark relief.

I know you're here. A snarl traveled with my thought.

Are you okay? Bryn's plaintive question only made fear bite harder into my trembling muscles. In the next moment she ran beside me.

I told you to leave. I bared my teeth but couldn't deny my sudden relief at her presence.

I could never abandon you. Bryn kept pace easily. *And you know I'll never betray you.*

I picked up speed, darting through the deepening shadows of the forest. I abandoned my attempt to outrun fear, shifted forms, and stumbled forward until I found the solid pressure of a tree trunk. The scratch of the bark on my skin failed to repel the gnat-like nerves that swarmed in my head.

"Why did you save him?" she asked. "Humans mean nothing to us."

I kept my arms around the tree but turned my cheek to the side so I could look at Bryn. No longer in her wolf form, the short, wiry girl's hands rested on her hips. Her eyes narrowed as she waited for an answer.

I blinked, but I couldn't halt the burning sensation. A pair of tears, hot and unwanted, slid down my cheeks.

Bryn's eyes widened. I never cried. Not when anyone could witness it.

I turned my face away, but I could sense her watching me silently, without judgment. I had no answers for Bryn. Or for myself.

Join the Hunt with Books by
Andrea Cremer!

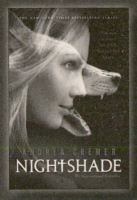

NIGHTSHADE
ANDREA CREMER

WOLFSBANE
ANDREA CREMER

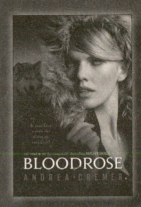

BLOODROSE
ANDREA CREMER

ANDREA CREMER
RIFT
A NIGHTSHADE NOVEL

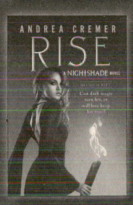

ANDREA CREMER
RISE
A NIGHTSHADE NOVEL

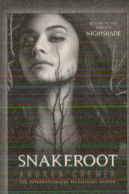

SNAKEROOT
ANDREA CREMER

And look for Andrea's next series:

THE
INVENTOR'S
SECRET

KEEP READING TO PREVIEW

DAVID LEVITHAN'S *NEW YORK TIMES*
BESTSELLING NOVEL WITH **JOHN GREEN**.

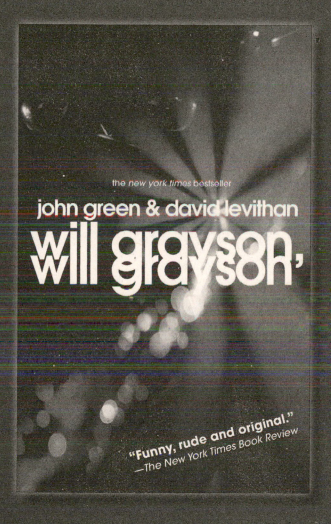

chapter two

i am constantly torn between killing myself and killing everyone around me.

those seem to be the two choices. everything else is just killing time.

right now i'm walking through the kitchen to get to the back door.

mom: have some breakfast.

i do not eat breakfast. i never eat breakfast. i haven't eaten breakfast since i was able to walk out the back door without eating breakfast first.

mom: where are you going?

school, mom. you should try it some time.

mom: don't let your hair fall in your face like that — i can't see your eyes.

but you see, mom, that's *the whole fucking point*.

i feel bad for her — i do. a damn shame, really, that i had to have a mother. it can't be easy having me for a son. nothing can prepare someone for that kind of disappointment.

me: bye

i do not say 'good-bye.' i believe that's one of the bullshittiest words ever invented. it's not like you're given the choice to say 'bad-bye' or 'awful-bye' or 'couldn't-care-less-about-you-bye.' every time you leave, it's supposed to be a good one. well, i don't believe in that. i believe *against* that.

mom: have a good d—

the door kinda closes in the middle of her sentence, but it's not like i can't guess where it's going. she used to say 'see you!' until one morning i was so sick of it i told her, 'no, you don't.'

she tries, and that's what makes it so pathetic. i just want to say, 'i feel sorry for you, really i do.' but that might start a conversation, and a conversation might start a fight, and then i'd feel so guilty i might have to move away to portland or something.

i need coffee.

every morning i pray that the school bus will crash and we'll all die in a fiery wreck. then my mom will be able to sue the school bus company for never making school buses with seat belts, and she'll be able to get more money for my tragic death than i would've ever made in my tragic life. unless the lawyers from the school bus company can prove to the jury that i was guaranteed to be a fuckup. then they'd get away with buying my mom a used ford fiesta and calling it even.

maura isn't exactly waiting for me before school, but i know, and she knows i'll look for her where she is. we usually fall back on that so we can smirk at each other or something before we're marched off. it's like those people who become friends in prison even though they would never really talk to each other if they weren't in prison. that's what maura and i are like, i think.

me: give me some coffee.
maura: get your own fucking coffee.

then she hands me her XXL dunkin donuts crappaccino and i treat it like it's a big gulp. if i could afford my own coffee i swear i'd get it, but the way i see it is: her bladder isn't thinking i'm an asshole even if the rest of her organs do. it's been like this with me and maura for as long as I can remember, which is about a year. i guess i've known her a little longer than that, but maybe not. at some point last year, her gloom met my doom and she thought it was a good match. i'm not so sure, but at least i get coffee out of it.

derek and simon are coming over now, which is good because it's going to save me some time at lunch.

me: give me your math homework.
simon: sure. here.

what a friend.

the first bell rings. like all the bells in our fine institution of lower learning, it's not a bell at all, it's a long beep, like you're about to leave a voicemail saying you're having the suckiest day ever. and nobody's ever going to listen to it.

i have no idea why anyone would want to become a teacher. i mean, you have to spend the day with a group of kids who either hate your guts or are kissing up to you to get a good grade. that has to get to you after a while, being surrounded by people who will never like you for any real reason. i'd feel bad for them if they weren't such sadists and losers. with the sadists, it's all about the power and the control. they teach so they can have an official reason to dominate other people. and the losers make up pretty much all the other teachers, from the ones who are too incompetent to do anything else to the ones who want to be their students' best friends because they never had friends when they were in high school. and there are the ones who honestly think we're going to remember a thing they say to us after final exams are over. right.

every now and then you get a teacher like mrs. grover, who's a sadistic loser. i mean, it can't be easy being a french teacher, because nobody really needs to know how to speak french anymore. and while she kisses the honors kids' *derrieres*, with standard kids she resents the fact that we're taking up her time. so she responds by giving us quizzes every day and giving us gay projects like 'design your own ride for euro disney' and then acting all surprised when i'm like 'yeah, my ride for euro disney is minnie using a baguette as a dildo to have some fun with mickey.' since i don't have any idea how to say 'dildo' in french (*dildot?*), i just say 'dildo' and she pretends to have no idea what i'm talking about and says that minnie and mickey eating baguettes isn't a ride. no doubt she gives me a check-minus for the day. i know i'm supposed to care, but really it's hard to imagine something i could care less about than my grade in french.

the only worthwhile thing i do all period — all morning, really — is write *isaac, isaac, isaac* in my notebook and then draw spider-man spelling it out in a web. which is completely lame, but whatever. it's not like i'm doing it to be cool.

Edison Junior High Library